A PLACE WITHOUT YOU

By Jewel E. Ann

Copyright © 2018 by Jewel E. Ann
ISBN: 978-1-7320897-7-8
Print Edition

Cover Designer: ©Sarah Hansen, Okay Creations
Photo: ©Rafael Catala
Cover Model: Adrián Pedraja Barrientos
Formatting: BB eBooks

DEDICATION

For Mom

I'm glad you located the G-spot.

CHAPTER ONE

*D*ON'T SWEAT IT. *Everything is temporary.*

I stare at the words on my thoroughly dented metal water bottle as I wait for my dad in the crowded, three-star hotel lobby filled with music enthusiasts. This will be the most epic three days I've ever had with my dad, and we've had a lot.

"Where are you?" I answer my phone, picking at the frayed hem to my high-waisted cutoffs accompanying my red crop top and tons of beaded bracelets, necklaces, and dangly earrings.

"Sweetheart, I'm still at home. I think I ate some bad sushi last night, and since then I've been praying to the porcelain god. I'm afraid I can't go. Can you still get back home? Has the plane left?"

"Wait. What? You're not coming?" His home in Oceanside, California is only a two-and-a-half-hour drive to our hotel in Indio. He *has* to make it.

"Henna, I'm drenched from a cold sweat, painful stomach cramps have crippled me, and I'm not sure I can make it to the bathroom without shitting my pants, let alone spend hours in the car. I'm so incredibly sorry."

"Oh, Dad … I'm sorry. That's awful." And gross. I drop down onto a chair that a gentleman vacated when his wife arrived with their key cards.

"Next year. I promise. No sushi." He tries to laugh, but all

1

I can hear is the physical strain and weakness in his voice. "I'll fly you out in a week or two, and we'll do something else before school ends. Then we'll have two weeks on the beach together this summer."

I nod to myself, biting on my gray painted thumbnail to channel my disappointment into something more sympathetic. "That's fine. I'll send you video and some photos."

"Henna, you have to go back to Colorado. You can't be at Coachella alone. It's not safe for a young girl like you to be there without a chaperone."

"Dad, I'm an adult. It's a music festival. I'll be fine."

"You're eighteen. That's not really an adult."

"I'll be smart."

"Still. The answer is no."

"Mom sent …" I stop myself. General Mitchell Lane is not as free-spirited as the mother of his child. Something tells me that the stock of condoms my mom sent with me is not going to comfort him.

"Mom sent what? A bodyguard?"

"Not exactly." I wrinkle my nose.

"Then get back on that plane and go home. Okay?"

I shake my head. It's *Coachella*. The lineup is so sick. I could die just thinking about it. There's no way in hell I am going back home before the weekend is over. "Okay. I'll go home."

In three days.

"Thank you, Henna. And again … I'm so sorry."

"No apologies. *I'm* sorry you're not feeling well. I'll see you in a couple of weeks. Love you."

"Love you too."

THERE ARE TWO groups of people: those who love Coachella and those who have no clue what they are missing. I belong to the first group.

Me: *You're the coolest mom ever, right?*

I grin, swiping out of my messenger screen to order a ride as I wait outside the hotel. Sushi-sick dad cancelled our reservation. Not cool.

Juni: *Your dad just called me.*

Juni ... because my mom is too cool to be lumped into the "mom" group. So I call her Juni.

Me: *Of course he did.*

Juni: *I'll arrange your transportation home.*

Narrowing my eyes, I frown at the screen.

Me: *Such a waste of a dozen ready-to-use condoms that* YOU *sent with me. My first April as an adult—what happened to telling me to just "live?"*

Juni: *Yeah, yeah. I already made arrangements for you to stay with Lauren, unless you have friends there who have room for you. Now that your dad's not there, I'm feeling more maternal anxiety and worry.*

Me: *I'll figure something out.*

Juni: *BE SAFE!!!*

Me: *Will do. <3*

Sliding into the backseat of the Prius, I hug my bag to my

chest as the opposite door opens.

"Uh?" I slip out one of my earbuds, pausing my music, as I glance in the rearview mirror at the driver. "Did I get in the wrong car?"

"You clicked ride share," the driver says.

"Oh. Okay." I shrug and give the blond guy sliding in next to me a smile and an exaggerated once-over because he's quite the snack.

Jeans and cowboy boots are an interesting choice for a day in the desert.

A few seconds later, he catches me assessing him and his hair again—buzzed close to his head on the sides and longer on the top. Did he forget his cowboy hat? That's the real unsolved mystery in my head.

His lips move. I stare at them for a few breaths before I realize he's talking. My hand tugs out my earbud again.

"Sorry. Did you say something?"

"What are you listening to?" he asks in a voice as smooth as his Mediterranean eyes.

"That's kind of a personal question. Like asking my underwear color."

He grins. It's all kinds of wicked. "Personal?" He shrugs. "I don't know about that. Depends on the song … and the color."

"Amy Shark, 'Adore.' And red and silver polka dots."

"Mmm …" He nods slowly. "Good choice."

"The song?" I bite the corner of my lower lip to control my grin.

"The underwear."

My heart wakes up as if to say, *"Whoa, is something going on here I should know about?"*

"Wanna see mine?"

My eyebrows lift a fraction. "Your underwear?"

He digs his phone out of his front pocket. "Do I look like a perv? My song."

Damn. He's good. My tummy joins in on the little dance happening inside of me.

Twisting his wrist, he shows me his phone screen.

"Apocalyptica, 'Nothing Else Matters.' Hmm ... that's unexpected." I let my gaze fall into his, a dangerous place to be. "You going to Coachella?"

He nods several times, glancing over the seats to the road before us. "I'm working there."

"Oh, cool. Doing what?"

He inspects my hair. I'd planned on changing clothes and doing something a bit more original with my crazy, dark auburn hair than a messy braid over one shoulder, but sushi dad took away my hotel room. Sexy stranger grins like either my question or my messy hair pleases him. "I'm an in-house tech—audio, lighting, video."

Dear God, he's the full package, especially when that grin of his grows as I continue to violate him with my eyes. Maybe it's just the lollipop I had on my way to the hotel. Everything seems aesthetically pleasing when I'm a little high.

"So, I'll know who to blame if the sound is a bit off while one of my favorite bands performs."

"You'll know who to thank when it isn't." He leans toward the middle of the backseat. I follow his lead because I'm curious if he smells as good as he looks. "But I get this feeling that in your state, everything will sound good."

Ignoring his whispered accusation that I'm high, I sniff. "You smell like lemon."

He sticks his tongue out, revealing a half-melted lemon drop.

I grin as we sit straight again. "Last year my mom brought back lemon drops from the Limoncello factory in Sorrento. They were amazing."

Sucking more intensely on his sour goodness, he nods slowly. "I'm sure they were. Sadly, I don't think my lemon drop was made in Italy."

"That *is* incredibly sad."

He chuckles. Is he laughing at me?

"Nice tats." He nods to my arms.

Holding them out, I admire my art. "They're henna, like me."

"Like you?"

"Yes. My name is Henna. And these will be much more intense tomorrow."

"Like you?" His teeth scrape along his bottom lip. It's ridiculously sexy.

"Are you flirting with me?"

He chuckles. "We met less than five minutes ago. I have a little more tact than that."

"Tact? Like asking the color of my underwear?"

He runs his hands over the legs of his jeans. Is he sweating? Am I making him sweat? That possibility gives me a whole other kind of high.

"I didn't ask. You freely offered that information. Besides, I have rules about flirting."

"Well, I despise rules, but you must share your rules anyway."

"Never flirt with someone who is not sober." He stares out his window like his rule is the end of our friendly conversation.

"Sober? Dude, this is as sober as I get." Leaning forward, I shove down the waist of my shorts in back, exposing a long L-shaped scar.

He glances over, forehead wrinkled.

"If I sit too long or stand too long or do anything too long, life kinda sucks. But a little high can go a long way with making said life a lot less sucky."

Sitting back, I exhale. Sexy stranger seems at a loss for words.

"Tell me, tech guy, do you have a name?"

The driver stops at the crowded entrance.

"Thank you," we say while getting out of the car.

Digging out my Coachella bracelet and All-Access Pass, I slip on my backpack and make several failed attempts to put the bracelet on my wrist amongst the other gazillion bracelets on my arms.

Long, tan fingers take over, attaching it for me. I look up and go all gooey inside at how amazing my ride-sharing stranger looks with the wind messing up his surfer hair.

"All-Access Pass. Lucky girl."

I nod without elaborating. Instead, I just stare at his eyes because they are worthy of my attention.

"Bodhi." He grins. "My name is Bodhi."

"Bodie? Like the ghost town in California?"

"Bodhi like the sacred fig tree."

"Shut. Up." My eyes pop out of my head. "For real? Your name is Bodhi. B.O.D.H.I?"

He grins, but I can't tell if it's a duh-that's-just-what-I-said grin or a you're-so-gullible grin.

"Henna and Bodhi. It's so fucking poetic. Now comes the part where I inform you that we will marry some day and live in a small house nestled into the cliffside of Italy, overlooking the Amalfi coast, where we'll have terraced groves of lemon trees, olive trees ... and tomatoes. I love tomatoes."

Bodhi's brows inch up his forehead.

"And before you say no and get all weird on me, I'm not suggesting we do this right away. I have some serious traveling to do before settling into one location with a hot guy." A long two-second delay later, I realize what I've just said.

Amusement grows along his mouth like the sun sliding up the horizon in the early morning, giving me the brightest smile. I slip on my sunglasses. Bodhi and the desert sun are a bit too intense, even for me.

"Henna, are you flirting with me?"

A group of girls gather around us and snap a few photos of me before blending back into the sea of humans funneling toward the entrance. Bodhi gives them a narrow-eyed look and shifts his gaze to me for an explanation.

I ignore the girls and his curiosity. "Yes, Bodhi, I'm shamelessly, unapologetically, working-my-ass-off flirting with you. The universe has spoken. We can't ignore *the universe*."

A bold laugh escapes him. "Fate?"

"Fate? No. Fate is nothing more than another word for happiness. We're more than fate. We *sound* like something undeniable—Romeo and Juliet, Johnny and June, Beyoncè and Jay Z ... *Henna and Bodhi*."

His parents have to be awesome like mine. I can't wait to

meet them.

Glancing at his watch, he gives me that goodbye smile that should be outlawed. "Whatever strain of weed you're on is clearly a good one. Don't forget sunscreen, a hat, and if you don't want a nasty cough by Monday, you should cover your nose and mouth with a bandana or scarf."

"Like … are you kidding me? Did you just give me a parental speech?"

"I have to go."

"How will I find you?"

He starts to walk toward the far entrance, tossing me a flirty grin over his shoulder. "Fate. Right?"

"Fate. Schmate. Now you're mocking me. Not cool, bae, not even a little."

I wait for him to look back at me one more time. I wait … and wait …

Yes!

As the crowd engulfs him from twenty yards away, he gives me one last glance.

Dead. I'm dead because that's the guy I'm going to marry. Henna and Bodhi—perfection! After taking a long swig of water, I stare at the words on my water bottle again.

Don't sweat it. Everything is temporary.

CHAPTER TWO

Afte SLATHERING ON a ton of sunscreen and covering my braided hair with a big-ass hat, I make my way through security. Spilling into a diverse crowd milling in every direction, I shoulder my way to the first stage.

Within hours, my clothes are drenched in sweat as the sweet smell of Coachella hangs heavily in the dusty desert air. Still—I love it.

The intense energy of the festivalgoers has its own pulse that can be felt past the rhythm thumping from the various stages. It's not a mingle fest. Everyone moves from stage to stage, dancing, singing their favorite lyrics, and drifting to the next stage to do it all over again.

"Shit!" A familiar voice grabs my attention.

Waiting for the next act to set up, I glance past the barricades to the right of the stage and giggle at the man frowning at ketchup dribbled down the front of his white T-shirt. A blue-eyed gaze shifts from the mess on the white cotton to meet my gaze. Biting my lips together, my eyes widen as I snort another laugh.

"*Fate* is working her ass off today."

He grins a unique blend of something goofy and incredibly sexy. Surfer sexy. No … it's cowboy sexy. The blond hair and tan skin say surfer, but those perfectly fitted jeans and boots scream cowboy. And the name is that of my future husband.

"I shouldn't have gotten the fries."

My sober alertness mixed with the timbre in his voice has me taking a mental count of all the condoms in my possession.

He steps toward me, using another french fry to wipe off the ketchup. It only makes it worse.

"Henna." Patricia, the tour manager for the band getting ready to take the stage, nods and smiles at me as she walks past ketchup guy.

Bodhi looks over his shoulder at her and then back at me with a hint of confusion on his adorable face. I still can't decide if I want to see him on a billboard wearing board shorts and holding up a surfboard, or if the thought of him on the back of a horse makes me weaker in all my girly parts.

I smile at Patricia before quickly returning my attention to the mess of a man before me. "No." I lean over the roped-off area, winking at the security guard eyeing me a few feet away. Stealing a french fry and popping it into my mouth, I lick the salt from my lips. "You just shouldn't have gotten the ketch-up."

He lifts an eyebrow. "Help yourself."

I grab another fry. "Thank you." Tapping it on my bottom lip, I inspect his shirt. "You should take that shirt off before anyone else sees what a mess you've made."

He smiles. I like it a lot. Smiles are nothing new to me. I've seen a lot of them—mostly arrogant ones.

"I don't have another shirt here." Dipping three fries at once into the ketchup, he tosses them into his mouth.

"Your point?" I take two more fries, leaving him with two.

"I'm pretty self-conscious about my body."

Biting the fries in half, I grin—a girl-meets-boy flirty one, just for ketchup guy aka my future husband. "Do you love what you do, or do you have dreams of being in a band? Being the one in the spotlight instead of the one adjusting it?"

"This isn't what I do. It's a break I take every spring. And for your information, I was in a band." He eats one fry and hands me the last one.

It's oddly the most romantic thing a guy has ever done for me. The final french fry trumps a single red rose. At least, that's how my mind works.

"Thank you." I take the fry. "Singer?"

"Drummer."

Drummer...

I press my hand to my bag over the exact spot where I have a condom. "Well..." I lick the salt from my fingers "...what a coincidence. I happen to have a thing for drummers."

"Are you still flirting with me?"

"Always. Even when our kids think it's gross and we're too old to flirt, I'm going to tease you with my sexiness."

"Cute." He tosses the french fry container in the garbage just behind him before turning back to me.

"You think I'm cute? See, Bodhi, you have flirting skills too."

This earns me the full smile, the kind that should be accompanied with at least one dimple. No dimples. That's fine. He has sex appeal beyond any dimple I have ever seen.

With the back of his arm, he wipes his brow. It's hotter than a pot of Devil's stew. Rubbing his lips together, his gaze meanders along my body. It's a more potent high than any strain of marijuana. Bodhi might be my new favorite painkiller.

He stares at me for so long I feel completely translucent. "I have to get going." He nods toward the stage. "Enjoy Coachella, Henna."

"Wait!"

With confident strides, he walks away.

"Seriously! You have to stop walking away from me, acting so savage."

"Savage?" He glances over his shoulder.

I snort a laugh. "It means cool, Bodhi. You're just too cool."

He winks.

Dig a hole in the ground and pile dirt on me. I'm so dead.

My fingers run along the outline of the circle of protection in my purse.

Bodhi and Henna. *Sigh…*

I grin, retrieving my phone.

Me: *OMG I met a drummer. And his name is Bodhi! BODHI!!! Are you reading this? HIS NAME IS BODHI!*

Juni: *Condoms!*

I giggle.

Me: *Lol. Right? #dead #bestnameEVER*

CHAPTER THREE

A FTER RUNNING INTO a few friends from school and a few more from my mom's and stepdad's social circle, I'm high on Coachella, high on gummies, and really high on thoughts of Bodhi.

The night air is electric with energy from the dancing crowds packed around the venue, the bass, the screaming, and the technicolor of lights from the stages and big screens.

Well done, tech guy.

Aside from the art features and stages, Coachella at night is quite dark and chilly. As my favorite ballad plays from twenty yards away, and everyone around me sways to the slow rhythm, I lift onto my toes to see the stage. Every girl around me is on some guy's shoulders, blocking my view.

I frown, as my song hits the halfway point and all I can do is hear it, but I came here to *see* it too. Dodging and bobbing, right and left, up and down, like a hyper dog, I crane my neck for a glimpse that eludes me with every attempt. Just as I decide to use my All-Access Pass to get a better view, something stops me.

"Ahh!" I nearly fall on my ass a split second before strong shoulders hoist me toward the sky. Warm hands steady my legs. I grab a fistful of blond surfer hair to regain my balance as a clear view of the stage comes into focus because *my* guy is taller than the guy holding the girl up in front of us.

Lucky me.

When I look down, ketchup guy tips his head back to give me that hybrid grin. We don't say anything. Instead, I hold up my arms and sway to the song along with the tall cowboy beneath me.

My head spins and I love every minute.

The high.

The energy.

The lights.

The music.

The large hands gripping my bare legs.

Bodhi holds me for the next two songs as well. When the band takes their final bow, he lowers me to the ground. I turn toward him, stumbling a bit from the bodies bumping us as the crowd filters out. My hands make claim to his arms as his fingers slide into the belt loops of my denim shorts.

"My favorite fry guy." I smile, but it fades into a contemplative frown as I inspect his shirt. "Where's your stain?"

Releasing just one of my hips, he twists his torso, showing me the stain on his back.

"Genius." I giggle. "Now it looks like someone else's fault, not yours," I yell over the hum of the crowd and the buzz in my own head. I should have only had half a gummy an hour earlier.

"Exactly."

"This is the best night ever. The best weather. The best crowd. The best bands ... It's all just ..."

"The best?" He laughs.

I nod on a slow sigh. "*You're* the best for loaning me your shoulders."

"You're welcome." It thrills me that his fingers are still hooked in my belt loops. I have no solid opinion on love at first sight, but this definitely feels like sparks flying, chemistry, *something* magnetic that makes my heart do funny acrobats.

"I'm starving. I haven't had anything to eat today except a few french fries from this dude I met earlier." A very sexy dude with a killer smile and mischievous look in his eyes that makes me think he has less than appropriate thoughts going through his mind.

Good call on the condoms, Juni.

He leans down. I suck in a breath. An inch over my lips, he hovers before relinquishing the full killer smile. After I surrender my own grin, he lowers his mouth to my ear—such a tease—sending crazy shivers along my skin.

"I have to help tear down." He smells good. No one smells good after a day at Coachella, but kudos to Bodhi ... he's still irresistible.

"I'll wait for you."

He stands tall again. "It could be another hour or two."

I'm willing to eat all ten of my fingernails and even gnaw on my own fist if that's what it takes to pacify my stomach long enough to share my next meal with him. "I don't mind."

His eyes narrow for a brief second. "How old are you, Henna?"

"Old enough to know never to eat ketchup while wearing white."

Coughing a hearty laugh, he nods. "Fair enough." His lips twist as his gaze ping-pongs from the empty stage to me. "Wait for me?"

Taking a step back, I shove my fingers into the back pockets of my shorts. "Take your time. I'll be here."

An hour and twenty minutes later, two sexy denim clad legs walk past me. "I'm still starving."

He turns. A flash of relief ghosts over his face. I hold out my hand from my spot on the ground next to the front of the stage. Pulling me up, he stares at me for a few seconds. He smells like lemon again. It's officially become my favorite fruit of all time.

"You waited."

Brushing off my backside, I chuckle. "Yes. Why? Do you get stood up a lot?"

"Not exactly." He rubs his lips together. "Let's go."

I take his proffered hand, and I'm not sure who initiates it, but we slide our fingers to interlace them as if we've done it a million times before. Everything about this night feels natural. At this exact moment, I'm so damn happy I could scream like a little girl on Christmas.

He leads us to the exit.

"Shuttle?" I ask.

"Yes, my van is at the hotel."

I laugh. "A van, huh? As in a minivan? Do you have a wife and two kids?"

On an easy chuckle, he shakes his head as we step onto the shuttle bus. The throng of people sandwich us together as we hold onto the rails.

I look up and smile at him.

He smiles back.

We do this every minute or two all the way back to the hotel. We've mastered flirting like we were born to flirt with each other. Keeping ahold of my hand, he helps me off the bus and guides me to the far end of the parking lot.

"Oh my god …" I whisper.

"Before you judge me—"

"Shh!" I release his hand. "Don't say anything. You'll ruin this for me." Walking slowly around the fine vehicular specimen, my heart nearly explodes from my chest.

She's stunning.

A classic.

Well-kept.

The perfect shade of cornflower blue like my mom says about my eyes.

Not a single dent.

Even in the dim light of night, the chrome shines.

"Okay." I stand a foot from the front of her. "*Now* I'm judging you. Don't ever let anyone tell you that you have anything but impeccable taste. Even when you're wearing your shirt backward … just show them a picture of this beauty, and any person in their right mind will know you're a god of good taste."

A Volkswagen van—vintage and total perfection.

"1972. I'm glad you approve. You're in the minority." He opens the passenger door.

I ease into the seat. It's immaculately kept as well. "Bodhi?"

"Yeah?" He pauses before closing my door, and a shy smile instantly steals his lips.

Bodhi.

Fate is killing it today.

"I have a dozen condoms stashed in my purse and backpack, but it's too late. I think I'm already pregnant. Nothing could feel as good as sitting in this beautiful van."

A tiny blush crawls up Bodhi's face. "Lucky van."

Bodhi

I HURT SOMEONE that I love, and now I'm paying the price. This is it. Once a year I get to escape and pretend for a few days that my life didn't change forever because I did something so astronomically stupid.

"Tacos are life." Henna moans, chewing her huge bite of taco as we sit at a picnic table next to a food truck that's getting ready to close up for the night—or early morning. She's a stunning glimpse of the life I could have had before I fucked it up. God … I don't want to blink.

"They are to die for." I wipe my mouth, grinning at her from behind my napkin. "So why are you at Coachella by yourself?" But really I wonder why were people taking her picture and why did one of the most well-known tour managers in the music industry acknowledge her earlier today?

Henna holds up her finger, rattling the slew of bracelets on her wrist, while she finishes chewing her food and taking a swig of water. She's a reincarnated goddess from the seventies. "My dad was supposed to meet me here. He was a *drummer…*" she smirks "…in a band that played here at the very first Coachella."

"Ah, that's why you have a thing for drummers."

"No." She shakes her head. "That's just why I was meeting my dad here. We love music. I have a *thing* for drummers for other reasons."

I grin, feeling just as high as she probably was this morning. Can I just stop time and stare at this girl? Count the freckles along the bridge of her nose, imagine what her long auburn hair might feel like with my fingers in it? Decipher the meaning behind her henna tattoos? "So where's your dad?"

She finishes her last bite of taco and takes down the rest of her water. "He ate sushi. I highly recommend you never eat sushi. I'm just not sure it's a good idea to eat a gutted fish before cooking it. Ya know?"

On a soft chuckle that feels so fucking incredible, I nod. "California veggie rolls are the closest I get to sushi."

"Oh my god! I love California veggie rolls. We should go find some." Of course she would say this. I'm not sure what Henna's world is really like, but she doesn't seem to have any boundaries, and at this very moment, I want to live in that world with her.

"It's after two in the morning." I glance at my watch, making a weak attempt to be responsible. "I feel like I should get you back to your hotel."

"Dude, how old are you? It's Coachella. We can sleep Monday." She stands and piles her trash onto mine. "Tonight ... or this morning, we get California veggie rolls."

Yeah, she's a torturous glimpse at a life I would have loved to live.

"Where are we going to get them at this time?" I toss our trash into the garbage can.

She types a message into her phone and gets a response within a few seconds. "I know someone, who knows someone, who knows ..." She slips her phone into her bag and looks up.

"Well, you get the point, right?"

I look at my watch again.

"Bodhi, Bodhi, Bodhi … my really far into the future husband and baby daddy … stop looking at your watch." Grabbing my wrist, she takes off my watch and tosses it into her bag too.

I lift an eyebrow. "You're trouble." Do I want trouble tonight? Do I want to go down this rabbit hole? Giving her the once-over while she does the same to me, the answer is clear.

Interlacing our fingers, she pulls me toward the van. "Oh, you have no idea."

I drive us to our destination, fighting my natural inclination to worry about everything and feel guilty for this huge smile on my face. She rolls down the window and turns up the radio. She doesn't ask me where I live or what I do. She doesn't ask me if I have ten siblings. We simply live in the moment.

"Uh … Henna, there's a security gate. Are you sure we're at—"

"Push the button and say Katy Perry's Teenage Dream."

"What?" I stop at the gate, giving her an incredulous look.

Unfastening her seatbelt, she crawls over me and rolls down my window.

"Henna—"

"Shh …" She pushes the button and glances back at me. "You're not staring at my ass are you?"

"You kinda have it in my line of vision." *And yeah, I'm staring at your ass, your legs, and every other part of your body that my hands are itching to touch in ways that would probably piss off your sushi-sick dad.*

She grins, and my dick hardens. "Katy Perry's Teenage

Dream."

The two wrought iron gates open.

"See?" She plops back into her seat. "Step on it, dude. California rolls are waiting for us."

I shake my head and step on the gas.

"Oh…" she twists her lips "…the party is still going on. I wouldn't let the valet park our baby. Go right and we'll find a good, safe spot for her."

"Our baby?" I turn right. "And every car here costs at least sixty-grand. I'm pretty sure we could have trusted *our* baby with the valet."

"No way. Right here." She points to a spot with lots of room on both sides then rolls up her window.

"Henna?"

We get out.

"Yes?"

"This looks like a really fancy party, a really expensive house, and a really exclusive invitation list."

She takes my hand. "Probably."

I chuckle. "My shirt is on backward and there's ketchup on it. I'm not sure this is a good idea."

She stops, tapping her finger on her chin. "You're right." She sighs. "I can't take you anywhere. I'll get on your back to cover the stain."

"Henna—"

She hops onto my back. I like her on my back. I'm certain I just like her body touching mine in as many places as possible. I grab her sexy legs.

"Problem solved."

I walk us toward the front door. "So you're just going to

stay on my back for the whole night?"

Teasing her nose along the shell of my ear, she squeezes me with both her arms and legs. "Is that a problem?"

I swallow hard. "Not at all." She's going to ruin me in less than twenty-four hours.

"Henna!" A brunette, maybe in her forties, greets Henna as I carry her into the house.

"Hey. Lauren, Bodhi—Bodhi, Lauren."

I let go of her right leg long enough to shake Lauren's hand. She gives Henna a sly grin and wide eyes. "I feel like I should get a picture of this and send it to your mom."

I stiffen. That sounds like a terrible idea.

"Yes!" Henna rests her cheek on my shoulder as Lauren fishes her phone out of her bra and takes a picture.

"Beautiful." She grins. "California veggie rolls are in the kitchen. Have fun."

"Thank you." Henna points toward the kitchen.

"Is this Lauren's house?"

"Yes," she says in my ear over the loud music. "And Rex's."

"You know some rich people."

"Sort of."

"So you're rich?"

"Nope. I don't even have a job at the moment. I just know people. I told you ... I know someone, who knows someone, who—"

"Yeah, yeah, knows someone."

"Exactly. Right there." She points to the platter of California veggie rolls and three different dipping sauces.

"Where are the plates?" I ask.

"Whoa! Plates? We're not sharing. Just grab the whole platter."

I look left then right, waiting for someone to see us stealing the platter.

"Left. Up the back stairway. If I'm too heavy to carry up the stairs, you can put me down."

I don't respond. Instead, I easily carry her up the stairs.

"The last room on the right."

"This is where you're staying?" I ease her to the ground, and she takes the plate of California rolls from me.

"Yes. My dad had a room at a hotel close to the venue, but when he got sick, he cancelled it, um … assuming I'd go back home to my mom. But I wanted to stay and everything was booked, so … I know someone who—"

"Knows someone, who knows someone." I roll my eyes as she opens the doors to a private balcony overlooking the Colorado desert. "Five-star accommodations," I say more to myself than to her. This is a different life than I've ever known. I came close to this life, but … I fucked it up.

I follow Henna outside and take a seat on the sofa next to her while she snags one of the rolls from the tray before setting it on the table in front of us.

We eat in silence for a few long minutes, taking in the starry night. How did I get here?

The house.

The view.

The woman. God … the woman. I don't even know if she's real. Maybe she's this ethereal creature sent to tempt me then punch me in the gut again for my epic mistake.

"I feel like I should ask you about …" I let out a long breath—one that holds a lot of something. A very *heavy* breath.

"It's a good night. Don't feel obligated to do the small talk thing with me. I rather like us without it."

Yeah, she's not real.

"Us ..." I say the word like I need to test it out.

"Bodhi and Henna." She unties her shoes and slips them off, tucking her feet under her. "And Alice."

"Who's Alice?"

"Duh. Our blue baby with big round eyes and an awkward but adorable little VW emblem nose. Unless..." she digs her teeth into her lower lip "...you already named her. Didn't you? That's cool. Alice could be a middle name."

I stare at her mouth, desperate to taste it. If this is a dream, I'm going to fight to never wake up.

The longer I stare, the more she squirms. Henna grabs another California roll and shoves it into her mouth. My gaze shifts to her brilliant blue eyes. She knows I was staring a bit too long at her tempting lips.

I grin. "I didn't name her."

"Aw ... see?" Henna mumbles over a mouthful of food. "You were waiting for me." She wipes her mouth and sets the napkin on the table. "Are you good with Alice? We can discuss this, but I'm not gonna lie ... she totally looks like an Alice." She pulls a package out of her pocket. "Gummy?"

I frown. "I'm good." She's ethereal, sexy, and as close to perfect as she could be while still being a pothead. Okay, that's not fair. Maybe she really does have pain from whatever caused that scar on her back. Either way, I can't go down that road again. But she can't be a road in my life because my life is a dead end.

Henna stares at her gummies with a contemplative look

then slides them back into her pocket without eating one. Now I feel like a dick. What if she's in pain?

"Just pot?" I ask.

She shrugs. "I can get you some beer or really probably anything you want from downstairs."

I shake my head. "I mean, is pot the only thing you use?"

"Oh ..." she laughs. "Yes. I was getting dependent on opioids. Juni suggested I try marijuana instead."

"Juni?"

"My mom."

"You call your mom Juni?"

"Yes. She's my best friend. Juni makes me feel open to share my darkest secrets. *Mom* makes me clam up."

Juni? I cock my head to the side. "I think there was a model or actress with that name. Juniper? Tall, blond ...?"

"Oh ..." She nods several times. "Yes. Juniper Carlisle. She was an international supermodel; now she has a fashion DIY show on cable."

"I don't watch much TV."

"No?" She mirrors my head-cock. "I had minimal TV growing up. Basically National Geographic for kids. My parents were very liberal about most things, then ultra conservative about other things. But ... lately I've been bingeing on *Riverdale*."

I nod toward her pocket, unable to shrug the nagging feeling that I came across as a condescending jerk. "If you need that ... don't let me stop you."

Her hand covers mine between us, closing her eyes for a few long seconds. "I think I could take one Bodhi before bed every night and never lose sleep over pain again."

Well, fuck me ...

"I should go." I stare at her hand on mine.

"There are probably a bunch of crazies on the road. You could fall asleep driving. And I'd hate to see anything happen to you and Alice." She grins and so do I. "Besides, I want you to tell me what it's like to be a surfer or a cowboy."

I bark out a belly laugh and melt into the back of the sofa, running my hands through my already messy hair. "Oh ... wow." I lace my fingers behind my head.

Her gaze drops to my chest. Curiosity and something even more intimate flashes across her face.

"Funny you should mention those two things. I love to surf, and I can ride a horse with the best of them."

"Bullshit."

"Bullshit? Why are you calling bullshit when you brought it up?"

"I was joking. Just being stereotypical. Naked, you look like a surfer, but dressed in these jeans and boots, I can totally see you in a cowboy hat, mounted on a horse."

"Wait. When have you seen me naked?"

Her skin turns pink all the way to the top of her ears. "I *mean* your actual physical appearance looks like a surfer."

"I see." I scratch my chin. "Hmm ... what do I think you look like?"

Her entire body seems to come to life as her back straightens when she rearranges herself so she's sitting on her knees, facing my side.

"You have an artsy-ness to you. I'd bet you did your own henna tattoos. But you're young ... I'm not sure I really want to know how young." My nose wrinkles a bit. It hits me. This girl could be sixteen.

She rolls her eyes. "I turn nineteen … soon."

"Fuck …" I still cringe, running my hands through my hair again. "Young."

She grabs my wrists and throws a leg over my lap, straddling me.

"Henna—"

"Finish telling me what your first impression of me was."

I shake my head slowly. "I can't." Swallowing hard, my gaze slips to her mouth.

"Why?" She interlaces our fingers and curls our hands around her back, forcing us closer together.

"I think you're trouble."

"Some say I'm Hell."

"Hell?" I whisper as she inches closer to me, finding my mouth just as mesmerizing as I find hers.

"Yeah." She searches my face. "Henna Eve Lane. H.E.L."

I grin, the kind that grows by the second. "Perfect." I lean in toward her lips.

She pulls back. "Take your shirt off. I can't stop thinking about the ketchup on the back of it, and I need to know if you have any tattoos."

"No tattoos."

But yes, I will take off all of my clothes for you if you just ask.

"Good."

"Good?" I cock my head to the side.

"Yeah. They're too permanent. I don't know if I could be into a guy who feels so strongly about something that he makes a permanent mark on himself."

"Interesting."

She nods. I lean in again.

"I'm serious. I need you to take your shirt off." She curls her fingers around the hem of it, waiting for me to give her permission.

I lift my arms without a second's hesitation.

"Damn ..." she whispers. Then her gaze shoots to mine as if she just realized she said that aloud.

She folds my shirt one way, then another, and yet another.

"I can put it back on." I take it from her shaky hands.

Henna

THIS IS THE part where I'm supposed to confess my virginity, but I don't want to be a virgin with Bodhi. I want it to be *us.* Henna and Bodhi. I want a weekend of living—a weekend of not being judged by my past or my family. But more than anything, I want to enjoy the incomparable high that I feel with Bodhi. It's a high greater than anything in my pocket.

I reach for my braid, but he stops me, sliding off the hairband and setting it on the sofa next to us. He loosens my braid, and as wavy auburn strands fall around my shoulders, he threads his fingers through it.

A playful smile tugs at his lips when I shiver. Bodhi makes me feel vulnerable and so alive. "I think I could like Bodhi and Henna," he whispers, pulling me to him, ghosting his lips over my face, touching me with his mouth everywhere but on my mouth.

I feather my fingers along his abs, closing my eyes to just

29

feel *us.*

No pain.

No past regrets or future worries.

We've known each other for *hours.* This is insane, but my compass has never pointed directly north, so I just don't give a shit. This attraction is something stronger than just physical. Bodhi is a force greater than anything I have ever felt. We were meant to meet, if only to share a few days. I'll never be able to explain it with words. *We* are a feeling.

And when it happens—the kiss—I feel it like a lost part of myself finding its way back home. His kiss is slow, and just like when we hold hands, it feels familiar and so right.

He pulls back, keeping his hands threaded in my hair. "Bodhi and Henna," he whispers, brushing his nose against mine. It feels like a promise, but I don't think it is because there's too much pain in his voice.

"Henna and Bodhi," I whisper back a breath before my mouth finds his again.

We kiss for what feels like hours. His hands caress my face, my hair, down my arms, and occasionally they find the curve of my butt, pulling me closer to him. I feel him hard against me, and I would give Bodhi everything, but for this night, that isn't Henna and Bodhi.

After our lips are thoroughly swollen and the morning hours approach sunrise, he removes his boots and socks and lays us down on the sofa—my face buried in his neck. My hands mold to his bare chest, our legs scissored together, and his arms encase me in something so unexpected I can't imagine the inevitable goodbye.

CHAPTER FOUR

Bodhi

F IVE DAYS OF freedom. Not guilt-free freedom, just freedom. My expectations reached no further than a weekend
of immersing myself in the life I once loved so much. Until …

Henna.

She blinds me with a light I haven't seen in years. Eighteen
is young. Even when I round her age up to nineteen, it still
plagues me with guilt, but there is something she has that I
need.

Air.

It feels amazing and unfamiliar to breathe again, even if for
only a couple of days.

"Who did this?" I trace the lines of her temporary tattoos as
the sun climbs up the horizon over the desert. My lips press to
the top of her head, and she leans into me, her back flush to
my chest.

"Me."

Elation settles into my chest. I was right—she's artsy.
There's a part of her no one will ever understand unless they
see how she expresses herself without words.

"Well, that's disconcerting."

Her body shakes with a soft chuckle. "Why?"

"I called it, which means I must be right about you being trouble."

"You only have to deal with me for two more days. Unless ..." She rolls over to face me.

I pretend that her wild hair, sleepy eyes, and smattering of freckles don't make my heart hurt for a few seconds when it really hits me—we are going to go our separate ways. I let myself enjoy a glimpse of the life I could have had before I messed up.

My mind wants to go there so badly because Henna isn't some girl I met at a concert, she's *the* girl, and every part of me knows it. When I hold her, my arms know it. I kiss her and my lips know it. When I look at her, something behind my ribs knows it too.

One day.

Henna made her mark on me in one day.

"Unless?" I palm her butt with one hand to keep her from falling off the edge of the sofa.

Her eyes widen. Yeah, I have a severe case of morning wood. Totally her fault, but I don't mention it and neither does she.

"Unless you're tired of me. I know you probably have to work today. I'm not clingy. Really, I just—"

I silence her with a kiss. She hums and slides a leg between mine which doesn't help my situation down there.

"When do you leave?" I ask after leaving her breathless.

"Monday."

"What time is your flight? Do you need a ride to the airport?"

"Um ..." She chews her lower lip. "Sure. What time are you leaving?"

I chuckle. "I'm driving. My schedule has some flexibility. What time is your flight?"

"Where are you driving to?" It's the first time she asks something that could link us beyond this weekend.

After the night we've spent together, I want to know where she lives, who waits for her at home, and if she feels the same ache in her stomach and chest that I feel knowing our time together is about to expire.

"East." I slide my hand from her butt to her lower back while my other hand fists her hair so I can kiss a thousand tomorrows out of her. When I have to release her, she forces something resembling a smile—the brave kind. I recognize it because it's the same one I have on my own face.

"Let's eat before we leave. I'm sure there's quite the spread downstairs."

"Rich people breakfast?" I ask.

She furrows a brow for a few seconds. "Yes. I suppose so." Rolling away, she swings her legs around and stands up, stretching like a cat.

"Do you eat rich people breakfast every morning?" My curiosity has been piqued.

After a long yawn, she cocks her head to the side, lips slightly twisted. "Shredded Wheat with cut-up banana and almond milk. Is that a rich person's breakfast?"

I sit up, doing a bit of my own stretching, loving the way her gaze roams along my bare chest, her lips parting ever so slightly. "No. I think that's a solid middle-class breakfast."

"Middle. That's average. Average is good, right?"

"There's nothing average about you, Henna." I stand, following her into the bedroom.

"I'm going to shower quickly, and by quickly I mean I need an hour. Do you have an hour?"

"To shower with you?" I try to play it cool, like I'm serious. I'm a little serious.

The color leaves her face. "Oh, um ..." She twists her fingers together, drawing her shoulders inward.

"I'm kidding."

A little kidding.

Henna's posture relaxes as her cheeks pink up again. "We could." Her gaze darts around the room before landing on mine for two seconds only to wander around the room again.

"My clothes are at my hotel. I'll shower there. I need to get going."

A slow sigh deflates her chest as she tries on a smile that misses the confident mark by a few centimeters. "Okay."

"But thanks for the offer." I wink.

More color paints her cheeks, and it looks stunning on her. "I kinda sorta thought we'd have sex last night, but we didn't, and that's fine, but now I don't know what comes next."

Does that make me the world's biggest idiot for not taking what she was planning on offering? Or does that make me a gentleman? I've already fucked her a hundred different ways in my head, so I'm going to shy away from the gentleman label.

"How about you put my number in your phone and I'll call you later today? That feels like a good next, don't you think?"

Henna nods and turns, walking toward the bedroom door. Digging through her purse, she retrieves her phone. When she pulls it out, a string of three condoms comes out with it. "Oh jeez." Quickly snatching them off the floor, she shoves them back into her purse.

I don't respond because I'm not sure what the correct response should be.

"I was conceived at Coachella." She hands me her phone with the contact screen open, ready for my information.

Taking her phone, I give her an expectant look, but she withholds all elaboration.

"And by conceived, you mean physical conception, not merely an idea kind of conception?" I hand her phone back and give her mine.

"In the shadows behind a stage. I know more details than most people should actually know about the moment they were conceived." She lifts a shoulder in a small shrug. "But Juni is my best friend. She's the absolute coolest mom ever, and the story of how she met my dad is my favorite story ever."

I nod as she keeps her chin tipped toward the screen to my phone. "Why is that?" I take my phone back when she holds it out to me.

"Yin Yang. Opposites. Laws of the universe." She wears a satisfied smile. "My parents were temporary. I was permanent." Holding out her arms, she inspects her henna tattoos as if seeing them for the first time. "My mom had henna tattoos on her body when she met my dad. Henna grows in intensity over a few days before fading to nothing. It's magical and beautiful and then it's gone. My parents say that about their love for each other. It grew quickly into something deep and intense, but over time it faded. Their love—like most everything in life—was temporary."

"We're temporary."

Her empty stare shifts to meet my gaze and she nods. "Don't sweat it. Everything is temporary. But today…" she walks into my chest, and my arms wrap around her as she looks up at me "…we should be at our brightest, our most intense."

"Intense?" There is a hyperawareness of every feeling in my body—my heartbeat, my quickening breaths, a tingle in my fingers eager to touch her in new places.

"Intense." She lifts onto her toes, wrapping her arms around my neck and guiding my mouth to hers.

Our kiss grows into something demanding. She hums into my mouth as my hands slide down her back to her ass, grabbing it with both hands to bring her body flush with mine. Her fingernails claw at my neck, my back, and my chest. Filled with desperation from many months of not being intimate with a woman, I lower my grip on her backside and lift her up.

"Bodhi." Her breathless voice unravels me as her mouth devours mine.

I walk us to the nearest wall, letting my itchy hands explore the rest of her body. When her back hits the solid surface, she releases the sexiest grunt and rocks her pelvis into me, grazing the head of my swollen cock uncomfortably confined behind my jeans.

"Henna …" I come up for air, but she fists my hair and pulls me back in for another mind-blowing kiss. With her pinned to the wall, I let my right hand slide under her top and cup her braless breast. It's so fucking perfect.

Latching her ankles behind my back, she grinds herself into me again. I'm ready to die right here on the spot. I pinch her hardened nipple.

"Bodhi!" Her head falls back against the wall as I suck and lick the skin down her neck to her bare shoulder. "Condoms … I have lots of condoms …"

"I saw that." Grinning against her delicate flesh, I press my body harder to hers, allowing my other hand the chance to claim her other breast.

She arches into me, hands tugging my hair, encouraging me to keep going.

It's funny how my mind went from feeling guilty about her age to working overtime to justify everything I want to do to her in this moment. She's an adult. A consenting adult.

With condoms.

Lots of condoms.

I only need one, and if she continues to make those desperate little noises while rubbing herself against my dick, I'm not going to need any condoms.

The girl makes me so weak in the knees, I fear I might drop her. I lower both of our bodies to the floor. There's a king-sized bed, a sofa on the balcony, even a chaise lounge in the corner of the bedroom, but I'm so damn desperate and high on Henna, the floor is as far as I can get us.

I settle my body between her open legs and push her top above her breasts with one hand while supporting my body over hers with my other hand. "You're so fucking beautiful." My attention lifts to her blue eyes.

The tip of her tongue darts out to wet her swollen lips. I want that tongue tasting me. My hips rock into her.

Fuck … I need inside of her.

"Take …" She swallows hard, her cheeks filled with heat. "Take off my shorts, Bodhi."

Stealing a few moments to let those words sink in, I dip down and taste one of her nipples with a slow slide of my tongue over it before flicking it several times then sucking it hard.

"Jesus, Bodhi!" Her back bows off the floor, her hands clawing my back and my shoulders.

I do the same thing to her other breast, making her squirm and pant beneath me as I inch down her body, teasing her navel with the tip of my tongue, tracing the swirl of henna leading me even lower. Her hands return to my head, making claim to my hair, her bracelets clinking together.

Biting the material of her shorts, I tug it until the button comes undone. "What do you taste like, Henna?" I run my tongue along her skin just above her delicate polka dot panties.

Her heavy breaths fill the space around us as she lifts her pelvis from the floor. I run my nose along the inseam of her shorts, torturing myself as much as her, yet loving every second of it. God ... I don't want it to stop.

"Henna? Henna's sexy friend? Breakfast!" Lauren calls from some place relatively close to the bedroom door that I feel fairly certain is not locked.

I freeze.

"In a minute," Henna says in a voice so weakened by lust, there is no way Lauren hears her. "Don't stop."

I wince as Henna tugs my hair, trying to keep my head between her spread legs. She pushes her pelvis an inch higher.

I want to keep going—so much it hurts in very restricted places. Looking for my watch that isn't on my wrist because she stole it last night, I'm reminded that I probably don't have time for breakfast, and if I don't get back to the hotel, I'm not going to have time for a shower and clean clothes—a ketchup-free shirt.

But ... I only have two days left with Henna.

"Bodhi, please."

Closing my eyes, I grip her ass with one hand, holding her to me while my lips brush the soft skin of her inner thighs, my tongue teasing her so close to the top I about lose it when she jerks and moans, lifting even higher onto her tippy toes. Her desperation multiplies mine.

"Acai bowls, fresh juice, croissants." Lauren's words come from a farther distance, but they still dampen my resolve.

I ease away from Henna.

"No! God, no!" She sits up, hair wild and completely ineffable. Her shirt falls back over her breasts as she grabs my face and plunges her tongue into my mouth.

Tacos aren't life. This girl is *life*.

I kiss her, my hands conflicted as I try to push her away for one second before sliding back up under her shirt to claim her breasts again.

She releases my face and traces her fingers down my torso, her tongue sliding against mine as she works the button to my jeans.

Fuck ...

My watch chimes from her handbag a few feet to the left of us. My reminder to not be late. I pull away again, out of breath and out of my damn mind.

"Bodhi." Henna jumps to her feet after I stand, running my hands through my hair while trying to make sense of what almost happened with a girl I met *yesterday*.

I hold out a flat hand to keep her at arm's length. "Don't."

Said no sane man EVER!

A slow-building smile works its way up her face. Yeah, she's *all* kinds of trouble—Hell.

"The acai bowls are bland, and the croissants are dry."

I grin for a second, but it quickly fades when her playfulness sinks into my gut. The problem is I like every single thing about Henna, and I don't care that we've only known each other one day. Time is a weak force compared to other earthly phenomena like magnetism.

Attraction doesn't give a shit about time. It wants what it wants.

I know one thing for sure—long after our time ends, I will feel an invisible pull to her for the rest of my life.

Yin and Yang.

Positive and negative.

Bodhi and Henna.

"I'm not even sure it's physically possible to tear myself away from you," I say, taking a step away from her and feeling the immediate invisible resistance. "But I have to try because I have to be someplace in a short while, and …" I shake my head as she tries to move toward me again. "Per your warning about the acai bowls and croissants, I'll just grab a glass of juice before I go."

Her mouth twists as her eyes narrow a fraction. "Okay."

"Okay?"

Henna nods. "Yep. Okay."

It feels like a trap. The smile she gives me isn't a submissive okay. It's evil and no doubt a hiding-something-that-will-probably-ruin-me kind of smile.

"I'm leaving now." I jab my thumb over my shoulder toward the door, eyes wide in anticipation of her next move.

"Okay." She laces her fingers behind her back and rocks back and forth on her heels.

I squint, nodding slowly. "O—kay."

"Oh!" She holds up a finger and jogs to the balcony, re-trieving my shirt. "Don't forget to stain treat it."

I take the shirt, slipping it back on with the ketchup in the front again. "I think it's headed for the trash."

"Well, I'm headed for the shower." Fishing my watch from her purse, she hands it to me and lifts onto her toes, stamping a quick kiss on my cheek before retreating to the bathroom. "Bye, Bodhi."

CHAPTER FIVE

Henna

WHITE CROP TOP tied in front.
Ample cleavage.
No bra.
Denim miniskirt.
White ankle boots.
Hair down.
Flower crowned head.
Mission: find Bodhi.

"Hey, Juni." I answer my phone as I worm my way through the festivalgoers after surviving the cluster fuck of security.

"Sunscreen?"

"Yes." I wait for the real reason for her call.

"Hat?"

"In my bag."

"How many condoms do you have left?"

I glance behind me, frowning at the shadow that's been following me since I left the hotel after my dad cancelled.

"Should I be worried about the gray-haired man following me who looks completely out of place?"

"I'm a cool mom, but I'm still a mom. Ignore him. I want you to have fun, but safety is my first priority."

I pull out my hat and swap it for the flower crown. It's going to be a freakishly hot day. "Thank you. I think."

"So … I got the picture from Lauren. He's adorable. Bodhi?"

I smile, sighing like a lovestruck fool. "Yes. He's … life."

"He's an experience."

I snake my way through the shoulder-to-shoulder crowd in one of the tents. "I know. And he's … everything. God! I had the best night of my life."

"And you were—"

"No condoms. We didn't get that far." I roll my eyes.

"So tell me everything about him."

"Not much to tell. We didn't share our bios."

"Smart. You might not see him after tomorrow. Just have fun. Have you seen a lot of friends?"

"Some. I sorta got distracted by Bodhi yesterday."

"Mmm … I remember those days."

Dad. She remembers my dad. That makes me grin again.

"I'll call you later, unless I get distracted. But I'm sure the gray-haired shadow will keep you appraised of my whereabouts." Glancing back, I watch the poor guy try to battle the sea of bodies to keep up with me.

"Love you. Be safe. Have fun. And condoms, Henna. Don't forget them."

"Yeah, yeah, bye." I slip my phone into my bag and hunch down to find a few holes to maneuver my way to the stage. Within minutes, the crowd goes wild as lights come to life and the lyrics to one of my favorite songs spill from the stacks of speakers.

After hours of milling around the tents, getting lost in the pulse of the crowds, and scoring a cold drink, I set out to find ketchup guy. But … no luck.

I snap a selfie with only the bottom half of my face to allow my cleavage to have the focus, then I text it to Bodhi.

Me: Missing my sidekick.

A few minutes later, he responds with a selfie of himself drenched in sweat, another white shirt sans stain, and sipping a sports drink. It looks like he's sitting on the edge of a stage, but I can't tell for sure.

Me: I bet you have your own screaming crowd. Location please? I called dibs on you today.

He sends me a short video of his surroundings.

Bodhi: Come find me.

I grin. This isn't my first Coachella. I know exactly where he's at. Spewing off apologies for my shoving and pushing to break free from the crowd, I take long strides to another stage that isn't set to have a show start for a while. Everything vibrates inside of me as I wear a permanent grin.

"Sorry, miss. This is a restricted area." A security guard holds up his hand as I make my way toward the side of the stage.

I retrieve my pass from my bag. Mr. Security Guard inspects it then gives me the nod while stepping to the side.

Rounding the corner to where I feel certain Bodhi is at, I

freeze. A blonde wearing a shirt that says *Crew* on the back throws her head back in laughter as Bodhi animatedly talks to her.

"You're too much." She nudges the toe of her shoe into the toe of his boot.

I have a place I want to stick my foot as well.

"Let's get a drink as soon as you're done."

"Um …"

I jump behind a large speaker as he turns his head to look around.

"I think I have plans."

"Well, if you don't, text me."

"Yeah. Absolutely."

I peek around the speaker just as he returns a genuine smile to the other crew member.

"Cool. Later." She sashays off in the other direction.

Bodhi lifts his shirt to wipe the sweat from his brow and blond girl shoots him an admiring glance over her shoulder. The hair on the back of my neck stands erect as my claws inch their way out. I had no idea I was catty, until now.

I'm not trouble. Bodhi is trouble.

Returning to my hiding spot, I contemplate just walking away. We only have two days—really more like one and a half. He's going his way, and I have school in the fall. There's no room for promises or cattiness. We are temporary—*don't sweat it, everything is temporary.*

"Let's stop time so we don't have to say goodbye."

I jump as two familiar arms wrap around me from my backside.

How the hell did he sneak around here and find me?

"Bodhi ..." I sigh his name, closing my eyes and relaxing my head back onto his chest.

"Henna." He kisses my neck.

My arms cover his. I don't want him to let me go, and I have no idea what to do with that realization.

He whips me around and pins me to the speaker, holding my hands behind my back. "No bra. Interesting choice when wearing a thin white shirt." His tongue makes a lazy swipe across his lower lip.

"I wore it for you."

A twitch of a grin nudges his lips, eyes alight with mischief. He hums. "For me?"

I nod.

He takes his time letting his gaze roam along my body. "If you dressed for me..." he looks around before leaning closer to my ear and lowering his voice "...you'd be naked."

Feeling extra flushed, I hold my breath until I can speak without stammering a bunch of nonsense. "I offered you naked Henna. You wanted a glass of juice and a quick getaway."

A throaty laugh escapes him. "Clear lapse in judgment on my part."

I let my thoughts simmer into secrets I will never be able to share with him. Something about him makes me want to get all sappy and sentimental. Probably the same something that had my claws curling, ready to attack an innocent blonde just minutes ago.

"When are you done?"

He glances at his watch. "Five hours."

I frown.

"But I have forty-five minutes to grab some food. Can I

feed you too?"

With only hours remaining, I want to spend Bodhi's forty-five free minutes making out with him. I can't get enough. New attraction is like the first glance of an exquisite view or the first bite of the most delectable dessert. I want to indulge on Bodhi, but lunch is fine.

It's safe.

"Lunch sounds perfect."

He takes my hand, letting our fingers intertwine, and we grab two Korean BBQ bowls and ice cream on the way back to the stage where Bodhi has to work.

"It's melting. You'd better hurry up." Bodhi points to the blue ice cream melting down my wrist. "You're gonna get— OH!" He fists his hand at his mouth as it drips down the front of my *white* top.

"Shit! Shit, shit, shit!" I lick it as fast as I can, but the desert heat is one step ahead of me. "Help!" I hold it away from my stained shirt as it continues to drip.

Bodhi grabs my wrist and starts licking the ice cream in the cone, the pools of it running down the sides. Then he licks my fingers and forearm, eyeing me with a mischievous grin around his lapping tongue.

I want that tongue. I want those lips. And when my smile fades, I think he knows exactly what I'm thinking.

Without taking his eyes off me, he, too, loses all playfulness. It's replaced with the same need I have. I *know* this because I'm certain Henna and Bodhi is a phenomenon greater than the simplicity of fate. We are a definable law of nature like those that came before us from Newton, Ohm, and Mendel.

He tosses the rest of my ice cream in the trash and pulls me around to the side of the tent. There are a few people, maybe fifteen yards away, vaping and chatting, but …

We don't care.

Bodhi grabs my face and kisses me. Our tongues and hands lose all control, feeling each other everywhere.

"Get a room," someone says on a laugh in the distance, followed by a few whistles and snickers.

We don't care.

Every crazy emotion stays caged in my head and my heart because that's what they are—crazy. I want to beg him to tell me everything.

His last name.

His address.

His age.

His greatest childhood memory.

And his most daunting fear.

But we are temporary. I need to keep reminding myself of that one truth.

His hand brushes over the thin material of my crop top. I moan into our deep kiss while he skims his thumb over my hard nipple.

More whistles and catcalls ensue.

We need someplace more private. Someplace that requires a condom to prevent nine-month surprises.

"Hen—"

I fist his shirt to keep us attached at the mouth as he tries to pull away. There isn't enough time to get my fill of him. There will never be enough time.

"Henna—"

I kiss his neck, tracing my tongue along his collarbone.

"Let's go somewhere more private." I slide my hands around his back and poke them down into his pockets, giving his nice ass a firm squeeze.

"Fuck …" He rests his forehead on mine, breathless. "Trouble. *Hell.* You're my complete undoing."

"What do you think I taste like?" I whisper.

"What?" he says with a strained voice.

"You asked me what I tasted like." I shrug. "I don't know what I taste like. But …" My heart knocks wildly against my ribs as I realize I want Bodhi. I want to use those condoms. All of them. "I want you to tell me what I taste like."

"Henna … I …" He pushes me so my backside is almost touching the tent, his body guarding me from our audience in the distance.

We stare at each other with drunken eyes and parted lips as his right hand squeezes my ass, sliding my miniskirt up a bit.

I swallow hard, knowing that if someone were to walk around the tent they'd see my half-exposed ass, something that the whistlers down the way can't see.

"Tonight." I kiss him, letting my tongue tease his lips first to ask permission.

He returns one last kiss that liquefies every inch of my body, leaving me a mere pool of a girl on the ground. "To-night." He grins. "I'll call you when I'm done."

FOR THE NEXT five hours, I meander around the festival, higher than I've ever been after any form of pot. Every ten minutes, I post a snap, resisting the urge to hashtag with *#CountdownToLosingMyVirginity.*

Showered, waxed, and covered in a thin layer of lotion, with nothing more than a long, flowing sundress covering my otherwise naked body and pink Birkies, I wait by the exit we took last night. I know Bodhi should be calling me at any moment as the scant, lingering crowd filters out at the end of night two.

Over my shoulder and a safe but protective distance away, Mr. Bodyguard watches me. He's not here to adjust my moral compass or rat me out for a few gummy bears; he's here to make sure no one harms me. That's it. That's just how cool my mom and stepdad are.

Bodhi's name illuminates as my phone rings.

"Hurry up. I'm wearing nothing and I mean *nothing* under this flimsy sundress. I'm getting cold. You need to warm me up with your body."

"Henna," he says in a strained voice.

"What is it? What's wrong?" I step away from the entrance, planting myself under a light, but away from everyone else.

"I'm on my way home. I left three hours ago. I tried to call you, but—"

"My phone died." Too many photos posted to social media. "I left to charge it in time for you to call now, not ..." I shake my head, feeling this grinding pressure in the pit of my stomach. "Why?"

"Something personal came up. It's my dad. I couldn't wait."

"Is he okay?"

"I hope so."

"Bodhi ..." What can I say? This terribly selfish part of me wants to get mad at him for leaving without saying goodbye.

The irrationally emotional side of me wants to cry. I do neither. "I'm sorry. I hope he's okay."

"Me too."

"Maybe …" Maybe what? I pinch my eyes shut.

"I'm not sure I've ever enjoyed being with another human as much as I enjoyed every second with you. Just … always know that. Okay?" he says, and I feel every ounce of his honesty and disappointment.

"What if we—"

"No what ifs. I'm sorry. My life doesn't leave room for any more what ifs. It's complicated."

"Can I …" Tears burn my eyes. I found *him*. Two days is not enough. Everything is temporary, but Bodhi can't be two days of my life. No … that's not okay.

"I'm sorry." So much pain bleeds from his voice. "We were perfect. *Bodhi and Henna …* I want every memory to be perfect. Let's let it end this way. It *was* so fucking perfect, and …"

Don't be sorry.

I wipe the tears from my eyes. "And temporary."

"Only our time together. But you, Henna Eve Lane, the mark you made is permanent."

"You'll forget about me. Henna fades."

"Never …" he whispers.

I choke on my emotions while I nod a goodbye I can't actually say aloud.

He waits on the line, but I can't speak. I can't even take a single breath, so I press *End*.

CHAPTER SIX

May (4 weeks later)

Henna: Hi. Remember me?

Bodhi: Hi. I'm pretty sure you're still my greatest memory.

I die.

Henna: How's your dad?

Bodhi: Better.

Henna: I'm in Italy. Where are you?

Bodhi: The barn.

Henna: LOL What if I swing by on my way home?

Bodhi: You'd wreck me. I'd have to start the getting-over-you process all over again.

Henna: How's that going?

Bodhi: Pretty shitty.

Henna: I listen to Hedley "Pocket Full of Dreams" at least ten times a day. Makes me think of this ketchup guy I met.

Bodhi: Hozier "Jackie and Wilson"

Henna: Someday ... I'm going to find you.

Bodhi: Wouldn't that be something?

Henna: Oh, it will be.

June *(4 weeks later)*

Henna: Hi. Remember me?

Bodhi: Hi. I'm pretty sure you're still my greatest memory.

Henna: How's your dad?

Bodhi: Obnoxious and grumpy.

Henna: I'm in California visiting my dad—the ex-drummer. You'd like him.

Bodhi: I've met his daughter. I'm sure he's pretty great.

Henna: Where are you?

Bodhi: Under Alice. She's getting her oil changed.

Henna: I miss Alice.

Bodhi: She misses you.

Henna: Are you over me yet?

Bodhi: Not even close.

Henna: I listen to Clean Bandit feat. Julia Michaels acoustic "I Miss You"

Bodhi: One Republic "Something I Need"

Henna: Someday … I'm going to find you.

Bodhi: Wouldn't that be something?

Henna: Oh, it will be.

July *(4 weeks later)*

Henna: Hi. Remember me?

Bodhi: Hi. I'm pretty sure you're still my greatest memory.

Henna: How's your dad?

Bodhi: Tired. Snoring.

Henna: I'm home. It smells like pine trees. Where are you?

Bodhi: Kitchen. Smells like garlic bread.

Henna: Are you over me yet?

Bodhi: Trying. Failing miserably.

Henna: I listen to Liza Anne "1000 Years"

Bodhi: Elvis Costello "She"

Henna: Someday ... I'm going to find you.

Bodhi: Wouldn't that be something?

Henna: Oh, it will be.

CHAPTER SEVEN

After staying faithfully high most of the summer, henna tattooing every inch of my body with Bodhi's name in fancy script, a ketchup bottle, Bodhi + Henna, even an unopened condom packet right below my navel—that is definitely a low point, even for me—I stop texting him. If he really misses me, he'll initiate contact.

I have obligations for another year, and he clearly has something that doesn't involve chasing me on his white horse and bending a knee. Not that those exact thoughts ever go through my mind.

"Happy Birthday, Hell!" Carley screams over the phone. She's my closest friend except for Juni, but she graduated the previous spring, which means we aren't in school together this fall.

I hold the phone away from my ear as I near the gates of a different kind of hell. "Thank you. How's college? Tell me it's awful and all the guys are ugly. Tell me the classes are really hard. Tell me absolutely anything to make me feel better about having one last year of high school."

"Sorry, chica. College is lit. And my Econ teacher is a nice snack. Gah! I wish you were here."

Rolling my eyes, I sigh. "Would it have killed you to lie to me? Just this once?"

Carley laughs. "Sorry. I know it doesn't help that you're officially the oldest student in school this year, which means all the guys are younger, but have fun, stay high, and live up to your nickname."

"You suck."

"Love you too, babe. Bye."

Ending the call, I toss my phone into my bag before getting sucked through the front doors with all of my eager peers.

Senior year of high school.

Yay me.

I have a lot of senior friends, but with Carley off to college, not any close ones. I am the girl who gets along with most everyone. Guys like me, some girls think they want to be me, and a few probably despise me for purely jealous reasons. Oh well ...

"Miss Lane, I anticipate a good senior year from you." Principal Rafferty smiles at me as I shuffle into calculus.

"Gail." I return a toothy grin.

Her smile fades. "Mrs. or Principal Rafferty, Henna. Let's try to get it right this year."

"Why? You didn't get my schedule right. I have like three study halls. How am I supposed to graduate with three study halls worth zero credits?" I hold up my paper schedule.

Gail frowns. "After calculus, go see Mr. Malone."

"Okey dokey." I wink, really needing to give more fucks about school, but I have too many distractions, like wanting to travel the world before even thinking about college—and Bodhi. I still have Bodhi stuck in my head.

After talking about everything we're going to do in calculus this semester, without actually doing a damn thing, the bell rings and I make my way to the new guidance counselor's office. The door is shut, so I knock and trace the name on the plate outside of it.

Mr. Malone

Another year. Another new counselor. I may be partially to blame for the frequent turnovers of this position. I spend more time here than in most of my classes. I enjoy chatting about my nonexistent problems, basically anything to get out of class.

"Come in," a muffled voice calls.

I open the door.

Sea blue eyes lift from the computer screen to meet my gaze.

Da faq?

He narrows those blue eyes for a few seconds, scratching his cheek. "Henna?" Bodhi's (Mr. Malone's) uncertain voice sounds.

I step into his office, slowly closing the door behind me before holding up my schedule.

His eyebrows push together as he looks at his computer screen, fingers pecking at the keyboard. "You-you're a student here?" He clicks the mouse a few times. "But you're ... nine-teen." With wide eyes, he stares at the screen while stilling his hands. "Today. You're nineteen today. Uh ..."

Rubbing my lips together, thinking of all the ways Mr. Malone is going to make things up to me for his summer of radio silence besides the three texting conversations *I* initiated, I wait for his stuttering to transform into coherent words.

"Jesus, Henna, say something." He runs his hands through his sexy blond hair that's a bit shorter than it was the last time I saw him. His face is shaven instead of stubbly, and his shirt is white again, a button-down with a sharp blue tie hanging from his neck.

"Isn't this *something?*" I grin. "But to the point ... I have three study halls, *Mr. Malone.*" I toss my schedule onto his desk. I want to cry and scream. I want to throw myself into his arms. I want to fist pump the hell out of the air because ... he's here. I found him! But mostly, I want to get high until this all makes sense, because right now I hate the cold, awkward air between us along with the pained expression on his face that doesn't look like he's happy to see me.

He blinks away his cloudy gaze. Is he also thinking of how our mouths devoured each other or the way he grabbed my ass to guide me over his hard-on beneath those sexy jeans he wore?

Crossing my legs to deal with the physical side effects of my thoughts, I shoot him a tight-lipped smile.

"We need to talk," he whispers.

I step closer to his desk, twisting my lips to the side. "I know. There's no way I'll graduate without adding at least one class. I won't have enough credits."

Bodhi rubs the back of his neck.

Resisting the urge to internalize his obvious stress, I choose the glass-half-full route—I'm going to lose my virginity to a guidance counselor. Such an interesting twist of fate.

"If you say anything—" He grimaces.

I snort a soft laugh. "I'm good at keeping silent, *Mr. Malone.* I had your number all summer, yet I never called you. And you never initiated a single text. Thanks for that."

The pain along his face deepens. "Henna, I ..." He shakes his head.

"It's fine. I like the twist this story of ours has taken." A smirk lifts the corners of my mouth. "It's like in a movie or a book when you think your favorite character has died, but they come back."

There's a knock at the door.

"Come in," Bodhi says with knee-jerk desperation like the person on the other side is here to save the day.

"Mr. Malone?" A boy in my class peeks his head inside.

Bodhi holds up his finger. "Have a seat in the hallway. I'll be with you in just a sec." He focuses on the computer again, tapping keys and clicking the mouse. "What classes do you want to take?" Mr. Malone is all business.

"If my calculation is correct, I only need one. Do you teach any classes, Mr. Malone? I feel like I'd learn a lot from you."

He clears his throat. "A class, Miss Lane."

"Miss Lane?" I glance over my shoulder to make sure the kid next in line shut the door behind him, then I rest my hands on the desk, leaning in and lowering my voice. A summer's worth of anger and resentment bubble to the surface. He tortured me by wanting me without really showing me more than words, and I want him to pay. "You can call me Miss Lane while we're here, and I'll call you Mr. Malone, but when you're fucking me in the back of Alice, we'll be Henna and Bodhi."

His throat bobs. "Henna."

"Nope." I stand erect. "Save it for later." I wink before turning toward the door. "Find me a class, any class, Mr. Malone. Whatever you think will be a good fit for me. I'll be back after biology."

CHAPTER EIGHT

Bodhi

I HAVE A master's degree in secondary school counseling and a PhD in fucking up my life. After surviving the onslaught of students and their schedule changes, I grab my sack lunch and eat it in Alice with the windows down. Yeah, I call her Alice.

It takes less than five seconds on my laptop to get results of an internet search engine for Henna Eve Lane. I managed to go all summer resisting the urge to type her name into an internet search, but now I need to know everything.

Rich? She said no, but I disagree. If your mother is an international super model—Juniper Carlisle, go figure—and your stepfather owns ZIP Tunes, the most successful record label in the world, you are rich in my book. I don't appreciate her lying to me.

Halfway down the screen, I find an article about a helicopter accident she survived. It was just her and a friend.

"Jesus …"

They were on their way to a concert in L.A. and the helicopter had engine issues. It crashed. The pilot died and so did her friend. Henna was in the hospital for months. That might explain why she's a year behind in school for her age.

"Alice, I missed you."

I jump at Henna's voice. Closing my laptop, I set it aside and shove the other half of my sandwich into the brown paper sack.

She hops into the passenger's seat.

"Henna, what are you doing?" I glance around. "You can't be here. Someone could see us."

"True." Slipping off her yellow flip-flops, she shimmies herself into the back, sprawling out on the bench seat. "You can take these seats out and put a mattress back here. Have you ever thought of doing that?"

"Henna, I have to be back in ten minutes, and you have automotive class in fifteen." I twist my body to see her.

"Automotive class. Yeah, thanks for that, Mr. Malone. I wasn't too happy when I got my new schedule, but after some careful thought, I realized you must have fantasies of me covered in grease working on Alice. It's cool. I'm on board. I'm also the only girl in the class, and that seems to please a lot of guys."

I didn't think about that little nugget. A bunch of horny guys all after Henna. Well done, me.

"I'm sorry," I whisper.

"I said it's—"

I shake my head, pinching my eyes shut for a brief second. "I'm sorry about this summer. The way I left. Not calling. I ..." Opening my eyes, I lift a shoulder. "I just didn't know what to do. I had nothing to offer you. And it would seem maybe that was for the best. But you need to know that unlike you, I don't have a rich family. I *need* this job. If anyone found out about what happened at Coachella, I'd be fired. I can't get fired, Henna."

She sits up, fixing her long auburn hair while her face morphs into a pensive expression. "How's your dad?"

"He's fine."

I half expect her to tell me more, like her address, her current favorite song, and how she *found* me.

She nods slowly, trapping her bottom lip between her teeth. "I can't pretend that weekend didn't happen."

"You have to."

She balls her hands. "You can't ask me to do that. I was going to give you my virginity for God's sake!"

My head jerks back. "W-what?"

Wincing, she releases a heavy sigh and stares at her bare feet. "Never mind. I have to get to class." She slides open the side door and slams it shut.

"Henna?" I jump out.

She turns.

I hold up her flip-flops.

Looking down at her feet as if she has no clue that she's not wearing them, she walks back to me. "I can't wear flip-flops in automotive class. Or short skirts. You kinda fucked up my whole wardrobe for my senior year. Thanks, Mr. Malone." Taking the shoes, she walks to the building, holding them in her hand.

Henna is a virgin.

Fucking *Hell.*

AFTER SCHOOL, I hurry home to get my chores done before

sunset. When I'm drenched in sweat and ready to pass out, I drag my ass into the house and take a shower.

"How was your first day as a high school guidance counselor?" my dad asks as I slip on a shirt while walking down the stairs.

"You're awake."

He nods from his wheelchair in front of the television.

"You were snoring when I got home. Etta said you've slept a lot today. I'll start dinner."

"You didn't answer me." He scratches his scalp over his full head of graying blond hair. Everyone thinks he looks just like a fifty-something Robert Redford. I can see that.

I retrieve a casserole dish from the fridge and preheat the oven. "It was chaos, but I'm sure things will settle down in another week once everyone has their schedule changes made."

"I bet those high school girls are pretty smitten with you."

I shake my head, hiding my grin. The whispers were too loud to ignore. Apparently, I'm quite the *snack* and *totally fuckable*—according to a few girls who waited outside of my office. "Girls. Yes. Women? No." Except Henna. She's nineteen and her mouth tastes like strawberry bubble gum and the feel of her nipples on my tongue gives me an eternal erection.

"Did you feed the horses?"

"Duke did." I chop some lettuce for a salad.

"The fence to the north needs to be repaired."

"I repaired it yesterday."

He hisses, adjusting in his wheelchair. I don't know what to do or what to say. Every offer I make to help him is met with "*I'm fine.*"

"You should get out, Bodhi. You never date."

This is true. But I do occasionally use a website for a quick hookup. It's not how I ever imagined meeting my sexual needs, but I also never imagined my father being confined to a wheelchair and the responsibilities of the ranch landing on me.

"I'm good."

"Bullshit."

I ignore him. He likes to bait me, get me riled up. My father isn't simply confined to a wheelchair ... he's battling cancer. And on the not-so-good days, he deals with depression and suicidal thoughts.

"We should eat out on the porch. Have you had any fresh air today?"

"I smoked some weed out there for ten minutes. Does that count?"

"Sure." I sigh, keeping my back to him as my hands pause from chopping lettuce. Closing my eyes, I go to the place in my head that brings a sliver of joy to my existence—Henna.

Bodhi and Henna.

CHAPTER NINE

Henna

"**G**OOD MORNING. YOU were asleep by the time I arrived home last night. I hate that I missed your birthday. I get the Worst Mom Ever award. My flight got delayed because of weather." Juni kisses me on the head as I poke at my plate of eggs and toast. "What brings you to the main house this morning? You're not usually a breakfast person." She sits next to me as Fiona brings her a cup of coffee.

I live in the upstairs of the guest house on the Phillip's estate—Zachary Isaac Phillips, ZIP Tunes. It's smaller, like an apartment, and it gives me a sense of autonomy since my closest friends are at college while I turn nineteen and still have to finish my senior year.

"Bodhi is Mr. Malone."

She sips her coffee. "I'm not following. Bodhi from Coachella? Bodhi who spent the summer tattooed to various parts of your body?" She smirks.

I roll my eyes. "Yes."

"And who is Mr. Malone?"

Tapping my fork on my lower lip, I cringe a bit. "My new guidance counselor."

Juni's eyebrows jump up her forehead. "Are you serious?"

I nod.

"Oh my God, Henna! You had sex with your guidance counselor?"

"No! Why do you refuse to believe me? I haven't had sex with anyone. At least..." I rub my lips together "...I haven't had *intercourse*."

I'm a virgin, but not a saint.

Juni studies me. It's not that I don't get it. A lot of girls my age are not virgins.

"Well, if that's the case, then I have to recommend that you not have sex with Bodhi. Find another nice boy."

Only *my* mom advocates for her teenage daughter to lose her virginity. Even if I don't take heed of her advice, I find it really cool that when the day does come, I can tell her all about my first time without feeling an ounce of guilt.

"I don't want to have sex with another nice boy."

"Henna ..." She shakes her head. "He could get fired, and not just fired, it could ruin his whole career. You're a bit of a hellion, just like I was at your age, but you've also been raised to care about people."

"It's only an issue if we get caught."

"Henna ..."

I drop my fork and grab my bag. "I know. I know. I'll behave."

"Do you need John to drop you off at school?"

"I'll walk. It's only a mile."

"It's almost a mile to get off our property."

"Fine, it's two miles."

"You'll be late."

I head to the door. "It's just calculus. I highly doubt I'll ever use it."

"But you need to pass."

"Bye, Juni."

I make it to school with ten minutes left in calculus—a stellar start to my senior year. The pot cookie I had this morning doesn't help me give a shit about my day or my whole year for that matter.

"I got a study hall pass to come visit you." I hold up my pass as Bodhi looks up from his desk.

"Schedule issues?"

Stepping inside, I close the door and drop my backpack onto one of the two chairs in front of his desk while I take a seat in the other chair and pluck my earbuds out of my ears. "This is a nice office." I smile on a contented sigh. "I've been in here…" I twist my lips "…a lot. But I see you repainted it."

"No. I didn't repaint it."

"No?" I move my attention to Bodhi. He looks so handsome in his gray button-down and black tie. I grin, almost giggle. Why? Well, I'm a tiny bit high.

"Your eyes are a little bloodshot."

"Yours are sexy." I grin, sinking down into the chair a little more and pulling out my sketch pad and pencils. "Surfer and cowboy sexy. Are you wearing boots?"

"Are you high, Henna?"

"It's Colorado. Everyone's a mile high." I continue working on a sketch I started several days ago.

He leans back in his chair, crossing his arms over his chest. "You could get expelled."

I nod slowly, shifting my focus to the paperweight on his

desk. Do people really use paperweights? I always think of them as unsuspecting weapons in murder mysteries.

"Is that what you want? To get expelled?"

On a laugh, I shrug. "I don't care. But they won't expel me. It's my last year. I'm the bane of Gail's existence. She wants me out of here, but for good, not so I fail and have to come back yet *another* year. God ..." I rest my head on the back of the chair, staring at the ceiling. I feel certain someone painted it as well. "I'm so sick of this place. There's a whole big world out there and I'm stuck here."

"You should go home."

"Home? Nah ... I'm good. I have automotive class. Lots of guys want to look under my hood." I tip my head forward to watch Bodhi's reaction.

The only part of him that reacts is the slight muscle twitch of his jaw. I think ... Yeah, I'm definitely a wee bit high. It's the best state of mind for handling my senior year.

"I read about your accident. I'm very sorry about your friend."

Blinking at an extremely slow pace, I let my mind play with his confession. He read about me. Was that in a file? Or did he search up things about me? Do I care? Not at the moment. My breakfast cookie made sure of that. "Robbie was the daughter of one of Zachary's friends."

"Your stepfather?"

I nod, gaze unfocused on Bodhi's desk. It's a bit messy.

"Our birthdays were in the same month, so our dads arranged for us to go to a concert in L.A. A sweet sixteen gift. An unchaperoned concert. Sort of. Zachary seems to always have eyes on me."

"We don't have to talk about this. I just wanted to let you know how sorry I am. The anniversary of that day is this Friday. If you need to talk ..."

"Nope." I prop my feet up on his desk, filling in more details on my sketch. "Not about that anyway. Tell me about your summer?"

"Henna—"

"Mine was crrraaazy. As you know, we went to Italy, then Monaco. I spent two weeks on a yacht. Parasailing, snorkeling, oh ... and I made out with a guy. He might have been related to a prince or something. I don't remember. But he wasn't a good kisser like you. And the food was just meh. Lots of fish. I managed to score a pizza on shore from this little hole-in-the-wall place up the street from the church where Grace Kelly got married."

I exhale slowly, feeling calm and snarky at the same time— an interesting state I'm not sure I've been in before. "How about you, Mr. Malone? Did you make out with someone this summer? Was she a better kisser than I am?"

"Where are your keys? You need to go home, but you can't drive."

I giggle. "You are right about that. I can't drive. A—I don't have keys because B—I don't have a car because D or um ... C—I don't have a driver's license. I like to walk. Sometimes I bike. Sometimes I ..." I stare at his tie. "I bet you hate that tie. You're not a tie person. No one who owns cowboy boots likes to wear a tie. Surfers don't either. Which ..." I hold up my finger.

"I'll call your mom. Will that get you in trouble? I don't want to get you in trouble."

"Oh, that's really sweet that you care if I get in trouble. That's what made us so great. Henna and Bodhi."

"I can tell her you have a stomach ache."

I laugh. "She knows about the pot. She's the one who gets it for me. I don't have a stomach ache, but I'm really hungry. Whatcha got in your desk drawers? Chips? California veggie rolls?"

"Henna—"

"Did you like it?"

His eyes narrow.

"Did you like kissing me? Did you like holding my hand? Holding me in your arms? Did you like *us*? I liked us ... so much." I change my mind. That cookie didn't do shit for the pain today. Thinking of *us* makes me hurt all over, just like the regret I see on Bodhi's face.

I'm ready for a nap and chips. I really want chips. They'd be much better than his sour face. Maybe he's sucking on a lemon drop. God ... I can taste the lemon in his mouth, the warmth of his breath, and the slide of his tongue.

He moves around the desk in front of me, leaning back on it, hands resting on either side of him. "Yes."

"Yes," I whisper, repeating his answer but not remembering the question.

"Yes, I liked us. Too much. Too soon. Too hard to explain, but yes ... I liked every second with you. But ..."

"Now we're forbidden." I scoot to the edge of my chair and look up at him. "Forbidden is thrilling." I set my sketch pad and pencils on my lap and rest my hands on his legs.

He shakes his head, stopping the ascent of my hands with his hands. "Forbidden can ruin my life more than it's already been ruined."

"I'll wait for you."

"It's not that simple."

"It's a year, not even a year. They can't say anything if I'm no longer a student. You can travel the world with me. I want to step foot on every continent and immerse myself in as many different cultures as possible, learn different languages, and see life through a wider lens. And I want to do this before I go to college—*if* I go to college—or get married or have kids. *We* could do it together. Wouldn't that be amazing?"

Bodhi's wince softens into a tiny smile. "It would be amazing. But it's not an option for me. Not in this life."

"Why?"

There's a knock at the door. Bodhi stands to his full height and straightens his tie as he walks to the door.

"Mr. Malone, can you—" Gail pauses. "Henna."

Bodhi clears his throat. "Henna and I were just talking about—"

"The accident." Gail frowns. "I'm sorry. I know this Friday will make three years. I'm truly sorry, Henna. Has Mr. Malone been helpful? I don't want to see you spiral downhill this year. We are here for you if you need help in any way."

I need Bodhi's lips on mine and his hands holding the weight of my breasts while his tongue flicks my nipples. I need his arms around me and his soft whisper in my ear calling me beautiful.

"You wouldn't happen to have a bag of chips, would you?"

Her eyes narrow as Bodhi stifles a tiny laugh as a cough.

"No. Sorry."

"No problem. Someone in my automotive class will have

some."

"Why are you in an automotive class?" she asks.

"Hot guys. Need I say more?"

Gail rolls her eyes. Bodhi doesn't share her response. His subtle reaction involves muscle twitching and teeth grinding.

Gail sighs, never happy with my response, never happy with my total lack of interest in school. "Are you feeling okay? If not, you should go home."

She knows I'm high, just like she knows my stepfather's name is on the new gymnasium. The two facts are always at conflict. I don't care. I should, but I don't. There are too many days that I have no interest in graduating or doing what it takes to get the diploma. I want the world, my freedom, and a break from expectations.

Expulsion would be a gift.

"I'm good. Hungry but good."

Gail adjusts her black-haired bun and pushes her white-framed glasses up her nose while sharing a look with Bodhi. "You should get back to class, Henna. Mr. Malone has other students."

"I have fifteen minutes left of study hall." I lean back in the chair again. "And no one else has knocked on *Mr. Malone's* door except you."

Gail purses her lips.

"Dr. Rafferty, I have a few things to finish discussing with Henna. I'll make sure she's not late to class." Bodhi to the rescue.

I try and fail to not grin. And seriously ... *Dr. Rafferty?* Is she really worthy of such respect?

"Thank you, Mr. Malone. Please come see me when you

have a few spare minutes."

"Absolutely."

She exits his office, making sure to leave his door wide open.

"*Mr. Malone ... Dr. Rafferty.*" I snort. "Why do humans feel the need to be so damn formal? We all shit, fart, burp, and pick our noses. I'm sure even *Dr. Rafferty* has lost at least partial inhibition in the throes of sex. Do you think her husband says, 'Dr. Rafferty, I'm about to come'?"

Bodhi takes a seat behind his desk again, twisting his lips to restrain his amusement. "Respect isn't necessarily a bad thing."

"I would respect her more if she didn't get such a stick-up-her-ass expression every time I call her Gail. Respect can be honored without the formalities. I just don't like it when people need holes in their ego filled with stupid shit like *Dr. Rafferty.*"

Bodhi returns a soft expression, but he doesn't say anything. Minutes pass as we sit in silence, and I *respect* him for that. He's not condescending or trying to fix my problems. He doesn't lecture me or rush me into sharing my feelings.

"I miss us. I know it's stupid because it was two days." I lower my voice, staring at his chest over my sketch pad because I don't want to see pity in his eyes. "It was just..." I try to focus on my thoughts that want to fade into other random thoughts "...something really powerful I felt. You probably think I'm young and impulsive. You probably think it was a crush. I'm sure you have a million girls with crushes on you, but it didn't feel like a crush. It felt ..."

"It felt what?" he whispers with the vulnerability of the Bodhi that held me in his arms on the sofa at Lauren's house.

I let my gaze inch up to his. "Vital. Like that *feeling* would own a piece of me forever. Like that feeling would never go away. Never fade. Like my existence suddenly depended on having that feeling, like a pulse—a breath."

He nods slowly for several long moments. "I need this job," he says like the most heartbreaking confession.

I think I just fell in love with Bodhi Malone. "I need this job" is his painful reality as to why we can't be together. "I need this job" says he *wants* to be with me, but he needs to be employed. "I need this job" says it all, and it hurts so badly because I selfishly want our needs to only be each other.

"I have class. Thank you, Mr. Malone." Standing, I grab my bag, wait until my balance gives me solid footing, and leave his office.

CHAPTER TEN

F OR WEEKS, I work on weaning myself off the weed, but it's not so easy. I've tried it a million times before, but the pain is real. My injury is real. The budding grownup inside of me wants to impress Bodhi with my ability to stay in school and not be high all the time. I manage to hold off until after lunch, making it through my hardest classes and my first study hall, in which I spend most of it in Mr. Malone's office. We don't say anything. I do homework or sketch something while he works on his computer, usually with earbuds in his ears.

"Warren asked me to homecoming."

Bodhi glances up, removing his ear buds. "What?"

"Homecoming. Warren Adams asked me to be his date."

"Okay."

"Okay." I scrape my teeth along my bottom lip.

"You said yes?"

I nod.

"Warren is a nice guy. Good call."

"You've known him for like three or four weeks. How can you say he's a nice guy?"

Bodhi shrugs, returning his attention to the computer screen. "Good grades. Nice parents. Nothing on his record shows that he's had issues in school. And he's your school's best running back. I've heard rumors that he could get a full-ride scholarship to play for UCLA."

"Yay, Warren." I give Bodhi a toothy grin when he makes a quick glance up at me. "Let's back up. What does *my* record say? Would you tell Warren I'm a *good call?*"

"No way. I'd tell the poor guy to use his running skills and never look back."

"You're an ass, Mr. Malone."

"You should show me more respect, Miss Lane."

I open a can of ginger ale and gulp half of it down. "Yeah, well, you should work a little harder to earn my respect." I burp the most unladylike burp.

"Noted."

"You seeing anyone? I heard the volleyball coach has been eyeing you. She's nice enough, but I also heard she's been engaged twice but never married. Clearly there's an issue."

He meets my gaze. "I heard you took an actual typewriter to your history class last year to take notes, causing all sorts of distraction with its noise."

"My laptop's battery was dead."

"Take notes on your cell phone."

"I didn't have one. I just got my first cell phone this past Christmas."

Bodhi squints at me.

"True story. I rejected technology for a while." Okay, I had it withheld from me, but I like to make it seem like it was my choice.

"I heard you took an abacus to trigonometry last year for your semester test."

I smirk. "You sure have heard a lot of things about me. How thick is my file?"

"I have four filing cabinets for the senior class. One is just yours. If you get held back another year, the school will have to build an addition—the Hell wing."

Laughter from both of us fills the room. Neither one of us says it, and maybe it will never be anything more, but in this moment we are Henna and Bodhi. What we share is so natural and easy, the only part that feels wrong is our thinking that it's wrong.

I glance at my watch. "I have to get to class."

Bodhi's smile remains firmly attached to his face. He doesn't ruin the moment by jumping back into Mr. Malone mode. I wonder if third period is his favorite part of the day too.

"Have a nice weekend."

"You too, Mr. Malone."

His eyes widen a bit. "I earned your respect today?"

He's earned my love, my affection, my desire, my every thought. How can he not know that? "You did."

After school I wait for Warren by his car. He has forty-five minutes for a break before he needs to be back for the game.

"Hell, I figured you'd be out shopping for a dress. Surely your mom knows a gazillion fancy designers."

I roll my eyes. "I'm wearing two floral pillow cases sewn together. You good with that?"

He leans down and kisses me on the cheek. "I asked *you* to homecoming, not your dress. Clothing is optional." Tossing his bag into the backseat of his Subaru Outback, he flashes me a cocky smile. Warren is going to have any girl he wants for the rest of his life. If his outgoing personality doesn't cinch the deal, his athletic build, hazel eyes, and thick dark hair will guarantee it.

"I need a ride. Pretty please."

"I don't have much time. Where to?"

I look across the parking lot to the area where the teachers park. "I'm not sure. I need to know where Mr. Malone lives. He should be coming out of the building soon. We need to follow him."

"You're going to slash his tires? I heard he put you in automotive class."

"No tire slashing." I keep my gaze on Alice.

"Tee Pee his house?"

"Maybe."

"Make a peace sign in his lawn with grass killer?"

Giving Warren a quick sideways glance, I grin. "That only happened once."

"He's pretty cool. What's your problem with him?"

"Who said I have a problem with him?"

Bodhi and his faded gray messenger bag head toward Alice.

"Sometimes it's a good idea to keep tabs on people who can make or break my senior year. He's getting in his van. Let's go."

Warren opens my door. I smile. He's a nice guy. If I have to find makeshift dates for my senior year, Warren is a solid choice.

"His dad's in a wheelchair."

I nod, keeping a close eye on Alice as Bodhi heads down the road. "Yeah, I heard that."

Warren turns down the radio. "My mom knew his mom. I guess after his dad had his accident, he went through some bad times and their marriage started to fall apart. She stayed to take care of him, but a year later, she died of a heart attack. She had a heart condition."

"Seriously?" My stomach falls, thinking about Bodhi's life.

"Yeah, so keep your revenge to a minimum. I think Mr. Malone has been through a lot."

I nod slowly as Bodhi turns into a long gravel drive. "Bella's Stables? What's he doing here?"

Warren chuckles. "Maybe he likes to ride horses."

Yes. That makes perfect sense for my sexy cowboy. "Stop. Let me out here."

"Do you want me to wait?"

I open the door. "Nah. My house is literally a mile up the hill."

"True."

"Thanks, Warren. I really appreciate it."

"You coming to the game tonight? Wanna hang out afterwards?"

"Maybe and maybe."

He chuckles. "Okay, then *maybe* I'll call you after I'm out of the locker room."

I hold up my hand in a friendly goodbye as I shut the door.

I don't know a lot about Bella's Stables. We're not equestrian people at my house. I'm fairly certain this place is more for tourists who want to horseback ride the trails in the mountains.

Walking the gravel lane, I pass stables on my right with a field of grazing horses behind it. Farther down the way, there is an old house I assume is abandoned. Stopping just round the bend, I spy Bodhi, parked next to an old silver minivan. He gets out of Alice, slings his bag over his shoulder, and walks up the wheelchair ramp.

Bodhi lives in that old house with his wheelchair-bound father. I press my hand to my chest, feeling an aching pain in my heart.

"Can I help you?"

I jump, keeping my hand to my chest. "Oh, um ..."

The middle-aged man with messy brown-gray hair peeking out from his black cowboy hat wipes his hands on a rag and shoves the rag into his back pocket.

"You wanna ride?"

"No, thank you. I just live up the way. I can walk."

He nods toward the stables. "I meant a horse. Did you come here for one of the trail rides? It's been a slow day. I'll knock thirty dollars off if you're interested."

I glance down at my jeans and sneakers I have to wear for automotive class, thinking they'd work for riding a horse. "Sure."

He starts walking and I follow. "Do you own the stables?"

"Nope. I'm the manager. My name is Duke, by the way. The Malone family owns everything, but after Barrett had his accident, things were neglected. They tried to sell it all, but they couldn't get a fair price, so they kept it and hired me to run things. Their youngest, Bodhi, helps out in the evenings and early mornings, but he has a job at the school now."

"Is his dad home by himself during the day?"

Duke saddles a chestnut horse with one white sock on its front right leg. "Etta, my wife, stays with him. We own that trailer just beyond the farmhouse. It's not much, but we don't have kids, just Howie." He nods to the dog pacing by the black gate to the horse fields.

"Howie is a beautiful dog."

"Australian Shepherd." He tightens the saddle. "Have you been on a horse before?"

"Once. On a beach with my mom for …" A photo shoot. But that sounds weird and getting into my family's professions isn't something I like explaining. "A short ride."

"Well, Angelina is a great fit for you. She'll give you an easy, slow ride." He looks me over. "Are you eighteen? I'll need a waiver signed."

"Nineteen."

"Oh, college?"

"No. I'm … not in college. I have some living to do first."

"I hear ya." He grabs a clipboard off a hook and hands it to me. "Read and fill out the three lines at the bottom. It'll be sixty-five with the discount."

I fill out the form and pay him.

"You can leave your bag right here. Ain't nobody around to take it. I'll have Leo take you from here. Give me one sec." He disappears around the corner.

I smooth my hand over the white area just above Angelina's nose, and her ears twitch. My innocent stalking has turned into a horseback ride with someone named Leo. I suppose in my own little part of the world, I'm just living.

"Hello."

I turn to the fine specimen in snug-fitting jeans, a tight tee, and blond hair a little darker than Bodhi's. He slips on a baseball cap. It almost makes me laugh. He needs a cowboy hat to complete his own sexy cowboy look. He has to be younger than Bodhi by a few years. His body looks like it's just coming into its own.

"Hi." I force my eyes to meet his gaze instead of comparing him to my favorite guidance counselor.

"I'm Leo. I'll be your private guide today." He holds out his hand.

"Henna." I shake his hand, it's nice, but not ... I internally scold myself. My life will suck if I spend the rest of it comparing every man I meet to the one I want the most. The one I can't have.

"Duke said you don't have much experience around horses. I'll give you a few simple ways to guide her, but she'll pretty much do exactly as you want without you doing much of anything. And Claud and I will be right next to you." He nods to the large black horse behind him.

"Cool. I'm sure we'll be fine."

Leo helps me onto Angelina, grabbing not only one of my legs, but my ass too when I fail to pull myself up into the saddle.

"Let's go." He clicks his tongue and Angelina follows him and Claud out to the trail.

Leo takes me on a ninety-minute ride where I discover that he's Duke's eighteen-year-old nephew who dropped out of school when he "fell into a bit of trouble," of which he doesn't elaborate.

"Come back tomorrow and I'll let you ride for free with me and Claud on the morning tour, 9:00 a.m."

My ass, lady bits, and inner thighs are thoroughly bruised. I will not be riding anything for a long time. "Thanks for the offer, but I can't."

"Another time?" He guides us toward the stables where a sexy guy in another stupid white tee and jeans stands with a sponge in his hand and a sudsed-up horse in front of him.

"Maybe," I whisper, a little breathless because Bodhi looks hot as fuck even with the slacked-jaw expression on his face.

"Mr. Malone." Leo nods as our horses slow their gaits.

"Leo …" Bodhi replies while looking at me with all kinds of questions etched into his forehead.

"I was going to do that, but I had a tour come up," Leo explains, dismounting from Claud.

"You can finish." Bodhi tosses the sponge in the bucket—still staring only at me—before taking Angelina's reins from me and guiding us into the far stall of the stable.

I want him to speak because I'm not sure how to explain my late afternoon ride on *his* property. He runs a calming hand down Angelina's neck a few times before holding out his hand to me. I take it and slide off the horse with very little grace, landing into his chest.

"Henna." He gives me an expectant look as I peer up at him.

"S'up?"

"S'up?" He cants his head.

"She's a great horse," I whisper.

He nods once, keeping me flush to his body.

I swallow hard and press my hands to his chest until he releases me. He takes off her riding gear and hangs it with the rest of the tack, his back to me. "Did you follow me home?"

"Yep. I sure did."

He pauses his motions, glancing over his shoulder. The truth is usually more shocking than a lie.

"Don't give me that look. You know what my nipples feel like against your tongue."

Crimson races up his face as he turns back to hang stuff up. "I needed to know where you live. How you live in my community, yet I met you at a concert with 100,000 spectators in the middle of the desert. And much to my complete shock, you literally live a mile from me."

"I'm the stable boy and you're the princess on the hill."

"Dude, no. I'm not a princess. I live in the guest house— not even the whole house—just one bedroom, a bath, and small kitchen. I walk to school, even when it's snowing. I have snow shoes, for real. Granted, I've caught a ride a few times in the rain, but that's rare. And clearly Leo is the stable boy, a juvenile delinquent stable boy, but nonetheless a stable boy."

Bodhi shakes his head, releasing a soft chuckle. "He's not a juvenile or a delinquent. He had sex with a woman much older than him when he was sixteen. Small town. Lots of gossip. So he dropped out of school and moved to Colorado, close to his uncle and aunt."

"That sucks."

Bodhi shrugs, sliding his hands in his back pockets while leaning his shoulder against the side of the stall. "Duke—and eventually Leo too—taking care of all of this is what allowed me to get a degree, a job, an extra source of income beyond the unreliable trail rides."

I stare at him for a few silent moments. "I want to know you, Bodhi what's-your-middle-name Malone."

He grins. "Bodhi Kaden Malone."

"Bodhi …" I take two steps toward him. "Kaden …" Another step. "Malone …" I rest my hands on his chest. They seem to know exactly where to touch him—where they fit so perfectly. "Do you regret this coincidence? Me being a student at your school? Do you wish we weren't in the same town? Do you worry about someone finding out? About losing your job?"

"Yes."

I tip my chin down, letting my hands fall to my sides, letting my heart bleed out.

"Yes, I worry about someone finding out, and I worry about losing my job, but I don't regret the coincidence. This sadistic, glutton-for-punishment side of me is so ridiculously elated that you're here, that I get to see you most days."

"Mr. Malone?" Leo calls.

I take a step back as Bodhi brushes past me, his finger intentionally ghosting along my hand for a breath. "Just a minute," he says to me.

After a few minutes, he returns. "I have to get some chores done and pay a few bills. Duty calls."

"Then what?"

He narrows his eyes in question.

"After your chores and writing checks. Then what are you doing?"

"Fixing dinner for my dad."

"Then what?"

Bodhi sighs. "Help him get ready for bed. Give him his meds and put him to bed. Clean up the kitchen from dinner, take a shower, check my email, then crash."

"It's Friday. Don't crash. Meet me in Alice."

"Henna, I can't." He runs a hand through his hair, tugging at it before letting his arm flop to his side.

"You can. It's your fear and guilt telling you that you can't. Just ..." I grip his shirt, resting my forehead on his chest as his arms lie limp at his sides. I love him beyond reason, and it's so damn exhilarating and so fucking heartbreaking, but … I can't pretend that he's not here in my life. My heart won't let me. "We don't have to do anything but simply *be*." I glance up. "Can you give me that? Can you just *be* with me?"

Conflict wars along his face and deep in his eyes. It's not a setup. I'm not baiting him. My need to be with him in any way possible is real, and it makes me think about something besides getting high, hating that I have another year of school and feeling guilty for feeling anything in life aside from lucky that I wasn't the one who died.

"Wait for me in Alice."

Alice. He still calls her Alice. I love that.

"I'll be there." I smile and a tiny grin breaks through all the worry on his face.

CHAPTER ELEVEN

Bodhi

"STOP PUNISHING YOURSELF," my dad whispers as I set a glass of water on his nightstand and adjust his covers.

"I have a job. The students like me. We turned an actual profit this summer. I didn't burn dinner tonight, and you seem to have a little less pain than you've had previous nights. I don't feel punished."

He shoots me a look, the one where he sees through my bullshit. He always sees through it. But we are also very much alike, so as much as he hates my self-inflicted punishment, he understands it.

"I love you, boy."

I grin, resting a hand on his shoulder before turning out the light. "I love you too."

My usual dragging-ass pace to clean the kitchen, shower, and respond to email from students and parents is replaced with a hurry-my-ass-up pace to get to Henna.

I pause on the porch when I see her in a hoodie and jeans, standing by Alice with her head tipped back, looking at the stars. My hands will always remember the silky feel of her long, auburn hair, and my face will never forget how it feels when that hair tickles it as we kiss. And my lips … they're ruined for eternity.

"There's nothing like this view."

She turns as I approach, her gaze making its own perusal of me with my wet, showered hair, clean jeans, and a hoodie too. "No boots?"

I glance down at my white Converse high-tops with the laces loose instead of tied. "Nah. There's no work to be done." I open the passenger door, and she climbs inside. Releasing the lever, I lower the back of her seat as far as it will go.

Her eyes shoot open wide.

"Get comfy." I shut her door and jump into the driver's seat, reclining my seat back as well. "There was a football game tonight."

"There was," she answers, both of us staring at the ceiling.

"You should have been there watching Warren play or your classmates march in the band or a million other things that don't involve me."

"Probably."

I turn my head toward her, and she mirrors me with a big grin.

"Do you think about us?" she whispers. "Because I do."

I nod slowly.

Possibly satisfied with my confession, she turns her gaze back to the ceiling and so do I. After a few minutes of silence, I drop my right arm, letting my waiting hand hang between the seats, but it doesn't wait long. Henna's hand slides into mine, lacing our fingers.

"Did you have fun with your dad over the summer?"

"Yes." She sighs. "We went to the beach, camped, and

fished. He taught me how to fly fish when I was eight. I don't know … it's two different worlds. When I'm with Juni and Zach, taking elaborate trips and seeing the world from a yacht in the Mediterranean Sea, it's pretty spectacular. But being mesmerized by the flames of a campfire or the ripple of the water as I cast lines with my dad is spectacular in its own right. Juni gives me wings. She encourages me to experience life to the fullest. Dad grounds me, and sometimes I need that too."

"I love that you call your mom Juni." I chuckle.

"I told you, she's my friend. I can tell Juni everything, but there are some things *Mom* doesn't need to know."

"Juni is a great name. You should call her that just because it's such a great name. And I think there's a model or actress with the name Juniper—Juni."

Henna giggles. "You'd be correct."

I squeeze her hand, and she looks at me. "Why did you lie to me?"

The smile fades from her mouth. "I didn't really lie. I just didn't tell you the truth." One shoulder lifts into a half shrug. "I didn't know if we could be *us* if we were completely forthcoming. But …" She exhales. "I was wrong. *We* are greater than you and greater than me, and we are definitely greater than our life's circumstances."

I want to believe her. Henna's innocence feeds my soul. It calls to me like a savior offering forgiveness. She deserves the truth, but dashing her hopes isn't how I want to love her. And the indisputable fact is … I love her. It didn't happen. It just is, was, and always will be.

"So your mom is Juni, but your dad is just Dad?"

"Yes." She returns her gaze to the ceiling, stroking her

thumb over the top of mine. "It's different with him. He was highly ranked and well-respected in the Marines. Calling him something as personal as Dad feels like an honor."

I like that. I like Henna's mind and how it works outside of the box. Her take on life is the cool breeze I love so much on long rides in the mountains. She makes me want to close my eyes and just feel her presence. I guess I, too, need the comfort of just *being* with her.

We stay in Alice until 2:00 a.m., mostly enjoying the silence of sharing space, mixed with the occasional random thoughts about school or living in Colorado.

"You don't have a curfew?"

Henna chuckles. "I'm nineteen and they don't call me Hell for nothing. No. I don't have a curfew. Do you?"

A hearty laugh ripples up my chest. "Midnight. I could be grounded when my dad wakes up. So ... we'd better call it a night—or a morning." I release her hand and lift the back of my seat while she does the same thing.

When I open her door, she slides out and instantly wraps her arms around my midsection, resting her cheek on my chest. "Thank you for putting me in automotive class. I'm quite the natural."

I grin, giving my arms permission to hug her back. "Why doesn't that surprise me?"

"It shouldn't. Clearly, you thought I would be good at it. Right? Surely, you didn't put me in a class you thought I'd fail just to teach me some bullshit lesson."

She doesn't see me cringe. "Never." I release her.

Henna pulls her hoodie sleeves down to cover her hands. "Tell Duke and Leo thanks for the ride."

"Speaking of rides. How are you getting home?"

"Two legs."

"No." I shake my head.

"It's a mile. No big deal."

"It's dark and two in the morning. That makes it a big deal. I'll drive you." I open the door.

She rolls her eyes and climbs into Alice. Less than five minutes later, we're parked at the gate to her estate. I jump out and open her door.

"Such a gentleman." She climbs out, pulling her hood over her head.

I glance at the gate. "Katy Perry Teenage Dream?"

"Retina scan or fingerprint."

Shaking my head, I rub the back of my neck. "Such a different world."

"I told you I live—"

"I know. You have a bedroom *all to yourself*, a bathroom *all to yourself*, and a kitchen *all to yourself*."

Her head whips back. "Wow. Could you be a bigger dick about it?"

I take a step toward her, and she steps away from me. "Henna, I didn't mean it like you think."

"Spoiled rich girl. Entitled. Self-absorbed."

"Those aren't my words."

"They're implied when you say things like that about me. I didn't ask for this life, and I'm not complaining about it either. My shoes are off bargain racks, and my clothes are from thrift stores because that's my personality. That's the life I've chosen regardless of the one I was born into."

"Okay." I hold up my hands. "I was really just joking

around. Clearly, I hit a nerve, and I apologize."

"Don't say that." She deflates. "Now I feel like a bitch for going off on you."

"It's fine. I'm tired. I'm sure you're tired. Let's just call it a night." I take slow steps back to the van.

"Bodhi." She frowns.

"Goodnight."

"Bodhi ..." She shuffles toward my van.

I shake my head. "We're good. Get through the gate so I know you're safe." I shut the door, letting my mind sort out the night's events, my emotions, and my reality. She's a student of mine. We have no business spending most of the night together.

Henna exposes whatever body part magically opens the gate, and she gives me a final wave. I lift two fingers from the steering wheel to wave back and drive my insane self home.

CHAPTER TWELVE

Henna

M Y NEW DAILY schedule …
Third period in Mr. Malone's office during the week
and weekends with Bodhi in Alice. This keeps me equally
satisfied and painfully tortured at the same time. He holds my
hand in Alice. I hug him goodnight, pressing a kiss to his chest.
That's what he gives me. Since I do love him, I let that be
enough.

"Do I want to know?" Mr. Malone asks me as I enter his
office the Monday of homecoming week.

I pop out my earbuds. "It's superhero day." I close the door
behind me.

"Leggings, a cape, and a diaper?" He scratches his chin,
pushing back in his chair and propping his red boots up on his
desk. Captain America has never looked so sexy.

"They're underwear. Don't be stupid."

"Underwear? Still doesn't make sense."

"Captain Underpants."

Bodhi coughs on a laugh. "Why doesn't that surprise me
about you? Of course, you're mocking superhero day in your
own special way."

"I take offense."

He crosses his superhero arms over his red, white, and blue chest. "When did you come up with that idea?"

Looking at my watch, I shrug. "Forty-five minutes ago."

"Well, Thursday will be your day—the seventies."

"Are you done making fun of me, Mr. Malone? It's so unprofessional. I feel bullied. Should I report you for bullying?"

He grins. "Do you have a dress for the dance?"

"I will."

"Seriously? You don't have one yet?" His eyes widen.

"Juni will have something. It will be too OTT, and I'll end up grabbing something from a thrift store. It's not my first school dance, Mr. Malone. Besides, since it's after the game, there's no real dress code. You'll see some kids quite casual and others dressed to the nines."

He nods as his smile dies. "I saw you and Warren getting coffee yesterday afternoon. I was in town getting supplies with Duke."

I adjust the tablecloth I'm using for large underpants. "Warren is a sweetheart. We get coffee most Sundays."

Lines form along Bodhi's forehead. "You were getting into his car."

"Yeah. He drives since I don't."

"He kissed you." Mr. Malone disappears. It's just Bodhi and Henna.

"It was a kiss. He likes to kiss me. It doesn't really mean anything."

Bodhi rubs the tension from his wrinkled forehead. "He's going to want to do more than kiss you this weekend. And I know this because I'm not that old, and I remember my senior homecoming. So it doesn't make him a bad guy, just a guy."

"Well, I trust him. And he's not going to take anything that's not his to take."

"I'm not ..." He sits up, resting his elbows on the desk. "I'm not implying that. I'm saying you're clearly attracted to him. Maybe it's not something he takes. Maybe it's something you give him because you want to."

"I don't."

"Henna—"

"Don't Henna me. It's not his. It's yours. And nothing will change that."

Burying his face in his hands, he grumbles something undecipherable.

"Since we met in the spring, have you dated anyone else?"

Bodhi glances up, confusion marring his handsome features. "No. My sister came to stay with our dad while I was at Coachella. It's the one time each year I can leave. The rest of the year I spend with him. Duke's wife, Etta, watches him when I'm here, but after that, he's my responsibility. I don't have time to date. That's not my life. But *you* can and you should."

"Well, if you're not having sex, then why should I need to have it?"

"Henna ..." He shakes his head. I didn't think he could look more pained. I was wrong. "It's not that I ... what I mean is ..." Bodhi sighs.

My stomach tightens and my chest constricts my lungs, making it hard to breathe. "Sex," I say on an exhale of disbelief. "You don't *date,* but you ... Jesus!" Standing, I slide my bag over my shoulder. "I feel so stupid. Just..." I shake my head

"...so fucking stupid."

"You're not stupid."

I grunt. "You're right. I'm smart. Clearly, you've seen my grades. Straight A's so far this semester, even in automotive class. Ha!" Letting my palm bounce off my forehead, my jaw hangs in the air a few moments. "Now it makes sense. Put Henna in a class with all guys and surely one of them will find their way into her pants." Choking on the words, I will away the true emotion that's like a machete slicing through my heart. "Does giving my body to someone else make you feel less guilty for hooking up with random women while your dad naps, or is it that you just don't want to have sex with someone as inexperienced as me?"

"Hen—"

"No." I hold up my hand and grab the doorknob with my other hand. "Don't answer that. *We* are done. I'll text Warren and let him know he's the lucky recipient of my virginity." I make it out the door and halfway to the restroom before the first tear falls. I made up the story about making out with the guy in Monaco. He tried to kiss me, but my lips weren't his to kiss. I just wanted to make Bodhi jealous. But what did it matter? Bodhi was fucking complete strangers. I wouldn't relinquish a single kiss, while he gave disgusting, skanky women *everything*.

Resisting the urge to skip out on the rest of the day, I finish my classes and walk home in my Captain Underpants outfit, earning a few honks along the way, mostly from kids who know me. Juni and Zach are gone until Friday. She'll swoop in with a dress that costs several grand, and I'll surprise her by actually wearing it because Warren deserves to see me in

Christian Dior before I give him my virginity.

When I'm no longer a virgin, I'll tell Juni all the things most girls can't tell their moms. I'll tell her how it hurt and how he finished five seconds after we started. But because it's Warren, I'm sure he'll hold me and make me feel special. Warren actually thinks I am special. Maybe "Henna and Warren" is a better fit.

I contemplate all of this as I get so high I pass out, not my usual MO with marijuana, but sometimes the only thing that takes the pain completely away is the loss of consciousness.

CHAPTER THIRTEEN

Bodhi

"YOU GONNA TELL me what's wrong?" my dad asks as I sort my mixed vegetables into their own piles on my dinner plate.

"Nothing's wrong."

"My legs don't work, but my mind is just fine. I'm not elderly, suffering from dementia, or flat-out stupid. I know you. Something has you more miserable than your normal self-inflicted doom and gloom."

I can't tell him about Henna. That's not a road I can go down now or maybe ever. Keeping him alive involves never letting him think I'm miserable because of his circumstances. College was for him, not for me. Sure, we needed the money, but he needed to feel that I was doing something for myself. Now I have a job, and I only share the good things about it.

"I have a student that's suffering with some personal issues. It's frustrating for me to not feel like I can really help her without overstepping my role as her guidance counselor." Truth.

"I'm sorry to hear that."

I nod, forcing a smile. "I see that Etta made brownies.

What are the chances that you let her make them without marijuana?"

He chuckles. I've missed his laugh. He seems to find it when he senses I'm happy. It's a daunting responsibility to know that not only does his physical wellbeing depend on me, but his emotional one does too.

"No pot. And she made ice cream too. Does that make up for your bad week?"

It's Friday. There will be a game. A dance. And the woman I love will have sex with someone else. Maybe Etta should have put pot in the brownies. It's been a fucking miserable week without seeing Henna. I hurt her, and I don't know how to make it right.

Forcing a smile, I nod to my dad. How can I be his everything and hers too? That's just it … I can't. So I make the only choice there is to make.

"Brownies and ice cream it is." I go through the motions, living the life I earned.

Henna

"STUNNING." JUNI SMILES at my reflection in the mirror.

"It's beautiful." I smooth my hands over the soft blue dress.

"Your eyes shine so bright in it. Warren will love it." She hands me my silver clutch before adjusting a few pins holding my hair up in a messy bun. I pop another gummy into my mouth.

Juni frowns, stilling her hands. "Are you dealing with pain

tonight?"

Chewing slowly, I nod, but it's not my back. It's my heart.

"I'm sorry. Of all nights…"

I shrug. "It's fine. I'll be fine."

Concern cuts deep into her perfect face. "Are you sure it's your back?"

I nod, finding it hard to speak because I'm in a sexy dress for a guy who's not Bodhi, and nothing has ever felt more wrong in my life.

"Henna," she presses. "It's him. Bodhi?"

Swallowing, I take a deep breath before speaking slowly. "I can have perfect makeup tonight …" Taking in another shaky breath, I continue, "Or we can talk about this."

Juni nods in understanding. After a few silent seconds, she gently wraps her hands around my bare arms. "A wise young girl once told me, *'Don't sweat it. Everything is temporary.'*"

I laugh a little. "Yeah … well, it started with you, but I think it's also the mantra of everyone who experiences chronic back pain. It's how we wake up each morning."

"As your mom, I'm so grateful that you do in fact wake up each morning. And…" she holds up a hand before I speak because she knows what I'm going to say "…I'm saying it for myself, not for you. So don't feel like it's a speech about you needing to look on the bright side or to show a little more gratitude. I'm so incredibly proud of all that you've accomplished in the past three years."

The doorbell rings. It's Warren. Here goes nothing … just my virginity. I navigate my way down the stairs.

"Wow!" He stumbles back with his hand over his heart.

Juni and Zach smile. I don't have to read their minds. Of

course they want to know why I can't fall for a nice young man like Warren. Well, they'll have to ask Bodhi Malone. He just sort of happened, and as much as I wish at this moment that I could make him un-happen, I can't. So even if I take off my clothes for Warren and give him my body ... even if I try to love him in my mind, my heart will always know the truth.

"You look very handsome, Warren," Juni says, bringing me out of my wandering reflections.

"Yes." I jump to agree. "You do."

Warren smiles.

"Good game tonight," Zach adds.

"Thank you, Mr. Phillips."

"Well, we'd better get going." I hug Zach and Juni.

My *mom* whispers in my ear. "It's your night. It's whatever you want it to be. It's *your* decision. Just be safe."

For once, I know she's giving me her blessing to stay Henna the Virgin, and her *be safe* is not a condom reference. It's a good old-fashioned "fasten your seatbelt and don't drink and drive."

"Love you," I whisper back. "Ready?"

Warren nods, looking truly handsome in his black suit as he offers me his arm. I take it and follow him to his Subaru all washed up for the evening.

We meet several other couples for a quick dinner before the dance. My high keeps me smiling but fairly mute during dinner. Warren occasionally reaches under the table and squeezes my hand, giving me a reassuring smile that I try to return. By the time we make it to the dance, I'm wholeheartedly resigned to the fact that I'm going to do this ... I'm going to have sex with Warren tonight—and I'm going to hate Bodhi for it the whole time.

"Have I told you how beautiful you look tonight?" Warren whispers in my ear as we dance to Bazzi's "Mine."

"A few times, but can a girl ever hear it too much?"

He grins, brushing his lips along my bare shoulder. It feels nice, especially when I pretend those lips belong to a messy guy who dribbles ketchup down his white T-shirt. Closing my eyes, I let my high take me back to April when the hands on me were Bodhi's.

Over the next two hours, Warren is crowned homecoming king and for whatever really crazy reason, I'm crowned queen. Then we chat with friends and dance more, and the more we dance, the more kisses Warren steals and the more brave his hands get, feeling intimate places of my body over my dress.

I kiss him back because in my head he's Bodhi.

His touch turns me on, makes me want more because in my head, his hands are Bodhi's hands.

"Wanna get out of here?" Warren whispers as Ariana preaches in her most seductive voice about God being a woman.

My head spins. "Yes." I grab his face and kiss him, flicking my tongue against his, but he doesn't taste like lemon. I pretend he does because all these months later I can still taste Bodhi.

Warren groans, sliding his hand over my ass to pull me closer to him. He's firm, but not hard like Bodhi. He's tall, but not as tall as Bodhi. His hand grips my ass like a football that he could fumble. Bodhi grips my ass like he owns it.

Warren pulls away, eyes heavy with lust, as he takes my hand and leads me out to his car. Our hands are clasped, but he doesn't move to interlace our fingers. When he puts me in the car, he leans in and kisses me. It's desperate, but sloppy. I can already feel that he's not going to last. He's losing control too quickly.

I kiss him back, refusing to keep entertaining this ridiculous comparison in my head. I'm going to let Warren fuck me if for no other reason than I want to march into Mr. Malone's office on Monday and tell him how an eighteen-year-old senior got the job done—the one Bodhi failed to accomplish at Coachella.

Warren breaks our kiss as I keep ahold of his hair. "I have a hotel room."

"Does this seat recline?"

He nods, a bit of confusion flitting across his face.

My lips move to his ear. "Guess what I'm wearing under this dress?"

"What?" He breathes heavily.

"Absofuckinglutely nothing. So we don't need a room, just a little creativity."

"Sweet Jesus," he says as his hands start working the button and zipper to his pants.

We won't be the first or last couple to not make it out of the parking lot after homecoming.

CHAPTER FOURTEEN

MONDAY MORNING I stand outside of Mr. Malone's office, holding my pass from study hall, but it takes me a full ten minutes to work up the courage to knock on his door.

"Come in," he calls when I do.

I open the door slowly with half the confidence I usually have when visiting his office. He doesn't say anything as he looks up from his computer screen, but his jaw pulses as if he's biting back the words he wants to say.

"Hi." I slip inside and shut the door behind me.

"Hi." He returns a monotone greeting.

I had this grand entrance planned. I'd hoped he would be blinded by my afterglow. Instead, I'm hurting so badly, I struggle to keep taking my next breath. How can he not know what he did to us?

"Did you have a good weekend?" I drop my bag and fall into the chair.

Bodhi nods once, chewing on the inside of his cheek as he returns his attention to the computer.

"I was crowned homecoming queen. Can you believe it?"

His eyebrows knit tightly, but he doesn't look at me. "Congratulations."

"Thanks," I murmur.

For the next thirty minutes, he uses silence as a weapon to

make me pay for what he practically told me I should do with Warren. I wait it out and say goodbye when the bell rings. We repeat this standoff for the remainder of the week.

Every day after school, I'm hell-bent on walking to Bodhi's house and letting him know exactly how much he hurt me. Instead, I get high and the marijuana does its job. After a while, I just don't give a shit. All is right in the world when I'm high.

Except today, I don't get high. It's Friday, the best day to binge-watch Riverdale and get high. Instead, I go for a sunset ride with Leo and a small group of tourists. I had no idea I was a horse person, but Angelina is a great creature. When my ass isn't throbbing with pain from the saddle, we're a match made in equestrian heaven.

"Do you have plans for later tonight?" Leo asks as the three other people follow us back to the stables.

I glance over at him. He gives me a very flirty smile. Bodhi could take a few lessons from Leo. "Not that I'm aware of. Probably getting high." Something tells me Leo won't judge me.

"Want company?"

I was right.

"Sure." I grin back at him.

"Sweet. It will take me about forty-five minutes to finish up here. Meet me at the end of the lane in say ... an hour?"

"An hour it is."

After dismounting Angelina, I start to walk in the direction of the road, but a dark figure on the porch of Bodhi's house catches my attention. My feet overrule my common sense, and they carry me toward the porch. There's an older man in a wheelchair entranced by the sunset.

"You lost?" he asks as I reach the bottom of the ramp.

"No."

He brings a joint up to his lips and takes a drag. "You take the tour?"

I nod, ambling up the whiney ramp.

"Was it good?"

"Sure." I shrug.

"That Leo kid is full of shit. You didn't actually believe anything he said, did you? Tourists are so gullible. No offense."

I laugh. "I live up the hill about a mile. And Leo is totally full of shit, but it's mildly entertaining shit that seems to amaze the tourists, so you should keep him around."

He inspects me for several seconds, his joint paused a few inches from his lips. "I'm Barrett."

"Henna." I hold out my hand.

He doesn't shake it. Instead, he offers me his joint. Can't say I've ever smoked pot with a guidance counselor's father before. I take it. I guess there's truly a first for everything.

"Have a seat." He nods to the wooden rocker beside his wheelchair.

I hand the joint back to him and take a seat.

"How did you end up in a wheelchair?" It's weird how I've never had the courage to ask Bodhi the same question, but when a stranger offers you a drag of his joint, nothing's off the table.

"Fourteen marble stairs."

"You fell?"

Barrett nods.

"That sucks ass."

He looks over at me.

I shrug. "Don't look at me like that. I speak the truth, and you know it. Any way you look at it, falling down fourteen marble stairs and permanently landing in a wheelchair just *sucks ass*."

A grin works up his face. "What do you know? You're clearly just a pretty, young pothead."

I turn to the side and lift my shirt, showing him my scar. "I know about things that suck ass."

"Mmm …" He inspects it for a long moment. "But you can walk."

"True." I put my shirt back down and sit straight again. "So, I suppose I only know about things that half-ass suck."

A laugh rumbles from Barrett again. "I like you, Henna."

"Dad, dinner's—" Bodhi stops on the opposite side of the screen door. "Ready," he finishes.

"'Bout damn time. It better be good and not instant shit for as long as it took you." Barrett winks at me. "You have somewhere to be or can I talk you into more than a joint with me?"

I glance over at Bodhi frowning at me. *Yeah, I smoked a little weed with your dad. So what?* I grin. "I'm starving."

"Follow me, young lady. Bodhi, Henna. Henna, Bodhi. Smile, Son. There's a bona fide woman having dinner with us. And she's not old or a relative, so step the hell up and show her some Malone manners."

Bodhi holds open the door as Barrett rolls in the house.

"Nice to meet you, Bodhi." I give him a toothy grin.

"The pleasure's all my dad's." He narrows his eyes as I pass him.

Looking over my shoulder, I stick my tongue out. He rolls

his eyes, biting back a grin.

"Spaghetti? It took you an hour to make spaghetti?" Barrett jabs Bodhi.

"The meatballs are homemade, Dad."

Barrett bites into one of the meatballs as I take a seat next to him and opposite Bodhi. "These are good. There's really nothing like juicy balls."

"Dad!" Bodhi flinches, scratching the nape of his neck. "Don't invite someone to dinner and be so crude."

"It's fine." I bite into one of Bodhi's made-from-scratch meatballs, and it's just as juicy and amazing as Barrett said it is. "Mmm … these are good balls." I wink at Bodhi.

He looks up at the ceiling, drawing in a slow breath.

I grin and so does Barrett.

We spend the next hour having the best conversation about how Barrett met his wife. I love that even though their marriage started to fall apart before she died, he speaks of her with such adoration. At first, Bodhi seems uncomfortable listening to his father talk about his deceased mother, but eventually he warms up and even adds to some of the stories. Cecile, his mom, stayed home while Barrett ran the ranch. She was an excellent cook and a prankster.

I melt listening to Bodhi and Barrett share their trip down memory lane with me.

As I help Bodhi take the dishes to the kitchen, there's a knock at the door. Bodhi answers it. I recognize Leo's voice.

Shit! Leo.

I totally forgot.

"Hey, there you are." He looks over Bodhi's shoulder as I approach the door. "My uncle said he thought he saw you walk this way."

"Yeah, I'm sorry. Barrett invited me for dinner, and the time slipped my mind."

Bodhi crosses his arms over his chest, watching Leo and I have a conversation with him in the middle.

"You still want to … uh…" he gives Bodhi a quick look "…hang out?"

Bodhi squints at Leo and then at me.

"Yeah, sure. Let me just say goodnight to Barrett."

"Really?" Bodhi's question stops me.

"Really what?"

Leo watches Bodhi with a bit of apprehension. He clearly knows who's the boss.

"You're just going to eat my food and run? Leaving me with the mess to clean up by myself?"

"Oh," Leo speaks up. "No. She's not."

Why does Leo feel the need to answer for me?

"I'll do it for her."

"What?" I shoot Leo an incredulous look. "No. You didn't eat dinner here. Just …" I frown at Bodhi, but he ignores my glare, staring back at me with a blank expression. "Another night, Leo?"

Leo takes a step backward on the porch. "Absolutely. Um…" he shoves his hands in his pockets "…have a good night."

"We will. Thanks." Bodhi shuts the door.

I cross my arms over my chest, mirroring Bodhi's stance from earlier. "Boy, your juicy balls sure do come with a price."

He grins. I pivot and march back to the kitchen. After saying goodnight to Barrett, I finish drying the dishes while Bodhi puts his dad to bed. Their old house is quite run-down, but there's still a warmth to it from all the family photos on the walls and the fireplace mantel. A beautiful multi-colored quilt lies folded on the back of a rocking chair. I wonder if Cecile made it?

"Smoking pot with my dad, huh? Have you no shame?"

I turn from the wall of photos—many with Bodhi. Ignoring his efforts to shame me, I point to a photo of him surfing. "So it's true. You can surf."

Sliding his hands into the pockets of his jeans, he lifts his shoulders, giving me a tight-lipped, I-told-you-so smile.

"Where's your sister?"

"Bella's in Kentucky."

I turn back to the photos, staring at one of her on a horse. She must have been ten or so. "Bella ..." I whisper.

"Daddy's girl. I've always liked horses, but to her they are life. Like tacos are to you."

I grin, but he can't see it with my back to him. "So why is she not here ... at *Bella's Stables?*"

"She dreamed of training horses, the kind that could win major stake's races. Last year's derby winner? She trains for that family."

"That's quite the dream come true."

"Yes."

I face him again. "And you don't ever feel a tiny bit of resentment that she's doing that while you're here responsible for your father all but one weekend out of the year?"

Bodhi blinks a few times. "Nope."

"You're a nice son."

"It's getting late." He glances at his watch. "Can I give you a ride home?"

"If I say no, are you really going to let me walk home by myself in the dark?"

"No."

"Maybe Leo could drive me home. I feel bad for standing him up."

Bodhi draws in a long breath, the muscles in his jaws flexing several times. "Then call him."

"I don't have his number. Maybe you could give it to me."

Those muscles pulse a few more times. Bodhi looks almost feral. The last time I saw feral-looking Bodhi was Monday after homecoming weekend. I'm so drained from wanting the man before me but constantly being turned away by his silence.

I step closer to him and a little closer yet until I have to crane my neck to meet his gaze. "Call him, please. Call Leo and tell him I'm ready to hang out."

Bodhi's nostrils flare.

"Tell him I'm ready to smoke a little weed and throw all inhibitions to the wind."

"Shut up," he says with a strained voice, through gritted teeth.

I ball my hands that ache to touch him. I try to ignore the tingle of my skin that begs to be touched by him. "Call him."

Bodhi shakes his head, emotions red in his eyes, jaw set.

"Call him. Tell him you don't want me, so he can have—"

"Just shut the fuck up." He grabs my head and kisses me, pushing me into the wall, rattling the picture frames beside my head.

I can't breathe. I. Can't. Breathe. All the oxygen leaves my body, replaced with Bodhi. Clawing at his head, I hold his mouth to mine by two fists full of his hair as we angle our heads to find the perfect position that allows our kiss to deepen. I climb up his body, wrapping my legs around him. He grabs my ass with both hands, not like a football—like he owns it. Devouring my mouth, he walks us to the stairs and drops to his knees, sprawling my body out above him.

Shoving my shirt and bra up at the same time, he reacquaints himself with my breasts.

I bite my lips together to keep from crying out. It's almost painful, but just as he pushes me to the very edge, he flattens his tongue over my nipple that he bit so fucking hard.

"Bodhi …" I pant his name, looking down at him as he looks up at me with hooded eyes.

"Shut up, Henna." His eyes are filled with so much anguish, I have to fight back my own emotions. He unfastens my jeans and peels them off me. "If you want me to stop, then say stop. Otherwise, just…" he tosses my jeans aside "…shut up."

Resting my elbows on the stair, I peer down at him as he pauses … waiting.

"Don't stop," I whisper.

Bodhi slides down my panties and spreads my legs. His eyes flit between my middle—wet and completely exposed to him—and my steadfast gaze. Lowering his head, he keeps his eyes locked to mine.

"Ung!" I bite back my reaction as his tongue makes a slow swipe.

He does it several more times before plunging it into me. His eyes roll back in his head and he hums his pleasure. My eyes do the same thing as he quickly and expertly claims my orgasm.

This sends me higher than I've ever been. The kind of high that could make me pass out. Before I completely come down, he picks me back up and carries me the rest of the way upstairs, kissing my mouth the way he kissed me between my legs.

"Tell me to stop," he whispers in my ear as he lays me on his bed. "Tell me, Henna." He crawls between my legs, resting his forehead on the mattress next to mine as his fingers slide between my legs.

I jerk my hips, sensitive to his touch after my orgasm.

"Please ... tell me." He slides a finger partway inside of me then pulls it out and spreads my arousal all around.

I'm a lot of things, but tonight I'm not his savior.

"Get a condom," I whisper in his ear.

"Henna ..." He says my name like the most desperate plea.

I reach for his jeans. He brings his body up so he's hovering over me, both of us watching my shaky hands unfasten his jeans. When they're fully unfastened, I flit my gaze to his. He parts his lips, letting his tongue make a lazy swipe over his lower lip. We say things in this one look that don't require words.

My fingers push the elastic band of his briefs down just enough to expose the swollen head of his erection. His eyes flare, watching me, breathless, with every muscle in his body flexed and hard as steel with anticipation.

"More," he says on a jagged breath.

I ease the black material down the rest of the way, completely releasing him. Our eyes meet again—his glazed over, mine slightly widened.

"Fuck," he seethes as I wrap my hand around him.

I'm so inexplicably fascinated by his reaction to me touching him, and I'm surprisingly comfortable with it as well.

Henna and Bodhi …

It's like my body knows that he's mine to touch. My nerves dissolve into a confidence that I can't explain. I slide my fisted hand up his full length, watching his facial reaction the whole time. He's mine. Even if he doesn't really know it yet—he's mine.

After a few more slow strokes, he stands on his knees between my spread legs, shrugs off his shirt and rids me of the rest of my clothes. Sliding out of his briefs and jeans, he rolls on a condom and kneels between my legs again. He grabs under my knees, pulling my pelvis and my whole body toward him. I hold myself there as he guides his cock between my folds, sliding it up to tease my clit before sliding it back to my entrance.

He does this over and over, stopping every so many times to press just the head of it into me an inch or so.

"Henna?" He continues to stimulate me with his full length, adding his thumb to circle my clit when he presses into me an inch or so.

My lips part to let out ragged breaths that come faster as the heaviness grows again between my legs. "Huh?" I lift my hips higher, approaching another release.

God … he feels so good. I close my eyes.

"Henna?"

I force them open, teetering on the edge of my orgasm.

"Look at me, baby."

I look at him. All the pain and worry have been replaced with something else.

"Henna Eve Lane …" He inches into me a little more.

My breath catches.

He pulls back out, leaving just the head of his cock kissing my entrance. "I love you."

Tears sting my eyes.

"No matter where I am on this earth, I'm loving you … *forever.*" His thumb circles my clit faster and my hips buck. He slows his circles when I come undone, a deep pulse spreading in all directions like the Mediterranean painting the shores of Italy. "Bodhi and Henna …" he says while grabbing my hips and plunging all the way into me.

"Fuck—"

He covers my mouth with his hand and stills himself, buried completely inside of me. He bends down, ghosting his lips over my ear. "Thank you," he whispers.

Tears run down my face, but not just from the pain of him inside of me. I cry because he knows that I gave *it* to him—not to Warren, not to Leo, and not to a hundred other opportunities before him.

"Forever," he says over and over as he kisses the tears from my cheeks and slowly begins to move inside of me.

CHAPTER FIFTEEN

Bodhi

S HE'S EVERYTHING I can never be. It's all I think as I watch her sleep. She's also Hell, and taming Hell is a job for the Devil. Right now, I feel like the Devil—stealer of innocence, breaker of rules, keeper of lies.

"Bodhi ..." She stretches her arms above her head, arching her back.

I remain on my side, propped up on my bent elbow, admiring the way the early morning light dances along her fair skin.

Henna's blue eyes flutter open, making her look ethereal with her red hair fanned out around her on my white sheets. I grin, fighting with the guilt I feel for *not* feeling more guilt over what happened last night.

"Good morning." I press a featherlight kiss to her lips.

She smiles and it chases away all the misplaced guilt. I *do* believe we are meant to be ... something. I just feel bad for her that she's destined to experience this part of life with *me*. As long as I'm tethered to my own unfortunate fate, I can never give her the life she deserves.

And Henna deserves everything.

"I love you, Bodhi Kaden Malone."

I grin, a really damn big one. It takes superhuman force to not jump on the bed and bang my chest. This girl in this moment is mine, and I'm over the fucking moon about it. I don't know if I'll have a job on Monday, or if she will hate me tomorrow, but *right now* ... we are perfection.

Bodhi and Henna.

"Say something." She bites her lip, concealing her grin as she pulls the sheet up to cover her breasts. "Don't just stare at me with that cocky grin, looking all perfectly messy and utterly intoxicating this morning."

My grin intensifies as my fingers brush away a few strands of hair from her face.

"Seriously ... Say. Something. I haven't woken up in a guy's bed before. I don't know what the protocol is. Do I get dressed and leave? Should I not have stayed? Do we have sex again?"

"I love you." Pulling her into my arms, I bring our naked bodies flush. She nuzzles her face in my neck and slides a leg between mine.

"I won't let you get fired."

"Shh ..." I kiss her head, tickling her back with my fingertips. "We'll deal with your guidance counselor later. He's kind of a dick anyway. Today we're—"

"Henna and Bodhi." She giggles.

"Yeah."

"Was it ..." She pulls back just enough to see my face. "Good? Last night?" Worry wrinkles her nose. "I mean, I just sort of lay there while you um ... did your thing. Because it um ..."

"Hurt?"

Rolling her lips between her teeth, she nods.

"I'm sorry. Was I too rough? I tried not to be, but it's also really hard to go slow at a certain point."

"No. It's ..." She shakes her head.

I love that my untamed Hell has fire in her cheeks, that our intimacy makes her blush. I love how a woman who could rule the world surrenders her confidence to me—trusts me with her complete vulnerability.

"I'm worried you didn't enjoy it."

I exhale a laugh, eyes widening. "Henna, you don't have to worry about that."

"But I do. I just laid there trying not to grimace. In my mind, I was so turned on by what we were doing. You inside of me. *Us.* But my body refused to cooperate. I just watched the clock, counting down the minutes until it was over. That's not sexy, Bodhi. It's like having sex with a corpse."

Rolling onto my back, I chuckle, covering my eyes with my forearm. "I haven't had sex with a corpse, so I can't confirm or deny anything, but I'm inclined to say it was not at all like that."

She rests her head on my chest, tracing the outline of my abs. "Well, you were incredible. Dare I say the best I've ever had?"

I laugh, smoothing my hand over her hair. After a few moments of silence, I ask the question. "What happened with Warren?"

Turning her head, she drops light kisses to my chest before peering up through her long eyelashes at me. "I said no."

"You said no ..." My mind plays with the meaning behind

her words. "Did he ask?"

She rolls her chin against my chest, side to side. "Not exactly. It just sort of naturally went in that direction."

I hate hearing this, but not knowing will eat me alive. "How far, Henna?"

On a slow blink, she returns her gaze to my chest. "Pretty far."

My stomach tightens, and I have to remind myself that I pushed her away. "But he stopped the second you said no?"

She nods, regret pulling at her brow.

"Then that's all that matters."

Henna scoots up, lining her body on top of mine, grinning when she feels my uncontrollable dick stiffen beneath her. "That's all that matters?" Her face hovers over mine, canted a fraction to the side.

"Yep."

She shakes her head. "That's Mr. Malone talking. My Bodhi would need to know every detail."

"Then your Bodhi is an idiot."

"Careful ... call him names like that and you'll have me to deal with."

I smile. "Oh, Henna ... I thoroughly enjoy *dealing* with you." My hands slide down her naked body, palming her ass.

She wrinkles her nose, giving me another head shake. "No *dealing* with me today. Too many parts of my body have been dealt with a little too much in the past twenty-four hours. I'm going home to shower, numb the pain with a tasty snack, and binge-watch *Riverdale* while wolfing down a bag of chips."

I hate that she's leaving me to go get high. I also hate that she has pain that requires her to crave the numbness that marijuana provides.

"On the stairs ... did I hurt your back?"

"No."

"Henna ..."

She brushes her lips over mine and whispers, "The stairs were my favorite part."

I grin while cupping the back of her head and kissing her. "Well, *you* were my favorite part."

Henna giggles. "I should get going before your dad wakes up." Easing off me, she sits on the edge of the bed and hisses in a tiny breath.

"Sorry." I don't know what else to say.

Glancing over her shoulder, she returns a half smile. "It's only partly your fault. Angelina worked out that area pretty good before dinner." She stands.

We stare at the streak of blood on the bottom white sheet.

"That's embarrassing." She cringes, trapping her lower lip between her teeth.

It kills me to see her flushed with embarrassment over this. "It's beautiful."

Her gaze finds mine. I sit up, swinging my legs off the bed while pulling her to stand between them. Henna rests her hands on my shoulders, gazing down at me like I'm her whole world. And I want to be that for her, but it comes with this huge responsibility that scares the living hell out of me because I don't want to ever be her disappointment—but that's inevitable.

"It's beautiful," I repeat, pressing a soft kiss between her breasts.

Her fingers slide up my cheeks and into my hair, caressing

my scalp.

My mouth navigates to her breasts, taking the utmost care to be gentle with her. "It's us ..." I softly blow on her wet nipple, eliciting tiny bumps along her skin. "It's Bodhi and Henna." Moving lower, I trace her navel with my tongue before continuing south. "It's life ..." The tip of my tongue finds her clit.

"Bodhi ..." She breathes, curling her fingers around my hair.

"I'm not going to hurt you," I whisper over her skin, working my way back up her body. I'm just showing her that I can be gentle. When she leaves, I want her to crave my gentle touch, not fear that every time will feel like the first.

She bends down and kisses me, framing my face with her hands. "I hate you for being with..." her throat bobs "...other women when I promised I'd find you."

"I hate myself too." My chin drops to my chest. They weren't just a means to fill a sexual need; they were a way to try and forget about Henna. I'm so fucking stupid because this woman is eternally unforgettable. How could I not know this?

"But I love you more." She slides her finger below my chin and tips my head up to look at her.

I don't deserve her, and time will remind me of that. But right now, I want her and that's all my selfish ego cares about. "I love you too." I stand, looking down at my beautiful Henna. The pad of my thumb traces her lower lip. "I'll get the rest of your clothes. I think they're near the stairs."

A blush crawls up her neck. I'm totally good with her thinking of us and what I did to her every time she sees a flight of stairs. I know I sure as hell will think about it.

CHAPTER SIXTEEN

Henna

"**I** HAD SEX."

Juni glances up from her coffee and phone screen as I walk into the main house dining room, freshly showered and primed for my afternoon high. It takes edibles a bit to find their way into my system. So for now, I grimace while taking a seat at the table.

She studies me with a cautious look. "It hurts *that* badly?"

"A horse."

"Please don't tell me you had sex with a horse. Or at least tell me the horse is in reference to a stud, but a human one."

I chuckle as Fiona gives me a warm smile and sets a cup of coffee in front of me. "Thank you."

"Okay, back to the horse sex story."

"Yes. That." I take a sip of coffee and add more sugar. "I can *only* have this conversation with Juni. My mom would be way too disappointed in me. Are we clear?"

Juni gets this nauseous expression.

I roll my eyes. "No. I didn't have sex with a horse."

She relaxes. "Then Juni is all ears."

"I've ridden Angelina, this beautiful horse at Bella's Stables."

Juni pauses mid-sip. "Down the road?"

I nod. "It's like cycle class; there's a definite breaking-in period."

Juni laughs. "I've done both, so I completely understand."

"Well, after a long ride yesterday afternoon, I had dinner with the stable owners."

"Oh, that's nice. I don't know anything about them."

"An older gentleman, fifty-ish, I'd say. He's in a wheelchair. His son lives there and takes care of him."

"It's weird how you can live so close to people and know nothing about them."

"Weird. Yes." I sip my coffee. "But you and Zach travel a lot, and we live completely gated off from everyone around us, so we've probably missed the neighborhood potlucks."

Juni shakes her head, grinning. "Moving on ..."

"I had sex with the owner's son."

"Oh ... that's ..." She twists her lips. "Random? You've known Warren for years, then you go and have ..."

I grin, knowing she's thinking exactly what I'm thinking—Dad.

"Tell me the story."

Juni shakes her head. "It's your story day, not mine. I've told you mine a million times."

"And I'll ask you to tell it to me a million more times."

"Henna, you're a romantic."

"I'm not." My head inches from side to side. It's possible to love a good romance without being a romantic. I ignore the tiny detail that I happen to be so in love with Bodhi Malone right now my heart will never find a normal rhythm again.

Every time she shares this story, I wonder how she can look at me and not think of my father. I'm a spitting image of him. If she hadn't shown me the video of my birth, I'm not sure I'd believe I'm really her daughter.

She smooths her silky blond ponytail over her shoulder, taking a big breath. Nearly twenty years earlier, my mom fell for a young drummer at the inaugural Coachella, a music and arts festival in California.

"It was a stifling hot day ..." she begins. I love the way her face lights up when she tells the story, almost as much as I love the story itself.

Sexy, redheaded drummer eyed tall blonde at the front of the stage.

Tall blonde stalked sexy drummer after the final act.

Sparks flew.

A few mind-altering drugs may or may not have been involved.

Sex in the shadows behind the stage.

No condom.

A baby girl named Henna was born nine months later.

I frown, loving and hating the next part.

"The band broke up. Your father enlisted in the marines and proposed to me on the same day."

"You said no." I sigh, always wondering "what if?"

She curls a few strands of hair behind my ear as her mouth turns up into a bittersweet smile. "He wanted his career. I wanted mine."

"But you both wanted me."

She nods a few times. "Yes. And we wanted each other, but ..."

"You were a temporary love."

Mom bops the end of my nose with her finger and clucks her tongue once. "Exactly. Timing guides our lives more than love. Love is just an emotion—timing is our destiny. Missed opportunities. Serendipity. Fate ... it's all about timing, not love."

"You still love Dad."

She returns a single nod. "Always."

"But you love Zach too."

She presses her hand to her heart. "Eternally."

My mother has loved two men, just in different times. I think that will always be my favorite part of the story.

"Don't call me a romantic." She knows I'm a realist. "But ... I want to love like that. And I think I may have found it."

"Henna ..." She leans over and kisses my forehead. "*Live,* my beautiful butterfly. Love freely, but don't ever let it anchor you. Don't ever choose love over life."

"What if I can have both? Like you?"

"Is this guy you just met willing to let you find yourself? Is he going to follow you to the far corners of the world and let you be you ... or will he try to clip your wings?"

I focus on my cup of coffee.

"If you just met him, you can't possibly know."

"That's the thing ... I didn't just meet him."

"No? Does he go to your school?"

I grunt a bit of sarcasm. "As a matter of fact, he does."

"Why didn't *he* ask you to homecoming?"

"It would have been frowned upon."

"By whom?"

"I'm pretty sure everyone."

Her head jerks back. "Why?"

Scrunching my nose, I glance up at her. "He's the guidance counselor."

Remaining statuesque, she blinks quickly several times. "*Bodhi?*"

"Yeah."

"Jesus, Henna ... you had sex with Mr. Malone."

"No." I shake my head. "I had sex with Bodhi. We're going to let Mr. Malone stay out of it."

Juni chokes on a laugh, resting her elbows on the table while rubbing her temples. "You're high."

I bob my head side to side. "Not completely, but I'm getting there."

"If you guys get caught, this ridiculous *Mr. Malone isn't Bodhi and Bodhi isn't Mr. Malone* thing isn't going to work with the principal and the school board."

"We're not going to get caught."

"Henna ..." She shakes her head, giving me a solid dose of *mom* disapproval.

I knew I shouldn't have trusted her to keep Mom out of this.

"You thrive on breaking rules, taunting authority, and proving that you can get away with murder. I know you ... and you'll let it slip to someone because what's the fun of doing something forbidden if no one knows about it? We have gotten you out of a lot of sticky situations, but we can't protect you *and* Bodhi from the possible ramifications of this."

The bad news? She's overreacting. I should have told Carley instead. Maybe I will later, and she can give me a timeline for how long it will be before I don't dread having sex again with the man I love.

The good news? The more *Mom* drones on, making me sound like a completely irresponsible rebel, the more I don't care because I'm starting to feel totally chill about *everything*.

"Don't sweat it. Everything is temporary." I smile on a content sigh.

She shakes her head. "You're going to learn the hard way on this one, but I'll remember to repeat those same words back to you when everything falls apart."

I nod slowly. "Okey dokey."

Juni stands, pressing a palm to my cheek, a sad smile steals her perfect lips. "I'm sorry, baby. I'm so incredibly sorry that you have to spend so much of your life checked out from reality."

I shrug. Reality is overrated when I'm not with Bodhi.

CHAPTER SEVENTEEN

MONDAY MORNING. THIRD period.

I take long strides to Mr. Malone's office. We haven't talked since Saturday morning. It's not that I've been waiting to see if he calls or texts me—like a test—but *if* it were a test, Bodhi would have a solid F.

"Good morning," he says, keeping his attention glued to his computer screen as I close the door, drop my bag, and sit in the chair opposite his.

"Good morning, stranger. Ever heard of a phone?" Okay, I suck a little at not starting shit that doesn't need to be started. I blame it on my youth, an excuse I plan on riding until I'm thirty.

"I'm not texting you. We don't need a traceable record." He leans back, folding his hands on his abs.

"But you can use it like a telephone."

"Traceable."

"Wow ... have you been talking with my *mom*?"

"Jesus, Henna ..." He cringes. "Please don't tell me you told your mom about us."

"I told Juni, but my *mom* butted in and took over our conversation."

He shakes his head, like he's trying to clear it. "Cut the Juni and mom crap. Why would you do that? You want to see me lose my job?"

"What? No. She's not going to say anything to anyone."

"*You* shouldn't have said anything to anyone. It wasn't supposed to happen like that. Not while you're a student here." He stands, running his hands through his hair while pacing the tiny windowless office.

That's it. I'm calling Carley as soon as I get home. Someone needs to be happy that I'm in love, that I saved myself for the man I want to marry. I'm nineteen for God's sake. We were two consenting adults. Bodhi's a guidance counselor, not my teacher or principal. What's the big fucking deal?

"Your not calling or texting has nothing to do with someone finding out. You regret what happened. Don't you?"

"No." He stops, resting his hands on his hips, chin dropped to his chest.

"Well, that's a convincing answer. Nothing about your defeated posture would *ever* lead me to believe that you regret what happened."

"It's not black and white, Henna. What do you want me to do? Tattoo your name on my forehead and fuck you on the lunchroom table?"

"No." My lips twist. "We're not even allowed to sit on the lunchroom tables. And I don't know what the weight threshold is for them."

"Henna ..." He rubs his hand over his mouth.

I stand, making my way around his desk. "Are you grinning, Mr. Malone?" I pull his hand away from his face, revealing his grin.

"I'm serious, *Mr. Malone*. If we broke one of the lunchroom tables, Principal Rafferty would not only expel both of us, she'd report us to the police for vandalism. Besides ... I'm not ready to let you inside of me again. I'm going to get a graduated series of dildos in various sizes to prep that area a little better. If you know where you'd fall on a chart compared to the approximated mean penile dimensions ... that would be helpful."

He attempts to wipe another smirk from his face before I see it. "Go bust someone else's balls. I have work to do."

Someone knocks on the door. I back up a safe distance.

"Come in."

"Mr. Malone, I need to talk to you," Danielle, a girl in my class, says.

"Okay. Henna was just leaving."

Keeping my back to Danielle, I grin. Bodhi maintains his neutral guidance counselor smile as his gaze returns to me, but something in his eyes changes, a spark of adoration that I'm certain only I can see. I mouth, "I love you."

He returns a barely detectable nod and a tiny twitch at the corner of his mouth.

"Hey, Danielle. Keep an eye on Mr. Malone. I caught him sitting on his desk. He has no regard for school property. We'd hate for him to get caught by Principal Rafferty." I flash her a smile without looking back at Bodhi.

Before she shuts the door, she says, "Yeah, Mr. Malone. Principal Rafferty is a real stickler about that stuff."

I giggle.

"Hey, Barrett." I carry a batch of my favorite cookies up the ramp to the Malone's porch.

Bodhi's not home from school yet. Just as well. The cookies aren't for him.

"Hey, young lady." He sets his can of pop on the table next to his wheelchair.

"What did you say?" a lady calls from inside the house.

"Talking to my young friend, not you, Etta."

"I thought *we* were friends." She looks out the screen door at us.

I give her a shy wave with one hand while I hold the cookies in my other hand.

"We're friends, Etta, but sorry ... I can't call you young when you're older than I am."

She shakes her head, tightening her gray-haired pony tail at the nape of her neck. "He's a pill. Good luck, *young* friend." Etta walks back in the house.

"Brought you some cookies." I hold out the plate.

Barrett eyes them. "They smell like the good kind."

Of course he can smell them. Carley thinks they smell disgusting, but she sure likes how she feels after eating one.

"My favorite cookies."

He takes one. "Thank you."

I sit next to him.

"You're not having any?"

"I brought them for you. I have school work to do tonight."

"Freshman year?"

"Seni—" I swallow my answer and cough to buy a few seconds to get my shit together. "Sorry ... yes. Freshman. Just some online classes. I'm not really ready for college full-time. Next year I'm going to travel."

"Travel, huh? Where to?"

"The world." I shrug. "I have this restlessness. It's not something that I've always had, but my accident changed something for me, and I just can't be part of the herd anymore. I'll go crazy."

Barrett stares at me. I'm sure I already sound crazy or just like a typical young person with no direction whatsoever. "If I could get up out of this wheelchair and walk, I'd sell everything I own and buy a boat to travel the world … and I'd never look back."

"YOLO."

"You only live once." He nods. "You going for a ride today?"

"No. I'm a little sore from Angelina." *And your son.*

"I'll have Duke get you a padded seat for the saddle. And he probably needs to adjust the stirrups so you can spread your weight more evenly between your legs and your bum."

And how about sex with your son? What do you recommend to ease that pain? I smile. "Thanks. I'd like that."

"Here comes trouble." He nods to Alice as Bodhi pulls down the lane.

"I love his van."

"Really?" Barrett sounds surprised.

"Really." *And I love your son too.*

Bodhi gets out, slinging his bag over his shoulder and loosening his tie. I've never seen anything so sexy in my life … except naked Bodhi.

"Henna here likes your van. You should let her drive it sometime."

Bodhi's lips purse as he walks up the ramp. "Hmm … I'm

not sure that's a good idea."

"When a pretty young thing like Henna shows interest in your van, you should jump on that opportunity. Ask her out on a date or something like that."

"I don't date." He gives his dad a look. I can't quite decipher it.

"And I don't have a driver's license." I give Barrett a tight grin when he shoots me the same incredulous look he gave me when I said I liked Bodhi's van. "My accident happened around the time other kids my age were learning to drive and getting their permits. I went to physical therapy instead. Walking was a pretty big accomplishment."

I hold out the plate of cookies to Barrett. He winks at me and takes another cookie. It's our wordless exchange that I know, at least in part, how devastating it is to not know if you'll ever walk again.

I did.

He didn't.

And that's just the suck ass part of life.

"Teach the girl how to drive, Bodhi."

Bodhi glances down at me. "How about I make dinner instead?" He returns his attention to his dad.

"Too late." Etta comes out the door. "Chili's in the Crock-Pot. It should be ready in about an hour. You're welcome." She pinches Bodhi's arm before heading down the ramp. "Goodnight."

"Goodnight and thank you," Bodhi says.

"Well, there you go. You have an hour to start Henna's driving lessons."

"Etta just left. I can't leave you."

Barrett holds up his hands. "I'll be right here, being good."

Bodhi seems conflicted. I don't know what to say.

"Go." Barrett takes the cookies from me.

"One more is your limit. Okay?" I warn him.

He winks. "Yes, ma'am."

"We'll be right back." Bodhi keeps giving his dad a look.

"And I'll be right here. Promise."

Bodhi nods slowly and heads down the ramp while I follow him. He opens the driver's door for me. I hold back my scream because BODHI IS LETTING ME DRIVE ALICE!

I fasten my seatbelt and look over at him as he continues to hold the door open. "Bodhi Malone, I have never loved you as much as I do in this very moment."

"Don't kill Alice." He lifts a brow in warning just before shutting the door.

I start Alice.

"Whoa …" He jumps in and fastens his seatbelt. "You need to wait until I'm ready for you to start her."

"Dude, I'm in automotive class. I can start a vehicle all by myself."

"So you've never driven a car … like at all?"

"Well …" I put Alice in drive and ease up on the brake.

"Well what?"

"Nothing." I wave to Barrett and he waves back.

"Both hands on the wheel."

I smirk, placing *both* hands on the steering wheel as we crawl down the gravel lane.

"Let's go to that old road that runs just north of your house. Very little traffic."

I nod, pulling out onto the main road.

"Good job."

I chuckle. "Thanks, teach."

"You've driven a car before, haven't you?"

"Driven. Borrowed. Stolen."

"Henna Eve …"

"Bodhi Kaden …" I mock him. "Before you go all guidance counselor on me, the stolen car was not technically stolen; it was borrowed. But the owner and I disagreed on that little detail, so it got reported as stolen, and I did a little community service and wrote a long letter of apology. No biggie."

"What have I gotten myself into?" he mumbles.

"Tell me about Alice. Why did you choose her? I mean … you know it makes you undeniably irresistible in my eyes, but she's a lot of awesomeness for the average guy."

He shrugs. "She was my mom's."

"I would have loved your mom."

Bodhi nods. "She would have loved you too."

That gives me more than a moment's pause. It's a beautiful sentiment that makes me feel incredibly special.

"Why does leaving your dad by himself for an hour freak you out so much? I saw the looks you gave him. What's up with that?"

"He's unpredictable."

"I'm unpredictable."

"He can be a danger to himself."

I know what he means, but it's not my favorite topic because it hits close to home. "Well, that ramp is a little steep. Is it up to code?"

Bodhi misses my humor. Instead, he stares out his window. "Where are we going?"

I park at the entrance to the Phillips estate.

"I'm not ready to meet your parents."

"Let's go." I climb out and open the gate.

"Henna?" He follows me.

"Hush. We have less than an hour." The gates open. I look back and offer my hand.

He shakes his head.

"You're not meeting my parents."

Bodhi wastes another thirty seconds of not trusting me before taking my hand. I guide him down a trail to a breathtaking lookout area probably forty feet above the stream. A fallen tree connects our hill to one on the other side of the stream. I step up onto it and start walking across it like a balance beam.

"Henna, don't do that."

"Come on." I stop and hold out my hand again.

"No. I can't die today."

I grin. "I can walk across this blindfolded. Wanna see?"

"No. I want you to come back here."

"You swim with sharks. That takes big balls and good balance."

"That's different."

My head tilts to the side. "I've seen your balls. They're huge."

He fights a grin.

I put my hands on my hips, not fazed at all by the forty-foot drop below me. "Okay. Let's say you die. Then what?"

"Then I won't be able to take care of my dad."

"So your sister has to do it."

He doesn't respond.

"Right?"

Bodhi nods once.

"The school hires a new guidance counselor. I find someone with a name cooler than Bodhi but that still sounds stellar with Henna." I hold out my arms, palms up. "There you go. Now you know."

"Know what?"

"That life will go on if you die. Don't sweat it. Everything is temporary."

He eats up another few minutes with his worry. I shrug and make my way to the middle where I squat and straddle the trunk, letting my legs dangle in the cool air. A grin pulls at my lips when he steps on the end of the log. Looking only at me, Bodhi walks with the ease of a cat to meet me in the middle. He straddles it, facing me. I glance between us at the carved letters in the log.

Henna +

Bodhi traces my name with his finger then glances up to meet my gaze.

I smile. "I carved it a week after I started to walk again. But ..." I swallow back the emotions that come with the memories. "I couldn't balance very well. Sadly, I didn't care. If I'm honest, I wondered what it would feel like to fall."

"Why? You were finally able to walk again."

"Yes, but everything hurt. Walking. Sitting. Going to the bathroom. Rolling over at night. Just ... everything. And while I wanted to walk, my reasons for it were much more different than what everyone thought." Giving him a sad smile, I lift a shoulder. "Just as I started to fall from this very spot, my stepdad, Zach, grabbed my arm. I didn't know he followed me. But my mom asked him to keep an eye on me when she couldn't because she said …" I drag in a shaky breath of courage. I'm not that person who wants to die anymore, but the memories of that person will never disappear. "She said I was a danger to myself."

A slight flinch pulls at Bodhi's brow.

With my finger, I trace the plus after my name, over and over. "Zach straddled the tree right here, holding me with my back to his front. I cried for the life I thought I'd never have. Who would love me when I hated my miserable existence? I was addicted to pain meds, a year behind in school, and in spite of it all, I was expected to have this gratitude for just being alive. Do you know how hard it was for me to not throat punch everyone who told me to *look at the bright side?*"

Bodhi scoots forward until our knees touch.

"Zach pulled out a pocket knife and handed it to me. He said I needed a goal, and he told me to make it personal, completely selfish, and a pivotal moment in my life. So I carved this because I knew if the day ever came that I finished it, it would mean that I was okay. More than okay. It means that the pain paid off. I'm still here, and…" I pull the keys out of my pocket and use one to carve *Bodhi* "…it means someone loves me."

When I finish, he takes the keys from me, wearing a grin as he glances down at the creek. It's entirely believable that I would accidentally drop them. I match his smile.

Bodhi grabs my hips and slides me so my legs rest on top of his. It steals some of my balance, but I know he's got me. I wrap my arms around his neck.

"Bodhi plus Henna," he whispers.

"Henna plus Bodhi," I whisper back a second before he kisses me.

CHAPTER EIGHTEEN

WE MAKE IT another week without our secret leaking to the powers that be.

Another week of watching Bodhi play his role as Mr. Malone during my third hour study hall.

Another week of me visiting Barrett after school each day to share edibles or share a joint.

Then I get my period.

Yay me.

I spend my after-school hours during period week at home getting high and eating chips while watching TV. I inherited my mom's awful periods.

Yay me again.

What I've discovered is that I don't have a needy boyfriend. Bodhi seems to love spending time with me, sexless time, but when we can't be together, he's focused on his dad, the ranch, or school responsibilities. It's a fascinating experience dating a true adult. I'm handling it surprisingly well.

"I'm done." I announce after fifteen minutes of silence in Bodhi's office.

He looks up. "Done?"

I sigh. "With the *thing* I had going on last week."

Wrinkles line his forehead as he shoots me a funny look. "You mean your period?"

I roll my eyes. "Yes."

"Oh. Well ..." He studies me. "Congratulations?"

I snort. "You're such a nerd."

"How are your grades?" His hands do their awkward fumbling over the keyboard, then he pauses. "Straight A's. Good job, Henna."

"Does that earn me a reward?"

He leans back in his chair, fingers laced behind his head. "Such as?"

Damn ... he's so sexy.

Bodhi narrows his eyes in suspicion, and most likely a little distrust, when I move from my chair to the door. "Henna ... no."

I lock the door anyway.

"I could get fired for having a student in my office with the door locked."

"*If* you get caught. You know everyone knocks. They don't even try to open the door until you respond." Prowling toward him, I slip off my denim jacket. "Remember that night at your house ... on the stairs?"

He shakes his head. "Not here."

"Carpe diem, Mr. Malone." I slide off my fitted neon yellow tee, revealing a black lace bra.

Bodhi's Adam's apple makes a slow dip as his eyes flash to the door. His nerves are palpable.

I kick off my flashy gold sneakers and unfasten my ripped jeans and shimmy out of them, luring Bodhi with my flirty grin. His lips part and I want to taste them, tempt them, and drive them so crazy they can't help but devour me.

"Henna ..."

"*Miss Lane.*" I sit on the edge of his desk. He rolls back in his chair just enough to accommodate me. "Today I'm Miss Lane, and you are Mr. Malone."

His gaze homes in on the apex of my legs as I plant each foot on the arms of his chair.

"The thong is new. You like, Mr. Malone?" I lean back on my hands, tossing my dark auburn hair over my shoulder.

The indecision on Bodhi's face has a way of slicing into my heart. He's twenty-six. No twenty-six-year-old should have to bear the weight of the whole world, but he does.

"You know…" I slide my finger under the thin strip of material and pull my thong to the side "…forbidden can be sexy."

Geez. It's like he's watching someone kill a litter of puppies. So much anguish. I press pause on the sexy scene I planned out in my head this morning.

Easing off the desk, I straddle his lap, framing his handsome face. "We live in a cage, and I hate it. The rules. The constant looking over our shoulders."

"The rules are there to keep bad things from happening," he says.

"The rules reward those who conform. They stifle independence, creativity, and freedom."

He shakes his head. "Without them, you would have nothing to break."

I blink several times. Bodhi grins.

The world doesn't understand *us*. They don't understand that someday I'm going to make babies with this man, and sitting on his lap, half-naked behind the locked door, is not wrong or forbidden.

It's basic.

It's simple.

It's us—Henna and Bodhi.

It's *life*.

"What's going through that head of yours?" He searches every inch of my face.

"I'm imagining what our kids are going to look like?"

Well, shit … there goes his smile.

"Don't." I rest my forehead on his, closing my eyes as my hands slide from his neck to his shoulders and down his chest. "Don't think about everything that stands between now and the future. Just … for the next fifteen minutes pretend that you can have absolutely anything in life you want." I feather kisses down his cheek to his ear and whisper, "For fifteen minutes, be limitless with me."

Warm hands rest on my hips as hungry lips claim mine. My fingers slide up his face, finding their favorite place in his hair. He releases a sexy growl when I tug to deepen our kiss. Greedy hands find their spot palming my ass—hard—scooting me closer. Like kneading dough, he squeezes it, pushing and pulling to work me over his erection.

I like out-of-control Bodhi. Unraveling him is an experience like no other. Lips, jaw, neck, shoulder—his mouth can't decide what it craves the most. "Our babies…" his lips pull into a grin against my neck "…will have fiery red hair, and they will be rock stars."

His words overflow my heart, dripping down … staining my soul with the most beautiful promise.

Grinning, I close my eyes and let my mind follow that dream. The artist in me paints it with vivid color. The hands of my imagination sculpt every tiny detail.

Bodhi eases down the straps to my bra while his lips brush along the swell of my breasts. He stops, pulling back an inch while lifting a single brow at the condom that I shoved into my bra this morning.

Relinquishing a sheepish grin, I lift my shoulders. "A girl can dream."

Blink. Blink.

I hold my breath, waiting to see if Bodhi can truly be limitless with me. He's going to clam up on me and say no. I deflate a little.

"Well, let's see if it fits."

My gaze shoots to his. "The condom on you or you inside of me?"

His grin doubles on a soft chuckle. "Both."

I crash my lips to his. "I love you. I love you. I love you," I mumble without moving from his mouth.

Bodhi squeezes my breast with one hand and his other hand snakes between us. I moan as his fingers play between my legs, getting me very, very wet. "Baby?" His heavy breaths fall against my cheek. "It kills me to rush this, but ..." He slides two fingers inside of me, twisting, stretching, and readying me for him.

"We have to hurry," I finish his thought with my own breathless words.

Bodhi nods. I rip open the condom wrapper as he frees his erection. My hands shake, nearly dropping it on the ground.

He glances up at me with a half smile. "Should I do it?"

Fire plumes along my cheeks. I shake my head, forcing my hands and mind to focus. "I've got it." I press it to the swollen head of his cock.

A PLACE WITHOUT YOU

"Other way," he says.

"Oh ... okay." I flip it the other way and try to roll it down over his length, but it doesn't want to cooperate. I rub it between my thumbs and middle fingers. "Shit!" I freeze.

We stare at the torn condom.

"My fingernail got it."

"Get another one." He bends down and sucks in my nipple.

My eyes fight to stay open when his mouth on my breast sends a jolt of pleasure straight between my legs. "I-I don't have another one."

He lets my nipple pop out of his mouth, eyes aimed up at me. "What?"

I shake my head. "Just one. Don't tell Juni. She insists on at least a twelve-pack."

Exhaling, he drops his forehead to my chest. "I'm so fucking hard and the stupid bell is going to ring in..." he glances up at the clock "...seven minutes."

I climb off his lap and kneel between his legs.

"Henna," he says in a husky voice filled with warning.

I rub my lips together as he strokes himself a few times.

"You're going to tell me no, aren't you?" I give him my most disappointed frown.

Eyes hooded, he draws in his lower lip with his teeth while his hand squeezes his cock, making slow, hard strokes. "I'm going to tell you you're down to five minutes, so don't lick it like one of your lollipops, suck it in hard and deep like the last drag of a joint." He keeps his gaze unwavering as one corner of his mouth curls a fraction. It's so wicked and so fucking sexy.

Honestly, the way he hisses when I take him as deep as I

145

can, I don't think he'll make it thirty seconds.

Two minutes.

He makes it two minutes. It's pretty impressive under the circumstances.

With three minutes to spare, we piece ourselves back together.

"You have to take this and throw it in the trash at home. Not in my office. Not in the restroom. Not on school property. Don't forget and leave it in your purse. Don't slip it in your pocket. And for the love of God, don't use it as a bookmark. Okay?"

I take the ripped condom and wrapper, squinting at him while I slip it into my bag. "You read a lot of fiction. I, too, heard rumors about a condom shoved into Moby Dick, but that's a bit too amateurish for me."

He opens his desk drawer and retrieves a lemon drop, pops it into his mouth, and closes the drawer. "Go be a good student. I have work to do."

I grab his tie and yank him down to my face. He grins. I grin. And I kiss him, sliding my tongue into his mouth just as the bell rings. He pulls away, rubbing his lips together then pausing.

My exaggerated, toothy grin shows him *his* lemon drop trapped between my teeth.

"You suck." He opens his drawer for another lemon drop.

I unlock the door and turn the handle. "You know it. Like the last drag of a joint." Glancing back over my shoulder, I blow him a kiss.

"Henna?"

I stop halfway out the door. "Yeah?"

His gaze inspects the hallway behind me for a quick second before those blue eyes land back on me. He mouths, "I love you."

Dead.

CHAPTER NINETEEN

Bodhi

"YOU WANTED TO see me?" I poke my head into Principal Rafferty's office.

"Yes, Bodhi. Come in and shut the door, please."

I take a seat in the faded black fabric chair. My master's degree should alleviate the stress of sitting across from a principal, but it doesn't. It still gives me flashbacks of my high school days.

She takes her time finishing up something on her computer. Then she signs a few papers and sets them on the top file on the corner of her desk before returning her attention to me. Clearing her throat, she interlaces her fingers, resting her hands on her desk. "How would you describe your relationship with Henna Lane?"

Oh. Fucking. Hell.

My stomach coils while my lungs constrict.

"Relationship? I'm her guidance counselor." I try to shrug, but my body is too rigid to even lift my shoulders. "So that would make it the same as my relationship with all my other students."

Her head bobs repeatedly in the slowest series of nods ever, like a large boat rocking in the ocean. My knee starts to bounce out of control. I rest my hand on it to steady my nerves.

"Why do you ask?" I try the proactive route. The what's-the-problem-because-I-have-no-idea-what-you're-getting-at route.

She sighs, smoothing a few stray black hairs back into her bun before pushing her white-framed glasses all the way up her nose. I prefer it to the way she looks judging me with her chin down, eyes peering over the top of them.

"One of the other faculty members reported seeing you and Henna in your blue Volkswagen van. Henna was driving. They said she parked at the entrance to her family's estate, and you both got out and went through the gates together ... holding hands."

Holding hands ... Holding hands ... Holding hands ...

Her words echo like we're at opposite ends of a long hallway with tall ceilings. My pulse pounds in my ears, and the past I can't escape whispers, *"You're a fuckup. A selfish child who never thinks of anyone else. You can't undo this."*

"She rides horses at my family's ranch. My dad's in a wheelchair. He befriended her. They both have tragic pasts. He's a relentless old man who won't take no for an answer." I refuse to make up a story that's not true, so I take the high road, even if it's more of a tightrope.

"He found out that she never took driving classes because of her accident, and he insisted I teach her how to drive. I know it was wrong, but not starting an argument with my father who will never walk again and who's battling cancer..." I find that shrug that I couldn't find earlier "...it seemed like the lesser of two evils."

Principal Rafferty blinks several times. "You weren't holding hands?"

"We were. She wanted to show me where …" I hate this. Henna's secrets aren't mine to share with anyone, but I'm trying to protect her—protect *us*.

"Where what?"

"Where she once tried to commit suicide."

Gail flinches.

"I didn't feel right about going onto her family's property uninvited by her parents. She—being Henna—grabbed my hand and persuaded me to go with her anyway."

She steeples her fingers, resting her chin on them. "I should have warned you about Henna. She's had issues for years, even before the accident. They've just been more extreme since it happened. Every guidance counselor before you knew her quite well. Her family has contributed a great deal to this school. But we can't show favoritism.

"However, navigating her chronic pain and emotional issues is a very unusual and delicate situation. If I'm honest, I really just want to see her walk across the stage, get her diploma, and …" She exhales.

"No longer be your responsibility?"

Gail gives me a regretful smile. "Yes." She clears her throat again, straightening her back. "I don't want this to get out. Nothing about Henna Lane is black and white. I'm not firing you … yet." She raises her eyebrows in warning. "I'll deal with your colleague who reported you. And while I like you and I want to trust you—I don't trust Henna. She's clearly fond of your company, and that's just something we can't have. So …"

She stands, resting just her fingertips on her gray industrial desk. "Mrs. Bateman will take over Henna's schedule and all of her other guidance needs. I will talk to Henna and her parents, strongly suggesting they find someplace else for her to enjoy her *equestrian hobby*, as well as finding her an actual driving instructor."

I don't respond because I have no clue what I'm supposed to say. All I can do is keep blinking, hoping that eventually I will awaken from this nightmare I call my life.

"In the meantime …"

I glance up at her.

"I suggest you not give her so much as a second glance if you pass her in the hall. Are we perfectly clear on this?"

"Perfectly," I murmur.

CHAPTER TWENTY

Henna

I SUCK ON a lollipop waiting for Bodhi to hurry up. He usually comes out of the school by four. It's nearly four thirty.

"There he is," I tell Alice. Pushing off her front bumper, wearing the grin I reserve just for Bodhi.

When he glances up from his phone, looking all hip in his tweed blazer, mismatched tie, and black Chucks, he stops. I crook a finger at him. This is the first time I've asked him for a ride, but I want him to take me shopping for some riding gear—boots, a hat, and maybe my own riding crop. Okay, maybe not the riding crop. I'll let his reaction to it dictate whether I get one or just pretend I'm joking.

Stopped a good twenty yards away, he just stares at me. No smile. Not a twitch of movement.

"Let's go!" I call.

The parking lot is basically empty. No one there to see us. What's his deal?

He turns and walks back toward the building.

"Bodhi?"

What did he forget? The tack store is going to close if he

doesn't hurry up. Collapsing again against the front of Alice, I shove my hands into the pockets of my jacket to keep them warm against the cool fall breeze. A few minutes later, Principal Rafferty struts toward me like an arrow headed for the bullseye.

What now? I've been on my best behavior. No skipping classes. Not so much as a late assignment.

The lollipop. Seriously? She's going to bust me for a lollipop at the far end of the parking lot, an hour after school's been dismissed? Gail needs a life.

"Henna." She pulls up the collar to her tan wool coat and lifts her shoulders to protect her ears from the cold.

"Principal Rafferty." I twist my lollipop in my mouth, hoping my respect in properly addressing authority buys me a free pass for my mildly illegal indiscretion.

"Do you need a ride? Can I call a friend or parent for you?"

I shake my head.

"Is there a reason you're leaning against Mr. Malone's van?"

Easing forward, I put enough space between my backside and Alice that I'm no longer *leaning against Mr. Malone's van.*

"I talked with Mr. Malone today, and I'm going to schedule a meeting with you and your parents. But in the meantime, I need you to stay away from Mr. Malone. Mrs. Bateman or I can handle your school needs. As for your after-school *activities,* such as riding the horses at Mr. Malone's family's ranch, I have to ask that you refrain from it and not be anywhere near the property or Mr. Malone and his family."

"What the *fuck!* Did you fire him?"

"Please don't take that tone with me or use such language. But no, Mr. Malone is still employed with the school district—

for now. If you want him to keep his job, I strongly suggest you heed my warnings and do as I request."

I'm kinda high and really pissed off. It's a terrible combination. I'm angry that I'm not angrier. My mind won't stay focused on one thing long enough to formulate an argument. I think I want to cry, but I'm not sure why because I haven't talked to Bodhi.

But ... he was there. Twenty yards away. And he walked back into the building. What if he didn't forget anything? What if this is his way of avoiding me? God ... what if he sent Gail out here to get rid of me so he didn't have to face me?

That scenario would hurt the most.

"I need to talk to Bodhi."

"You mean Mr. Malone."

I clench my fists, ready to jab my half-eaten lollipop into her eye. "Yes. Mr. Malone. Bodhi. Whatever, *Gail*. I just need to talk to him now."

"I'm sorry." She shakes her head.

Fuck. What does she know? Who saw us or heard us? It can't be that bad if she didn't fire him. It can't be blowjob-in-his-office bad. Can it?

"Henna, please. Let me take you home or find you a ride."

I shake my head, backing away from her, backing away from Alice, backing away from this life-snatching hellhole called school. "I'll walk," I murmur, staring over her shoulder at the door that Bodhi isn't coming out of, and the building where I know he's hiding *from me*.

From. Me.

There's pain. It's a dull ache inside of my chest. But my high keeps me from feeling the full impact. So I decide one thing's for sure—there is absolutely no solid reason to ever be sober again.

CHAPTER TWENTY-ONE

I STARE OUT the window as John drives us home. Zach sits in the front seat, talking on the phone, while Juni sits in the backseat with me, holding my hand but not saying a word.

What's left to say?

Yesterday Bodhi walked away from me—abandoned me.

Today Principal Rafferty made me feel like a child in front of Juni and Zach. She painted an ugly and forbidden picture of me and Bodhi.

It's not the rules or warnings to heed that keep me from Bodhi. It's him.

He *walked away* and I haven't heard from him since I left his office yesterday with a smile on my face and so much love in my heart.

It's scary how much can change in twenty-four hours. I thought the same thing after my accident.

Don't sweat it. Everything is temporary.

We pass Bella's Stables. My mom squeezes my hand. Leo's carrying a large metal bucket into the barn, probably oats for the horses.

"Leo dropped out of school," I say flatly.

"What?" Juni leans closer, trying to decipher my mumbling.

"Leo, the tour guide at Bella's ... he had an 'inappropriate' relationship with a woman and dropped out of school. I'm nineteen. I don't have to finish school now. I can do it later. Or never." I have no aspirations of doing anything in life that requires a college degree. Why do I *need* a high school diploma?

"Henna, don't ..." Juni stops. Of course she stops. *Juni* understands exactly what I'm saying. In her rational mind, she knows I'm right. She knows I've never shown a true interest in college. I tell people that I'm going to travel the world *first* because it's less shocking than a girl my age with good grades and "so much potential" flat-out rejecting college forever.

My *mom*, however, feels the social burden, the expectations, and the need to do right by me.

"I'm not living. You told me to live. I'm dying. I've been dying every day since the accident." Except for Bodhi. With Bodhi, I live.

I breathe.

I dream.

I imagine.

I'm limitless with him.

But without him, I'm ...

"So drop out."

Juni's head snaps up when Zach says those three words. I thought he was on the phone.

"Zachary." Her head whips back.

John parks in front of the house and opens my mom's door while Zach opens mine. I follow them into the main house, suddenly quite interested in Zach's opinion.

"Juni, really?" Zach slides off his jacket, continuing toward the living room.

She drapes her jacket over the banister, her heels clicking

on the granite floor after him. I shadow her, leaving on my hoodie.

Zach pours himself a drink and folds his tall body into a leather, claw-foot chair, holding his drink with one hand while running his other hand through his thick salt and pepper hair. "Where's your college diploma? What degree did you get?" he asks her.

"Zachary." She shakes her head, folding her arms over her chest.

"Because I don't have one, and..." he shrugs, looking around the impressive room filled with the most expensive furnishings "...I think I've done okay for myself."

I ease into the corner of the sofa, watching the court weigh in on my future.

Juni's face scrunches up with so much worry. Zach reaches out to her. After a few seconds, she sets her hand in his, letting him pull her onto his lap. It makes every inch of my body ache for Bodhi's touch.

"After the accident, we agreed we'd let her live *her* life ... no matter what."

Juni eases her head side to side, still wrought with guilt. "Mitch will never be okay with this."

"Where's his degree?" Zach levels her with a squinted look.

"He'll see it differently. He went into the Marines and made a career out of it."

Zach shifts his attention to me, giving me a sincere smile laced with sadness. He literally saved me during a very dark time in my life. Literally pulled me to safety. He loves me like his own daughter. "It's your decision, darling. Not because we say so or whether your dad does or doesn't give you his blessing. You're nineteen. It's legally your decision. But I guess what I'm saying is …" He lifts Juni's hand to his mouth and kisses it. She returns a soft smile and nods as if granting permission for an unspoken request. "We support you no matter what you choose to do in life. Our love for you will never be contingent on the choices you make. You're going to mess up. Hell, I still fuck shit up on a daily basis."

The closest thing I can find to a smile attaches itself to my face. They can offer me freedom and unconditional love, but they can't give me Bodhi, and right now he's all I want. Our life is still this cage, but now I'm on the outside and he's still stuck inside. He didn't clip my wings. He clipped his own.

"Say the words, Henna." Zach brings my attention back to the room, away from the cage. "Say the words and we'll put you on a plane and send you anywhere you want to go."

I CHOOSE MY little apartment over the guest house. For now.

I choose to get high.

I choose to litter my space with pages of sketches and painted canvasses.

I choose to stay in my space for weeks, thinking of Bodhi's choices—specifically the one where he didn't choose me.

When I'm high, I love him. When I'm not, I hate him.

By the holidays, I start to find that my new favorite high *is* hating him.

I've missed too many days now to get my diploma. I guess I dropped out without officially dropping out. There's probably some form to fill out or some *rules* or *guidelines* to follow. I'd be epically disappointed in myself if my last act as a student involved following protocol.

A girl's gotta maintain her reputation.

"Fiona restocked your fridge," Juni says from the doorway to my bedroom.

I pause my paintbrush for a few seconds then nod and continue my stroke of green. "Tell her thank you."

"Will do. Zach and I are going skiing with some friends. How about you come with us?"

"People with metal parts holding their bodies together don't ski down mountains."

"You know what I mean. I'll schedule you for a massage. Mani, pedi. Lunch. What do you say? Christmas is in two days. Put away your paintbrushes and spend some time with your family."

"Dad invited me to spend New Year's Eve with him."

"I know. Maybe you should come clean with him. You know … clean slate, fresh start, new resolutions."

"He's going to be pissed off at you for not telling him."

Juni exhales. "I'm not afraid of your father. You asked me to not tell him, so I didn't. The fact that you've let so much time pass without mentioning your dropout status to him is on you, not me. You're an adult. It's time he treats you like one, whether you choose to act like one or not."

"Whoa … throwing a little shade today." I glance over my shoulder, lifting my eyebrows.

"Grow up, *young lady*." She winks to soften the blow. Juni has a way of infusing just enough humor into the truth that no one can accuse her of being mean.

I wrap my brushes in a wet towel to go rinse them. "Have fun." I lean over and kiss her cheek while passing by on my way to the kitchen. "Thanks for the offer, but Carley is coming over in a few hours. It's my only chance to see her before she takes off for Texas with her new boyfriend."

Juni leans against the counter as I rinse the brushes in the sink. "Are you good?" Her face falls short of hiding all of her concern.

"I'm good." The vibrant colors fade together into an ugly mess of brown circling the drain. I know how they feel.

"Let's try this again." She shuts off the water and takes the brushes from me, setting them down in the sink.

My eyes stay glued to the pooled ugly brown.

"It's been months. You could be anywhere in the world, but you're still here. You could walk a mile down the road and knock on his door, but you haven't."

"You want me to leave?" I swallow hard.

"I want you to live."

Tears fill my eyes, and I try so hard to will them away.

"I don't want to be selfish," I whisper.

"What does that mean?"

"It means if I ask the..." I draw in a shaky breath "...question I'm dying to ask, the one I should know the answer to, it will sound incredibly selfish."

She rests her hand on my arm. "Say it."

The words come out in a sob. The words come out like a building crumbling. The words rip open my chest. "Wh-why doesn't he want me anymore?" My arms hug my waist, and my body buckles onto itself, trembling with emotion.

"Oh, Henna." My *mom* pulls me into her arms, lowering both of us to the ground.

I know, I just *know* in my mind that Bodhi loves me. I

know he's doing what he feels is right for his dad and his career. I know all of this—in my head. But my heart doesn't reason like that. My heart just feels, and right now it feels the worst kind of pain.

Rejection.

Abandonment.

And lonely.

I'm so incredibly lonely without him.

"H-he was r-right there. And he j-just ... walked away." I choke on a sob.

Mom hugs me tighter, kissing the side of my head over and over. "Shh ... I'm so sorry."

I love Juni. She's fun and cool. And she rarely judges me. But sometimes ... I just need my mom.

CHAPTER TWENTY-TWO

Bodhi

"YOU LOOK LIKE shit. Ever heard of a razor?" My sister showers me with compliments before ever stepping foot into the house.

I move aside to let her in. "Nice to see you too, Bella."

She tugs on my facial hair. "Scruffy."

"Kids at school like it."

"Pfft." She drops her suitcase at the bottom of the stairs. "Where's Dad?"

"Recliner. Sleeping."

She turns, exhaling slowly like the trip from Kentucky to Colorado is the longest trip ever. "How's he doing? What did the doctor say? Is he in pain?"

Scratching the back of my head, I chuckle. "For someone who makes the visit once, maybe twice a year, I find your concern a little dramatized."

"Just because I have a busy life, doesn't mean I don't care."

I sigh, feeling emotionally dead and raw with pain clear to my bones. "Let's not fight. He's doing fine. The doctors said the cancer is still slow growing, but they want to start treatment again after the holidays. Oh, and he's still a pain in the ass, but I think that's about it."

Bella grins and rolls her eyes. "Sounds about right." She rubs her arms. "Brr ... you have any coffee made?"

I nod toward the kitchen.

"How's your job?" She sits at the table while I pour her a cup of coffee and set it in front of her plate of Christmas cookies that Etta made.

"It's good." It's fucking unbearable. I can't walk in that building without thinking of Henna. I can't breathe for the entire forty-five minutes of third period. I can't understand why her parents let her drop out. And I can't do a damn thing about it.

If Henna's not a student, the school can't fire me for being in a relationship with her. But I'm not stupid. Principal Rafferty will not like being made to look like a fool. She'll know I lied, and she'll find some reason to fire my ass and destroy my career before I even get a full year on my résumé.

"How's the ranch doing?"

I shrug, taking a seat next to her. "It was a little slower this summer. The fires in the area didn't help. At one point, I thought we were going to have to evacuate, but they got it under control."

"Yeah, I worried about Dad when that was going on."

Dad. She worried about Dad. No need to worry about her fuckup of a brother.

"He's in good hands."

She frowns.

I sip my coffee. "So ... what's new with you?"

"It was a rough fall. Castaway had a knee injury. Ted is being an ass about it. Thinks it's my fault. Other than that.

Nothing much."

"Who's Ted?"

"The owner's brother. Doesn't know shit about horses, but he sure likes to throw his weight around."

"So is Ted next in line if Arnie dies?" Arnie is the billionaire who owns the horses she trains. He had a stroke last year, and Bella nearly had a heart attack when it happened. Arnie thinks the world of Bella. But no one else seems to agree with her style of training, which only matters if Arnie dies.

"Unfortunately, yes. And Ted just wants to cash it all in. So if you have a secret stash of money someplace, I might have a few good tips on some horses you could buy that will likely win some crowns."

I grunt a laugh. "I'm certain you make way more money than I do. Dad told me you got ten percent of the purses last year, and he suspects you're getting a percentage of breeding rights."

She smirks. "That's a lot of math for my brother who never liked math."

"Mmm ..." I give her a fake smile while rubbing my temple with my middle finger.

Her smile settles into something resembling regret. Our relationship has been ripped to shreds over the years, but it's still raw, and every jab cuts open old wounds. I wonder if the day will ever come when we no longer need the boxing gloves.

"You seeing anyone?" Another jab, but I don't think she means for it to be.

Twisting my lips to the side, I shake my head.

Bella traces the rim of her cup with her finger. "You ... at least hooking up with anyone?"

Pushing a tiny laugh through my nose, I roll my eyes. I once let it slip to her that I occasionally find someone to hook up with using a "dating" website. It's not like I've paid for sex, but some people—like Bella—seem to think it's just as bad.

"Maybe. But at least it's in my budget."

"What? I'm just asking. Looking for small talk."

"He's too obsessed with babysitting me to have time to find a good woman."

We look over at Dad wheeling himself into the kitchen.

"Hey, Daddy." Bella gets up and gives him a hug. "Merry Christmas."

"It's Christmas Eve," he says in his gruff, post-nap tone.

"Fine. Merry Christmas Eve." She ambles to the stove and lifts the lid off the Crock-Pot. "Mmm ... smells good, Bodhi. Beef stew?"

When Dad's awake, we treat each other with a lot more respect—usually.

"Yes."

"Did you invite Duke and Etta?" Dad asks.

"Of course. She's bringing dessert." I glance at the time. "I'm going for a ride before it gets dark."

"You guys have a ton of snow. I bet the trails are fun." Bella smiles.

I nod. They're an escape.

"Be careful," Dad says.

"I will."

After changing into my layers of riding gear and saddling up Snare, my favorite horse named after my favorite drum, I set out on the trail, walking through a glittering fresh blanket of snow. The air is crisp on my skin, the wind a soft whisper in my ears, and the sun a beacon of hope that I will survive this fucking life of mine.

Snare snorts, pulling to the right a bit. We slow down, anticipating another rider coming in the opposite direction. He snorts again.

"Easy ..." I pull back on the reins a little more.

It's not another rider. It's someone snowshoeing toward us, trekking at a pretty good pace. We stop and wait for them to pass in their neon blue snow gear, wraparound sunglasses, and auburn hair cascading beneath it. I wait idle in the saddle for her to pass.

Is it *her*? No. Not her. Maybe a dream? Shit ... what's wrong with me? She slows up upon passing us. My head follows her and hers follows mine, both of us looking back over our shoulders. Then she stops.

I don't have to see her whole face to know it's her. I *feel* her. She releases one pole, letting it dangle from her wrist as she slides her sunglasses onto her head.

My heart feels like Snare's standing on it. Those freckles along her rosy nose and cheeks, and those blue eyes so brilliant, framed with that wild red mane—it all hits me so hard I can't breathe. Without her, I'm not sure I want to breathe.

Her gaze drops to the ground between us. After several blinks, she slips her glasses back on and continues in the opposite direction.

"Jesus ..." I whisper, climbing off Snare. "That's it? You're just going to walk off?" I plod my way through the snow after her. "Stop!" I grab her arm.

She whips around with her pole, ready to decapitate me. I duck then lose my balance and stumble back onto my ass.

Henna straddles me with her snow shoes on either side of my body, forcing my head back into the snow by shoving the point of her pole against my throat.

"Just to be. Very. Fucking. Clear." Her voice drips rage like acid on my soul. "*You* are the one who walked off."

I can't see her eyes behind her glasses, but I don't miss the tear trailing down her cheek, and there's nothing I can do about it because I'm not sure how much longer I'll be alive as the tip of her pole digs a little more into my skin, making me work harder for oxygen.

She nods slowly several times as another tear appears on her other cheek. "I'm glad we ran into each other. I needed this closure." Inching the tip away from my neck, she swings a leg over my head and continues on her way.

"Well, I don't have closure!" I dig my ass out of the snow and chase after her, with nothing to offer, with no grand explanation, with nothing but a bleeding, aching heart and a need to feel *us* again.

Giving her a good ten feet radius from my throat, I run ahead of her and hold up my hands in surrender. "Please, just ..."

Henna holds her pole out like a sword and takes another step forward so that the point of it marks the center of my chest.

"It's okay," I whisper as emotions sting my eyes. "Without you, I'm already dead."

She clenches her teeth. "You don't deserve me."

"No. I don't."

Like a leaf slowly floating to the ground, she lowers her pole.

"I owe you an explanation."

"No," she murmurs so softly I almost don't hear her. "I know you have your reasons. I know they're probably very self-sacrificial in comparison to my indignation, but if I'm not at the top of your list, that's okay. I don't need to see your list because I'm leaving. I'm making my own list, and you're ..." her voice cracks.

She inhales a shaky breath and swallows hard before biting her lips together to keep them from quivering, but I already saw them losing their battle with her emotions. Her pole is no longer pointed at my heart, but I feel it tearing through my chest with each word she speaks.

"I'm not on your list," I say it for her.

Mr. Malone would be so proud of her for putting one foot in front of the other and walking away from a doomed relationship. He would commend her for having a list. But the man in me who simply loves this woman more than life, well ... that man can't seem to get his lungs to draw their next breath, let alone put one foot in front of the other and walk away from her.

Taking the two steps that puts me so close to her I can feel her warmth cut through the cold between us, I remove my gloves and slide off her sunglasses, revealing red, tear-filled eyes. "Where are you going?"

She swallows again and blinks more tears, silenced by her choking emotion.

"To experience the world?"

She nods once, keeping her gaze to the ground.

CHAPTER TWENTY-THREE

Henna

I'VE NEVER BEEN this sober, and I know this because I've never felt this kind of pain.

Bodhi slides his finger under my chin, lifting it until I look at him. I give him more tears since all the words are trapped in my throat.

"I hope the world treats you like the incredibly special person you are. I hope your list is long and daring. I hope you experience joy, surprise, anticipation, passion, and … love."

Bodhi … I already have …

"I hate you," I manage to get those three vitally important words out.

He nods. "I know you do."

Easing off my gloves, I let them and my poles drop to the ground. My cold hands press to his warm cheeks, guiding him close to me, so we share the same breath. "But I *love* you more."

His eyes search mine, and when he seems to find what he's looking for, he smiles. "I know you do."

The Law of Henna and Bodhi: When love breaks, fall inward, fall together, and fall hard. Then let time pick up the pieces.

I pull him to my lips because that's how we fall. He kisses me like my mouth was meant to be kissed only by him. When his lips finish with my mouth, he kisses my nose, cheeks, forehead, and jaw.

"When are you leaving?" He doesn't give me a chance to answer before his mouth covers mine again. My hands slide from his face to his neck, desperate to be closer to him.

In the distance, his horse makes a noise. Bodhi pulls away, out of breath and harboring a pang of disappointment in his eyes as he glances over my shoulder to his horse. "I have to get back."

"Yeah." I release him and grab my poles and gloves, putting them back on.

"Henna?"

After fumbling with my gloves, feeling shaken by his kiss, I glance up.

"When do you leave?"

"I'm uh ..." I shake my head. He's completely rattled my senses. "California. I'm going to California for New Years with my dad. Then I'm going to Japan."

"Japan?" He jerks his head back.

I nod. "Starting with places I haven't been. So don't expect postcards from Paris or Rome."

"You're sending me postcards?"

"No. Well, yeah, sure ... I can. I just meant ..."

He nods. "I get it. I know what you meant. I don't expect anything. Well, actually ..." Bodhi rubs the back of his neck. It's so Bodhi. He does it when he's nervous. "It would be nice to know that you're okay. But don't feel any obligation."

"Come with me." The words are out before I realize they were even on my tongue.

"I can't."

"Can't or won't? Because you could have said something in the parking lot that day, but you didn't. You could have contacted me, but you didn't. You could have done a million things that you just didn't do. And I don't think it's because you couldn't." It's just the beginning. I have so many questions for him, it would take several lifetimes to ask them all.

He exhales, sending a plume of evaporation between us.

"Don't." I shake my head and hold up my hands. "You know what? I think it's best if I don't know all the answers. I know the ones that matter and that's good enough."

"What answers are those?" He narrows his eyes.

"Well, just one I guess."

"And that is?" His head cants to the side.

"I asked you to come with me. You said no. That's the only question that matters."

"I said I can't."

"Yeah, well … that's just another way of saying no."

"No…" an edge of irritation hijacks his words "…I can't means I want to but I just *can't*. A simple no leaves it open for interpretation that maybe I don't want to go, but I *do*. I just *can't*."

"It doesn't matter."

"It matters a whole fucking lot, Henna!" I step back. He rubs his gloved hands over his face. "I'm sorry. I'm frustrated and angry and …"

"It's fine."

"It's not fine."

"Jesus, Bodhi ..." I shake my head, holding my hands out to the side. "What do you want me to say? Because for months I've wanted to knock on your door and ask you to just *be* with me, but I knew you'd choose your dad, your job, your reputation over me."

"That's not—"

"Then ask me to stay." I stab my poles into the snow next to my shoes, gripping them tightly. "Ask me to move in with you. Ask me to marry you. Ask me for absolutely anything that keeps us together."

He closes his eyes. "You deserve—"

"Stop assuming you know what I deserve or what I want! I want YOU! Don't you get that?"

"It's not that simple."

I unhook my boots from the snowshoes and bend down on one knee.

His brows knit together.

"Marry me, Bodhi. I love you. It's *just* that simple. I want to spend my life with you. I want to have kids with you. So, marry me. Please."

This hurts. Bending down and handing over my entire heart to him just hurts, but I know that the regret of not giving everything I have to offer him will hurt more.

His eyes fill with tears as his head moves side to side. "I don't have a life to offer you right now. You said it yourself. It's a cage. That's my life. That would be your life. And you can't live like that. I can't watch you live like that."

I stand and turn. Ripping my hat off my head and throwing it as far as it will go, which is only a few feet. "Why do you live in a cage? Why can't you hire someone to watch your dad so you can *live* too? Why is it okay for your sister to have a life, but your life is always taking care of your dad? It makes no sense!"

"I have to get back." He walks past me.

"Why you?" I follow him.

"Why not me?" he mumbles as his boots kick up snow behind him.

"Because you deserve a life too."

"I don't."

"Why?"

He stops when he gets to his horse. "Merry Christmas."

"Why you, Bodhi?" I ignore his holiday greeting.

He mounts his horse.

"Tell your sister you're getting married, and she needs to split the responsibility of watching your dad."

"I can't tell her that." He stares off into the distance.

"Why not?"

"Because he's my responsibility."

"Why?"

"Jesus … I just told you because he's MY responsibility."

"That doesn't answer my question, why? Why? Why? Why? Why?—"

"BECAUSE IT'S MY FAULT HE'S IN A WHEEL-CHAIR!"

The horse neighs and rears back a bit. Bodhi tightens the reins. After the horse settles down, Bodhi looks at me with regret. "In another life … I would be with you. Marry you. Have babies with you. Just … not in this one. I'm sorry." He gives the horse a gentle nudge with his feet and rides off.

CHAPTER TWENTY-FOUR

Christmas

WE OPEN PRESENTS. Juni and Zach got me new luggage for my new adventure—and clothes.

"I couldn't resist." Juni shrugs, knowing that our tastes in fashion are not the same.

"I love them." I fold the last item and set it next to me on the floor by the mammoth tree filling the spacious room with the scent of pine. "A new adventure calls for a new look. I'm sure you know what's trendy around the world more than I do."

"They're just clothes. You'll find your own *international* style as you make your way through new-to-you countries. God … the handmade items you'll find are just extraordinary. Nothing like you'd ever find off a rack here in the U.S." Juni gives me the best smile. Her excitement for me bleeds through every word.

We enjoy a small family dinner. It's the first year in nearly a decade that it's just been the three of us at the table on Christmas. It's usually filled with grandparents and close friends. This year everyone else had other plans, and while it's kind of a bummer that I won't get to say as many goodbyes, I find it perfect that it's just the three of us.

"We're going to watch a movie. Care to join us?" Zach asks as my mom makes hot chocolate.

"I'm going to watch something in my room if that's okay?" I slip on my boots, coat, hat, and gloves.

"Sure." Zach gives me a big hug and kiss on the forehead. "Merry Christmas, darling."

"Merry Christmas." I close my eyes for a second and just enjoy his embrace.

"Sweet dreams." Juni leans in while holding two mugs and kisses my cheek. "See you in the morning."

I nod and smile while closing the door. The snow crunches under my boots when I step off the last porch step. "What are you doing?" I whisper to the wind, to Bodhi a mile down the mountain from me. Is he with his family? Is he watching an old movie? Is he ...

Sliding my phone out of my pocket, I do something I haven't done in a long time. I message him because I'm leaving, and I don't give a shit about traceable calls and messages. I'm not his student. I'm not sure I'm his anything.

> **Me:** *I only wanted one thing for Christmas, but I didn't get it. Hope you got everything you wanted. Merry Christmas. <3*

Just as I start to slip my phone back into my pocket, assuming he won't respond, it chimes.

> **Bodhi:** *I'm parked at the end of your drive. I've been here for over an hour, trying to get the nerve to ask permission to enter the gates.*

I look up. The end of the lane is way too far and twisty to see from here, but it doesn't stop me from running toward it anyway. With shaky hands from my body jerking to keep its balance in the snow, I bring up the gate app and open the gate for him. Within seconds, headlights appear in the distance.

I keep running.

The van stops.

The second Bodhi steps out, I tackle him to the ground.

He grunts from the impact. My hair falls around our faces. I inhale his addictive wood and citrus scent and the warmth of his mouth so close to mine. Lemons. His breath smells like lemons.

"I opened a hundred gifts today, but none of them were you. I was looking for you."

"Me?" He grins.

"You." I kiss him.

He threads his fingers through my hair and slides his tongue against mine. I don't care if it sounds immature or ridiculous—we belonged to each other before we ever met.

"It's cold." He breaks our kiss.

"My bed is warm." I rub my nose against his.

"So is mine." He sits up, taking me with him so I'm strad-dling his legs.

"Mine's closer." I bite his bottom lip and drag it through my teeth.

"I disagree."

"Uh …" I give him my best confused look.

"Up." He lifts my hips and I plant my boots in the snow as he stands and brushes the snow off himself.

He opens the side door to Alice and flicks a switch.

"Oh my god …" I hold my gloved hand over my mouth.

Battery-operated LED lights line the back of the van, illuminating the mattress, pillows, and fluffy blankets that have replaced the backseats.

"Get in before all the heat escapes." Bodhi pushes me in onto the mattress with my boots hanging out the door.

I giggle as he slips off my boots and plops down on the mattress next to me to take off his boots as well with quick moves before slamming the door shut.

My eyes dance with delight at *this*. He did this for us—for me.

"I can't believe—"

Bodhi kisses me with urgency, covering my body with his. Our fingers intertwine above my head as his body settles perfectly between my legs like God made that space just for him. The mattress allows us one good roll in each direction, and we work the entire space to rid each other of our clothes without missing a single kiss, a single grin, or a single touch.

"Lock in the heat." He pulls the sheet and approximately ten flannel blankets over our heads.

As I giggle, I feel his grin along my skin a split second before his tongue teases my nipple, hands squeezing my breasts while he hums his pleasure.

A heavy ache builds between my legs, longing for him, even if I know it's going to hurt. And I just know it will. Maybe not as bad as the first time, but it's going to hurt. Still, I'm turned on, desperate to feel him all over me and completely inside of me. It's like getting a massage and the therapist hits a tight knot. It hurts in a good way. You want to scream *no* and *YES* at the same time.

I leave for California in a few days. And after New Years, I leave for … indefinitely. The unsettled part of my mind and my soul needs to do this. Traveling the world is all I've been able to think about for years. This is not an opportunity everyone gets. I've told my friends and family this is what I'm doing, garnering both reactions of envy and judgments of insanity—both drive my need to do this. Robbie didn't get the chance to do this. She died. The pilot with a wife and three children died. Settling for anything less than living an extraordinary life and seizing every moment feels like I'm failing them too, not just myself.

"Merry Christmas to me," Bodhi murmurs, taking his kisses down my body. He camps out between my legs, grinding his pelvis into the mattress at the same rhythm his tongue and fingers bring me to orgasm.

"Bodhi!" I wrap my legs around his head as my whole body convulses.

He throws the covers off and reaches between the two front seats, returning with a condom, like it's a race. Once he's fitted with the rubber, he crashes his mouth to mine, balancing on one arm while his other hand positions his cock at my entrance, making a few circles—spreading my arousal around.

"You're so fucking tight." He pushes into me one slow inch at a time, face strained.

I am tight. Apparently once isn't enough to get everything broken in.

Bodhi moves slow at first then speeds up. Harder. Faster. I claw into his back, wanting so desperately to build up another orgasm, wanting so desperately to be his every dream. When I realize that's not happening, I kiss him. This I can do. This I love. It takes my mind off the discomfort of feeling overfilled with Bodhi.

"Henna ..." He grunts my name, slamming into me one last time before finishing with a few short jerks. Collapsing onto me, he buries his face in my neck. "I love you. I love you so fucking much."

"I love you too," I whisper, feeling a terrible ache in my chest.

I'm leaving and he's staying.

He slides out slowly, sitting up on his knees to remove the condom. After disposing of it in a napkin from his console, he settles next to me, spooning his front to my back. Our arms tangle as we sigh.

"What did you do?" I ask because I have to ask. If I'm going to leave my greatest love behind to follow dreams that are starting to feel hollow ... I have to know why.

"What do you mean?" He buries his nose into my hair and inhales.

Closing my eyes, I imagine a life where I can be nothing but the next breath in his lungs, the metronome to his heart, the blood in his veins.

"Your dad."

He stiffens. I lace our fingers together, squeezing tightly.

"You can tell me *anything*. You know that, right?"

Bodhi hums his acknowledgment.

I want to crawl inside of him and pluck every ounce of pain from his heart like removing needles from a pin pad.

"I had some issues with addiction shortly after our band started getting some seriously respectable gigs. A year. That's it. After playing out of a basement while in high school, we got our chance. I got to play to real audiences, for a year. And then I fucked up. Hell ... we all did.

"I was drunk or high, usually a toxic mix of both. We went to this party. Ty was supposed to be the responsible one that night, but he ended up in worse shape than the rest of us. I remember feeling so fucking sick, I just wanted to go home. At the time, home was with my parents when the band wasn't traveling. Some girl found me vomiting all over myself. She offered to get help. I gave her my phone, and she called my parents. My dad came to rescue me."

He clears his throat. I squeeze his hand tighter, like the way his voice constricts each word, stealing all the oxygen around us.

"I couldn't even walk, and I only know this because the girl later gave a firsthand account of what happened. My dad tried to help me out of the house, but I passed out. And seeing as I was nearly as tall and big as him, when I went down, he went down—a whole damn flight of marble stairs. I landed on him with not so much as a scratch. He ... never walked again."

"Bodhi ..." The world spinning in my head, my hopes and dreams, they slow like they're dying as a heaviness suffocates everything inside of me. My tragedy was different. It wasn't my fault. My guilt is different. Everything is different.

"And as if that's not enough, my sister hates me. She not only blames me for what happened to our dad, she believes the stress of it all eventually lead to my mom's heart attack."

I turn in his arms, clutching his face in my hands. "I don't know what to say," I whisper.

He blinks a few times, a lifeless expression stuck to his handsome face. "There's nothing to say. I fucked up. I can't change it. Now, this is my life, and I have no reason to ever complain. I'm not in the wheelchair. I don't have cancer—"

"Wait..." I pull my head back "...cancer?"

Bodhi nods slowly. "He didn't tell you?" He grunts a laugh. "Of course he didn't tell you. He most likely had it before the accident, but they didn't discover it until the accident. He went through treatment ... Jesus ..." He closes his eyes briefly. "As if the paralysis wasn't enough, he's had to deal with feeling like shit while strapped to a fucking wheelchair."

Still, I have no idea what to say, so I let him have his moment, the one where he imposes more self-hatred upon himself.

"Anyway..." he blows out a slow breath "...he went into remission. A year ago they discovered it was back and spreading. Did you not wonder about his liberal use of marijuana?"

I shrug. "It's legal here. No big deal. I just thought he was the coolest guy in a wheelchair I'd ever met."

Bodhi grunts a painful laugh. "I love your innocence."

"You should since you took it." I try a small smile to lighten the mood, tempting him to step away from the gates of purgatory.

It doesn't work. He winces. "Henna, I ..."

"No. No ..." I roll on top of him. "Don't go there. Don't do it. No regrets. YOLO. Man up and show some pride for taking my virginity. So many men before you have tried and failed. You should get a prize or at least a bumper sticker that says *I was in Hell and never wanted to leave.*"

The most intoxicating laugh breaks from his chest, and in the dim lighting his perfect smile beams. My grin matches his. I love *us* so much it's hard to find a complete breath when I think about leaving.

"I don't want to go."

His smile dissolves into a frown, and the same regret he had for his dad reappears, but this time it's for me. I hate being his regret.

"Tell me you want me to stay."

His head eases side to side as his hands feather down my back to my bare ass. "I want *you*, but I don't want you to stay."

"What if I want to stay?"

Bodhi shakes his head some more. "You don't. We feel the same, and you know it. You want *me*, but you don't want to stay."

"You're right. I want to go. I want you to come with me. And I know it's selfish. And maybe nineteen is too old to play the young and selfish card, but even if it is, I can't help how I feel."

He presses his lips to mine, unmoving. It feels like he's stopped time. I want him to stop time. I want to live with Bodhi forever without taking a single blink.

CHAPTER TWENTY-FIVE

W E SPEND THE next three days talking on the phone, texting, and taking long walks along the snowy trails on the back of Snare. I find riding a horse with Bodhi sitting right behind me, holding me in his strong arms, is quite possibly the greatest experience I've ever had.

Between spending time with my family and him making an effort to be there with his sister, we don't find any more time to spend in the back of Alice.

"Maybe something came up?" Zach looks at his watch as he and my mom wait with me at the bottom of the stairs to ZIP's private jet.

I'm leaving today. California then ... the world. It should be the best day of my life. But instead, I'm dying inside because I'm leaving Bodhi. What's worse—he's not here to say goodbye. He said he'd be here. He's twenty minutes late.

"Sometimes goodbyes are too hard." Juni strokes my hair below my white beanie as I keep my eyes glued to the entrance of the small airport. "You can FaceTime him from your dad's house."

Tears fill my eyes. I don't want to FaceTime him. I want his arms. I want his lips.

Fuck ... I just want him.

"What if he got into an accident? I know he wouldn't miss

this. I just know. Something's happened. I can't leave until—"

Zach points to the blue van stopped at the security entrance. "I'll call down to have them let him in."

I drop my purse and take off running like I did on Christmas night. Alice speeds toward me. Bodhi stops at the barricade, jumps out, and runs toward me.

"Where were you?" I squeeze my eyes shut, letting the emotions flow down my face as he hugs me, lifting me off the ground.

"I'm so sorry," he says out of breath. "Alice wouldn't start. I was so fucking scared that you were going to be gone." Bodhi sets my feet back on the ground. He cradles my face, rubbing his thumbs over my tear-drenched cheeks before kissing the rest away, ending with a slow, miserable, my-heart-is-breaking kiss.

"I love you," I whisper when his lips release mine.

He rests his forehead on mine. "I love you too. Forever."

"Jesus ..." I blink more tears. "This hurts. I already miss you. It's already impossible to breathe. How am I supposed to get on that plane?"

"Show me the world, baby. Live like I'm there with you."

I grip his jacket and press my lips to his like he did our last night together—unmoving. *Time ... please just stop. Just give me this moment with him forever.* "You make me want to stay," I whisper past the lump in my throat.

Bodhi kisses every inch of my face before letting his lips find the center of my forehead. "You make me want to go," he whispers in return.

"Henna and Bodhi," I say on a painful sigh.

He hugs me to his chest, resting his hand on my head,

holding me like I'm his world. "Bodhi and Henna," he softly echoes me.

I ease back. He holds my hand, slowly letting go until it's just the tips of our fingers clinging to the final second.

"I love you," I mouth.

Bodhi's eyes fill with tears and his jaw clenches, trying so hard to hold it together. He starts to speak, but he chokes, shaking his head. He holds his fisted hand to his mouth. If he blinks, he'll cry. If he speaks, he'll sob. If he does either one, I'll never get on that plane.

Forcing myself to turn, I walk back to the plane.

"Call me when you get there." Mom gives me a final hug and so does Zach.

I climb the stairs to the jet and stop at the top. Alice's brake lights shine red in the distance. He turns right and disappears.

"Okay, world…" I take a deep breath and wipe the tears from the corners of my eyes "…show me whatcha got."

CHAPTER TWENTY-SIX

January and February – Japan

MY DAD TAKES my dropping out of school a lot better than I imagined. We spend a memorable New Years together, then he takes me to the airport for an emotional goodbye before boarding my non-private jet to Japan.

Bodhi messages me before I leave California.

Bodhi: *I hope you're wearing your best smile and lots of sunscreen. This is life, baby ... LIVE IT!*

I send him a short video of me kissing my hand and blowing it toward the camera.

Me: *Living it. Missing you. Xo*

Why Japan? Well, it's where Juni met Zach. It's a stunning mix of ultra high-tech and rich historic culture. I spend two months in Japan traveling from hostel to hostel, living like a nomad instead of a princess up the hill. Granted ... my expenses are covered by the music king and fashion queen, but I only splurge when adventure calls and live frugally on days that require nothing more than my sketch pad and sharpened pencils.

I'm living. But mostly ... I miss Bodhi.

"Hey!" I grin and it feels equal parts amazing and torturous as Bodhi's face appears on the screen. We FaceTime once a month and text once a day. That's what we agreed upon before I left. Anything less would have me running home and giving up on my dreams, anything more would distract me from *living*.

"Hey, yourself." Bodhi's smile could break my computer screen. "How was your last day in Tokyo?"

"Amazing. I can't believe how many friends I've made in two months. I didn't make that many in four years of high school." My lips twist. "Okay, I've made four new friends in a couple months, but that feels like a lot."

Bodhi shakes his head, his smile still beaming. "It looks like Japan suits you better than high school."

"Yeah, but I still miss third period."

His grin fades a tiny fraction. "I miss you too. *But* ... I'm so freaking happy for you and for me when I get to live vicariously through your postcards. Look ..." He repositions his computer screen to the wall behind his bed.

I send him a post card from every new city, no matter how big or small. He has them tacked to the wall above his bed. "What happens when you run out of wall space?"

He repositions the camera so it's back on him. "I have three other walls."

If I send him enough postcards to cover all of his bedroom walls, I'm certain it would take a decade, and after two months and one new country, I'm ready to go home to Bodhi.

But ... *life*.

"Have you picked up the language?"

I laugh. "Maybe sign language. I'm pretty good at charades.

The locals find me entertaining." I shrug. "I've mastered some of the language. Enough to not feel like a tourist every day."

"Are you going to tell me where you're going tomorrow? What new country?"

"Nope." I pop the P. "I told you, I'll tell you when I get there."

Bodhi chuckles, scratching his stubbly face. He looks so damn sexy with a neatly trimmed winter beard. My fingers ache, missing his touch.

"You don't know, do you?"

I roll my eyes. "I have a plane ticket in my bag. Of course I know where I'm going tomorrow." Releasing a long sigh, I ask the question that makes me the most nervous. "How's your dad?"

His brows draw together. "He's fine. The last round of chemo took a lot out of him, but he's bouncing back a little more each day. How about you? Where's your pain level?"

"Surprisingly not awful. I honestly didn't anticipate staying in a country so long with such harsh punishments for using marijuana."

"The acupuncture and herbs have helped?"

"God, yes ... so much. After that first miserable week here, which I'm certain it was the long flight that did a number on my back, I've been functional." I grin. "And sober. Okay, I may have shared some hot sake with a few of my new friends during late night gatherings at the hostel, but that's it."

"Sake, huh?"

"Not my cuppa, but this is a wasted experience if I don't try new things. I don't even want to tell you some of the foods I've tried. Sushi dad would never let me live it down."

Bodhi chuckles. It hurts ... all of it.

His laugh.

His smile.

That handsome face.

Those eyes ...

"I wanna come home," I whisper as emotions burn my eyes.

"Baby ..." He lifts his hand to touch the screen. "Japan is one country. The world is your dream."

"You're my dream."

He frowns. "It's just because we're seeing each other like this—live, like we're together when we're not. I've seen too many pictures of you over the last two months with the biggest smiles and your eyes beaming like you just discovered the meaning of life. Don't cheat yourself. You'll regret it."

We've never discussed how long. How long will I be gone? Before Bodhi, I thought at least two years with Juni, Zach, and my dad meeting me for visits in some of their favorite countries. If I go home, even for a quick holiday visit, I know I won't be able to get back on a plane again. I will make a beeline to Bodhi Malone, and that's where I'll stay.

So, I'm not going home until my travels are complete.

"Tell me about the rumors," I say.

"Rumors?" His head cocks to the side.

"There's always rumors. After I dropped out, what were people saying? Did they suspect us?"

He glances at his watch. Our different time zones suck. He has school soon, and I have bed soon.

"Kids are always talking shit. I ignore it, but ..." Bodhi chews on the inside of his lip.

"But what?"

"Some of the female students have been a little ..."

"Sluts! They're after you, aren't they?" Jealousy nips at my nerves.

"I've had to take care of some inappropriate notes and texts. That's all."

"I'd better go before I get the urge to kill something."

Bodhi rubs his chin, a triumphant grin playing along his lips. "I love you, Hell. I love you so fucking much."

I nod, choking on the emotion that always hovers like a dark cloud over our goodbyes. "Wait for me."

"Henna, I'm not going anywhere."

I know this, but time distorts emotions and breeds resentment. Time could destroy us. I cough a laugh to hide the impending sobs. "I leave early. Have a good day at work." My tears chase my goodbye. I try not to let him see how much this hurts.

"Have a safe flight to ... wherever."

I nod, plastering on a smile to mask the ugly cry climbing up my throat to escape my bleeding heart. "Bye." Pressing *End,* I completely fall apart. I will never be immune to my love for him.

> **Bodhi:** Close your eyes and let me kiss away those tears. Fall asleep in the memory of my arms wrapped around you. Dream of us.

This makes me cry more, but I do it. I find comfort and eventually sleep in the warmth of *us.*

CHAPTER TWENTY-SEVEN

M ARCH IN CHINA: Twelve postcards, daily texts, one FaceTime. I meet five new friends that I hope to see again someday.

April and May in Vietnam, Laos, Thailand, and Cambodia: Thirty-two postcards (I fall in love with Southeast Asia), texts most days but not every day, one FaceTime. Bodhi gets the flu, but still makes it to Coachella. I meet eleven new friends and a million friendly faces. I head for my next adventure forever changed because the aftermath of war, genocide, communism, and poverty is still etched into the faces of the locals.

June in Vanuatu: Six postcards, texts several times a week, one FaceTime. I meet three new friends, and ... a guy.

Me: Yesterday my diving instructor asked me to dinner. He's nice. Ten years older than me. I said no. He texted me this morning from my front door. He brought me breakfast. His name is Noah. I feel guilty for eating breakfast with him.

Bodhi: I worry that your guilt could get in the way. Don't feel guilty. Live, Henna. That's the point, right?

Why can't he be a little upset or show an ounce of jealousy?

Me: I want to say those same words back to you. When will you "live?"

Bodhi: I have to go. My dad has an appointment. Love you.

Me: *Love you too.*

Vanuatu is a paradise nestled off the coast of Australia. I chose it because I've been to Fiji with Juni and Zach, and I want this trip to be *my* new discoveries, not reliving old adventures. Paradise has a way of making the rest of the world seem nonexistent. On a tiny island so far from the life I left behind, it's hard to do anything but live in the moment, especially with my tan, dark curly-haired friend, Noah. Aside from being my hired diving instructor, he takes it upon himself to make sure I get private snorkeling in the afternoons, parasailing, and picnics on the beach.

"I call bullshit. There's no way you're a doctor. Like ... a real medical doctor." I toss a chunk of pineapple at Noah. It lands on his tan washboard abs.

He grins, blowing the little bit of sand off it, and pops it into his mouth, giving my bikini-clad body the once-over. I hide my blush beneath my wide-brimmed hat. "Total truth. I'm a third-generation doctor of medicine." He runs his toe along the instep of my foot.

"You're too young."

"Says the nineteen-year-old girl traveling the world by herself."

I give him a flirty smile, letting my eyes shift to his small boat anchored fifty yards from the abandoned beach. The day is perfect. And while I miss Bodhi *always*, in this exact moment, it doesn't cause physical pain to my heart. Noah gets the credit—or the blame—for that.

"Fine, Dr. Noah, why are you on a beach with a nineteen-year-old nomad instead of saving lives?"

He stares out at the pristine Pacific, chewing on the end of a toothpick while the breeze ruffles his dark wavy hair. "My wife …"

I stiffen.

"I met her when she was about your age. I'm not sure how you feel about love at first sight, but I just knew I was a goner when she gave me this guilty smile after accidentally taking my black coffee instead of her latte at the hospital cafeteria. She was a nurse on the oncology floor. I was a resident in the ER. We married three months later." He smiles. It's equally sad and romantic at the same time. "She was pregnant by the next month. But she went into labor at thirty weeks." His brows knit together as his gaze sinks to the sand between us. "We were traveling. She told me to save the baby." Noah shakes his head. "I couldn't save him, and … I couldn't save her. There was just so much blood."

Reaching across the sandy divide, I grab his hand.

"It changed me so profoundly I couldn't walk back into another hospital."

I know about love at first sight. And I know about things in life that change you *profoundly*.

"I'm so sorry."

He squeezes my hand. "Nothing lasts forever, right?"

"Yeah …" I release a slow breath as our gazes meet. "Everything is temporary."

Noah eases to sitting, holding my gaze in his dark eyes. And when he leans toward me, I don't move. When his lips press to mine. I don't pull away. With one hand, he steadies his body between us while his other hand slides through my hair, cupping the back of my head. My hat falls off.

I pull back an inch, breaking our kiss. My chin dips in shame. "There's someone."

Noah's hand slides from my head to my arm, feathering his touch to my hand where he traces the beads of my bracelets with his fingers. "At home?"

I nod.

"Can I ask why he's not here?"

"Timing. We just met at the most impossible time in our lives." I glance up and share my own heartbreaking smile.

"And now? Are you just passing time waiting for the right moment?"

"I don't know. Maybe."

"And he's waiting for you?"

It's my turn to look away. "I think *he* thinks he's waiting for me, but how long can one wait?"

"Do you want him to wait?"

I just want *him*. It's always been that simple for me.

"Well, he owns my heart, so yeah ... I want him to wait. But I'm quite good at wanting the impossible."

"Hmm..." he nudges my bare leg with his "...I don't need your heart. I'd take absolutely anything you had to give. So, you've got my number."

"You did catch that I'm not exactly hanging out in one spot forever, right?"

He takes the last piece of pineapple and holds it up to my lips, while grinning. "I have a boat. I can purchase a plane ticket. Train? Bike? As I said ... you've got my number."

I slowly open my mouth and let him slide the juicy fruit onto my tongue. As I close my mouth around it, he lets his fingertips linger on my lips. When he leans in to let his lips steal the spot where his fingers rest, I let him.

As soon as I get back to my rented bedroom and shared kitchen, I message Bodhi.

> **Me:** Noah kissed me and I let him. Don't respond right now. I think it would kill me if you did. Missing you has become a full-time job for my heart. The only thing keeping me from coming home is knowing that we will never be us again until I see this journey through. So it's okay to hate me. But please … love me more. Xo

CHAPTER TWENTY-EIGHT

Bodhi

"NEVER SEEN YOU work so many hours. Not sure I've seen you sweat so much either," Dad says as I bring my bone-tired body through the door just before seven at night.

I've channeled all my energy into fixing fences, replacing boards in the barn, and re-siding the house. Summer is my time to get this stuff done. It keeps my mind from going to places like Henna kissing some guy named Noah half a world away.

Ignoring him, I toe off my boots and wipe my brow while taking the steps up to my bathroom—the same damn steps that hold memories of Henna naked on them.

"Is this about the girl? Henna? She still finding herself?"

I shake my head. "It's just work that needs to be done before school starts this fall."

"You were showing me pictures of her every day, but two weeks ago you stopped showing me pictures and you've been grumpy as hell since then. I'm old, not stupid. It's about the girl."

Yeah, it's about the girl—the way the sun feels on my skin,

the whisper of the breeze when I'm on Snare, the reflection of the full moon, the air in my lungs, the rhythm of my heart … it's all about *the* girl.

After I shower and eat dinner in silence and under the relentless scrutiny of my dad's curious glances, I clean up and put him to bed before making my nightly trip outside to lie on the mattress in the back of Alice. I leave the doors open to welcome the breeze, a breeze I want to think kissed Henna's skin and whispered through her long auburn hair. Basically, I do anything to connect *us*.

It's been two weeks since Henna messaged me. Two weeks since she kissed Noah. Two weeks since she told me not to respond right away. I don't know what the time frame is on responding to that, especially when I don't know what to say. The world is filled with men who can offer her a life I can't even begin to give her.

She'll come back. This I know. Her home will always be Colorado, but I don't believe she will truly come back to me. *Don't sweat it, everything is temporary.* I'm temporary, but Henna could never be temporary.

As if she knows I'm thinking about her, my phone chimes with the first text since the Noah text.

Henna: *Hi. Remember me?*

I take a deep breath. Maybe I need to let her go. Maybe *she's* looking for permission to let go. If only it were that easy.

Bodhi: *Hi. I'm pretty sure you're still my greatest memory.*
Henna: *How's your dad?*
Bodhi: *Nosey.*

> **Henna:** *I landed in Madagascar. I'm going in search of le-murs tomorrow.*
>
> **Bodhi:** *I landed on a pile of hay when I fell off the roof of the barn today. I'm going in search of my lost watch tomorrow.*
>
> **Henna:** *Seriously? OMG did you get hurt?*

My heart hurts too fucking bad to feel anything but the pain of missing Henna.

> **Bodhi:** *I'm fine.*
>
> **Henna:** *Listening to The Fray "Never Say Never"*

Fuck ...

> **Bodhi:** *Colony House "This Beautiful Life"*
>
> **Henna:** *Someday ... I'm coming back to you.*

I stare at her words, then I play "This Beautiful Life" on my phone at full volume.

> **Henna:** *Bodhi?*

After a few blinks, I put this song on repeat and set it on the seat next to me. "What are we doing?" I whisper, closing my eyes.

HENNA SPENDS JULY in South Africa. Juni and Zach meet up with her in Cape Town. She posts pictures on Instagram, including one of everyone on the beach—three other couples I've never seen and a guy standing next to Henna with his arm draped over her shoulder.

She looks incredible. She looks … happy.

To end the month on a real high, my dad finds out his cancer is progressing again. We have our usual argument over treatment. He says no. I say yes and threaten to call Bella. I win until I get home and find him writing a suicide note. That makes the fourth time since the accident. At least this time, I catch him before he does anything more than write a note.

We fight.

He cries for me and my "wasted life."

I cry for him and his "wasted life."

We fight some more, and he gets high and passes out. I contemplate getting drunk for the first time since the night he tried to carry my wasted ass down those marble stairs. Instead, I give in to a very weak moment, and I call Henna. I have no clue how much it will cost to call her, but I don't care at the moment. I can't FaceTime her and let her see me like this, but I'm certain if I don't hear her voice, I could take my own life.

"Bodhi?" she answers in a groggy voice.

I always forget there's a huge time difference.

Choking on emotions that feel like razor blades in my throat, I let her voice cover my skin, sinking into my desperate soul.

"Bodhi?" Her voice gets a little stronger as she clears her throat.

Falling back on my bed, I press the phone to my ear with one hand and cover my heart with my other hand. "Hi."

I should probably start with *Sorry I've been a selfish, jealous dick ignoring your texts and attempts to FaceTime me for a whole month*, but all I can manage to get out is "hi."

Long moments pass with painful silence. This isn't Bodhi

and Henna. This is just fucking torture.

"Tell me to come home," she whispers as if she knows I'm ready to break.

Come home. I have nothing to give you except me. Just please ... come home.

Closing my eyes to suppress a new round of tears, I pinch the bridge of my nose. Today ... hell, this whole month has kicked my ass physically and emotionally. I'm so fucking tired.

"It was a kiss. That's all. And I didn't tell you to hurt you. I told you because I don't want anything between us."

Except miles of ocean, hours of time, months of separation, and so much pain. Henna can be anything, do anything, live an extraordinary life. If I love her, I'll let her go. I know what I have to do, I just don't know what happens after it's done, after we're done. The love doesn't just vanish.

What do I do with these emotions I have for her?

"You knew ... you knew we were temporary even when I didn't want to believe it."

"Bodhi," she says my name with caution and uncertainty. "Jesus ... there's someone else."

I shake my head. How could she think that? It takes everything I have to not correct her assumption. If I say no, she'll know something else is wrong, and she'll come home to me.

Me—the man who has nothing to offer her.

If I say yes, I'll break her heart. But hearts mend. Maybe not my mom's heart, but Henna is stronger than my mom was. Hers will mend, probably without a single scar.

"I should go."

"Go? Are you kidding me?" Anger builds with each one of her words, slashing my chest, cutting me open. "You woke me up after not responding to me for over a month, just to tell me that you've found someone else? No. That's not okay. You owe me more than a fucking phone call. You—"

My face distorts as I fight the pent-up emotions, shaking from my silent sobs as she lets me hear her pain with a choking cry.

"I'm sorry," I manage to let two words slip past my swollen throat, letting them slip off my idle tongue that wants to tell her the truth, but the truth would not set her free, and Henna Eve Lane needs to fly. She needs to be free.

No matter where I am on this earth, I'm loving you ... forever.

"I hate you."

Hate me. But this time, hate me more than you love me. Then ... let me go.

Henna lives with such passion. I used to think it was her youth, but it's not. She's going to say what she means no matter what. When she's eighty, I'm certain she will live her life with an uncensored tongue.

"You're going to be fine."

She laughs out a sob. "Sure. Whatever helps you sleep at night."

The line goes dead.

CHAPTER TWENTY-NINE

Henna

One Year and Eight Months Later
Indio, California—Coachella

"DAD!" I FLY out of the cab and run straight into my father's arms. The festival goers around us stop and stare for a few seconds before funneling toward the entrance. "Finally!" I kiss him on the cheek just before he sets me back on my feet.

During my more than two years traveling the world, he only met up with me twice—in Germany a year ago and Ecuador last Christmas. Coachella is my last stop before I go back to Colorado after being gone for over two years.

"I stayed away from the sushi this time."

"Good call." I tuck myself under his arm as we make our way to the entrance.

"Kiddo, we have a lot of catching up to do."

"True."

We hold out our bracelets to be scanned.

"But we'll do that at the hotel later. Right now, it's all about THE MUSIC!" I skip out in front of him and twirl in circles, my bracelets jingling, my hair whipping in the wind.

Dad chuckles. A few girls around us do a double take, but not because of me. My dad with his Marine-sculpted body, red hair, and crooked smile bears an uncanny resemblance to Kevin McKidd, Owen Hunt's character from *Grey's Anatomy*.

I don't see it, but it's probably true. It's just that a few of my friends binge-watched the show and fell in love with Owen, so I can't let there be a connection. It's just too wrong.

For hours we drift from stage to stage. My dad is rock and roll to the core. He lifts me up on his shoulders, and I feel like his five-year-old daughter again, but at the same time I feel a dull pain from the past—my last time at Coachella and the shoulders that lifted me toward the sky.

I miss those shoulders. I miss everything about Bodhi Malone.

He obliterated my heart with one phone call. It took me a week to leave the hostel. It took me a month to find the strength to tell Juni without breaking down. But I'm certain it will take a lifetime to forget him. Glancing around, I can't help but wonder if he's here, working the lights and sound. Did Bella come home to stay with their dad for the weekend, or are Etta and Duke watching over him?

"I'm starving." Dad drinks the rest of his bottled water as we shuffle out of the tent after the last concert of the night.

"Me too. Tacos?"

"Absolutely." He wraps his arm around me.

"Ew ... no." I pull away laughing. "You're a saturated sweat rag. Just ... no."

We take the shuttle back to the hotel and find the nearest restaurant still open and serving tacos.

"Margarita blended and two chicken hard-shell tacos." I hand the waitress my menu.

Dad gives her his order then shakes his head at me. "Margarita blended. When did my little girl grow up? I can't believe you're old enough to order alcohol. For God's sake, it feels like yesterday that you were OD'ing on fruit punch."

I grin. "That's just an age thing. I'm not sure how grown-up I feel."

"Your mom and Zach spoiled you by funding your little hiatus from real life."

Laughing, I roll my eyes. "Real life? I'm not even sure what that is anymore."

"So what now, Henna? What are your plans?"

"Well, I met a woman in Greece who sells art to major home goods stores. She connects artists to retailers. A lot of retailers are looking for something that can be exclusive to them and limited print designs. Like she literally just happened to walk by me while I was perched on a bench sketching."

"That's fantastic."

The waitress sets our drinks on the table.

"Yeah." I take a sip of my margarita. "I'm not sure if that's how I want my art to be sold long term, but for now, it could be a really great starting point for me."

"Starting point? Henna, you're going to have your art sold to potentially hundreds of thousands of people. That's more than a starting point."

I grin around my straw and shrug. He's right. If I'm honest, my travels taught me a lot about life, the importance of connecting with other people, and taking chances even when they're way out of your comfort zone. When I wasn't dying over Bodhi for those two years and three months, I was living—like *really* living.

"So I'm going to call her when I get home. Home ..." I shake my head. "I'm going home to a guest house and a very empty estate."

"Yeah, Juni said they'd be in L.A. until September. Why don't you go there? Surely there's an extra bedroom." He smirks. "Or you can stay with me. No extra bedroom, but you know you love my sofa bed."

I roll my eyes.

Zach owns many homes. He purchased the one in Colorado for me. At least that's what Juni said, but it's her favorite place too. Most of the time, they're in L.A., closer to the epicenters of their professional lives. I don't hate L.A., but it's not my Rockies.

"My favorite strain of marijuana can only be found in Colorado."

"You're full of shit." He rolls his eyes. "Are you really still a pothead?"

"Pothead? Thanks, Dad." I suck down more of my margarita. "I'm really still in pain if that's what you're asking, but I've found other ways to deal with it out of necessity and lack of medical marijuana available during my travels."

"I'm extremely grateful I didn't get the phone call that my only daughter is in some third-world country's prison on drug charges."

"Yeah, well, me too." I giggle, gathering my hair off my neck and leaning back to stretch. It's been a long day. As I release my hair and straighten my back, my gaze falls over my dad's shoulder to the bar.

My heart stops. Completely, emergency brake, brick-wall stops.

Bodhi.

He laughs before taking a drink of what looks like water. The blonde next to him talks animatedly with her hands in the air, then she leans toward him, laughing hard as she balances by putting her hand on his leg.

I knew coming home might involve seeing him again. I've both dreaded it and craved it. As I sit here, I don't even know what my heart is feeling because it's simply idle in my chest. Maybe it's waiting for my brain to process all that's happened over the past three years since I met Bodhi in this same city.

"What are you looking at?" Dad turns, looking over his shoulder.

"Nothing."

Nothing? Is that a lie? Are Bodhi and I now nothing? I don't know because a lot happened after that phone call. When I managed to crawl out of my dark hole, I lived.

I lived in constant motion, immersing myself in my surroundings, always looking for the next adventure. I lived in the laughter of new friendship, and sometimes ... I lived in the arms and the beds of other men.

But not once did I ever want their names carved beside mine in a fallen tree trunk above my creek in Colorado.

"Is *nothing* the blond guy?" Dad turns back around. I told him about Bodhi and Mr. Malone, minus the stair sex and blowjob in his office at school.

I didn't even tell Juni those details. She knows there was sex and other "intimate acts," but no matter what name I give her, my conscience will always see her as Mom. Does *Mom* really want to know what Mr. Malone tasted like going down my throat? I think not.

"Maybe," I say cautiously, adjusting my chair so Dad blocks me if Bodhi looks our way.

"Do I need to kick Nothing's ass?"

I grin, in spite of the pain. I grin because my dad's never had that chance to be protective of me like this. He's never confronted a date of mine at the door and threatened to castrate them for so much as looking at me for too long.

"No. But thanks for the offer."

"It's a standing offer."

I chuckle, tipping my chin and stirring my drink with the straw.

The waitress brings our food, and because every hungry stomach in a restaurant homes in on out-coming food, Bodhi looks our way.

Two seconds.

I give him eye contact for two seconds. Possibly the longest two seconds of my life. And from the way the color drains from his face, I'm certain this is the first he's noticed me.

"So ... you dating anyone?" I ask my dad, vowing to not look in Bodhi's direction again, even if I feel his heated gaze all over me.

"Not at the moment. I can't get a handle on these dating websites. I think they're for your generation, not mine."

I nod, before taking a huge bite of my taco. Bodhi's still staring at me. I *feel* it. I've lost my appetite, but I need something to focus on, so I shovel in food, fiddle with my napkin, and gulp down the rest of my margarita and my ice water.

"And these women do not put accurate profile pictures on

the sites nor do they post accurate facts about themselves. Last month I went on a date with a woman who said she enjoys all things outdoors, hiking, biking … Then she practically dies on me during dinner because she forgot her inhaler, and the walk from the car to the restaurant exhausted her."

I nod, tackling my next taco like a savage ripping apart its prey.

"Henna?"

I nod.

"Henna!"

I snap my head up out of my hunched, cavewoman position. "What?" I mumble over an entire taco shoved into my mouth.

"Have you heard a word I've said?"

I nod a few times then shake my head. "Sorry." I chew slower and wipe my mouth with my shredded napkin.

Dad glances over his shoulder again. I don't. I can't.

"Who is he?"

He's life.

My dad is no idiot. He made reading the enemy a profession.

"If I tell you, can you refrain from injuring him?"

He takes a pull of his beer, eyeing me with suspicion. "Probably not."

"Then he's *nobody.*"

I return to my last taco.

"So you know I'm going to do some serious bodily harm to him. Give your old man a break and at least give me motive for when they arrest me."

He took my virginity, my heart, and my whole fucking world.

Then he gave it back. But I didn't want it back.

"I think you should let Juni fix you up with someone. She told me she's offered to do that for you."

"Changing the subject will not change the outcome for that young man behind me, but in response to your ridiculous suggestion, the answer is no. I'm not having the mother of my child set me up on a date. It's ..." He shakes his head, wearing a sour look on his face.

"Yeah, I can see how dating one of Juni's supermodel friends could be a little torturous."

"We're done talking about this." He dives into his food, and we let the rest of our dinner disappear in silence.

After the check is paid, he slides back in his chair. "Just one more order of business ..."

"No!" I reach over the table and grab his arm.

"Who is he, Henna?"

Finally, I risk one more glance up, but Bodhi and his pretty friend are gone. I exhale.

"Doesn't matter. He's gone. I'll order a ride. Let's go."

The driver is three minutes away. As we emerge from the restaurant, I almost run into the blonde standing next to Bodhi a few feet from the curb.

Shit.

And there it is, the pain I couldn't completely feel before. But when Bodhi looks over at me as Dad and I wait next to them, everything hurts the way it did when I got on that plane to leave him over two years ago, the way it did when he called me to let me go.

"Hi," he says politely because he's older and more mature than me.

I can't find a single word, not even a noise that could resemble one because I'm ready to fall apart after working so hard to piece myself back together. With one word, he's threatened all of that.

The blonde gives me a tiny, confused smile as her eyes flit between me and Bodhi.

"Hi." My dad offers his hand to Bodhi.

What the fuck?

"Mr. Malone, right? You were Henna's guidance counselor, right? She's told me so much about you."

Okay, now my dad's just being an asshole. I love him, but he's still an asshole. He knew exactly who Mr. Nobody was when he saw him in the restaurant. He just thought it would be fun to toy with me.

Not fun.

Not cool.

Total asshole—that I, of course, love.

Bodhi shakes my dad's hand, again being a grownup while I flounder wordlessly. "Bodhi. And yes, you are correct."

"Mitch, I'm her dad."

"Our car!" Yay, look at me, finding two solid words.

Dad gets in the front, and I hop in the back, but Bodhi grabs my door before I can shut it. I look up at him.

He doesn't grin. Doesn't show any emotion in his expression. "Ride share."

I glance at my phone. Really? Is my stupid app on a default ride share setting or am I just that clueless when tapping the options? It's history repeating itself in the worst possible way.

Scooting over to the far side, Bodhi gets in the middle with blondie on the other side. The night couldn't get any worse.

Ugh!

Dad glances over his shoulder with a single brow raised. I squint at him as I plaster myself against the door. Bodhi's arm presses into mine as he fastens his seatbelt. My lungs collapse.

"Buckle up." He gives me a look, not a smile, not really anything other than the way the driver might look at me if he were the one telling me to buckle up.

I fumble with the seatbelt. When did my hands start shaking? Bodhi covers my hand with his. I glance up at him and tears sting my eyes, so I focus on the seatbelt again. He takes it from me and fastens it.

"Thank you," I whisper.

His touch ripped off the Band-Aid I've had over my heart. One touch and I want to cry. I hate time right now. We were stupid, young, and naive to think we were immune to its effects. If only my body were immune to his touch.

"Jax and Harper are in the bar at the hotel. Do you want to hang out with them for a while?" Blondie rests her hand on Bodhi's leg like she did at the restaurant.

Am I jealous? Absolutely.

Can I justify my feelings? No.

Still, my mind does its own thing.

Bodhi doesn't drink. Of course he doesn't want to hang out in a bar.

Oh, and did you know he's mine? Yeah, I made that claim years ago.

Did you know we have our names carved into a log?

Do you like California spring rolls? I bet you eat raw fish.

Turning away from her hand on his leg, I watch the traffic outside of my window for a few seconds before closing my eyes.

I'm not this person. The woman on the other side of Bodhi is probably very kind. And maybe he likes her hand on his leg. I left him. It wasn't fair to ask him to wait for me.

If only realizing this—the truth—could ease the blow. But it doesn't.

"Sure," he answers her.

The truth tightens its hold on my heart.

"So you were Bodhi's student?" She leans forward to see me.

I pull in as much air as my weak lungs can take, and I turn to face her without looking at Bodhi, who I know is staring at me. "For a few months, then I dropped out."

"Oh." She gives Bodhi an awkward look like she said something wrong.

"I had the chance to travel the world. So I did. Mr. Malone..." I grin "...Bodhi, encouraged me to do it."

It's half the truth.

My dad glances over his shoulder, shooting Bodhi a scowl. Bodhi adjusts in his seat, likely feeling every ounce of my father's disapproval.

"Dude..." the blonde nudges Bodhi "...you're a guidance counselor and you encouraged a student to drop out of high school. That takes some big balls." She laughs.

Things I learned in my travels: After seeing three other sets of balls, Bodhi's are large and so is his cock; they're not all created equally.

He clears his throat. "I'm not certain that's how it played out."

I give him a quick glance before looking back out my window. "It was a couple years ago. I don't recall the specific details." I shrug.

"So did you travel the world?" she asks.

"Yes."

"That's awesome. Are you going to finish school?"

I shrug.

"Well, I'd put my plans on hold if I could afford to travel the world. Did you go to Paris and find a handsome French man to steal your heart?"

If she could stop talking, said heart would appreciate it.

I shake my head. "I didn't go to Paris."

"Really? That's the first place I'd go."

Of course she would. I close my eyes again and give myself a good scolding for being this way, showing my claws.

The driver stops in front of the hotel. And of course, it's our hotel *and* Bodhi's.

Thank you, fate. You suck tonight.

I jump out my side instead of waiting for Bodhi and his friend to get out.

My dad stretches and yawns, waiting for me to come around the car. "Damn ... I'm too old for this."

"You are." I smirk, pushing his back to nudge him toward the revolving door, leaving Bodhi and his friend behind us.

"Are you Henna?" blond friend calls, saying my name slow-ly.

Blowing out a quick breath, I turn just after we get inside the hotel lobby—fake smile pinned to my face. "Yes?"

She narrows her eyes. "Are you ... I mean you look like ..."

Here we go.

"Zachary Phillips's daughter and ..." Her eyes widen with each word.

My dad's chest presses to my back, his hand rests posses-sively on my shoulder.

"And Juni Carlisle's. That's you, isn't it?" She shares her questioning look with Bodhi.

"My daughter. Henna Lane is Mitchell Lane's daughter. I'm Mitchell Lane."

Down boy.

I give him a slight elbow in the gut. He gets along well with Zach. I'm not sure why her slight misstep in wording has him going all Papa Bear.

"This is my dad, Mitch, and yes, Juni is my mother. Zach is my stepdad."

"Oh my gosh!" She gives Bodhi a WTF look. "You had Zachary Phillips's daughter as a student and you didn't say anything?"

My dad starts to correct her again. I give him a slight head shake and another nudge with my elbow.

"Honestly ..." Bodhi shrugs, sharing a tight-lipped smile and eyebrows peaked, "I didn't know at first. I don't keep up with that stuff."

"You *need* to come have a drink with us." She puts her hands together in a prayer fold at her chest. "Oh ..." She cringes at my dad. "Is she ..." She looks at me. "Are you twenty-one?"

I nod. "Yes, but—"

"Please, please, please."

Dad grumbles something under his breath. I think it's "tell her no," but I miss it.

"Just one."

Bodhi's face tenses just before I turn to my dad. "Go to

bed. I'll be up later. Don't wait up." He yawns again. I don't think it will be an issue.

I know he's dying to say something protective, but he knows it would be ridiculous at this point in my life.

"Be smart." He bends down and kisses my cheek.

I smile.

When I turn back around, blond girl shoves her hand toward me. "I'm Rayne by the way. And thank you for saying yes. I'll try not to talk your ear off, but I have so many questions for you." She grabs my arm like we're BFFs and pulls me toward the bar with Bodhi in tow. "Have you met ..." She spews off every major music act to grace the charts in the last decade.

While we wait for a booth, along with their friends, Jax and Harper, I blow Rayne's mind with just how many famous people I know or have met. It didn't hit me until now just how honest and simple my relationship was with Bodhi. We met through our shared love of music. There was an instant connection, but it never had anything to do with my family, their connections, or what he could gain by befriending me. Because he had no idea who I was, yet ... he knew me better than anyone.

We're seated in a small round booth.

"Bodhi, you'd better sit between Henna and Rayne, so she doesn't scare Henna away. I'm like totally frightened for her." Harper winks at Rayne.

Rayne flips her the middle finger while sliding into the booth. Bodhi slides in next to her, and I, in fact, end up next to Bodhi. And when I say next to Bodhi, I mean our arms and legs are touching because I'm the fifth wheel in a booth made for four.

"I'm sorry," Bodhi mouths while Rayne chatters with Jax and Harper.

I shake my head and give him an it's-okay smile.

"Sooo ... Henna was Bodhi's student." Rayne shifts the conversation back to me.

Hurray.

"Student?" Jax grins at Bodhi. "Thought you were a guidance counselor. Who was stupid enough to give you students?"

Bodhi sips his water. "They're all my students. I'm the keeper of schedules and sanity. The school would not function without me."

I laugh a little, welcoming the small crack in the tension.

"My guidance counselor sure as hell wasn't the fine snack that Bodhi is." Rayne leans into Bodhi playfully, which causes him to lean into me. Which causes me to feel tingly all over— and warm. I'm ready to spontaneously combust.

The next hour turns into Henna fest. *Henna did this. Henna did that.* Anyone who didn't know the truth would think Rayne was in fact my best friend because she seems to know a lot about me, and what she doesn't know she manages to drag out of me like a million details about my travels. I feel a little guilty that they are hearing this before my dad.

I keep my gaze on Bodhi's friend more than him, but when I give him an occasional quick glance, he has a smile on his face like he's proud? Maybe even happy?

I don't know. But I guess if his intention was to break my heart so I would follow through with my plans, then he should feel good about the outcome.

Too bad I don't. It's hard to explain. I don't regret anything. It was a once in a lifetime opportunity and I'm grateful beyond words that I was given that opportunity. But here I am, two years later, and the man that I love is being touched by another woman, and all I have are memories that won't hold my hand or keep me warm at night. They won't take me on horseback rides. They won't eat California spring rolls with me. They won't ask me to marry them. And they won't love me back.

"Well ..." I nod my head toward the exit. "I'm going to call it a night. Thank you. It's been fun."

"Thank *you!*" Rayne leans over the front of Bodhi and pulls me in for an awkward hug.

I stiffen as Bodhi's hand slides along my leg. Is he doing it intentionally? Is he just trying to find a place to put his hand since Rayne and I are practically hugging on his lap? His warm hand on my bare leg does very embarrassing things to me.

My cheeks flush instantly, and I'm wet between my legs, so hungry for his touch.

As Rayne releases me, so does Bodhi. Tipping my chin to hide my embarrassing reaction to him, I mumble another quick goodbye and speed walk out of the bar.

CHAPTER THIRTY

L AST NIGHT I slipped into the hotel room and grabbed my nightshirt while my dad snored like a champ. Then I took a twenty-minute shower and fingered myself into a Bodhi-induced orgasm.

This morning I feel better. Calmer. And ready for another day of Coachella with my dad. The heat is off the charts. They say the hottest spring on record. In true Hell, I-don't-give-a-shit fashion, I'm wearing an Alice blue, strapless sundress that doesn't cover much, my silver Birkies, and lots of bracelets. My travels didn't allow for my henna tattoos, which sucks because they would look amazing with all the skin showing today.

"Bethanne?" My dad nods for me to follow him over a few feet as we wait for the next act to come out on stage.

A dark-haired woman turns. "Mitchell Lane." She grins and falls into his open arms.

"How long has it been?" he asks, setting her back on her feet. It was quite the hug.

"At least ten years."

Dad turns. "Bethanne, I'd like you to meet my daughter, Henna. Henna, this is Bethanne. Her husband and I were in the Marines together."

They share a sad smile. I don't ask, but it's pretty obvious that said husband is no longer alive.

"Nice to meet you." I smile.

"You too. And don't let your dad lie to you. Alan and your dad were in the same band before they both enlisted."

I raise my eyebrows. Dad grins, nodding slowly like he's remembering the good ol' days.

"You here by yourself?" he asks her.

"Will you judge me as a pathetic old woman if I say yes?"

"You're younger than me." He bites his lower lip.

Is he *flirting* with her? Okay, I'm out of here. "So ... I'm going to see if I can find um ... Carley. I'll text you later?"

Carley is not here. I grasp for the easy excuse.

"Yeah, sure. Be careful."

"It was nice meeting you." Bethanne holds up her hand.

I mirror her gesture. "You too."

Instead of looking for a friend who I know is not even in California, I worm my way toward the front of the stage just as an electric guitar cuts through the stacks of speakers. The crowd comes to life and the technicolor of lights start to dance around to the building beat.

"What's up, COACHELLA!" the lead singer yells before diving into the lyrics.

I throw my arms in the air and give my own scream because the energy is contagious. But I can't stay. I'm on a mission: find Bodhi and see why he touched my leg.

I'm not going to ask him that in those exact words, but I need to know why and if he felt it like I did. I need to know why he let me go, even if I know it's because of his dad and his self-induced prison sentence. He needs to tell me to my face that he doesn't want me anymore, that he's met someone else.

Swallowing a year and half of pride, I message him.

Me: *Where are you?*

He doesn't respond right away, so I bob my head to the beat and envy those around me who are ten stories high on weed. I could use a little hit at the moment.

Bodhi: *Hotel.*

I start to type something, but wait … why would he be at the hotel? Unless he's with Rayne and they're …

My stomach starts to reject the last meal I fed it. I don't respond. He's a grown man. We ended. He has needs. Rayne clearly is capable of filling them.

A few minutes later, my phone chimes.

Bodhi: *Why?*

Me: *Nothing. Sorry to disturb you.*

I told him Noah kissed me. He should just tell me he'll talk later after he gets done fucking Rayne. That's fair. I deserve it.

Bodhi: *Room 312*

Please be alone and not inviting me for a threesome.

I don't text back. Instead, I hop on the first shuttle back to the hotel. Am I ready to be alone with him? No one to distract us from the elephant in the room? Probably not, but I take the elevator to the third floor and knock on room 312 anyway.

After a few seconds, he opens the door.

"Hey." His gaze eats me up. "Nice dress."

If before I showed up I wasn't acutely aware of how little it covers, I am now. "Thank you."

He holds open the door. I take cautious steps into his hotel room, inspecting my surroundings for any signs that a woman has been in here with him.

"Why are you here?" I ask, pulling open his shades to check out his not-so-awesome view of the roof to the pool area.

"Job injury."

I look back at him as he bends at the waist and parts his hair just behind the crown of his head. There's a row of stitches.

"I took a hammer to the head this morning. Some guys working above me dropped it. Five stitches."

My nose wrinkles. "Ouch. Are you okay?"

"Yeah. No big deal. But I was told to take the rest of the day off. So ... instead of baking my wound in the sun, I came back here." He plops down on the king-sized bed. Leaning against the headboard, he turns on the TV. "Figured I'd binge-watch something."

I grin, taking a seat in the desk chair. He's mocking me.

"Where's your dad?"

"Hanging out with an old friend. A woman." I smirk. "He started acting all flirty with her, so I decided to ditch him for the day."

"To come see me?"

"No. Yes." My teeth trap my lower lip to stop my rambling. "I don't know. I thought you were probably there, so I was just seeing if you ..."

Touched me on purpose.

Miss me.

Love me.

"If I wanted some fries with extra ketchup?"

Yup. I love him. If there was any question about it before I walked through his hotel room door, there isn't now.

My cheeks burn again like they did last night. Bodhi can touch me without lifting a finger. I feel him in ways I've never felt anyone before. "Yeah. That." I grin, keeping my eyes on him while I reach for the phone and press room service. "Hi. Can we get an order of french fries with extra ketchup and two bottles of water? Thank you."

The hum of the air conditioner gets really loud in our awkward silence. French fries seemed like a good start. Now what do we do or say while waiting for room service?

"Last night I enjoyed hearing about your travels." Bodhi knows what direction we need to go with this awkwardness, but now I can't find all those brave words I wanted to say because I just want to hug him and ask him if there was someone else. If he made it up. If he fell out of love with me. So many questions.

"I felt like I was dominating the conversation. But Rayne had so many questions."

He chuckles. "She was pretty elated when she figured out who you are."

"So … how do know Rayne?"

"Coachella. We met years ago. A lot of us did. This is our annual gathering now. Strangers who became good friends through music."

"Friends," I repeat to myself more than him.

"Is there something you want to ask me?" He cocks his head a bit.

I shake my head.

"You want to know if Rayne is more than a friend?"

Well, she's very pretty. Of course I want to know. But

when my parting words to him included *I hate you,* I think I lost the right to know.

My heart is completely out of control, making my chest tighten. I thought I could do this, but I can't. Digging into my bag, I pull out some cash and toss it onto the desk. "The fries are on me." I stand and make my way toward the door.

"Jesus, Henna. That's it?" He flies off the bed and presses his hand to the door over my head.

With my back to him, I look at my feet, holding my breath.

Don't cry.

"I let you go. There wasn't anyone else."

"Why?" I say with a strained voice, teetering on the edge of losing it all.

"Because I had my dad, and he wasn't doing well. Because I had a ranch to take care of and a job at the school to keep. And because you had the whole world and nothing holding you back … except me."

I turn around, not caring that with one blink my tears race down my face. "You weren't holding me back!" Anger fights with the pain. I don't know which wants out more. I just know that they both hurt.

His face scrunches while he shakes his head several times. "I was. You weren't living. You were tethered to me. I knew it when you told me about Noah. The guilt. That's not living." He rubs the tension along his forehead. "Trust me. Guilt robs you. It eats at you. It was going to destroy us eventually. I just … I wanted you to be free in every sense of the word."

"That wasn't your choice to make." I wipe the endless flow of tears from my face.

"You've been gone for more than two years. Did you find someone?"

I lied. I still hate him. I hate him for asking me that.

"I found lots of people. I made lots of friends."

"Did you find love?"

Biting my quivering lip, I shake my head.

"Did you let another man inside of you?" His eyes turn red, filled with unshed tears.

We stand toe to toe while years of emotions fill the air around us, while so much pain bleeds from both of us without saying a word.

"You let me go ..." I whisper.

He takes a step back. My answer to his question is clear on his face. "I did. And that's why."

I cough a painful laugh. "You let me go so I'd have sex with other men? That's fucked up."

"My life is fucked-up, Henna!" He swallows hard. His face distorts as more unshed tears fill his eyes. "My father has cancer, and if I turn my back, he tries to end his life. My sister hates me. I hate my job because it reminds me of you. I hate every second of every day except the ones where I'm with you. And you left and I didn't want to hate myself any more for holding you back. I didn't want to be your dream that would never come true!"

"You. Don't. Get. To. Choose. My. Life!" I ball my hands, so angry that he shut me out of his life. I'm so angry that he feels the need to suffer in silence. "I would have come home. You should have told me everything."

"Sure." Sarcasm drips from his voice. "I should have told the girl who was suicidal a few years ago to come home and hold my hand while I deal with my suicidal father. That would have been way more fun for you than surfing in South Africa or parachuting in Spain. Waiting for me until the wee hours to get my shit done just to watch me pass out would have been way more romantic than sex with a man who had something to give you in return."

Running my fingers through my hair, I sob. "It was sex. They had sex to give me. Empty, meaningless sex."

Bodhi takes another step back and another, resignation settling into his face. "I won't apologize for what I did. I was there last night. I heard the excitement in your voice when you talked about the places you saw and the people you met. I wanted that for you. Everyone wanted that for you."

"Funny ..." I shake my head. "Because after two years, a million new faces, and countless cities ... every place was simply a place without you. So it doesn't matter that everyone wanted that for me. I only wanted you."

There's a knock at the door. Bodhi frowns, brushing by me.

"Thanks," he murmurs to the guy delivering the french fries. After shutting the door, he brushes by me again, setting the covered plate of fries on the desk.

"Life House, 'Broken,'" I whisper, reaching for the door handle to leave.

Bodhi wraps his hand around my wrist to stop me. His lips brush along my ear. I draw in a shaky breath.

He whispers, "Snow Patrol, 'Chasing Cars.'"

Snow Patrol for the win. I turn slowly into his embrace. He presses his forehead to mine, threading his hands through my hair. We close our eyes for long seconds. In my head, Gary

Lightbody sings about just forgetting the world. In the next breath, Bodhi kisses me.

So this is what it feels like to understand that the world is not a place or a destination. It's a moment. When we touch, it's the world. It's life.

I slide his shirt up his torso. He breaks our kiss long enough to let me ease his shirt over his head, being careful of his stitches. Kissing him again, I run my hands down his chest. He groans deep in his throat. I love that I still can affect him this way.

My mouth moves from his lips to his jaw, neck, chest, and then … I stop.

Oh my god …

My fingertips ghost along his skin to the black letters stacked up his torso just above his hip bone.

H
E
N
N
A

Inked *permanently* into his skin. I look up.

He cradles my face in his hands, brushing the pad of his thumb across my lips. "In spite of what you believe, *my* Henna could never be temporary."

His mouth replaces his thumb, and we kiss harder than we've ever kissed each other. He palms my breast over my dress for two seconds before he shoves it down. Hungry lips devour the skin along my neck, one breast then the other while he works my dress over my hips so it drifts to the floor, a blue puddle at my feet.

"Bodhi ..." my knees turn to jelly as my first orgasm starts to throb between my legs, desperate to be set free.

"Henna ..." he whispers, lowering his body to lick and suck my belly button while sliding off my panties.

No words can describe how it feels to be physically worshipped by a man who has my name permanently tattooed on his body—like he wants to always feel me on his naked skin. Like he wants to make sure every other woman knows he's *mine*. Bodhi let me go and kept me forever at the same time.

"You're so beautiful." His hands palm my ass and his tongue teases my clit, stopping just before I let go. He tastes his way back up my body, letting his hands follow every curve and line like he sculpted me and he's admiring his work.

We kiss again as he walks us the few feet to the bed. I unfasten his jeans. He breaks the kiss to watch me, each one of his breaths ragged with anticipation.

I rid him of his jeans and briefs, stopping on my way back up his body to taste him the way he tasted me. Hooded eyes watch me as his lips part. My gaze stays connected to his while my tongue makes a slow, wet swipe up his erection. I give him a devilish grin.

"Don't lick it like one of your lollipops, suck it in hard and deep like the last drag of a joint."

He smirks, knowing exactly what I'm doing. Fisting the base of his cock, he guides it into my mouth. "Fuuuck ..." He hisses when I take a hit, sucking him hard.

My skin heats like I'm melting. I've missed him—his warmth, his gentle hands, and hard body. I've missed the familiarity of *us*.

Bodhi's abs contract while his breaths become harsher. I release him and press my lips to his hipbone for a few seconds before dotting a kiss on each letter of my name.

"My Henna could never be temporary."

Emotion stings my eyes. The way he loves me is more beautiful than anything I've seen in the whole world—and I've seen a lot.

Bodhi sits on the bed, taking the weight of my breasts in his hands. His mouth makes love to them while I straddle his legs, up on my knees, rubbing myself along his erection. Licking and biting his way up to my neck, he palms the back of my head and whispers in my ear, "Let me grab a condom." He sucks in my earlobe, biting it and dragging his teeth across it.

My heart freezes because my mind decides to wander into dangerous territory. He didn't know I was going to be at Coachella. Yet, he has condoms. I know, I really know that it makes total sense. After all, it's Coachella. The year I met Bodhi here I had twelve condoms with no name in particular assigned to any of them. It was just the smart thing to do because ... it's Coachella.

I sit back on his lap, resting my forehead against his chest, eyes shut.

He kisses the top of my head. "Henna, what's wrong?"

My mind hates me. Why does it have to go there? And why does my heart have to follow it? I purchased condoms over the past two years—more than once. I have absolutely no right to be upset or feel hurt by Bodhi having condoms. Where's the off switch for my mind?

But ... this is Bodhi. I told him about Noah, and if he asks,

I'll tell him about every man who ever touched me. *We* are greater than every mistake, stronger than any lie, and our love is embodied in the truth.

That is Henna and Bodhi.

"You have condoms, but there's no way you bought them for me." That's all I say. I don't need to apologize for how I'm feeling. He'll know. Bodhi will understand.

His strong, calloused hands cradle my jaw, lifting my gaze to meet his. "Yes." Deep lines of pain form along his forehead. "So what are we going to do about it?"

My heart will trip over a million things while chasing Bodhi Malone. I need it to get up, dust off, and keep running. At times like this, it needs to outrun my mind. I need to let my heart win.

Keeping my blue eyes locked to his, my hand wraps around his cock, stroking it slowly. His eyes leaden.

"Henna ..." He watches me touch him. "What are we going to do about it?"

I lift onto my knees again, whispering my lips over his. "You didn't buy those condoms for me." My tongue traces the seam of his mouth. He opens up for me. Our mouths fuse as I sink onto his erection.

Bodhi's hands grab my hips to stop me for a second. I drag my tongue along the roof of his mouth and curl my fingers into the hard muscles of his back. He groans into our kiss and pulls me completely onto him.

My breath catches as he fills me—my body, my mind ... my heart.

Within seconds we become a tangled mess of arms and legs destroying the sheets while our moans and the relentless creaking of the bed frame fills the air. Bodhi drives into me hard. Every muscle of his body is ridged and demanding just like his kiss. We roll in every direction, desperate for more, for it to last, for time to stop.

"Bodhi ..." I beg for *more* and *harder*. He gives me more, so much more that it feels like he's trying to crawl inside of me to capture my entire soul.

Covered in sweat, with the sheets ripped entirely off one side of the king mattress, my name rips from his chest as his warm release fills me.

"I love you so ... damn ... much ..." He pants into my neck with the weight of his collapsed body pinning me to the mattress.

I've never felt so thoroughly fucked, claimed, owned, desired, needed, and *loved.*

"Bodhi?" My fingers slide through the back of his hair, feeling something stickier than sweat. "Your stitches."

"Fuck the stitches." It's as if even lifting a finger is too much work for him.

"I fear they've torn open and you've lost your mind. We can't *fuck the stitches*. They're kind of important."

He lifts his head from the crook of my neck. "I'm fairly certain I lost my mind approximately three years ago."

"Funny." I wrinkle my nose. "But seriously, you're bleeding."

He rolls his eyes and groans, easing off me onto his back. I inspect his stitches. They're still intact, but the cut is bleeding a bit. "I think resting for the afternoon didn't involve what we just did."

"I think you're full of shit," he mumbles with his eyes shut, both hands resting on his chest.

Ignoring him, I clean up in the bathroom and wet a wash-cloth to deal with the blood.

"Does it hurt?" I blot his head.

"Nope." He doesn't even flinch.

I set the wash cloth aside. Kneeling behind his head, I bend over and kiss him upside down. "I missed you beyond words," I whisper.

His eyes open, looking a few shades darker blue beneath the curtain of my hair around us. "You hated me."

"Yes." I drop soft kisses all over his face. "But I loved you more."

CHAPTER THIRTY-ONE

Bodhi

WHEN I SAW her in the Mexican restaurant, I felt certain that I was dead and she was a dream. I was good with that. If she came to me only in dreams, then I never wanted to wake up.

Still, I had nothing to offer her, but that didn't take away from how badly I wanted her. Life without Henna is nothing short of my heart trying to beat against a wall of broken glass. Slowly bleeding out.

"Everyplace was simply a place without you."

Since the day I fell down the stairs, breaking my father's back, I've felt pretty damn unworthy. Until Henna.

"They're cold." She walks her naked body over to the desk and grabs the fries. "I say we eat them anyway."

"I like how you think."

Henna pops one into her mouth and struts her sexy self back to the bed, completely comfortable in her own skin. Straddling my midsection, she dips two fries in ketchup and feeds them to me. Then she kisses me. "I missed you."

I think she's said it at least a dozen times, but I don't complain. It's pretty fucking spectacular to be missed. But the way she says it makes me think that she's saying it more for herself than for me, like she needs to keep reassuring herself that I'm here and she no longer needs to miss me.

Kissing the tip of her nose, I grin. "I missed you too. Is your dad going home Monday?"

She nods, eating another french fry.

"Are you going home?"

Licking her fingers and giving me a hard-on, she nods again.

"How would you feel about riding home with me and Alice?"

She tosses me the biggest grin. It hits me smack in the middle of my chest. "Do you make the fifteen-hour drive straight through or would we stop to have sex in the back of Alice?"

I love her. So much ...

"I have to be home by Wednesday." My lips twist, hiding my ridiculous smile. "But I think we might be able to stop once or twice ... or a hundred times."

As much as I can't help but be deliriously drunk on Henna's insatiable desire to have sex, in the pit of my stomach, I know her newfound enjoyment is the result of other men *breaking her in*, and it kills me. I just can't let it kill *us*.

My abs tighten as Henna nibbles on a fry and traces the letters of her name with the pad of her finger. I curl her hair behind her ear, just watching her and the way that beautiful freckled face comes to life seeing her name tattooed on me.

"When?" Blue eyes find mine.

"I got it the day you left."

She nods, her brow furrowing. "Did you regret it after you

dumped me?"

Coughing a laugh, I pinch her sides, making her jump. "I didn't *dump* you. And I have not regretted marking myself with Henna for a single second."

Leaning in again, she sucks in my bottom lip, and her nipples graze my chest. Little Miss Seductive Nudist is literally seconds from getting thoroughly fucked again.

"Your name has been all over my body. The summer after we met, I painted you *everywhere*. I may have been a little obsessed. And I've sketched you." She teases her fingers down my abs, biting her lip. "And painted you ... and fingered myself thinking of you."

Aaannnd ... french fry time is over. I snatch the plate from her and slide it onto the nightstand.

"I wasn't done."

I grab her face, bringing it a breath from mine. "You are now."

Henna

"IT'S MIDNIGHT." DAD flips off the TV, pinning me with an expectant look from the bed.

So much for sneaking in. "It is." My nose wrinkles. I feel incredibly guilty for spending the day in bed with Bodhi. Okay not *incredibly* guilty, but moderately guilty and thoroughly satisfied. "I'm sorry."

"Do I want to know where you were all day?"

"I messaged you."

"I'm not saying you didn't. But you never said what you were doing. Do I want to know?"

I set my bag on the desk and plop down on the bed. I'm twenty-one. He shouldn't be able to make me feel like a child, but he does.

"Bodhi got an injury. He needed stitches."

Dad squints. "Mr. Malone?"

I roll my eyes. "Duh."

"So you spent the day doing what? Licking his wounds?"

No, his body. Giving extra attention to his cock.

"We talked. I haven't seen him in over two years. There was a lot to be said." And done. We had a lot to do, and we did it very, very well, in my honest opinion.

"Why is your hair wet?"

Because about thirty minutes ago I was having shower sex with Bodhi in his hotel room while he wore a shower cap to protect his stitches—which I must say, he *still* looked like sex on legs even in a shower cap.

"I went swimming."

"Where's your suit?"

"I went skinny dipping." I toss him a toothy grin.

"Henna Eve Lane ..."

"Here's the thing, Daddy Dearest, you're in denial that I'm all grown up. And you're asking questions that you probably don't want the answers to. So ... would you really like me to elaborate on my day, or do you want to hear about my trip around the world since you fell asleep last night and we didn't get to talk?"

He rubs the back of his neck, grimacing. "You're going to be the death of me. And I'm *still* planning on killing that guidance counselor."

"I love him."

The grimace on his face intensifies. "Henna …"

"I do. So you'd better make nice with him because he's going to be in my life for a very long time."

Forever, just like the tattoo of my name.

He deflates. I move from my bed to his, nestling under his arm.

"Love, huh?" He kisses my head.

"Yes. The kind that makes the hair on my arms prickle when he's near. The kind that flutters in my chest when he looks at me. The kind that brings me to tears when I go *years* without seeing him. You know how you used to hate the way Mom and Zach would buy me stuff on a whim? You thought I needed to want it for at least thirty days because young minds are fickle and they jump from one want to the next. Well …" I glance up at him. "I've wanted Bodhi since the day we met three years ago."

"Henna …" His lips form a sad smile.

"Don't." I press two fingers to his mouth. "Shush. I don't need the 'he's going to break your heart' speech. He could easily break it."

He already did.

"But he's worth the risk. I'd rather have my heart broken than never risk giving it to someone. He's the ultimate high. And …" I smirk. "I'm a bit of an expert on a good high."

Dad rolls his eyes. "You're going to be the death of me."

Sliding my hands around his midsection, I hug him tightly.

"Let's hear it. I want all the details of your trip."

I grin and dive into the memories of the previous two years.

After hours, I glance up, my voice a little hoarse, and he's asleep.

"Night, Dad." I lean over and flip off the light.

CHAPTER THIRTY-TWO

THE ELEVATORS DING a million times as I wait next to them in the lobby. With every set of doors that opens, my heart rate doubles only to be shot down when Bodhi's not on it. I should have just gone to his room, but I wanted to surprise him with coffee and ... me.

Ding.

And there he is. Bodhi looks up from his phone.

"There you are!"

I turn toward the female voice that stole my line.

Rayne charges toward the elevators, holding two coffees. "Oh, hey, Henna. Bodhi, I got you—"

Bodhi holds up his finger to stop her from speaking. I start to step back, not sure if he's meaning for me to not talk either or if our relationship needs to remain secret.

"I need Henna for just a sec ..." He grabs my hand and pulls me into the elevator. Before the doors completely shut, he takes my face and kisses me with the most demanding lips.

I can't move because I have a cup of coffee in each hand, so I just let him keep me upright with hands that were made to hold me and his body pressing me to the wall of the elevator.

"Good morning," he whispers over my lips with a generous smile capturing his mouth.

And there it is ... the prickling along my skin and the butterflies going crazy in my tummy. He sucked all the words from my mouth. I start to speak, but my smile gets its way first.

"Is this for me?" He takes one of the coffees like he didn't just violate my mouth, leaving me a goop of runny paint on the wall. "Mmm ... it's good. Thank you." He pushes the button to the lobby.

"I-I wasn't sure if you wanted anyone to know about us."

The elevator dings, and the doors open to Rayne waiting with a long list of questions on her face.

"Yes. I think I want people to know." He gives me the best pearly white grin and takes my hand, interlacing our fingers as we step into the lobby.

Rayne's jaw slowly unhinges. "You ... you're ..." Her eyebrows inch up her head.

I hide my happiness behind my coffee cup.

"I, uh ... thought she was your student?"

Bodhi shrugs. "She was. But she's not now."

My heart does a pirouette. You don't realize how much you miss someone until you're with them after a long time apart and your heart can finally beat again.

"Well ..." Rayne takes a slow inhale. "Okay then, looks like you have your coffee needs taken care of this morning." She winks at me.

I wrinkle my nose in a tiny apology. But the thing is, I want to meet all of his needs. Always.

"She's the best." Bodhi presses his lips to the side of my head.

"You taking the shuttle? Or grabbing a car?" Rayne asks.

"Car. So we don't spill our coffee." I hold up my cup.

Rayne nods.

"I'll order one. You can ride with us." Bodhi takes my coffee so I can dig out my phone.

When we get to Coachella, Rayne gives me a hug and whispers, "Lucky girl," before heading to the entrance.

Bodhi pulls me into his arms. "Where's your dad?"

"He had a breakfast date with Bethanne."

"Yeah?"

I nod before pressing my lips to his chest over his heart. "I love you. Will you wear a hard hat today?"

He chuckles. "Definitely."

"I want us to have dinner with my dad tonight before he goes home tomorrow. I know it will be late, but if he stops wanting to kill you for two seconds, I think he'll really like you."

"Alrighty then ... sounds promising and a little scary."

"I'm an only child." I glance up, squinting against the sun. "Lots of people feel very protective of me. You'd better be careful."

Bending down, he brushes his lips along my cheek. "Bodhi and Henna are a lot of things, but careful is not one of them."

Closing my eyes, my heart dances in this moment, not wishing for the next one. It's not a destination, and it's not even a journey. It's a moment. Life is a moment. Who says we have to go anywhere in life to experience it?

I have never felt more alive than when I'm with Bodhi.

MY DAD AND Bethanne meet up with me by lunch, and we spend the last day at Coachella together. I like her silent confidence and her sick knowledge of music. She reminds me a lot of my mom. Dad clearly has a particular taste in women.

After the last performance, all four of us have dinner together. Bethanne is the perfect buffer between my dad and Bodhi. It goes unexpectedly well. My dad even gives Bodhi a friendly squeeze on the shoulder when we say goodnight.

"We're going to grab a quick drink in the bar." Dad nods toward the hotel bar as Bethanne stands behind him, rocking back and forth on her heels.

I have a feeling Bodhi and I are not invited. Part of me wants to pull a Juni and hand my dad a box of condoms with my blessing to hook up with his old friend tonight. But ... I don't go quite that far.

"We're taking off early in the morning, so if I don't see you again, it was nice meeting you." I smile at Bethanne.

"Why are we taking off so *early*?" Dad squints at me.

Bodhi squeezes my hand.

"Oh ... did I forget to mention that I'm riding back to Colorado with Bodhi?"

"You did." Dad's eyes narrow a fraction more.

This is ridiculous. He knows where I was last night and what or *who* I was doing. I'm twenty-one. His infatuation with playing protective dad needs to come with a large side of reality.

"We'll drive the speed limit, sir." Bodhi assures him.

I manage to hold out for a full two seconds before bursting into laughter. Bethanne joins me.

"Come on, Mitch. I'm sure they'll be just fine." She pulls at his arm as he maintains a scowl.

Bodhi keeps his composure. Smart guy. I release his hand and lift onto my toes to give my dad a kiss on his cheek.

"I'll see you after a bit."

"Don't wait up for me since you're leaving so early. We'll say goodbye in the morning. Early." He frowns again.

Bethanne's cheeks turn rosy.

"Yeah …" I nod slowly. "I won't."

My dad's face turns pink as well. Oh my gosh … this is too much.

"Night." I twist my lips to keep from letting the gotcha grin slip.

The elevator door dings. Bodhi tugs on the back belt loop to my shorts as I watch my dad and Bethanne walk toward the bar. She slips her arm around his waist.

Yeah, he's getting laid tonight.

I turn toward my guy when the door closes. "I guess this is goodnight." My shoulder lifts into a half shrug.

Bodhi inspects me with a restrained smirk. "Guess so."

We lean against opposite walls of the elevator with the sexual tension so thick it's hard to breathe. I'm on the fifth floor. He's on the third, so it stops on his floor first. The door opens.

"Nighty night." I grin.

His eyebrows lift into a slight challenge. "Night." He steps out of the elevator.

I let it go up to my floor then I push the button to the third floor again. Why? Why doesn't he insist we have a goodnight kiss or something like … sex!? He plays me better than I play him. I suck at cool. I just want him. Period.

When the door opens, he's standing right there, waiting for me. "Jerk." I grin.

Bodhi pulls me out of the elevator and tosses me over his shoulder. "Tease." He smacks my ass and carries me to room 312.

This moment. This is life.

CHAPTER THIRTY-THREE

W E MAKE IT back to Colorado by Wednesday. And because life is meant to be lived and not chased, raced, or saved for another day ... Bodhi lets me drive Alice without a driver's license. He may have agreed to it while buried inside of me in the back of Alice—sandwiched between my luggage—but he kept his promise. That's all that matters.

"You don't have to carry them upstairs. I don't remember how I left my room two years ago."

Bodhi ignores me, carrying my two large suitcases up the stairs while I follow him with a smaller suitcase and my backpack.

He stops at the doorway to my room. "Fuck me ..." he whispers.

"That bad?" I cringe.

"Henna ..." He sets down my suitcases in slow motion.

Jeez, how bad can it be? I look around him as he blocks most of my view.

"Oh ..." My teeth dig into my lower lip.

"You..." he takes a step into my bedroom "...sketched me. And painted me. A lot." With wide eyes, Bodhi inspects the easels with paintings, the sketches pinned to my walls, and a few on my bed. Most are him or us. Some are my memories of our first Coachella. There are two of his dad, a handful of

Alice, and one of Angelina—my favorite horse.

"You think I'm obsessed. I'm not. Well ... I am, but not like you think. I just had a lot of time on my hands after I dropped out of school. If it helps my case, I was a little high when I did most of these."

"I think ..." He picks one up. It's us reclined back in Alice, staring at the ceiling and holding hands.

"What? You think what? If you want to run, then run. But I'm not crazy, or a stalker, or—"

Bodhi turns. "Jesus, Henna." He shakes his head. "You're talented as fuck. You were always sketching in my office, but you kept your book tipped away from me. I just had no idea. And then you told Rayne about your job offer to sell exclusively to certain stores, but even then I just didn't grasp exactly ..." He trails off, taking another slow glance around my room.

I hug his back, and he interlaces our fingers over his abs. "You're my favorite muse."

"I'm flattered. God, that's not the right word. I'm something beyond flattered. There's probably not even a word for what I feel right now."

"I told you I sketched and painted you. In the hotel when we were eating cold fries."

He turns in my arms, coughing out a laugh. "Yeah. I vaguely remember something, but it didn't really register with me because, as I recall, you were sitting on me naked."

"Oh! Speaking of that. If you really don't think I'm a freak, then I'll show you my private collection."

"Private collection? You mean these are not yours? Have you sold them or something?"

"No." I retrieve several sketches from the top of my closet.

"When I say private, I mean *private*."

Bodhi

HENNA SHOWS ME a sketch book with a dozen or so sketches of me and us ... naked. But not just naked, in sexual positions. I don't know how I feel about seeing myself sketched this way. She's fucking gorgeous and I'd easily get off after staring at these for a while, but I'm just a little unsure how I feel about my dick sketched in full detail. You can see a large vein.

"These are ..." I flip through them. She has one of me going down on her at my house on the stairs. It's from her perspective, so I don't see her head, just her breasts and my face between her legs, eyes heavy with lust. "I don't know what to say. I feel like Rose, only I didn't ask you to sketch me."

"Rose?"

"Yes, Jack."

"*Titanic*?" She chuckles.

I nod, unable to peel my gaze from these sketches. I'm in shock and awe. And horny. I want her on the steps again, tasting her for the first time. "Have you shown these to anyone?" With hard effort and some pain, I make myself look away.

"They're part of my portfolio on my website, and I have a Tumblr page with them on there."

"Jesus, Henna!" I jerk my head back. Students. Faculty. Principal Rafferty could find these.

She snorts. "You're so gullible."

Narrowing my eyes, I toss the sketchbook on the bed and step toward her.

"I don't like that look." She steps back.

"What look is that?" I say with the most eerie voice I can make.

I step forward. She steps back. Then I lunge at her, but I miss. Henna runs out of the bedroom, squealing all the way down the stairs. I chase her through the main room, into the kitchen, and back up the steps, hooking her waist before she can shut the door on me.

"No!" She giggles as I tickle her.

I love her giggles, her smile, the shimmer of life in her blue eyes. I love that she kisses me to stop me from tickling her. I love that the kiss turns into clothes being discarded onto her bedroom floor. I love it when she says my name as I sink into her beautiful body.

"Bodhi ..."

And I love that when I'm inside her I feel worthy of something so much better than the life I've given myself.

"I love *us*, baby ..." I kiss her neck, interlacing our hands above her head.

She draws her knees back more as I thrust deep into her, her breath catching for a few seconds before releasing with a small moan.

This woman ... I love her in a way I still can't comprehend.

"I HAVE TO go." I try to untangle our naked bodies, but I swear she's an octopus with more than four limbs.

"Let's spend the summer in this bed. Juni and Zach will be gone for months. I'll get you access to the gate, and we can basically chill and watch Netflix all summer."

"Chill and watch Netflix?"

"Sex. That's code for sex, Mr. Malone."

Biting her nose until she loosens her hold on me, I wriggle out of the bed. "Speaking of Mr. Malone, I have school tomorrow."

"Boo." She sticks out her bottom lip as I step into my shorts and tug on my shirt.

"And I have a horse ranch to help run and a sick father ... and I'm guessing a healthy dose of shit from my sister because I said I'd be home hours ago."

She sits up, letting her sheet fall from her chest. I tell my dick *no* when it decides to perk up again.

"I want to meet your sister."

"No. You don't."

"Why? Are you embarrassed of me?"

"Duh," I say in my best teenage-girl voice.

Henna throws a pillow at me. "Your dad loves me. I'll bake up something extra special for him." She winks.

I roll my eyes, tying my shoes.

"And I'll pop in for a visit in say ..." She glances at the nonexistent watch on her wrist. "An hour?"

"Hmm ... shoot. That's not a good time. Maybe another day or year or like ... never."

"Bodhi Kaden Malone!" Naked love of my life leaps from the bed, giving my dick unnecessary hope again. Penile insatiability is a real thing with Henna in my life.

"I confessed to my dad how much I love you. I arranged

dinner because I said he needs to get used to you being in my life. But now you're freezing me out of yours." She plants her hands on her naked hips.

I toss her a blanket from the bottom of her messy bed. "Cover up because I have to go."

She throws it aside. "I'm not covering up with a blanket. I'm going to get dressed and come to your house."

God! My fiery little redhead knows how to torture me.

"It's not personal, Henna. And when my sister leaves, you can hang out with my dad all you want. But I'm serious ... my sister will see how much I love you, and she will do everything in her power to strip you from my life because she thrives on my misery."

"She wants you scarred and guilted. And the greatest power she has over you is that you let her do it. You let everyone make you feel guilty."

I don't need this right now.

"You're right. I'm going to rectify that right now by not letting *you* make me feel guilty for not inviting you to my house to meet my sister."

After getting no further than putting on her bra and panties, she sits on the edge of the bed. "It's the Coachella curse. We're Henna and Bodhi there. We're amazing. The world doesn't matter when we're in the middle of a desert, surrounded by music. But as soon as we get home, I'm your dirty little secret."

On a loud exhale, I squat down in front of her, resting my hands on her hips. "This is my life, Henna. And I want you in my life and not as my dirty little secret, but the fact remains that my life is not like your life. I can't take off on a private jet on a whim. I can't pretend that my father is not my responsibility. My sister didn't get wasted, high, and completely shitfaced. She wasn't the one who landed on my father at the bottom of a marble staircase. And I get it ... I should forgive myself, but it won't change my father's condition. It won't change my responsibilities."

"So, I'll just never meet your sister? That's going to be our life?"

I shrug. "She rarely visits."

"Bodhi ..." Henna shakes her head, pressing her palms to my cheeks. "She can't take me away from you. Not her. Not your boss. Not anyone."

"I know." I kiss her quickly and stand.

"So I'll head that way after I get something made for your dad?"

"Yep." I walk out of her room and down the hall. "After school tomorrow would be perfect."

"Bodhi!"

I keep my ass moving. Everything she said is true, but I'm still not ready to let Henna meet my sister. My Henna high is too good. Bella will kill that high, then she will chip away at Henna's love for me.

"Love you!" I call just before shutting the front door.

CHAPTER THIRTY-FOUR

Henna

I BAKE COOKIES, the good kind that I haven't had in years. After putting them in a basket like I'm Little Red Riding Hood, I take them to Bodhi's house.

"Well, look what the cat dragged in." Duke ties the chestnut horse to a post and ambles toward me as I make my way down the long drive.

"Hey. How are you?" I keep walking as he joins me.

"Mighty fine and yourself?"

"Never been better." I toss him my best smile.

"Ya been baking?"

"Sure have. I'd offer you one, but I think you should wait until you're done with work. They're the *relaxing* kind of cookies."

"Ah, I see. Barrett will love you."

"I hope so."

Because I sure do love his son.

"He's not doing well."

My steps falter. "The cancer?"

"Yeah. They want to do more chemo. Barrett says no, but Bodhi insists he keep fighting."

I nod slowly. "And what about Bella? What does she want?"

"That girl is hard to read. She don't come around but a couple times a year. And for a few days, she fusses over Barrett then leaves. I can't say for sure if her distance is because she doesn't care enough to be here more or if she can't emotionally handle it. Seeing your dad fight cancer from a wheelchair has to be hard. Bodhi is a saint."

If only he felt like one.

"Well, I'm going to see if I can get the Malone family high so they all chill for a bit."

Duke barks a hearty laugh. "I like you."

"I like you too, Duke. See ya later." I give him a parting smile as he heads back toward the barn, and I continue to the house.

There's a gray car parked next to Alice. I assume it's Bella's rental car.

Raised voices leak through the partially closed door like this old house is bleeding. I rest my hand on the screen door handle, trying to hear what's being said, but I can't make it out.

"Those for me?"

I jump back. Barrett opens the door the rest of the way and wheels out onto the porch.

"You scared me. I wasn't eavesdropping."

"You were." He takes the basket from me.

"Okay. I was." My nose wrinkles as I slide my hands into the arms of my sweatshirt and sit in the chair next to him.

"Henna, right?"

I nod. Damn it's chilly this evening.

"Haven't seen you in a long time. Bodhi said you were exploring indefinitely. He used to show me the postcards ... then it stopped." Barrett's vacant eyes give me a sluggish inspection as he takes a shaky bite of a cookie, slumped into his chair slightly to the right like his spine won't let his fragile body remain upright any longer. It's sad because he also looks like he's lost half his body mass. His thick blond-gray hair is gone, and so is the easy smile he used to share with me. In two years, he's aged a decade, maybe more.

"Yes. I traveled the world exploring."

"Atta girl. You said you were going to do that. I'm proud of you, kid. Did you learn anything along the way?"

"Hmm ... you'd think so. Right?" I chuckle. "Nothing too scholarly. But I met a lot of genuinely amazing people, and in some small way they all imparted a bit of knowledge onto me. But more than anything, it gave me a greater appreciation for my home and the people in my own life like ..."

Bodhi. *Just say it!*

"Me?" Barrett winks.

I giggle. "Exactly."

He tries to straighten a bit, causing a grimace to wrinkle his face.

"Need help?" I take the basket of cookies from his lap and stand to help him.

He shakes me off. "I'm good in a dying-of-cancer-crippled-old-man sort of way."

Bodhi told me his dad is fifty-six. That's not old. But he didn't tell me about the chemo and Barrett not wanting to go through it again.

"What kind of cancer?"

"Hell if I know anymore. Started with my liver. I think it's working on attaching itself to every organ in my body and eating me alive."

"Maybe they'll find a cure."

He grunts, looking out at the horse barn while taking another bite of his cookie. "Sure."

I've got nothing. There's no grand response to *cancer is eating me alive.*

"Whose car is parked by Bodhi's?"

"Bella's. My daughter. She's leaving in the morning to go home to Kentucky. Bodhi goes to this big music thing every spring—well I make him go because I get tired of his grumpy ass. But ... he loves it. I can tell every time he gets home. He's a different kid. Usually Duke and Etta old-man-sit me, but Bella's no longer training horses full-time, so she came." He nods toward the house. "That's what you were eavesdropping on—my grown-ass kids fighting. I'm used to the occasional bickering, but today I'm certain they were trying to tear each other's throats out."

"Fighting over the TV remote?"

Barrett flips me a grin. "I like you, young lady. Maybe I could adopt you and get rid of those two in there. We could get deliriously high every day. And one day ... when I don't wake up, you can just bury me in the pasture and smoke a joint in my memory." He winks. "Deal?"

What can I say? There was a day when the idea of getting deliriously high until life ended appealed to me like it does to Barrett. I was recovering. He's not recovering. He's slipping away, and there's nothing anyone can do about it.

"Deal." I only half mean it.

Barrett bobs his head in agreement. "You're my person."

I haven't been anyone's person, so I'm not sure what all that entails, but I can bake cookies and smoke a few joints with Barrett if that makes his days a little better. Burying a body might not be in my personal repertoire, but I keep that to myself. He's happy at the moment, so that's all that matters because we are only a moment.

Nothing more.

Nothing less.

"Hello …"

I turn toward the door and the female voice.

"Bella, come meet my friend, Henna."

Bella is petite with a dark-haired pixie cut and sable eyes, nothing like Barrett or Bodhi. She's clearly the spitting image of the woman I saw in pictures on the living room wall.

"Hi." I smile.

Bella gives me a wary once-over before relinquishing a ghost of a smile. "How do you know my dad?"

"I live up the way, and we met after I took a guided tour on Angelina."

Her ruddy lips purse to the side. "What's in the basket?"

"Cookies," Barrett answers.

I give a stiff smile.

"Want one?" he offers.

Oh God …

"I'm good. The wine I had with dinner was a Moscato. I don't need anything sweet."

Phew …

"They're double chocolate. Your favorite. And Henna makes the best cookies."

Why must he press this? They're double chocolate to tame the cannabis taste.

"Maybe just half."

My nose wrinkles as I give Barrett a this-is-not-a-good-idea look. He winks at me, giving her a whole cookie."

Bella takes a bite, her nose scrunching a bit like mine. It's a recipe I've perfected over years. My mom says they're really quite good, and she's never been a big cannabis fan.

"Not bad." She shrugs.

"What's not—"

Bodhi freezes when he sees me. I return a toothless smile with wide eyes.

"Henna's back in town, Bodhi. She just brought over some cookies. I gave one to your sister."

Bodhi's gaze swells with concern as it ping-pongs between me and Bella.

His dad holds up the basket. "Bodhi?"

He shakes his head. Men who get high and totally shitfaced then put their fathers in wheelchairs for life don't touch drugs or alcohol.

Barrett shrugs. "Your loss. After embarrassing yourselves with your bickering while Henna could hear you, I think you both could use a cookie. Maybe two."

Bodhi tosses me an uneasy look. "I didn't know your friend was here."

It's probably strange that I'm oddly turned on by this game where I'm Barrett's friend until Bodhi has me alone with my clothes off. We're back to the forbidden. I didn't think I wanted that forbidden thrill anymore, but I was wrong.

"I prefer her to both of you at the moment."

Bodhi cringes like Barrett's little jab really pains him. Bella? She's finishing the whole cookie, inspecting it before each bite as if she's trying to figure it out. I don't think she's heard a word Barrett's said about their fighting.

"Did our dad tell you he's going to die without chemotherapy?" Bella asks.

"Bella. Don't," Bodhi warns.

Rolling my lips together, I wait for Barrett's reaction.

"Because he is…" she continues "…he's going to die without the chemotherapy. And he won't listen to Bodhi because he feels sorry for Bodhi." She coughs a laugh. "Which is utterly ridiculous because Bodhi's the reason he's in a wheelchair."

"Bella." Barrett narrows his eyes at his daughter while giving her a barely detectable head shake.

Bodhi looks out past the drive toward the horse barn while running a rough hand through his hair.

Bella sits in one of the wooden rocking chairs like a queen taking her place on the throne. "If Henna's your friend, then she should know the truth about the Malone family."

My heart and my head struggle with Bella's attitude. Yes, she's being cruel to both Bodhi and her dad, but I know it's because she's not only angry about the circumstances, she's hurting too. That makes me sad for her. She's lost her mom. Her relationship with her brother is toxic. And she's dealing with the real possibility she could lose her father.

Bodhi is her scapegoat.

"I'm going for a ride," Bodhi mumbles while walking down the ramp in his jeans and cowboy boots.

"You do that," Bella spits out. "I've only been watching him for the past week so you could escape, pretending you didn't mess *everything* up. But yeah ..." She leans back in the chair with her hands laced behind her head and a stiff smile carved into her bitter face. "Since I leave in the morning, you'd better squeeze every last bit of freedom that you can out of me."

"Fuck you."

"Bodhi!" Barrett's voice booms with more strength than I thought he had in him. "Don't you ever talk to your sister that way."

Resting his hands on the ramp railing, Bodhi hangs his head. Bella has the audacity to look offended while their dad releases a long exhausted breath. I feel so out of place, yet another part of me feels like I need to be here. I traveled the world to discover the place I wanted to be more than anywhere else is in Bodhi Malone's arms.

Easing out of the squeaky chair. I give Barrett a sad smile.

"Don't go," Barrett says while Bella keeps rocking and Bodhi remains statuesque with his head tucked between his outstretched arms and hunched shoulders.

The wood planks creek beneath my feet as I walk down the ramp. Bodhi doesn't move. I duck my head and slide my body between his arms so he's now caging me between his body and the railing.

"Henna," he whispers, closing his eyes. "Don't do this.

My palms slide up his cheeks. "Henna and Bodhi forever," I whisper.

The rhythmic wood-against-wood whining of Bella's rocking chair stops. I don't have to see her to know she's frozen, wondering what's going on between me and her brother.

"Take me for a ride, Bodhi." My thumb grazes across his

lower lip. I let us be in our own little bubble.

The pain deepens along his forehead, but he leans into my touch.

"Because I love you so fucking much, the rest of the world can't touch us."

His hand moves from the railing to cup the back of my head, and he brings our mouths together in a slow kiss. We kiss like no one else exists—slow and passionately.

Crickets are all that can be heard around us. Without looking at his dad or his sister, he grabs my hand. "I'm taking Henna for a ride with me. Don't wait up."

If there was any question whether or not I would forgive Bodhi for letting me go the way he did, there isn't now.

I forgive him. I love him. And it's so much more than temporary.

CHAPTER THIRTY-FIVE

Bodhi

"**Y**OU'RE TERRIBLE AT following instructions." I pull her toward the horse barn.

"I love you too."

I can't hide my grin. She erases all the pain in my life with a look, a word, a single touch.

"I think your sister swallowed her tongue."

With a grunt, I mumble, "If only …"

"By the time we get back, they'll be in a happy place. I bet she doesn't hate you in about … two hours."

I hold open the door for her, shooting her a lifted-brow look. "So kind of you to get my sister and my father high this evening."

"You're welcome." She lifts onto her toes and deposits a soft kiss on my lips before continuing into the barn. "Duke done for the night?"

"Probably."

"I can't recall seeing him walk to his mobile home."

I grab Snare's blanket, saddle, halter, and reins. "I'm guessing it's because you were too busy feeding my dad cookies."

Henna meanders around the barn, showing love to some of

the horses with their heads peeking out of the stalls. "Did you find anyone … when we weren't together?"

I lift the saddle onto Snare, glancing over at her to confirm that she's asking me what I think she's asking me, but her back's to me.

"Did I date? No."

"But you were …" She makes her way over to me, leaning against a wood post, arms crossed over her chest. "*With* other women. Right?"

My hands stay busy as I let her question hang in the air, hoping it will evaporate without an answer.

"Bodhi …" She slips her hands in my front pockets and rests her head on the middle of my back.

I close my eyes, pausing my hands.

"If you say no, I'll feel terrible like I cheated on you. If you say yes, I'll feel jealous, but at least …" She trails off.

I open my eyes without turning. I'm not ready to look at her. "Jealousy is a pretty fucking awful feeling. I'm not sure why you want me to answer you at all. Does it matter?"

Bobbing her head on my back, she exhales. "Were you jealous?"

"I don't want to go back there." I finish getting Snare ready for the ride.

"I'm sorry." She steps back.

This is not a conversation I want to have today or ever. It's not going to do anything but pound a wedge between us. And for what?

"There's no reason to be sorry." I walk Snare out of the barn.

"It felt like another world away. You know? I didn't feel

like Henna—*your* Henna."

"It's fine."

"Would you at least look at me?"

I stop. Holding the reins with one hand while resting my other hand on my hip, I gaze at the ground. After a few moments of silence, I turn toward her. "What do you want me to say, Henna? How am I supposed to be honest without coming off as angry or mean? If I'm willing to let it go, why can't you?"

"Honest as in you were jealous and angry? That's what you mean, right?"

I shake my head, releasing a painful laugh. "I can't win this game, Henna. There's no way I come out of it as anything but the unreasonable asshole. So let's let it go."

"Now you're talking like a guidance counselor."

"I *am* a guidance counselor."

"Not mine." She plants her fists on her hips.

"Okay ..." I say slowly. "Fine. I was jealous and angry. There. Are we good now?"

"Why?"

"Jesus ..."

"Just tell me why?"

"Because I was."

"That's a terrible answer." She pokes and pokes. "Was it because you loved me or because you were mad at me for leaving you?"

"BECAUSE I'M HUMAN!" Snare gets antsy. I pull on his reins to calm him down.

Henna jumps, tears rushing to fill her eyes.

"Yes, because I loved you. Yes, because I was mad at you

for leaving even if more of me was so damn happy that you were getting that opportunity. And because monotony sucks, but those are the cards I dealt myself. And because my dad was—*is*—battling cancer. And because he was trying to kill himself. And ..." Emotion burns my own eyes. "I'm human," I whisper in complete defeat. "Love is not a rational emotion. It jumps out of planes and dives off cliffs. It leaves a permanent mark on everything it touches. I can do the right thing or I can love you, but I can't do both."

She blinks, letting go of her emotions. I watch them stream down her cheeks. The right thing would be to wipe them from her face, an unspoken apology for me being human.

I don't.

Our love is forbidden and complicated. It's hard and un-forgiving. If we want it, we need to let it hurt sometimes.

I hold out my hand.

Henna doesn't wipe her tears either, but she takes my hand and lets me help her onto Snare. I mount him behind her. We take off on a slow gait, disappearing into the trees, letting the silence between us soothe our wounds.

After an hour without a single word spoken, we return to the barn by the last blink of daylight. Snare stops. The reins drop, and I hug her to me. I feel like she's mine—like she's meant to be mine. But I don't know why or how that even makes sense in the scope of events that have happened in my life. It's just this whisper along my skin when I'm with her— *don't let go.*

Henna leans her head into the crook of my neck. "I'm hu-man too."

My nose nuzzles her long hair until my lips find the back of her ear. "You're my *favorite* human." I kiss her warm skin for a long moment before dismounting Snare.

Henna shares a tender smile as I help her out of the saddle and into my arms. "Thanks for the ride."

In spite of the disastrous afternoon with my sister, I can't help but smile back before pressing my lips to her forehead. "Anytime."

"We'd better check on your dad and Bella," she says as I lead Snare to his stall and remove his riding gear. "I feel solely responsible for the impaired states they're probably in right now."

"You should." I put everything in its place and take Henna's hand, leading her back to the house. As we get to the front door, I push her up against the siding and kiss her like I can't get enough because I really can't.

"What was that for?" she asks, breathless and clenching my shirt to keep her balance.

"That's for now. *Right now* when it's just us and I get to pretend that you really are my whole world. In about thirty seconds…" I nod toward the door "…that's going to change."

"That's how I always felt about third period. In your office, with the door shut, I always felt like we were in our own little world. Henna and Bodhi."

I nod slowly. "Bodhi and Henna. I like them—quite a bit."

She pushes at my chest. "Let's go assess the damage."

We make our way to the living room.

"You!" Bella points a finger at Henna from the corner of the sofa. "You got me a little high." She sighs contently. "But at the moment. I'm okay with it. Shh …" She laughs a little. "Don't tell my dad."

Dad's asleep in his recliner. No big surprise.

Henna bites back her grin as I take a seat at the opposite end of the sofa and pull her onto my lap.

"So you're banging dad's young friend. How kind of you."

I frown and start to speak, but Henna beats me to it.

"I fell in love with your brother before we ever had sex."

"Yeah?" Bella returns several exaggerated nods.

Yup, she's high.

"Dad's going to die." Her downcast gaze mirrors her mouth. "I know we don't want to believe it, but he's going to die, and..." Bella leans her head back and closes her eyes "...maybe it's his time. Ya know? We all have our time."

"It's not his time," I murmur.

Henna rests her hand on my arm as my body tenses beneath her. Bella doesn't say another word. Instead, her jaw relaxes with the rest of her body, and she joins Dad in dreamland.

"Where does she sleep?" Henna turns her head to glance back at me.

"She has a room upstairs."

"You should carry her up the stairs."

I nod, not moving an actual muscle to get up. There's something so peaceful about being in the same room with my sister and my dad without anyone fighting. For a few minutes, I just want to enjoy it. "Thank you."

Henna scoots around until she's facing me, straddling my lap. "For what? Getting your sister high?"

"No. She's *okay with it* because she's still high. Tomorrow, I'll encounter a totally different Bella. The thank you is for coming here when I told you not to. Thank you for dealing with my fears when I couldn't do it. Thank you for being you. For being my dad's friend. And ..." Leaning forward, I press my lips to her neck, teasing her skin with my tongue. "Thank you for coming home *to me.*"

Her hands slide along my shoulders and up the back of my head to fist my hair. "Bodhi ... you're everywhere I want to be."

I'll take my sister to her room *after* I take Henna to mine and show every inch of her perfect body how incredibly thankful I am for her. She's the second chance I don't know if I deserve.

"Everywhere, huh?" I stand, hoisting her up with me.

She wraps her legs around my waist. "Everywhere," she whispers over my lips. "Where are we going?"

I start up the stairs. "I feel like *dealing* with you."

"Yeah?" She grins.

I nod, kicking open my half-closed bedroom door.

"Whoa ..." Her eyes bulge in their sockets as I set her on her feet. She crawls up to the head of my bed and runs her fingers along all the postcards she sent me. "I sent you a lot of postcards."

They cover most of the wall.

"There should have been more," she whispers just before twisting her body to look at me over her shoulder.

I shrug off my shirt and unfasten my jeans. "*Should have* is the most unproductive phrase in the English language." I let my jeans fall to my ankles and step out of them.

Henna's lips part and her tongue makes a lazy stroke along her bottom one.

"But *should* by itself is filled with endless possibilities.

Like … you should take off your clothes. You should let me touch you *everywhere …* because it's where I want to be." I flip off the light and shut my bedroom door. By the time I find her in the dark, she's completely naked on my bed. "You're so beautiful," I whisper into her neck.

Her hands slide up my bare back. "You can't even see me."

"Baby, I don't see your beauty with my eyes." I slide her hand up, pressing it to my chest. And for a few long moments, we remain idle with nothing between us but my heart kissing every one of her fingertips.

CHAPTER THIRTY-SIX

Henna

B ODHI WAS RIGHT. Bella didn't appreciate the high once it wore off. Lucky for everyone, she got on a 10:30 a.m. flight back to Kentucky, and Bodhi went to work.

By mid-afternoon, I have my suitcases unpacked and all of my laundry done. As I set a new canvas on my easel, Juni calls. I answer and put her on speaker phone so I can keep working.

"Welcome home."

I laugh. "Thank you. It's a little weird that you're welcoming me to my home in Colorado while you're at home in California."

"I know. It wasn't what I wanted. I'm coming out next week. Just for a few days, because I need to see my girl. How was Coachella?"

"You really don't know? Dad didn't call you?"

"Fine." She sighs. "He may have mentioned a certain boy crush."

"Bodhi is not a boy crush. He's every love song I've ever heard. He's all the colors of the rainbow. He's—"

"Temporary."

I squirt blue paint onto my palette. "Yes. I get it. I really, finally get it. Everything is temporary. We are nothing but now. Everyone and everything changes. And maybe Bodhi dies tomorrow. Maybe I go on and love again. But I don't think feelings are temporary. Even when we're no longer in love, or angry, or deliriously happy, we remember what that felt like. This feeling I have for Bodhi will linger inside of my soul long after we are no longer *us*. I will never forget what loving him feels like."

"Wow. You're not the same girl who got on the plane over two years ago."

"Nope. It's still me with a bit more clarity." I cock my head at my canvas before adding more colors to my palette. "The thing is ... Bodhi's family is a complicated situation. You know I told you about his dad having cancer? Well, he's also been suicidal."

"Henna ..."

"I'm fine. Really. I was in a bad place then. I'm not in that place anymore. Not even close. But because I was there, I understand Bodhi's dad. He's miserable, but not like I was miserable and frustrated that my pain wasn't getting better fast enough. He's miserable because his pain is getting worse; the cancer is spreading. I think he just wants ..." I draw in a shaky breath.

I remember wanting it. The look he has in his eyes ... I saw that reflection in my own mirror after the accident.

"To be done." My mom knows too, but I don't know if she can really understand it from Barrett's point of view. I think she might only be able to see it from Bodhi's point of view.

"Yeah."

"There's a reason they say *fighting* cancer. Or rehab is the hardest work you'll ever do in your life."

Just as I thought.

"I know."

"His dad is what … maybe ten years older than I am? Isn't he close to Zach's age? I can't imagine Zach having cancer and just letting him give up on life. We get one chance at life. You don't go down voluntarily."

Spoken like someone who has never had chronic pain. My mom gets weekly massages. Chiropractic adjustments. Acupuncture. And has a personal trainer. I love her, but she really has no clue.

"Well, I'm not him. I won't judge him. Everyone has to make their own decisions."

Juni hums like she's pondering my statement. "I suppose. Though, if you really love Bodhi, you'll try to help his dad in any way possible. Do they need money for treatment?"

"I don't think it's the money as much as it's his dad not wanting anymore chemo, and Bodhi and his sister don't agree with his decision."

"Well, maybe you could be an outside influence. Sometimes we value stranger's opinions more than those of our family."

"Maybe." I twist my lips at the painting. I find my brushstrokes turning into a picture of Barrett, but he's not in a wheelchair. Maybe it's a premonition, or maybe it's him in an afterlife.

AFTER I GET off the phone with my mom, I wash out my brushes and walk to Bodhi's house. He shouldn't be home for another hour.

"He's asleep." Etta greets me with a warm smile.

"Mind if I sit and wait for Bodhi?"

She shrugs. "Help yourself. Henna? Right?"

"Yes."

"Mind if I head home to make dinner early if you're going to be here?"

"Yeah. Sure. That's totally fine." I slip off my sweatshirt and retie my hair into a ponytail.

"Barrett talks about you." Etta slips on her shoes and jacket. "He told me this morning that you are here to save Bodhi."

"Oh?"

She nods.

"Save him how?" My eyes narrow a fraction.

"I'm not sure. But he hasn't napped this soundly in months. Something has given him a sense of peace. It's you." She shrugs.

I nod once but not really understanding at all.

"Thank you. Goodnight, Henna."

"Goodnight."

After the door closes, I curl up on the sofa with a Denver Bronco's fleece blanket and watch Barrett sleep in his brown leather recliner. I gave him cookies yesterday. Maybe he ate the rest of them today, and that's why he's sleeping so soundly. The longer I watch him, the more I question if he's sleeping. Doubt creeps into my head.

Am I just staring at a dead man? Does Etta check his pulse?

With that unsettling thought, I toss the covers aside and jump off the sofa.

"Please don't be dead." I check his wrist. I don't feel anything. But I'm not sure where I should feel something, so I press two fingers to his neck, moving them up, down, and side to side. Nothing? "Oh my God ..." I step back with one hand over my mouth and my other hand over my chest. "When did you die?" I whisper.

One of his eyes pops open, followed by the other.

"Oh my God! You're not dead." I drop to my knees and rest my forehead on the arm of his chair, grabbing his hand and squeezing it tightly.

"Not today, young lady. But Christ ... I hope the mortician does a better job of checking my pulse than you did. I don't relish the idea of being burned or buried alive." Barrett rests his hand on my head and gives it a few gentle pats.

After my heart finds a normal rhythm again, I lift my head.

"I'm not going to live forever." He squeezes my hand back.

"No one lives forever. It's just not your time."

"True." His lips pull into a tiny grin. "Maybe tomorrow."

"Friday? No. You can't die on a Friday. No one who knew you will ever be able to say TGIF again."

"Saturday?" He scratches his chin.

I give him a "really" look. "The weekend? You can't be serious."

"So Sunday is out. Monday seems to be a crappy day. Nobody likes Mondays anyway. I should die on Monday."

"*A* Monday. Not Monday as in this Monday. You're not ready to die."

"Oh?" He chuckles, but it fades quickly as he presses his hand to his side and grimaces. "And why the hell not?" he asks in a strained voice.

Because my mom has guilted me into keeping you alive.

"On a scale of one to ten, where is your pain level?"

"One hundred." He sighs as if the pain has let up.

"Barrett ..."

"Eight. But who the fuck wants to be alive to experience a ten?"

I stand, taking two steps back to the sofa where I sit and wrap up in the blanket again.

"When you're not high, where's your pain level?" Barrett asks.

I shrug. "Depends on the day."

"On your worst day."

I haven't had a worst day in a long time. I've learned to manage my pain through various means. "Five."

"Five I could live with."

"Then we need to figure out how to get you to a five and keep you there."

"Henna ..." He shakes his head. "A six is a rare good day. An eight is my bad day. Seven is my average. If you had to live every day with an average of seven, what would you do?"

Rolling my lips between my teeth, I shrug and give him three words that may not seem like an answer to his question, but they acknowledge what he's getting at and why I can't go there with him. "I love Bodhi."

He nods several times with a content smile. "You're his savior."

"I'm no one's savior, but I love him. And I want a life with him. Babies ... Barrett I want to give you grandbabies someday. If you're dead, how are you supposed to enjoy them?"

"Grandbabies?" He coughs a laugh. "Did that boy propose to you?"

I frown. "No."

"Good. I don't want you planning a wedding with me in the way. I don't want to be something to fit into your future with Bodhi. My days of being a burden are numbered. That boy of mine would go to his own grave without ever having anything that truly meant something. You ..." He points at me. "You mean something, and he sure as hell knows it. But I'm in the way. I want to get out of the way, and I want you to help me do it."

"Ha!" I huff, shooting off the sofa and pacing the room with my fingers laced behind my neck. "If by *in the way* you're suggesting that the chair you're sitting in is Bodhi's chair, then I'll help you to your wheelchair or to bed. I'll make you dinner. Bake you cookies. Share a joint with you. But if you're suggesting—"

"Henna ..." he says in a serious voice he hasn't used with me before. "If you love him, you'll help me do this."

I shake my head, continuing with my pacing. "Funny. Someone just told me before I came here that if I loved Bodhi I'd convince you to get the treatment. So ... I *do* love him. What's the right answer? What's the right way to show him? Something tells me it's not letting you die."

"When I die, he's yours. You can go anywhere together. Do anything together. Don't you want that? Don't you think he's served his time and that maybe he finally *deserves* that life? I die and my pain disappears. I get to see my wife again and make up for all the bad things I said and did. I die and Bodhi gets to live a good life with a good woman who loves him. I die and my kids can find closure to this battle they've been fighting for years. I *want* to die. I'm ready to die."

A million rebuttals and "what ifs" play tag in my mind, but before I can voice them to Barrett, the front door opens.

"Hey." Bodhi smiles, setting his bag on the floor by the infamous sex stairs.

"Hey." I rush to him and throw my arms around his neck before he can see the pain and indecision in my eyes. "How was your day?"

"It was fine." He kisses my cheek and sets me down. "Dad, how are you?" Taking my hand, he guides me back into the living room.

"Still alive." Barrett grimaces, trying to adjust in his seat.

"Need some help?" I ask, letting go of Bodhi's hand.

"He never wants help," Bodhi grumbles.

"Well, today I could use some goddamn help." Barrett seethes as he tries and fails to get his body adjusted where he wants it.

I start to help, but Bodhi grabs my arm and gives me a gentle tug away from his dad. "I've got it." He lifts the arm to the recliner and bends over, sliding his arms under Barrett's arms to transfer him into the wheelchair.

Barrett wraps his arms around Bodhi's neck. After he's in his wheelchair, Bodhi starts to stand, but Barrett grabs his son's head and pulls him closer to whisper in his ear. I swallow hard as my throat thickens with emotion. A dying man hugs his son. I have no idea what he's saying to Bodhi, but something about it is so incredibly tender it squeezes my heart to the point of physical pain. Drawing in a shaky breath, I blink away the stinging in my nose and eyes.

Barrett lets him go, and they just stare at each other for a few silent moments. Bodhi shakes his head slowly. "I can't do that." When he turns to me, his eyes start to redden, looking as hopeless and deflated as Barrett.

Shoulders curled inward, Barrett's gaze drifts to his lap, forehead wrinkled with clear frustration.

"I'm going to change my clothes. Would you like to stay for dinner?"

It takes me a few seconds to tear my gaze from Barrett. I nod to Bodhi. "I'd love to."

He jerks his head toward the stairs, a silent invite to follow him.

"I'll wait for you down here with your dad."

"You sure?"

"Yeah." I return my attention to Barrett.

"Okay."

When Bodhi's upstairs, I squat next to Barrett's wheelchair, resting my hand on his hand. "I can't. Bodhi loves you. He would never forgive me."

"He doesn't have to know."

I told Bodhi about Noah. Of course I'd tell him about his dad. I tell him everything. "That's not how I love your son."

"How do you love my son?"

My lips curl into a tiny smile. "Completely. Eternally. *Honestly*. But really just … beyond words."

Barrett seems to consider this for a few seconds before squeezing my hand. "Beneath the surface that he shows you, he's miserable. It won't change my mind about the chemo, which means things are going to get so much worse for not just me, but for him too. He blames himself for my situation. My pain is his pain. No one needs to suffer any longer."

The stairs creak and I stand, releasing Barrett's hand while giving him a tiny nod of understanding. That's the hard part ... I really do see this from both sides.

"Do you know how to make anything aside from cookies?" Bodhi calls as he heads around the corner to the kitchen.

I wink at Barrett. "I'm going to school your son on cooking. Enjoy the show."

Barrett doesn't respond. Not a nod. Not a smile. Not a word.

My heart drops into my stomach. It's like he's already checked out of life, his heartbeat echoed in his slow, emotionless blink. Heading toward the kitchen, I pull in a big breath to chase away the pain I'm feeling for him.

"So what *do* you do during third period these days?" I press my chest to Bodhi's back, running my hands up under the front of his *white* tee as he inspects the contents of the open fridge.

"There's a new girl in town who likes to sit on my desk and expose herself to me."

I curl my fingers, letting my nails dig into his flesh. Bodhi grabs my wrists to keep me from breaking his skin.

"I hate you."

He chuckles, turning toward me, letting the refrigerator door close behind him as he backs me into the counter, still holding my wrists to his chest. "I know you do." The mischief in his eyes challenges my scowl. Releasing my wrists, he clutches the back of my legs and lifts me up onto the counter.

My hands rest on his shoulders as he nuzzles his face into my neck, inhaling like I'm the breath he's needed all day.

"But you love me more," he whispers just before trailing kisses from my ear to my shoulder.

"So much more ..." I wrap my legs around his waist. "Bodhi?"

"Hmm?" His hands slide under the back of my shirt, his fingers dipping to the waist of my jeans.

"Your dad is not doing well."

Bodhi slowly lifts his head, meeting my gaze. "Because he refuses treatment."

"It's not a cure."

A line forms between his eyes as his gaze intensifies. "It can prolong his life. It *has* prolonged his life."

My fingers tease the nape of his neck as I nod once, lips twisted to the side. "What life?"

"What do you mean?"

Lifting one shoulder, I cringe. "He doesn't have a wife. He has a babysitter. His daughter is rarely here. You work at school and with the horses. And when you're here, the two of you seem to be at constant odds. He's in pain."

"That's why he needs the treatment. To fight the cancer and eventually the pain will get better."

"What if he doesn't want to fight anymore?"

Bodhi reaches around and releases my legs from his waist, stepping back until we're no longer touching. "What are you saying?" His chin drops to his chest as his hands rest on his hips. "I—"

"Dinner smells wonderful." Barrett interrupts us.

I slide off the counter, giving Barrett an apologetic smile. "Sorry. That's my fault. I think I saw some chicken in the fridge. Why don't you boys go into the other room while I make something magical with that chicken?"

Bodhi's gaze lifts to mine, filled with questions that I can't answer right now.

Barrett clears his throat. "Looks like Bodhi here doesn't trust your culinary skills."

Bodhi doesn't trust me at the moment, but it has nothing to do with dinner.

"My mom doesn't know a cheese grater from a colander, so assuming I don't either is a fair assumption. But while she was busy being her spectacular self all around the world, I was learning life skills from my nanny and our cook."

"I'll help." Bodhi snaps out of it.

I shake my head. "Go hang out with your dad. Really."

Because his days are limited no matter what you want or what I'm willing to do.

Barrett Malone is trying to check out of this world and that's just life.

"You don't know where stuff is at."

I close the distance between us and lift onto my toes, grabbing Bodhi's shirt to steady myself as I whisper in his ear, "Go. Pretending that it's not happening won't change reality."

When I release him, he searches my eyes for something. I'm not sure he finds it, but he turns and follows his dad into the living room.

CHAPTER THIRTY-SEVEN

AFTER A SILENT dinner with Bodhi and Barrett, where Barrett takes literally one bite of his food, I walk home before dark and Bodhi lets me because he seems more worried about leaving his father unattended than letting me walk home alone. Probably a good instinct. The following day I keep my distance from both of the Malone men. Bodhi doesn't call or text.

Saturday, I finally get a text from Bodhi.

Bodhi: *My dad is having a rough day. I'm not going to be able to see you.*

Me: *Need help?*

Bodhi: *Thanks. But I've got this.*

Me: *Love you.*

Bodhi: *Love you too.*

We repeat this conversation on Sunday. By Monday, I need to see what's going on at the Malone house. I don't expect to see Alice parked in the drive, but she's there, which either means she didn't start this morning or Bodhi didn't go to school.

"Hello?" I call, letting myself inside the house.

Etta comes down the stairs, holding her finger to her lips.

"They're both sleeping," she whispers, padding her way to Barrett's bedroom just off the living room. She eases his door shut and meets me back in the entry.

"Bodhi didn't go work?" I ask in a hushed voice.

Etta shakes her head while frowning. "He took a personal day after yesterday."

"Yesterday?"

Her forehead wrinkles. "He didn't tell you?"

I shake my head.

The frown on her face deepens. "Barrett refused to eat or drink, so yesterday afternoon Bodhi took him to the ER. They gave him IV fluids and had someone talk to him. Like ... a psychiatrist or something. They determined he was fine to go home given his condition."

"What does that mean?"

"I guess it's hard to get anyone to say that a terminally ill person is a danger to themselves. After all, they're ..."

I nod once. "Going to die."

Emotion grows in Etta's eyes as she returns a tiny nod of acknowledgment.

"I'm sorry."

She gives me a sad smile. "We all are. It's so hard to watch Bodhi and Barrett go through this. That boy just tortures himself with guilt. It's so heartbreaking."

"How is Barrett?"

"Gone." She wipes a tear before it falls. "He has such a vacant look in his eyes. His voice carries this monotone defeat. He doesn't want to live, and I don't know how you convince someone to live when they've lost the will."

I rest my hand on her arm and give it a gentle squeeze. "I

don't think he's lost the will to live. I think *his body* has lost the will to live. There's a difference. He's just lost the will to suffer and watch his kids suffer with him."

Etta nods. "You're wise for such a young girl."

Sharing a sad smile, I shrug. "I'm just prematurely experienced in matters like life and death."

"Sorry to hear that."

"It's fine." I nod toward the stairs. "I'm going to peek in on Bodhi."

"Okay. I'll put some stuff in the Crock-Pot for later." Etta gives me a kind smile before heading to the kitchen.

Easing open Bodhi's door at the top of the stairs, I pad toward his bed where he's asleep on his side, shrouded in darkness from the drawn blinds. I don't want to wake him, but my arms need to hold him. When he shuts me out like this, I feel like I did when he let me go over the phone half a world away.

I slip under his sheet and thick gray duvet, inching toward him as he breathes steadily with his arms slightly crossed on his black T-shirt clad chest. Before I let myself touch him, I watch him for a few minutes, wondering if he's at peace when he sleeps or if his dad and his past haunt him.

The palm of my hand touches his cheek so softly. His groggy eyes blink partially open.

"Go back to sleep," I whisper. "I just needed ..." I bite my lips together to hide the wave of emotion crashing into my heart as he looks at me with such sadness in his grief-stricken eyes.

"Me," he whispers back. "I hope to God you just needed me because I sure as fuck need you right now."

"I always need you ... in *all ways.*"

Bodhi palms my backside with his possessive hand, bringing my body flush to his before rolling on top of me, settling his tall frame between my legs. I drown in the exhaustion and frustration etched into his face ... but it's the need that wins over.

"*All* ways?" His gaze sweeps over my face, settling onto my mouth.

I nod once, feeling breathless, tingly, warm, and heavy with need.

Balancing on one hand, his other hand slides between us and down the front of my jeans in one quick motion that ends with two of his fingers buried inside of me. I gasp, my eyelids surrendering to the gravity of his touch.

"Do you need me like this?" Bodhi whispers over my lips as I arch my back.

"Yesss ..."

He kisses me hard with his tongue, making demanding strokes just like his fingers inside of me.

I am his canvas.

His instrument.

His making and his undoing.

Bodhi paints me with his emotions, plays me with his body, takes what's his, and gives me *everything* in return.

"Take me away," he whispers in my ear before dragging his warm mouth down my neck, "without leaving this bed..." he slides his fingers out of me and peels my shirt off, followed by my bra "...take me to another world where it's just ... Bodhi ... and ... Henna ..." He shrugs off his tee.

My gaze goes straight to the side of his torso where my

name crawls along the sexy curves of his muscles. I can't see well in this light, but I know it's there, an idle promise that we will never be temporary.

Sitting up, I lift onto my knees so we're facing each other. "Henna and Bodhi." My fingers thread through his hair, bringing his head to mine so our lips are a breath from touching. "Forever."

He unbuttons my jeans as I kiss his soft lips. "Forever," he echoes.

Bodhi

I NEED TO check on my dad, but I don't want to let go of Henna's naked body tangled with mine, so I indulge for a few more minutes on the floral aroma of her wild hair spread around my neck and the warmth of her cheek on my chest. Her fingers trace my ribs and abs. I love this girl with more love than I thought I had left in my heart. Henna takes everything that's good in my life and multiplies it.

"I'm worried about you." She turns her head just enough to press a kiss over my heart.

Stroking her hair, I take a deep breath and let it fall from my chest with a slow release. "It's my dad you should be worried about. He's not thinking straight. He's reckless. And he's lost all regard for his wellbeing. I don't know how I'm supposed to finish the school year with him in this mental state. It's not fair to ask Etta to be on suicide watch. She tends to his needs, but that involves turning her back on him. He needs constant supervision."

"What if he's just tired of..." she shifts her body to the side, head on her propped-up arm, blue eyes set on mine "...everything. The cancer. The chemo. This ..." Trapping the corner of her lower lip between her teeth, her nose scrunches.

"Life?" I roll onto my side to mirror her.

She nods.

"I know he thinks that right now. He's thought it before. It will pass. It always passes. In the meantime, can you do me a huge favor?"

"What?"

I curl her hair behind her ear and brush my knuckles along her cheek. "Can you be here as often as possible with him? Bring him cookies, smoke joints all day, hell ... I don't care. Just be here so he has something to look forward to, and so he has less time alone to do something stupid. He likes you. And I need to finish the school year, then I can be here for him."

"Bodhi, he's very sick. You get that right? He's weaker than I've ever seen him. His disposition has changed so much since before I left. I can't give him the will to live no matter how many cookies I bake for him or how many joints we share on the porch. Your dad is ..." She rolls onto her back and covers her eyes with her arm, but I don't miss the quiver of her lips or the tear that slides down her cheek.

"Baby." I pull her to me and she buries her face into my neck as her body shakes with silent sobs. I know my father is dying, but I'm not ready to say goodbye. There are a million unspoken words between us that I have to say before he's gone. I just haven't been able to say them yet, and if he dies before I get the nerve to tell him what's in my heart, it will destroy me.

"Can you just give me a couple more weeks until school is out?" I kiss the top of her head, and she slides her arms around my torso.

She nods.

CHAPTER THIRTY-EIGHT

Henna

"**Y**OU'RE THE BABYSITTER?" Barrett stares at the joint I offer him.

"Yes. Bodhi asked me to get high with you while he's at school. He's killing my sobriety." I ease into the chair on the porch next to Barrett's wheelchair and pull a sketch pad and pencils out of my bag. "How cool is that?"

"He's worried I'm going to kill myself."

Sharpening my pencil, I glance up at him with a gonna-give-it-to-you straight grin. "Yep."

"So you keep me in line until he's out of school. Then he forces me into more treatment. God ... that boy is delusional."

I shrug, working my pencil in short feathering strokes over the top of the paper. "Maybe he loves you. Let's go with that possibility."

"He was good, ya know. At the drums." A tiny smile steals his lips. I like where this is going. "His band didn't exactly play the kind of music that I enjoyed, but I wasn't blind. That kid had talent. Dumb as a box of rocks, though. Every one of them. They were on the cusp of becoming something really big and they knew it. That's why they were celebrating all the damn time. Booze. Drugs. Girls. Just … stupid."

I can't see that Bodhi. It's not that I don't believe history. It's just I've never seen him drink or even look the tiniest bit tempted by drugs. "What happened to the rest of the band?"

"Bodhi went to rehab while I was in the hospital. Two of the other band members got arrested for possession with intent to deliver. Then they just fell apart because they hadn't made a true name for themselves yet, so there weren't enough people invested in their future to care about saving them. Bodhi came out of rehab, and his mom and I insisted he go to college and get his life together."

"But …" I steal the joint and take a hit.

"But what?"

"But he's not exactly together." I stare at my barely started sketch then close it up, not feeling as inspired as I had hoped this morning.

"He would be if he'd let me go. You could help me help him."

I grunt a laugh, watching Duke carry a saddle out of the barn. "I told you, he would hate me forever."

"He doesn't have to know. Heck, you don't have to know."

I shake my head.

"I need to see my doctor. Maybe you could take me tomorrow."

I shake my head again, keeping my eyes on Duke to keep them from tearing up because if I look at Barrett and his helpless expression, I will break. "I don't have a driver's license. Besides, Bodhi said Etta takes you to your appointments when he can't make it."

"Maybe I just want to go for a drive. A girl with your resources can surely find someone with a handicapped accessible vehicle to take us for a drive that might just happen to go to my doctor."

My head continues to shake. "I can't."

Barrett doesn't say another word to me the rest of the day and only a few words the rest of the week.

"THIS ONE." JUNI holds up a shirt as we shop for something for me to wear for my headshots. Now that I've signed papers to have some of my prints sold through a major online retailer, I need to give them a headshot and bio.

"Maybe I should wear a dress."

"I love you in dresses, but you should look like what your art feels to the people who see it. Raw and original."

I smile at my mom because she's my biggest cheerleader in life—my very best friend. "Give me the shirt." Rolling my eyes, I take it and head to the dressing room, knowing Miss Fashion Extraordinaire is probably right. This shirt is the one for me.

"What time is it?" I ask as I try on the shirt.

"Eleven-twenty."

"I have to be to Bodhi's by one. Etta has an appointment."

"How's his dad feeling this week?"

I button the shirt, staring at my reflection in the mirror. "The past two days have been awful. It's not just that he doesn't want to eat. When he does eat, most of it comes back up. Etta said it's a blockage. Nothing is going through. They need to do surgery."

"But he doesn't want it?"

"Nope," I enunciate the word making it into three syllables.

"And you can't convince him otherwise?"

I open the dressing room door. "Yesterday he gagged and nearly fell out of his wheelchair while vomiting all over himself. It took Etta and me almost an hour to get him cleaned up and settled into his bed. When he fell asleep, he looked dead—pale, dry lips, emaciated from head to toe. When he woke up just before Bodhi came home, he assured me what I witnessed was nothing compared to what he feels when going through chemo. Then he made me promise to not tell Bodhi what a shitty day he had because Bodhi would lecture him on needing treatment right away."

"Jesus …" Juni's nose wrinkles.

I turn so she can see the back of my shirt as I give it one last inspection in the mirror. "This is the shirt."

"One hundred percent." She nods to my reflection in the mirror.

John drives us to grab a quick lunch. Then he takes me to Bodhi's house.

"Come meet Barrett."

Juni gives me a hesitant look. "I haven't even met Bodhi yet."

"Which is so wrong because he's my Mitchell Lane and Zachary Phillips all rolled into one awesome guy." I grin.

She nods, relinquishing her own smile because she knows exactly what I mean. "Fine."

John opens her door while I hop out the other side of the vehicle. She follows me up the ramp where I half expect to see Barrett smoking a joint or napping in the cool breeze, but he's not here.

"Hello?" I say softly as we step inside the house.

"In here, Henna."

I follow Etta's voice to the kitchen with my mom just behind me.

"Oh my god …" I stop, staring at the mess on the floor and all over the kitchen counter and walls.

Etta shares a sad, defeated expression. I look to Barrett who looks fraught with guilt in the middle of the mess.

"W-what happened?" I'm afraid to ask. The tension in the room is high, and my poor mom is meeting Barrett for the first time under really awkward circumstances.

Etta looks at Barrett. He drops his chin to his chest.

Her lips tremble with a nervous smile. "It's been a rough day. Barrett didn't want to eat, so I made all of his favorites, hoping he'd find something that he could eat."

It looks like they had a food fight, and they both lost.

"I just … lost my patience." Barrett glances up at Etta, sending her an apologetic and extremely sad smile. "I'm sorry."

She nods slowly, mirroring his expression. "It's fine. I'll just get this cleaned up. You have guests now." Her hands shake as she tries to pull a line of paper towels from the roll by the sink.

"I'm Juni, Henna's mom." She rests her hand on Etta's arm. "Can I have my driver take you someplace? Home? Henna and I will get this cleaned up and stay until Bodhi gets home."

Emotion swells in my chest as my mom befriends a stranger in need and offers to clean up when it's been years since Juniper Carlisle has lifted a finger to clean anything. Etta quickly wipes away her tears before they find their way down her face, and she nods.

"I'm Etta. And ... thank you," she whispers to my mom.

Juni nods and leads her to the front door. I turn to Barrett, not able to take a step without landing in either splattered food or broken pieces of dishes.

He looks at me for a few seconds before he starts to cough, holding his hand to his mouth. When he removes his hand, there's some blood on it, and it's smeared along his lower lip. Barrett's pained expression meets my gaze.

"Okay," I whisper.

He closes his eyes and nods several times on a slow exhale. "Thank you."

I'm choosing Barrett over Bodhi and Henna. And even if he never believes me or forgives me, I'm choosing Bodhi over *us*.

"John is helping Etta down to her trailer."

I glance over my shoulder at my mom. "Thank you."

She tiptoes through the mess to Barrett. "Hi. I'm Juni. It's nice to meet you. My daughter thinks the world of you and your son."

Barrett forces a smile and something resembling a bit of life into his spine as he tries to sit straight and offer her his hand. She stares at it then shoots me a look.

"Oh ..." Barrett fists his hand, having forgotten about the blood on it. "It's nice to meet you. I think the world of Henna too." His words are strained.

Barrett is in pain.

"Point me to a broom and mop." Juni holds her smile, and it's not fake or forced. It's filled with compassion.

Barrett nods to the tall pantry door next to the fridge.

I grab the cleaning supplies. "I'm going to clear a path to

get you out of the kitchen so you can rest while we clean up."

Barrett struggles to maintain eye contact with either one of us. He's clearly embarrassed. I can only imagine how degraded and completely stripped of confidence he must feel right now. For weeks he hasn't been able to go to the bathroom by himself, even with everything handicap accessible. Barrett no longer has the strength to lift himself onto the toilet or use the device to lift himself to pull his pants up and down. His sense of independence has vanished from his life. Life … Barrett doesn't have much of a life anymore.

I clean him up while my mom clears a path to the living room. We help him into his recliner where he quickly falls asleep.

It takes over two hours to clean up the mess in the kitchen and dispose of all the broken dishes. I hand my mom a glass of water as we lean against opposite counters, gross and sweaty.

"Thank you for …" A wave of emotion hits me before I can finish.

"He needs chemo. Maybe there's something experimental. I can have someone look into this. We can pay for his treatment."

"He doesn't want it."

"Henna … he thinks he doesn't want it because he's still battling the cancer, so he perceives everything he's done up to this point as a failure. If he had better doctors, more resources—"

"Mom." I shake my head. "He destroyed the kitchen today because Etta made all of his favorite foods. She did something nice for him. Can you imagine how he'll react if someone suggests he try a new experimental treatment?"

I drink the rest of my water and set the glass down. "But seriously…" I hug her "…thank you so much for what you did today."

She hugs me and kisses my cheek. "I'm here for you. Even though I'm leaving tomorrow, I can be here in a few hours if you need me. Okay? You are always my number one priority."

"Thank you." I pull back and smile. "Mom."

She gathers my hair and pushes it off my shoulders, stroking it a few times like she's done since I was a little girl.

"Hey."

Juni glances over my shoulder and I turn.

Bodhi looks past me to my mom.

"Hey." I immediately go to him, falling into his embrace.

"Everything okay?"

No. Everything is the worst everything could be. "Yeah. Bodhi, I want you to meet my mom, Juni. Mom…" I turn "…this is Bodhi."

Bodhi holds out his hand, but his body is stiff and awkward. I'm sure he's thinking that she knows our story and it's not one a guidance counselor should be proud of. "So nice to finally meet you."

Juni shakes his hand. "The feeling is mutual." Her eyes widen a bit as her smile turns into something fun and flirty, a much-needed change of mood after the previous two hours we've shared here in the kitchen. "I can see why my daughter is obsessed with you."

"Oh my god, Mom. I'm not obsessed with him." She knows how to make me act like a young girl embarrassed over a boy.

This makes Bodhi grin. "Thank you. The obsession is mutual."

I blush when Bodhi winks at me.

"Are you staying for dinner? I'd love to have you," he says.

"Oh, no. It's been ..." She glances at me as if she's not sure I'm going to share this afternoon's incident with him. "A long afternoon. I'm going to head home, get a little more work done, and maybe order in some food to eat while watching a movie." Squeezing my arm, she kisses my cheek one more time. "Breakfast in the morning?"

I nod.

"Again, a pleasure meeting you. Give your dad my regards when he wakes up."

Bodhi nods with a small smile. "Thank you. I will. Nice meeting you."

She lets herself out, and I fall back into his embrace, releasing a long breath.

"Deep sigh."

"Yes." I look up at him.

"And a crease between your eyes." He rubs his finger above the bridge of my nose. "What's going on today?"

"I brought my mom by to meet your dad."

He nods. "And he never woke up?"

Biting my lips together, I shake my head. "When we arrived he was in the kitchen with Etta. She made him his favorite meals, hoping something would sound good to him. He didn't want to eat anything."

Bodhi nods again, brow wrinkled.

"He sort of lost it. I didn't see it happen. We arrived after the damage was done."

"What do you mean lost it, and what damage?"

"He threw all the dishes of food around the kitchen, breaking most of the dishes." I step back and point to the wall by the small kitchen table. "The tomato sauce didn't completely come off. It's still tinged red."

Bodhi's lips part as he blinks several times at the stain on the wall. "Where's Etta?"

"She was a bit shaken, so my mom had her driver, John, escort Etta to her trailer while we cleaned up your dad and the mess."

He closes his eyes, rubbing the corners of them with his fingers. "Shit … I'm so sorry."

"Don't apologize."

He grunts a deep exhale of sarcasm. "*This* was your mom's first visit to my house. Her first impression of my family."

"Bodhi…" I grab his face "…your dad has cancer. There's nothing impressive about cancer. There's also no judgment. There's just pain and compassion. That's it. He's in so much pain, and all we can do is show him complete compassion."

Emotion reddens in his eyes. I press my forehead to his. "Make things right with your dad, Bodhi."

He shakes his head. "He's a fighter. He's just forgotten how to do it."

"Bodhi," I repeat with more gravity to my voice. "Make. Things. Right. Maybe it's what he needs to fight this. Maybe it's not. But you will never regret saying what needs to be said *right now*."

"He'll think it's permission to die."

I tighten my hold on his face and kiss him. "It's his life. He doesn't need permission to die."

"Henna." His voice breaks as he covers my hands with his

hands. "He's my dad. He's part of me, and I'm part of him. He needs *my* permission to leave me."

I press my thumbs just beneath his eyes to wipe away the tears that escape.

CHAPTER THIRTY-NINE

Bodhi

I LOST MY way.

That's it. There is no other grand explanation for how I got here. And now I don't even remember where I was going. Maybe that's the problem. I need to stop going anywhere.

I'm here.

He's here.

We have now.

Mistakes and dreams distract from reality. My reality is my father wants to die, but I don't know if it's for me or for him. I can't let him die for me.

"Hey." His greeting lacks oxygen. Every word he speaks feels borrowed. Every blink stolen.

"Hey." I find a genuine smile for him because he deserves the best of me.

His sluggish gaze lands on the beautiful woman asleep on the sofa with her head in my lap. "She loves you."

I nod once. "I love her."

Dad's shaky hand reaches for the remote to his chair. He raises the back a few inches.

"I love you too," I say just above a whisper.

He pauses, gray-blue eyes focused on me.

I've fought for so many years to be strong and brave, anguished and regretful, obedient and indebted. True emotions stayed buried in a dark place next to my soul. I felt guilty for loving him, so I never said it. I tried to show it, but after the accident those three words felt empty coming from me. I felt unworthy of saying them to him.

They wouldn't make him walk.

They wouldn't cure his cancer.

They wouldn't bring my mom back.

Stroking Henna's long hair, I let the tears go. Holding them back, not saying those three words ... it was so much easier than this. Vulnerability takes more strength than anything else in life. You have to be willing to *feel* absolutely every emotion. Vulnerability is the sharpest knife, the longest marathon, the highest mountain.

The lump in my throat makes it nearly impossible to speak. I can't hear anything beyond the pulse in my ears. And everything is blurred through the endless tears.

But ...

I say *everything.*

Sniffling, I clench my jaw a few times, forcing the words past the swell of emotion in my chest. "I do. I love you, Dad. And there's never been a single day of my entire fucked-up life that I haven't felt your love for me. I think that hurt the most. Mom called it grace. She once told me that's why she stayed. Because at the end of your very worst days together, she always felt your grace. And your hope."

As I swallow the fear that instinctively wants to protect my vulnerability, I use the back of my arm to wipe my face, but it's a lost cause because I've waited too many years to say these words to him.

"You told me to play my music when Mom thought it was wasted time. You sold your favorite horse to buy me my first drum set. Mom called you an enabler. You called it a chance. *Everyone deserves a chance in life.* That's what you said. And then you said *don't screw it up.*" I choke on a sob, hoping I don't wake up Henna. I'm not sure I can be this vulnerable in front of her too.

Dad's brow wrinkles as he tries to sit up more, but he can't, and I sense his frustration. Gently sliding out from under Henna's head, I ease onto my knees beside my dad's chair. Clasping my hand with his, I bend down, resting my forehead on our hands. He sets his other hand on the back of my head.

"I'd do it again. Knowing the outcome ... I'd do it again," he says. "I'd buy you the drums. I'd tell you to play your music. I'd get in my car and drive to that house. I'd climb those same stairs, wrap my arm around you, and try to carry you down the marble stairs. You're my boy, Bodhi. I might not be able to always catch you when you fall, but it won't ever stop me from trying. And maybe you're looking for my forgiveness, but I've told you a million times, there's nothing to forgive. There is no debt to pay."

"D-dad ..." Sobs rack my body.

He strokes my hair like I did to Henna's hair. "I just fear you've lost your will to jump. And maybe it's because you don't think I can catch you now. And maybe I can't. But don't you ever stop chasing your dreams. Chase them all the way off a cliff. But for God's sake ... don't be afraid to jump."

I cry like I've never cried before—not even when my mom

died. I've never let myself feel this deeply because it just. Fucking. Hurts.

"I'll j-jump, but you h-have to fight. And not because I need you to catch me. I just need *you*." I lift my head, squeezing his hand as I press my lips to the back of it. "You're the mom I lost. You're the sister who left. You're my friend, my father, my whole family." My words break apart. "You're my idol. I'd be so damn lucky to even be half the man you are."

His shaky hand cups the back of my head and pulls me closer so he can kiss my forehead. "My boy, you're already twice the man I am. You're smart and kind." He releases my head so he can look me in the eye. "And compassionate."

I shake my head. "I won't let you give up. I won't let you go."

He nods, giving me a sad smile. "I know you won't." Swallowing hard, he lets his gaze shift to Henna for a few seconds before returning to me. "Thank you for holding on when I wanted to let go. Thank you for loving me like that."

I smile through my pain. Henna was right. I needed to make things right with him. "Fuck the cancer." My hand squeezes his again. "We've got this."

"Fuck the cancer," he echoes.

I help him get ready for bed, and tonight it doesn't feel like I'm imprisoned in this life. It doesn't feel like a debt to pay. Helping my dad—being with my dad—feels like a privilege.

"If I can get you an appointment, I'm going to see if Etta and Henna will take you to the doctor so we can get a new game plan."

Hope.

It feels amazing to have hope again.

Dad nods as I pull the covers over him. "Yes. It's time for a new game plan."

"I'd take you myself, but I need to finish the school year, and I don't want to put this off any longer. You're too weak and in too much pain. They need to find a solution."

"They will." He gives me a reassuring smile.

"Goodnight." I shut off his light.

"Bodhi?"

I stop just shy of completely closing his door. "Yeah?"

"The girl. She's the one."

I grin even though he can't see it. "She's *life*," I whisper.

That life hasn't moved an inch from her curled-up position on the sofa. I pick her up and her sleepy eyes blink open, eyelids almost too heavy to stay open.

"You've been crying." Her forehead wrinkles as she tightens her hold around my neck while I carry her up the stairs.

I nod.

"Bodhi …" She reaches for my hand after I set her on my bed.

"I need a shower."

Henna releases my hand, lips trapped between her teeth.

"Shower with me?"

Henna

I LOOK UP. After a few seconds of searching Bodhi's red eyes, I return a sad smile that mirrors the residual pain on his face. What made him cry? I have a million questions, but I don't think he needs them right now. He just needs me, so I'm going to give him all I have to give until he hates me.

And he will hate me.

Taking his proffered hand, I follow him to the tiny bathroom. He turns on the water, letting the small space fill with steam. Without a second of hesitation, I remove my shirt. He removes his. Our locked gazes never falter. We strip and it's the start of something physical, but I have a feeling the mark he's getting ready to leave on me will be deep and emotional.

We step into the shower, and Bodhi closes his eyes as the water streams over his head. My hands rest on his chest, and my lips press to his sternum. "I'm sorry you're sad. If I could take your pain away, I would."

He tips his chin down and opens his eyes, drops of water clinging to his eyelashes. I've never seen him look this vulnerable.

"You were right." He smooths my hair away from my face. "I told my dad everything I never said before, and we're better." He presses his forehead to mine, rolling it back and forth a few times before kissing my cheek and slowly dragging his lips along my skin to kiss my face everywhere.

"That's good." I slide my hands up to his shoulders, curling my fingers into his muscles when he steps closer, rubbing his erection against my belly.

"Yes." He nips at my lips, teasing me like the fingers sliding between my legs. "I'm going to call the doctor tomorrow to see when we can start chemo again."

What?

My fingers ease up on his shoulders, but his fingers venture farther between my legs. His breaths become ragged, his lips hungrier. Bodhi's words swirl in my head, not making any sense, but maybe it's just because he's manipulating my body like only Bodhi can do.

Emotion wrestles in my chest, tugging at what I think he means and what I know can't be true. I saw it deep in Barrett's lifeless eyes. I heard every ounce of pain and resignation in his voice. There's no way he agreed to chemo.

My breath catches as he palms my ass with both hands. I moan, my mind dizzy with what I'm trying to *feel* and what I need to figure out.

The need to feel wins over.

I reach my hands back and mold them to his over my ass.

"Too hard?" He loosens his grip a bit, pulling his head back just enough to look at me.

My fingers flex, encouraging his to do the same as I shake my head. "No." I blink a few times and look away.

"Henna," his voice lowers. "Are you blushing?"

My gaze lands on his again. I shrug. "I love the way your hands claim my ass like their purpose in life is to manipulate my body exactly where and how you want it."

Bodhi's lips stretch wide, showing all of his beautiful white teeth. "Well, my hands love the way your body bends to their demands."

"Don't be cocky." I lift onto my toes and bite his bottom lip.

Those strong hands that I love on my body lift me up. Pinning me to the wall, Bodhi spreads me open, driving into me with one confident thrust.

"Jesus!" My head falls to his shoulder as I claw his back.

When I lift my head, he smirks, looking like a god who

owns my world. "I think you like me cocky."

"I like your cock *in* me." I kiss his neck, running my tongue up to his chin where my teeth tease the strong angle of his jaw. One of my legs slides down to balance on my tippy toes while he cups the back of my other knee, lifting it high to keep his body wedged into mine.

"I love Hell. It's my favorite place to be." Bodhi takes me hard and slow, crashing his mouth to mine.

Just after midnight, we're parked outside of my guesthouse. I promised breakfast with my mom before she leaves tomorrow, and if I stay all night with Bodhi, I'll never make it home in time.

Bodhi opens my door.

I grin, climbing out. "Oh, *now* you're a gentleman."

He slides the hood of my sweatshirt over my still wet head and tugs on the drawstrings. "I have no idea what you mean by that."

About twenty minutes ago, our first goodnight kiss in his driveway turned into our pants shoved down to our knees and my hands planted against the side of Alice while Mr. Gentleman gripped my hips and made the studs in the barn look like amateurs.

I'm not sure if his intensity with me tonight is really about me or his need to let everything go after talking with his dad. Nuzzling into his neck, I inhale a mix of pine, cedar, and Bodhi. It gives me a better high than any joint or edible. His chin has a few days' worth of stubble, and his hair looks like someone ran their fingers through it a million times, tugging and pulling. I might be that someone. My hands slip into the back pockets of his jeans.

"I like you gentle. It's sweet and my heart feels like it could burst. But ..." I glance up, meeting his devilish grin.

As if to say he knows where this is going, he palms my ass much harder than my grip on his backside.

"When you *need* me in the moment, when you physically can't hold back..." I wet my lips "...that's when I feel so alive I can barely breathe past my racing pulse. I *love* insatiable Bodhi."

"Insatiable." He nods, lips twisted a bit. "I think that's an incredibly accurate word for how I feel when I'm around you."

Cocking my head a bit, I blow out a slow breath. "Tonight you felt extra insatiable and ... intense. I feel like it's because of your dad."

He studies me for a few seconds then nods several times. "It felt like this huge weight has been lifted from my shoulders."

Maybe, just maybe Barrett had a coming-to-Jesus moment with Bodhi. Maybe Barrett decided it wasn't time to meet his maker after all, but I doubt it. And that breaks my heart for Bodhi.

"Speaking of my dad, I need to get home. What you did to me against poor Alice back at my house has me running late tonight."

My eyebrows inch up my forehead, jaw unhinged for a few seconds before I cough a laugh.

"Shh ..." He releases my ass and presses a finger to my mouth. "Don't say anything and ruin this moment for me."

My agape expression shifts into a grin. I said that same thing to him when I saw Alice for the first time. "Sometimes I wonder what my heart did before I met you, besides droning to the same old beat every day."

He slides his fingers between mine and ducks his head, closing his eyes and rubbing his nose against mine.

"What's going through your head right now?" I whisper.

"Lyrics."

"A song?"

He nods slowly.

"What song?"

"Our song."

"We have a song?"

"Dave Matthews Band."

I smile, he doesn't have to say the title. I already know. We are Henna and Bodhi. "You and Me."

"You and Me," he echoes the title in a whisper before capturing my lips just like he did to my heart years ago. As we kiss one last time, I think of the lyrics—packing a bag, disappearing, taking a boat and not stopping until we've reached the end of the world because together we can do anything. Those words are our life when we are limitless.

CHAPTER FORTY

"**G**OOD MORNING. I wasn't sure I'd see you." Juni winks. Fiona smiles while serving me a cup of coffee.

"You're flying back out to California today. Of course I'd be here for breakfast with you. Why would you think otherwise?"

"I got a firsthand look at Mr. Bodhi Malone." She grins behind her coffee mug.

My lips lose the battle at playing it cool. "It *was* after midnight by the time he dropped me off."

"He's hot."

Here we go. The conversation I always wondered if I could have with my *mom* even if I think of her as Juni, my best friend. I give it a go. "Yes. He's that and more."

"More?" She hums. "More is good."

I sip my coffee, feeling flushed from this topic. "More is …" My words skid to a stop before leaping off my tongue. Can I say more is what happened against the side of Alice last night?

She studies me for a few seconds. "Zach and I still go at it like rabbits."

I choke on my coffee. "Mom!" There's my answer. She might welcome this conversation with me, and I feel like the luckiest girl in the world for having this cool mom, but I don't think I can do this.

"Come on, Henna." She reaches across the table and squeezes my arm. "I've been waiting for years to have this conversation with you. I've told you to live life, and sex should be one of the greatest human experiences you have. Why do you think the world is so abundantly populated? Why do you think ZIP Tunes is the most successful record label? Humans are sexual beings. We are emotional beings. When we're not having sex, we're thinking about sex. When we're not thinking about sex, we're working hard so we can have homes, beds, cars, yachts ... jets." She smirks. "And all of these are just places to have sex!"

My laugh stays in for maybe two seconds before I lose it. Juni laughs too. We laugh together until we're in tears. I love my mom, my friend. While I know her sex speech holds a lot of truth, she preached it because she knew I needed this. After everything that happened yesterday, this sidesplitting laughter is exactly what I need.

Wiping the tears away, I giggle a few more times. My face and sides hurt from laughing so hard. "Bodhi *is* hot. And sexy. He's very ... *generous.*" My teeth dig into my bottom lip as I gauge her reaction. I can't believe I'm telling her this, but I am. "He touches me like he owns every part of my body and his large hands do it quite well. It's confident and so fucking sexy. Sometimes it's gentle as if we have something emotional to say, but we can't find the words. And sometimes it's ..."

I'm on fire. Fiona could fry an egg on my cheeks.

"Raw." Juni finishes my thoughts. "Primal. Like it pisses you off that you can't get any closer. Every sense comes to life, hungry to be satisfied. And when you're close to that moment, you don't give a single fuck about anything else in the world. Your brain shuts down, lending every ounce of energy to taking and giving the most indescribable pleasure."

My mouth hangs open, hands wrapped around my coffee mug.

Juni lifts an eyebrow. "And if it's not like that for you, then we need to talk some more because it should be like that. Don't settle for anything less."

I continue to stare at her.

"God ..." She shakes her head. "Of all the mornings for you to be sober. This is the one when I wish your tongue was a little more relaxed."

I chuckle, coming out of my stupor. "Fine. What do you want to know? Is sex with Bodhi good? Yes. It's mind-bending. What's my favorite part? When he goes down on me followed by that first thrust when he's inside of me while I'm still feeling the effects from my orgasm. It's when I feel completely possessed by him. Does he hold me when it's over? Yes. We sleep tangled in each other's arms. But ..."

Juni hasn't blinked. She's eating every morsel of information I give her while resting her elbows on the table, face perched in her hands like she can't keep her head up. And maybe she can't. I just gave her a mother lode of information about my sex life.

"But ..." She almost chokes on the word.

Have I rendered the confident super model speechless?

"*But* it's more. It's just more, and that more can't be defined." I swallow hard as my eyes fill with a new kind of tears, and my lower lip starts to tremble.

"Sweetie." She gets up and comes around to my side of the

table and hugs me from behind my chair, resting her chin on my shoulder. "What's going on?'

"I'm going to lose him." I choke on the last word and shake with a silent sob.

"No. Why would you lose him?"

Because I'm going to help his father die, and he's not going to see it as Barrett setting him free ... he's going to hate me—the kind of hate that's greater than any love.

"When his dad dies, I think it will change us."

Mom squeezes me tighter. "Ridiculous. He will need you more than ever before."

Closing my eyes, I let her comfort me even if she has no idea what that really means right now.

I GET TO Bodhi's house just as he reaches the end of the gravel drive at the main road. When he sees me, the huge grin on his face feels like a knife in my heart. He stops and gets out. Before I can say *good morning,* he has my face cradled in his hands, and his lips are fused to mine.

No lemon yet. He's all minty and his skin has that fresh, after-shower woodsy scent. I tell my hands to stay out of his hair since he's on his way to work, but they don't listen very well. He moans when I claim his slightly longer hair in my fists, deepening the kiss because every one of them feels like the last one.

"Good morning, Hell," he whispers, releasing my lips.

"Morning." I grin, stepping back to give my head some oxygen before I pass out. "You look sexy as fuck, Mr. Malone. I kinda want to pay a visit to your place of business and test out those cafeteria tables for weight load."

He adjusts himself while shaking his head. "You're going to destroy me. You know that, right?"

My heart pauses for a few seconds. He has no idea just how much I'm going to destroy him, and not in a sexy way.

"Is it wrong that I want Gail to know what we did against Alice last night?"

He looks at his watch then palms the back of my head, stealing one last kiss that leaves my knees wobbling a bit. "I'd be disappointed if you didn't want her to know." He grins. "Gotta go. Etta made oatmeal. See if you can get my dad to eat some. I left a message with his doctor's office this morning. Can you please go with Etta to take him to his appointment if they can get him in today?"

I nod slowly as he gets into the driver's seat.

"Thank you so much. You're the best."

I'm not.

"Have a good day. Don't let any skanky hoes in your office."

He pauses just before closing the door. A smile rides up his face. "Jealous?"

"Don't play with me, Mr. Malone. Your hands belong to my ass."

His gaze strips me in one heated sweep of my body. "Oh, Henna, we're definitely going to *play* later. But for now, I have to be professional and a *gentleman*." Bodhi shuts his door and mouths *I love you* as he pulls out onto the main road.

On a deep sigh, I make my way down to the house. As expected, it smells like oatmeal with lots of cinnamon as I slip off my shoes and set down my bag inside the door.

"Good morning."

Etta turns from the stove. "Good morning. Oatmeal?"

"I'm good for now. I had an early breakfast with my mom."

She turns off the gas burner and grabs her cup of coffee. "What you both did yesterday—"

I cut her off with a quick head shake. "Etta, we did nothing compared to all you did and what you endured. I'm a little surprised to see you here today."

"Barrett and I are good." She gives me a sad smile. "I've been through a lot with him. My reaction yesterday was grief for him and his struggle more than the breakdown that he had over the food I made. It's incredibly difficult to watch him fall apart and not be able to do anything to help him."

"It is." I nod, thinking of what we *can* do to help him. "He still asleep?"

She shakes her head. "Bathroom. He hasn't had a bowel movement in two weeks. He's miserable, and in his words *completely emasculated* since he needs help from me to get on and off the toilet."

I cringe. "I'm surprised Bodhi hasn't hired an in-home nurse to help take care of him. At least he'd feel like it was a professional helping him instead of the neighbor slash wife of his business manager."

"I don't think they can afford it. That's why they've tried to sell the ranch numerous times, but they've never gotten an offer that would allow them a new place to live and enough left over for extra care."

"Don't they have health insurance?"

"I can see you've never paid for any of your health expenses."

313

Now I feel like the sheltered princess on the hill. I have no idea how much chemo costs, or health insurance, or private in-home care. Maybe I've purchased clothing from thrift shops, but I've never paid an actual bill for something like a doctor's visit. "No." I frown. My mom asked if they needed help paying for expenses. Stupid, naive me said no.

Barrett's weak, defeated voice calls from the bathroom.

I start to follow Etta.

"I've got it. He hates when you see him like this."

I nod, stopping at the living room and folding my arms over my chest. It's been a long time since I've felt so helpless and insecure. So … *young*.

Etta helps Barrett out of the bathroom. He greets me with a grimace.

"Hey."

"Morning, darling."

Darling. That's what Zach has always called me. I don't want Barrett to call me darling. I can't let someone die who calls me that name. It will feel like letting Zach or my dad die.

"I'm going to change the bedsheets. Maybe Henna can get you some oatmeal?"

Barrett doesn't respond. I'm sure he's not hungry or can't imagine putting food into his body if it won't come out.

"Yes. I'll get him some oatmeal."

Etta nods after giving Barrett a long look that's not met with any sort of eye contact. When she's in the bedroom, I nod toward the kitchen and Barrett follows me.

"Is it the money?" I dish up a small bowl of oatmeal for him.

When I turn back to him, he holds a scowl of confusion.

"Money?"

"If money weren't an issue, if you could go anywhere in the world to get the best doctors, the best treatment, if you could have a male in-home nurse to take care of you, if you didn't have to think about selling the ranch or inconveniencing anyone financially or in any other way ... would you still want to die?"

His eyes widen as he grunts a laugh and gives me a knowing nod. "Your mom saw me yesterday and offered to save me?"

"No. I don't know if you can be saved. No one is guaranteed their next breath, not even if they have all the money in the world." I shrug. "My mom and stepdad don't have all the money in the world, but they have a lot of it. They would move heaven and earth for me. Your son is my heaven and earth, and you've become part of my world too. You have children who love you. If you want to experience as much of this life with them as possible, then let's try. Let me get you the resources. Don't allow your guilt or pride to stand in the way."

Barrett adjusts in his chair, a grimace distorting his face.

"Need help?" I walk toward him and halt when he buckles at the waist and vomits bile and blood onto himself.

"Etta!" I grab a towel.

Barrett coughs and coughs. "He's choking!"

Etta runs into the kitchen. She grabs his shoulder to help lift his torso. Her gaze shoots to me as I stand frozen, holding the towel. "Call 9-1-1."

My head nods half a dozen times.

"Barrett? Barrett?" She lifts him, but he slouches to the side, eyes rolling back in his head. "Henna!"

I jump.

"Call 9-1-1, now!"

Dropping the towel, I run to my bag, collapse onto my knees, and fumble with frantic hands to find my phone. Tears burn my eyes as I dial the three numbers.

After they arrive and he's loaded into the ambulance, Etta grabs my arm as I stand idle watching, wondering if he's alive, if he's going to be okay.

"Are you coming? Duke and I are following the ambulance."

I nod, not finding a word to say.

"Did you call Bodhi?" she asks as Duke pulls up to the house in his old truck.

"No," I whisper.

"I'll call him." Etta ushers me to the truck where I climb in the middle.

Duke gives me a sympathetic smile.

Life feels like it's in slow motion. It's how I felt right after I regained consciousness after my accident. Sometimes life packs a punch so hard it's disorienting.

"He wants to die." My gaze affixes to the ambulance lights in front of us as we pull down the long drive.

Maybe they didn't hear me.

"Bodhi, it's Etta. When you get this message call me. It's your dad. They're taking him to the hospital." She blows out a shaky breath. "He's not answering his phone. I'll call the school and see if someone can get him."

"Gail."

"What did you say?" Etta touches my leg.

I don't blink. If I blink the lights will disappear. Barrett will disappear. But that's what he wants. Right?

"Gail Rafferty." My own voice echoes in my head like this is not real. Like I'm in a dream or like life is just getting bad reception. "Tell her Mr. Malone's dad is dying." My voice sounds robotic. My pulse feels sluggish.

"Don't say that, Henna. He'll be fine." Etta holds the phone up to her ear and asks for Gail Rafferty.

I don't know why I said that. Whoever answers the phone can walk to his office and tell him there's an emergency. Maybe I want Gail to know that Bodhi's dad is dying and what she did to us only added grief to the stress in his life. For what?

I hate her.

And I hate how slow the ambulance is driving in front of us. Is he dead? No need to jeopardize any more lives if he's already dead.

"Here." Etta hands me a tissue. "He's going to be fine. We have to believe that."

I stare at the tissue that feels rough in my hand. Why do I need this tissue? That's when I see something drip onto my arm. My hand slowly touches my face. I'm crying. Why am I still crying? It's what Barrett wanted.

When we get to the hospital, they take Barrett into the emergency room. He looks so lifeless on the gurney. They won't tell us anything because we're not family, so we wait in the waiting room until Bodhi arrives.

Duke nudges me as I stare at the coffee stain on the tightly looped gray carpet in the waiting room. I look up as Bodhi runs through the entrance, straight to the desk. The lady nods, then shakes her head, says a few words, looks at her computer screen, and finally gives him a pathetic smile while pointing to the waiting room.

A grave expression steals his handsome face. I feel paralyzed for several seconds, unsure of what my place is at this moment. Does he need me? Do I sit in the corner and let the grownups figure things out? As he walks toward us, looking only at me, I know where I belong.

Standing, I meet him halfway and wrap my arms around him. We don't say anything. That's the thing with us: we don't need anything but each other. When life hits us hard, we find sanctuary right here.

I don't know how long we stand here. We have a way of making time stand still.

"Mr. Malone?"

Bodhi releases me and turns toward the brunette in green scrubs and a white coat.

"You can see your father now."

"Thank you."

"Just family for now." She holds her hand up to me.

Without a single second of pause, Bodhi takes my hand. "She's my wife."

I swallow hard as my mind goes back to that day on the snowy trail over two years ago when I asked Bodhi to marry me. It was spontaneous and desperate, but he probably never knew it was equally sincere. I know he just called me his wife so I could see his dad with him, but my heart can't find a normal rhythm now because it wants those words to be true.

"Okay. Follow me." The doctor leads us back to the ER and a room behind a heavy metal door where Barrett is hooked up to several monitors with an oxygen tube in his nose.

"Jesus ..." Bodhi whispers, releasing my hand and taking

cautious steps to the side of his dad's bed.

I pinch the bridge of my nose to ward off the tears that burn my eyes. Barrett looks dead, but his heart monitor beeping says otherwise. When Bodhi touches his hand, Barrett's heavy eyes blink partially open.

"Let me go," his dad rasps.

I draw in a shaky breath and turn my back to them and the doctor at the door because these burning tears need out so badly.

"This is bottom. Okay." Bodhi attempts to infuse optimism into his words. "There's nowhere to go but up. We've got this."

I continue to swipe away my tears. Maybe I don't want to be the fake wife in this room. The real girlfriend made to stay in the waiting room would be much easier on my heart. The doctor makes her way to the other side of the bed. I rotate again to keep everyone from seeing how much I suck at being brave.

"So here's what's going on …" The doctor shares very grim news, and that's just from less than an hour in the ER. She recommends an immediate consultation with Barrett's medical and surgical oncologists.

I tune out the rest and think of happy things, funny things, and sexy things about Bodhi. I think about getting high and painting while the music is so loud it shakes my canvas when the chorus hits its peak. Eventually, the tears dry and I bring myself to turn around again just as the doctor leaves the room.

Bodhi's moved a chair next to his dad's bed. He glances over at me and frowns while his brows knit together. My tears are done, but I'm sure my eyes are red and a little puffy. He holds out his hand. I press my lips together to keep the rest of myself held together as I take his hand. Bodhi pulls me onto his lap so I'm right next to Barrett's bed.

"Those tears…" Barrett starts to speak, but his voice is weak "…better not be for me."

I shake my head, swallowing past a lump in my throat.

"Once the doctor comes back with the prescription, we can go. Tomorrow we'll meet with the oncologists."

Barrett doesn't respond to Bodhi. He just stares at me with pleading eyes.

"Did you call Bella?" Barrett asks.

"No."

"You'd better call her, Son. If she finds out, she'll be mad no one told her."

Bodhi sighs.

"Go call her now. Leave me to chat with my girl here."

I glance around at Bodhi. He waits as if I need to give him permission.

"Go. We'll be fine." I kiss the corner of his mouth.

He nods and I stand to let him leave then sit back in the chair next to Barrett.

"It's time, darling."

He really needs to stop calling me that. It's too personal. The last thing I need to do is get more personal with a man who his hell-bent on dying.

"If your offer still stands."

I've recently made more than one offer. "Which offer?"

"I need some money."

My body relaxes. He's choosing to fight this. After what I saw just a couple of hours ago and the grave tone of the ER doctor's voice, I'm cautiously optimistic about his chances. But Bodhi wants him to fight, so if he's willing to do this for his son, I'll do whatever it takes to make it happen.

"I'll call my mom as soon as we leave. She knows a lot of people. We'll get you in with the best doctors and make sure you have everything you need at home, including someone qualified to tend to all of your needs. And—"

"Darling," he cuts me off, "that's not why I need the money."

"Oh?" I squint.

"I need a special medication. It's expensive. It also requires two physicians to agree that I can take it. An oral request. A written request." He coughs a few times and adjusts his oxygen tube. "A two week waiting period. But I not only need the money for the prescription; I need you to help me find the right doctors."

"But you have doctors. Two oncologists who are supposed to see you tomorrow."

He eases his head side to side. "This is a faith-based hospital."

"I … I don't understand."

"It's time. It's past time. I need doctors who believe I should have the right to die with as much dignity as possible, which…" he frowns "…isn't much at this point."

"Assisted suicide," I whisper.

"They call it death with dignity. Cause of death will be cancer. It won't be suicide."

"But Bodhi thinks—"

"He's delusional. He thinks what he wants to think. We're past miracles. I'm just tired, Henna."

"He'll hate me."

"He won't have to know. And don't tell me you have to tell him. You don't. He won't ask. He'll think I died in my sleep. It's not a lie. That's how I'll die."

I'll always know. Will I be able to take this secret to *my* grave too?

"Please."

I hug my arms to my chest, feeling a little cold—probably my body going into shock. After a few agonizing moments, I nod.

"Thank you, darling. And I need one more favor." He reaches for my hand and I give it to him.

As if death isn't enough.

"I want to see your mom. Privately."

My eyes narrow just as Bodhi comes back into the room. Barrett squeezes my hand like he's trying to squeeze an answer out of me. I nod again just before standing.

"Bella is flying home next week. I told her it wasn't necessary, but she insisted."

"Good." Barrett nods. "I want to see her before … I start treatment."

My gut clenches. This is how it's going to be. He's going to lie to his family because he can't trust them to support his decision to die with dignity.

"Well, the doctor called in your prescription. She'll be in to discharge you, and we'll stop on the way home and get it."

Barrett attempts a smile, but it looks like a grimace.

"I'm going to…" I point toward the door "…hang out in the waiting room while you help your dad get dressed."

Bodhi bends down to press a kiss to my cheek. "Thank you

for everything."

Don't thank me.

"Of course."

And if the truth comes out, please don't hate me.

CHAPTER FORTY-ONE

I CALL MY mom to see when she can fly back to Colorado to see Barrett. I have no idea what he wants, but his *privately* comment left me feeling like I wasn't supposed to know. Then I ask my mom for the biggest favor ever.

"You want me to help Barrett kill himself? No. I can't do that, Henna."

I put my phone on speaker and set it by my bed as I dig into my gummies. It's time to numb some of this fucking pain after two very long days. "Were you not here yesterday? Did you not see what happened? Had you been at their house today..." closing my eyes, I take a deep inhale and wonder if I will ever forget what I saw happen to Barrett "...you would understand. You would see that he's miserable. In pain. Embarrassed. And just ... done."

"Henna ..."

"Since I've been home, I've been researching this online. There's a process. It could take two weeks anyway. Two more weeks of him being in so much pain. And he has to have two doctors sign off and one send in a prescription. They won't do it unless they believe he's terminal with six months or less to live. And they won't do it unless they believe he's psychologically competent to make this decision and physically capable to do it when the time comes."

I don't tell her they strongly suggest he inform and discuss this with his family.

"Do you know what you're asking?"

"Yes. I know. I'm not asking you to kill him. He's going to die. I'm not asking you to do anything illegal. You'll have this on your conscience for a while, but I'm risking the most. I'm risking losing Bodhi. Yet, I'm willing to because …" I blink back the pain. "If you would have seen him today …" I swipe my finger along the corner of my eye.

"Okay."

"Okay?"

"Yes. I'm trusting you, Henna. If you believe this is for the best. I trust you."

I'm twenty-one. A part-time pot user. And I paint and draw shit all day. Should anyone trust me?

"Thank you."

"I'll make a few calls."

"Love you."

There's a moment's pause on the line. "I love you too. And I'm sorry."

"For what?"

"You will lose him if he finds out."

I sniffle and rub my eyes. "I know."

BODHI TAKES BARRETT to see the oncologists. He doesn't ask me to go. That's fine. I'm not sure I want to be in the room for that discussion.

When they get home, Bodhi helps Duke with the horses. They had an above average day with the tourists. I hang out with Barrett and start dinner. We're trying broth for him.

"What did the oncologists say? Bodhi seemed like he didn't want to talk about it, so I didn't ask."

Barrett sips some cannabis tea I brought him. "They had pretty good news."

"Oh yeah?" I glance over my shoulder from the stove.

He sets his tea on the table with a shaky hand. "They gave me three to four months to live—with treatment."

I frown. "That's good news?"

"It is for me."

I turn back toward the stove.

"You think I'm being harsh?"

I shrug. "Not necessarily. I think you're resigned to ..."

"Reality?"

I nod.

He's had two doctors tell him he has less than six months to live. That's what he needs to make an oral request for physician-assisted death. Of course it's good news to him.

"How did Bodhi react?"

"He thinks I should have the surgery and get opinions from other doctors. He's holding out for a miracle. I don't exactly hate him for that."

"So ... how are you going to hold off on the surgery?"

"I told him I wanted to wait until Bella comes to visit. That will buy me a week. If I can convince her to stay for a week and not end up in the hospital again, that will get me my prescription. But I need other doctors. I already know mine won't do it. Religious reasons."

"My mom is looking into this. And she's flying back this weekend to see you." I shut off the stove and take a seat next to

Barrett. "Can you tell me why you want to see my mom?"

"I could." He reaches for his tea again, and I hand it to him. "But I'm not going to."

I roll my eyes. After a few minutes of tea sipping in silence, I glance up at him. "Are you scared?"

He chuckles a little. "No. Pain robs you of that kind of fear."

I'm familiar with that.

"Eventually the only thing you fear is—"

"The never-ending pain." I finish for him because I know, at least in part, what he's feeling. "It's weird, planning your death. Don't you think?"

"It's not as much fun as planning a party or a vacation." He smiles. It's more relaxed.

"Have you thought about how you're going to do it? Like … are you going to take it as soon as you have the prescription? I'd say you should plan a special last meal, but you can't keep much down, so that sucks."

"Haven't given it much thought. I suppose I'll just know when the time is right."

"Are you going to tell me?" My knee starts to bounce. The timing of Barrett's death is giving me some serious anxiety. Maybe I need a cup of cannabis tea too.

"Do you want me to tell you?"

"Yes. No." I cringe. "I don't know."

He nods thoughtfully as if my indecisiveness makes sense. "Well, you have a little time to figure that out. I think it's best if nobody knows, if you just trust me to do it when I feel it's time."

"Probably a good idea. But … like will you give me a little

heads-up?" My bouncing knee speeds up.

Another soft chuckle escapes his chest.

"It freaks me out to think about walking into a room with a dead body. No offense."

"None taken." He has a little sparkle in his eyes.

I'm glad I amuse him.

"My boy—he loves you."

His words catch me off guard. A warmth spreads across my skin.

"He can't keep his eyes off you. While he's watching you, I'm watching him. I'd say that's how I used to look at my wife, but I'm not sure I've seen anyone look at someone like Bodhi looks at you. He was a miserable pain in my ass those years you were gone. It didn't make sense until you came back. With you, he's living his best life. Without you, I'm not sure he's living at all."

He won't always look at me like that, but I don't say that to Barrett. I think he has enough emotional shit going on planning his death. "There's been so many times that I've thought *this … this is the moment I've officially fallen in love with Bodhi Malone.* But every time I think it, I realize that it's not true because I feel certain I loved him before now. How can I feel like I've loved him forever when I haven't known him forever?"

"It's how love should be—no beginning and no end."

I return an easy nod. "If only life could extend the same courtesy."

"Nah … the earth would be overpopulated. If you believe in the circle of life, then it, too, really has no beginning and no end."

Leaning forward, I rest my hand on Barrett's hand. "I'm going to miss you. Our conversations. Getting high just to give the middle finger to our lows."

"Thank you. I've enjoyed our time together as well. So very much." He rests his other hand on mine. "I won't ask you to bury my body in the back of the house, but in the end table drawer I have my stash. While others are grieving, I want you to smoke, laugh, kick back on the porch, and know that I'm one of the brightest stars in the sky winking at you each night."

"A star winking at me." I grin. "I like that."

The timer on the stove beeps.

"Dinnertime. You need to try to keep some broth down."

He scratches his chin. "So I can live long enough to die on my own terms."

Grunting a laugh, I nod. "Yes. That."

CHAPTER FORTY-TWO

B Y THE END of the week, thanks to my mom, Barrett has two physicians willing to honor his oral request for physician-assisted death. There's a waiting period, and he'll need to submit a written request as well.

My mom's plane should be landing soon, and she's supposed to come straight here to meet with Barrett *privately* per his request—something Bodhi knows nothing about.

"Juni is coming by in a bit. Is that okay?" I ask as he buttons his jeans while I lie on his bed with one arm propped behind my head, enjoying the view.

"Of course it's okay. Is there a special reason for her visit?"

Damn! Will looking at his sexy body with my name on it ever get old?

"If you're going to stare at me this much, I might have to charge admission into my bedroom."

I grin, lifting my gaze to meet his smirk. "I'd pay full price."

"Okay, big spender. Now..." he slips on a blue Henley tee "...what's the reason for your mom's visit?"

"She's going to hang out with your dad while I show you something."

His eyebrows lift a fraction. "Show me something, huh?"

I nod, trapping my lower lip to hide my grin from his suggestive look.

Bodhi kneels at the end of his bed and grabs my ankles, tugging me until my butt is at the end of the bed.

"That's not what I'm planning on showing you." I giggle.

He hooks my legs over his shoulders so I'm spread open for him. When he looks at my exposed flesh like it's something he craves, I start to tingle and feel a heaviness work its way down my body. My lips part as my breaths quicken.

"Bodhi …" I whisper.

"I know, I know. This isn't what you want to show me. Fine." He grins, standing while my legs flop off the end of the bed.

"Oh my god! You're evil. Pure evil." I smack him with the pillow, but he turns to the side to avoid the direct hit.

"What do you want to show me?" He continues to chuckle as I swat him several more times.

"Nothing but my knee in your nuts for teasing me."

Bodhi snatches the pillow from me and tosses it on the floor before pinning me to the bed. "Good morning, beautiful." He rubs his nose against mine as his pelvis rocks into me.

He's going to have evidence of me on his jeans. How much evidence depends on how much longer he continues to dry hump me. I'm still pissed off at him for teasing me, but I'm also feeling desperate for a release.

"Good morning." I lift my head to capture his lips before he attempts to get away. My legs wrap around his backside just for good measure.

Our tongues do their favorite dance while fully clothed Bodhi grinds against completely naked me. I moan into our kiss as my orgasm builds again. He releases my wrists and slides one hand under me to grab my ass, guiding me exactly how he wants me to move against him, angling my hips so that the swollen head of his erection rubs my entrance.

We continue this erotic dance against his denim shield until he throws out a frustrated *fuck* and tries to hold his weight over me with one hand while his other hand fumbles with his jeans.

I put him out of his misery by unfastening them and pushing them down just far enough to release his hard cock. Before I can tease it, or even get a quick glance at it, he plunges into me with a more satisfied *fuck* and a slack jaw.

And fuck we do—hard and fast while sharing intimate smiles between kisses. I love these smiles. They're the subtle strokes of our love amidst a very bold painting of a crazy life together. These smiles say I love you beyond reason.

It's a good morning. A really, really good morning.

"HEY, SWEETIE." JUNI kisses my cheek when I open the door.

"Thank you for everything," I whisper next to her ear when we embrace.

She nods without saying a word as Bodhi walks up behind me.

"Juni, thanks for coming by to stay with my dad."

She glances at me.

I wrap my arm around Bodhi's waist. "Yes. It's so kind of you to stay with Barrett while I show Bodhi the surprise."

"Surprise," she says slowly as I pin a tight-lipped smile to my face. "It's no problem."

"Come in. He's just had a little breakfast. Hopefully he

keeps it down." Bodhi winks at his dad as we enter the living room.

It's such an everything-is-going-to-be-okay wink. Who knew a wink could feel like a jab to my heart?

"Hello, again. I'm going to do my best not to embarrass myself this time." Barrett turns on the charm even under such grave circumstances.

"Hi." Juni smiles. "There's nothing to be embarrassed about. You look a little better today?"

"It's a new aftershave." He rubs his chin and neck.

Juni laughs.

"Is John still outside?" I ask.

"Yes, dear."

"Great. I'll have him drive us to see Bodhi's surprise. Be back in an hour ... or two," I declare as I wait for Barrett to give me a sign as to if he needs an hour or two.

He gives me no sign. Two hours it is.

"Call us if there's any issues." Bodhi and my mom trade glances.

"We'll be fine," she assures him.

Bodhi follows me out front where John opens the SUV's back door. "I've never been driven like this before. Or in a fancy SUV for that matter."

I kick the tire to the Land Rover. "This old thing doesn't have anything on Alice."

He grins while nodding at John as I scoot across the backseat.

"Does the surprise involve anything illegal?"

"Illegal. Forbidden. Taboo. Basically, you're asking if the surprise is fun." I grab his hand and squeeze it. "To the main house, please, John."

John nods and puts the Land Rover in drive.

Bodhi tosses me a narrow-eyed glance, lips twisted to the side. He's dying to say something, but it must not be appropriate for John's ears. Within a few minutes, we've pulled in front of the main house.

"Thank you, John."

"Thanks," Bodhi echoes me as we hop out.

"We're going to have sex in your parents' bed, aren't we?"

I snort a laugh. "That wasn't the plan. But clearly it's on your mind, even after what happened..." I glance at my watch "...less than an hour ago." I open the front door.

Bodhi's gaze sweeps the grand two-story entry. "Such a different world," he mutters.

"Same world. Bigger house. More is just more. It's not better. It's not anything to envy, unless you're comparing a single-serving bag of chips to a large bag of chips. Then more is obviously better."

"Damn, I love you." Bodhi follows me down the hallway by the kitchen.

I grin even though he can't see it. He's going to love me harder in about ten seconds.

"The basement? Their bedroom is in the basement?"

I lead him down the stairs as motion-sensor lights illuminate our path. "Still thinking about more sex, huh?"

"Always." He tugs on my ponytail. When we reach the bottom of the stairs, his eyebrows leap up to his forehead as his jaw falls to the ground.

"You can't be shocked that the owner of a record label has a recording studio in his basement."

Bodhi's head inches side to side a few times. Then he nods just as slowly. "I probably shouldn't be, but I am." He walks to the glass door of the soundproof room and opens it.

I follow him, feeling like I'm watching a young child on Christmas morning. He inspects the row of guitars, the keyboard, the photos of all the famous musicians who have been in this basement. Then ... he takes a seat at the drums.

"Make it a good one, Malone." I grin.

He caresses the drumsticks much like his hands have touched my body so many times. I might even be a little jealous of them at the moment. His foot starts the slow, deep rhythm of the base drum like a heartbeat. I slide onto the bench by the keyboard and watch his sticks hit the toms, the snare drum, the crash of the cymbals. It builds until his whole body moves in sync, each part effortlessly doing its thing.

Bodhi's head bobs, eyes closed. He never misses a beat. By the time he flies through the finale and sets the sticks down with such reverence, it takes me a few moments to find a single word. They're not the words I ever imagined saying, and maybe they're even a bit too raw and honest.

I say them anyway, in a whisper to myself that he can hear. "You were a rock star, and you fucked it up."

Reality pulls at his brow as he returns a single nod. "I was a rock star, and I fucked it up. I had a fully functional father and I fucked him up. I had dreams, and I fucked them up. Does that make me a fuckup?"

Making my way across the room, I straddle his lap, wrapping my arms around his neck and kissing his cheek, his nose, and the corner of his mouth. "It makes you human."

"Human," he whispers.

"Bodhi, you're a guidance counselor. How does one go from owning the stage to counseling kids and fixing schedules?" I grin. "Was your Plan B really what you're doing now? Did you think, *I want to be a rock star OR a guidance counselor?*"

He grabs my ass and pulls me closer so I don't fall off his lap. Burying his nose in my hair, he exhales, pressing his lips to my neck. "My mom told me to make a difference. She told me my greatness didn't die when we fell down the stairs. I was a drug addict in high school. I even asked for help once from my guidance counselor. She said she would get me some help, but then she went into labor, and I never got that help. Never asked the substitute counselor. I just ... got drunk and high with my bandmates."

"So you chose to become a guidance counselor because you're a guy and you'll never take maternity leave?"

His laughter vibrates against my skin. "God, I love you. You get me. You just ... get me." After a few minutes of us just being *us*, Bodhi lifts his head, bringing us face to face. "Thank you for this. I haven't played in years."

"You're welcome." I return the same affectionate smile as though I'd been planning this surprise for a long time, instead of the truth which is I needed a distraction so Juni and Barrett could talk in private.

Gah! I wonder what he's saying to her? She'll tell me. We're best friends. She has to tell me.

"Let's make a song together. Jump on the keyboard or play something on a guitar, and I'll join you."

Poor guy. He has no clue.

"I don't play."

"What do you mean?"

I shrug. "I mean, I don't play."

"Just do something simple like Chopsticks."

"Can't. I've never played Chopsticks."

"How the hell is that possible?" His head cants to the side. "You always have music playing. You live with earbuds in your ears."

"I love music, but it's not my art."

"Henna, your dad was a drummer. Your parents conceived you at a music festival. This makes no sense."

Another shrug. "You know the saying: Those who can, do. Those who can't, don't."

Bodhi chuckles. "Yeah, that's the saying."

"Besides, even if I could master Chopsticks, it would be ridiculous. Like ... me asking you to create a sketch with me and you saying you can't. I wouldn't tell you to draw a few stick figures. No. Just ... no."

"It's a foundation. I can build on it." He lifts me off his lap and pulls me to the keyboard. "Two fingers. Start here. I know you have rhythm." Bodhi stands behind me, grabbing my index fingers and moving them along the keys to play Chopsticks. After a few times through, it's like riding a bike. He releases my fingers, and I play it on my own. "Keep going."

He runs over to the drum set and adds a beat and some more rhythm. Bodhi makes Chopsticks sound crazy cool. I can't stop grinning as we stare at each other to the rock version of Chopsticks.

Bodhi mouths *I love you.*

And of course ... I die.

AFTER A SOLID two hours of playing in the recording studio, John drives us back to Bodhi's house. Juni and Barrett are all smiles. It makes me uneasy. Bodhi just thinks our parents hit it off really well. Since Bodhi needs to give Barrett a bath, I ride home with my mom, waiting until we're at the dining room table to ask the question.

"So, what did he need to talk to you about?"

Fiona sets down two salads in front of us.

Juni smiles and thanks her before giving me her full attention. "He wanted to personally thank me for what I've done. And for raising such a loving daughter." She takes a bite of her salad.

"And?"

Wiping her mouth with a white cloth napkin, she mumbles, "And what?"

"You didn't need to fly home and have privacy for Barrett to thank you. That's an email or a quick phone conversation. What aren't you telling me? There has to be more."

"You know, I feel like you don't understand the definition of private."

My eyes widen. "I feel like you don't understand the definition of best friends. There's only one definition for best friends: two people who tell each other everything. Go ahead, check Merriam-Webster."

Juni grins, sipping her red wine. "All I can say is that if Bodhi adores you even half as much as Barrett, then you are a lucky girl."

I'm turning a blind eye to a man getting ready to end his

life. Being adored by him is not such a great thing for my heart or my conscience.

"Bodhi played the drums for me. He's so good."

"Good as in Zach needs to hear him?"

My lips roll between my teeth as I shake my head. "Yes, that good. But he's a drummer, not really a singer so much. And I'm not sure finding him a band is a good idea or even what he wants in life at this point." I shrug. "It's weird. I don't know what he wants in life. I'm not sure he knows or has even given himself a chance to think beyond his life at this moment. And maybe that's okay. Ya know? It's what makes his love for me so special."

I pause a moment, as I always have to do when I think of *us*. "Bodhi doesn't have a clue how I fit into his life. He doesn't think he has anything to offer me. Just him. Just his love. Holding hands on the sofa while we watch Barrett sleep. Horseback rides. Sunday drives in Alice."

"Alice?"

I nod, wearing a grin that feels fabulous on my face. "I named his VW van Alice. Right after we met. And he still calls her that. He loved me enough to let me go. Now he loves me enough to know that *loving me* is enough."

I can do the right thing, or I can love you, but I can't do both.

Bodhi probably has no idea that those words will always stay with me.

"Do you love him enough to let him go if loving him isn't enough? Because it might not be enough if he finds out how his father planned his own death."

I'm twenty-one. Playing the age card might be getting old, but I play it anyway because my love for him is more than enough. My heart can't let him go without kicking and scream-ing, begging and pleading. "We'll see, won't we?"

"Barrett said Bodhi never needs to know the truth. I agree. You're not making this decision for Barrett. You're not admin-istering the medication. You're simply abiding by his request. If it's not you, it would be someone else. And honestly ..." She blows a slow breath out of her nose, forehead winkled.

"Honestly what?"

"I'm very conflicted about this, and I told Barrett as much. I know he feels desperate, and he also feels a connection to you, but asking you to do this, putting you in this situation, is a bit selfish on his part. Yes, you're an adult, but you're a *young* lady. Bodhi aside, this will affect you for the rest of your life, just like your accident."

"I'm fine."

"Well, *fine* can be a very temporary state."

Taking a bite of my salad, I let her words settle in my head and my heart.

CHAPTER FORTY-THREE

B ELLA VISITS BARRETT, and he manages to stay out of the hospital in spite of his inability to maintain weight. I eat dinner with their family most evenings to help keep the peace between the two siblings. Barrett magically finds topics of conversation that bring back happy memories of their family. Occasionally, I even notice Bodhi and Bella trading knowing smiles about something. In those moments, I fight back the tears.

Barrett is content—weak, in pain, exhausted, oftentimes heavily medicated or high, and on good days he sleeps a lot. Bodhi's itching to get him scheduled for surgery and started on treatment again.

But that's not going to happen because today Barrett holds all the power. He's his own god.

"It's like staring at a loaded gun," I say as we keep our gazes affixed to the prescription bag on the kitchen table.

Barrett hums his agreement.

"How do you feel?"

He clears his throat. "I'm tired today."

"No." I scoot my chair closer to his wheelchair. "In here." I press my hand to his heart. "How do you feel about Bodhi and Bella? How do you feel about letting go when no one knows what happens next?"

He covers my hand with his hand. "I feel like I've nearly emptied every emotion I have left to give. I can't fix them if they're not ready to be fixed, but if I leave it all—all the love—behind, then maybe that will be enough for them to realize the fight is over. There are no winners or losers—only survivors. My kids ... they will survive me."

My nose and eyes burn with all my fears. "I want you to tell me w-when." My voice cracks under the heavy dose of reality. "I need to be prepared. *Kinda* knowing like I do at the moment is worse than not knowing at all."

"Soon." He releases my hand.

"Soon? Hours? Days? Weeks? What do you call soon?" Panic takes over. I thought I could do this, but with that bag right here on the table, I can barely breathe past the anxiety.

"Soon as in every goodbye matters."

"Soon as in today? Tonight? Are you going to do it before Bodhi gets home?" I glance at my watch. He won't be home for another three hours. That's plenty of time. Did he leave on good terms with him this morning? "Maybe I could make dinner." My hands shake. I fold them on my lap. God ... my heart might break through my chest. I can barely hear past my racing pulse. "Maybe today is too soon."

"It's a Monday."

I nod several times as my knee begins to bounce. My nerves won't be held back no matter how hard I squeeze my hands together. "There's a Monday next week too. But now that I really think about it, people have a lot to deal with on Mondays. Have you considered a Tues—"

And then it happens. My knee stills, my hands still, I think my heart even stops for a few seconds when Barrett leans forward, nearly falling out of his chair, to rest one of his hands on my leg and the other on my folded hands.

All that energy.

All the nerves.

All the pain.

All the fear.

It comes out as a sob ripping through my throat. I collapse onto my own lap, resting my cheek against his hand on my knee.

"It's okay, darling. Everything will be okay."

I spent so much time thinking about Bodhi and how he would deal with his father's death, I haven't checked in with my own heart. Right now it hurts because I don't just love Bodhi, I love his father too.

I'm going to miss Barrett Malone.

He squeezes my hands with what little strength he has left. "I asked Duke to get you a good saddle for Angelina, and I told him she's your horse. No matter what happens to the ranch, she's yours."

"H-horse? I don't w-want a horse. I want a miracle, just like Bodhi. The improbable. Th-the impossible. Why not? They happen. If anyone deserves a miracle, it's y-you."

He moves a hand to my head, stroking my hair as he mumbles something. It takes a few seconds for the words to register. When they do, I cry even harder.

"You're the miracle, Henna. Take care of my boy."

"YOU CAN'T STAY. He'll know." Barrett gives me a sad smile.

I nod. As much as I want to be here for Bodhi, my eyes are

too swollen. My heart is too broken. The moment he walks through the door, he'll know something is terribly wrong.

"I'm going to call Etta to see if she'll come stay with you and make a pot of soup for dinner." I grab my phone from my pocket.

"Thank you."

I can't even look at Barrett. Just his simple *thank you* puts me on the verge of losing it again.

Etta agrees to head this way, so I hide the prescription bag where Barrett can easily get it when he's ready. I put on my sunglasses and ready myself at the front door to make a quick escape before she can get a good look at me in my broken state.

I text Bodhi.

Me: *Etta is here. I'm leaving. I need to finish a sketch tonight. I'll see you tomorrow. I love you … so much. Xo*
Bodhi: *Love you too. Thanks for all you do.*

Thanks for helping my dad die. My conscience will never live through this.

"I'll leave the bottles in the empty bag right where it is now. You'll need to properly dispose of them before anyone goes through my stuff."

With my back to him, my hand on the front doorknob, I nod.

The drippy faucet in the kitchen marks time, punctuating the silence, cementing reality as I catch sight of Etta.

"I love you, darling."

Oh god …

I can't breathe, and I definitely can't speak, so I nod without looking back. Rushing out the door, I hold my phone up to my ear so Etta thinks I'm on a call. With my breath held hostage and my last bit of composure ready to shatter, I give her a friendly wave while passing her on the ramp. When the door closes to the house and I'm at least ten yards from the porch, I nearly vomit, choking on my grief.

CHAPTER FORTY-FOUR

I CONSUME ENOUGH edibles to get to sleep. Then I wake up at three in the morning, fully clothed. If—when—Bodhi calls, I want to be ready.

Sitting on the edge of my bed, I stare at my phone. I stare at it until my eyes fatigue. Collapsing onto my side, I rest the phone on my pillow and stare at it some more until I fall asleep again.

Dave Matthews "You and Me" blares from my phone—my new ringtone for Bodhi. Before I went to sleep last night, I turned the volume up all the way because I didn't want to sleep through his call. Now, as my heart stops, blocking all oxygen from my lungs, I rethink that decision.

I'm not sure how they find their way out so quickly, but tears stream down my face. This is it. I swipe the screen of my phone, bringing it to my ear slowly, prolonging the inevitable for just a few seconds longer.

"Hey." My hand flies to my mouth to stop the sob that threatens to trample my *hey*.

"Good morning, sexy."

My jaw drops, mid-sob. *Good morning sexy?* That's not what one says when their father is dead. Oh my god ... Barrett didn't do it. Why didn't he do it? I'm relieved that he didn't, but what does this mean?

I blow out a slow breath to steady my voice. "What's up?"

"I need a favor."

"Um … sure." I wipe my eyes, feeling like this huge weight has been lifted from my chest.

"Duke just called. Etta is under the weather today, and I woke up a little late. My dad and I were up late talking. Memory lane. It was great, but I missed my alarm." Bodhi's words are slightly clipped like he's hustling. "He's probably tired too, so I don't want to wake him yet. How soon could you be here? I just don't want him to be alone when he does wake up, and I'd rather not have to call in and use another personal day. I'll need those days for his surgery."

No … no, no, no.

This can't be me. The routine is Bodhi wakes his dad up, gets him to the bathroom, and dressed. *Then* Etta or I arrive just as Bodhi's leaving. We take over, making breakfast and attending to his daily needs beyond that point. Everyone knows this. Barrett knew this. That's why he chose nighttime, so Bodhi would be the one to find him in the morning.

"Henna? Are you still there? I'm sort of in a hurry. Can you help me out?"

No.

There's a good chance his dad is dead. Bodhi needs to take a personal day. Period.

"Uh …" I swallow hard, choking on this nightmare. "Yeah, just let him know I'm on my way."

"I'm not going to wake him. Just get here as soon as you can."

"Bodhi—"

"Please, babe, can you just do this for me?"

Rubbing my forehead, I close my eyes. "I'm on my way."

BODHI'S PULLING OUT of the drive by the time I get there. I force a smile when he rolls down his window. It's never hurt this much to smile.

"You're the best." He grabs the strap to my bag and pulls me flush to Alice so he can crane his neck out the window to kiss me. He's in such a good mood.

Pressing my hands to his cheeks, I kiss him. Will it be the last time he kisses me? I don't know how, but he'll find out. He'll know I knew about this.

"God ... I love you," he whispers over my lips before releasing me.

I return a smile that hopefully conveys my love for him. My chest is too congested with fear and dread to find words.

"Bye." He rolls up the window and pulls away from me.

Staring at the house for a few seconds, I will my legs to take me there.

One step.

Two steps.

I will never forget this day for the rest of my life. It's a feeling I can't quite explain, but I think it will change who I am.

The ramp boards creak as I walk up them to the front door. The front door whines on its hinges when I open it. And when I close it behind me, it's *dead* silent.

Dark.

Hallow.

Suffocating.

Taking slow steps, I stop in the middle of the living room

and stare at Barrett's bedroom door. It's cracked open a few inches. Threading my fingers through my hair, I draw in a shaky breath.

Maybe he didn't do it. What if their trip down memory lane convinced him to fight this? Sometimes all it takes is finding something that makes the fight worth it. I ease into Barrett's empty recliner, ghosting my fingertips over the worn black leather arms.

And I wait.

The mantel clock keeps me company for the next two hours.

Two hours.

I wait two hours for a cough. I wait two hours for the squeak of his bed frame. I wait two hours to find the strength to walk into that room.

My trembling hand presses to the faded-wood bedroom door. It's warm compared to my cold fingers. Chills vibrate my whole body, like when I'm outside on a winter day and I can't get warm. The ache in the back of my throat makes it hard to breathe. The need to *know* overrides my instinct to run, call Bodhi, and tell him his dad died.

Because ... what if he's not dead?

"Barrett?" His name catches in my throat, coming out as a stutter.

Nothing.

I step closer to the bed and gasp, turning quickly and pinching my eyes shut. My shoulders curl inward as my breathing becomes erratic. One hand goes to my stomach as a wave of nausea contracts my abs.

This picture of Barrett will never leave my mind—pale, jaw

relaxed, eyes partially open, and completely lifeless.

Dead.

Should I call 9-1-1? Is that what Bodhi would have done had he found Barrett this morning? CPR? I ... I don't know what to do. This wasn't my job. I wasn't supposed to be the one to find him like this. Folding at the waist, I rest my hands on my knees and try to even out my breathing.

"Think ..." I whisper. "What do I do?"

I run to my bag and grab my phone. There's this sudden sense of urgency, but I don't know why. I drop the phone because I can't stop shaking. Desperation pounds in my chest. No amount of preparation could have ever prepared me for this.

"Hey, sweetie," Juni answers.

Raw emotion has an impenetrable immunity to one's will. No matter how hard I will myself to keep it together, I can't. My answer to her greeting is an uncontrolled sob as I collapse to my knees.

"Oh ... Henna ..."

My cries drown all the words. The man I love to the ends of the earth, to the end of time, lost his dad and he has no idea.

"I'm on my way. I'll be there in a few hours. Where are you?"

"H-Here ..."

"Bodhi's house? How's he doing? He needs you, Henna. I'll be there soon—"

"H-h-he ... doesn't k-know ..." I choke. "He left ..." I hiccup. "He wanted m-me to be h-here when..." another hiccup "...Barrett woke up. But he's ..."

"Jesus, Henna. I'm so sorry."

"I don't k-know what to … to do."

"Breathe, I need you to breathe first. Okay?"

I nod, trying to calm myself down.

"Are you there alone?"

"Yes."

"Did you call 9-1-1?"

"You. I c-called you."

"Okay. Call 9-1-1. Then go get Bodhi. I'll have John come get you. This isn't something you tell him over the phone. He shouldn't be driving after hearing this news. Understood? And I'm already in the car on the way to the airport. I'm going to call your dad and Zach."

Bella. Duke. Etta.

Nobody knows.

"K." I wipe my cheeks and my nose while disconnecting the call and dialing 9-1-1.

"9-1-1 operator. What is your emergency?"

The answer stays lodged in my throat for a few seconds. "I … I need to report a death."

This dispatcher leads me through a series of questions as I grab my bag and head outside as John pulls into the driveway.

I press end and clutch my phone as John gets out of the vehicle. Without a word, he wraps his arms around me and kisses the top of my head. Every day thousands of people around the world die from cancer. That means every day thousands of families go through what I'm going through now, what Bodhi and Bella are about to experience. Cancer sucks ass. Just like helicopter crashes and falling down flights of marble stairs.

On the way to the school, I call Duke. Just what Etta needs

to hear when she's already under the weather.

"Want me to go inside with you?" John asks as he opens my door in front of the school.

I shake my head. "But thank you."

At the entrance, I press the button by the security camera. "Yes?" The voice isn't familiar. Must be someone new working in the office.

"I need to see Bodhi Malone."

The door buzzes and unlocks. The next set of security doors are at the office. They buzz open as well.

"Do you have an appointment with Mr. Malone?" the new receptionist asks.

I shake my head slowly. Every word she says sounds slow and echoed. Maybe it's because this isn't real. Maybe I'm going to wake up from this nightmare.

"Henna?" Principal Rafferty walks around the corner that leads to her office.

My gaze shifts to her, face long and incapable of a smile or anything even close to it.

"How are you?" Gail acts as if we're friends. We are not friends. I hate her.

"I need to see Bodhi."

She frowns. "Henna. I don't think that's a good idea."

I swallow hard to suppress the anger that's mixing with my grief. It's a toxic combination. "I don't care what you think. Never have. Never will. I just need to see Bodhi." I'm not telling her why. I refuse to tell anyone else before I tell Bodhi. "It's a family emergency."

"Well, you're not his family, so—"

I leave the office and try to open the set of doors to the

main corridor of the school, but they're locked. "Open the fucking door!"

"Henna. If you don't leave now, I'll have you escorted out of the building."

I jerk on the doors. "BODHI!" Tears burn my eyes as Gail tells the secretary to call the school security guard.

My fists bang on the glass. "BODHI!"

The security guard runs down the hallway toward the doors I'm trying to open. His hand is on his holstered gun.

What the fuck?

"Miss, step back from the door," he calls through the door before opening it.

My eyes stay focused on his hand as it flips the snap on his holster. Stepping back, breathless and shocked that I'm considered a threat worthy of a drawn weapon, I hold up my hands.

Keeping his hand readied, he opens the door.

I blink out more tears, silenced by how long it's been since I've been here and how unwelcome I am here, even now. But more than that, I'm still forbidden to see Bodhi inside these walls.

"Ms. Lane needs to be escorted to her car." Principal Rafferty steps between me and the school security guard.

"I love him," I whisper. "And he loves me. So go fuck yourself. I wish it were you that died today, not his …"

"Henna?"

I glance over Gail's shoulder and past the security guard at Bodhi. His brow is wrinkled, his eyes wandering as he tries to assess the situation.

"Bodhi …" my voice cracks as I push past Gail.

The security guard grabs me.

"Bodhi!"

"Pete, get your fucking hands off her!" Bodhi's booming voice sends all heads in his direction as Pete releases me and I run into Bodhi's arms.

"What's wrong?" he whispers in my ear as he cups the back of my head. Those two words stumble a bit like he knows something is wrong—like he's bracing for my answer.

No amount of bracing can protect him from the pain. It's just not possible. So I don't wait a second longer because I can no longer bear the burden of truth alone.

"He never woke up."

Bodhi releases me. His hands grab my face as his eyes narrow and fill with the truth. He knows, even if it hurts too much to admit. He knows.

"Henna ..." He swallows hard.

"I'm sorry."

His hands fall from my face. The few people around us step back.

Bodhi's jaw clenches as his face distorts to keep it together. He opens his mouth several times to speak, but swallows instead to keep his composure. "He killed himself?"

My nose and eyes burn as I blink out several big tears. "He didn't wake up, Bodhi. His body was just ... done." I hate that we're sharing these words in front of an audience. I hate that I so easily hand him a lie wrapped in the truth, and that there's no going back now.

He nods slowly, gaze on me, but not *really* on me at all. Holding out my hand, I wait for him to take it. Bodhi makes a slow, lifeless glance around at the secretary, Gail, and the security guard, then he takes my hand.

CHAPTER FORTY-FIVE

WE LAY BARRETT Henry Malone to rest next to his wife on a sunny Thursday morning in May. Bella stands next to Bodhi on one side while I stand on his other side, holding his hand. I'm surprised how many friends are here. Not just Barrett's friends, but most of the teachers from the school, including Principal Rafferty and a handful of students. Even Bella has friends from Kentucky who flew in for the funeral.

When the graveside ceremony ends, I join my parents and Zach by the limo while Bodhi and Bella watch the casket get lowered into the ground. Since she arrived the day after he died, I haven't seen Bella shed one tear. At first I thought she was angry, but it's just her personality. She's been very matter-of-factly making funeral arrangements, even helping friends and family find hotel accommodations.

But right now, she looks utterly deflated, just like Bodhi. Adult orphans before the age of thirty.

"Did I mess up?" I whisper to my mom as she squeezes my hand while we watch Bella and Bodhi.

Bella's ironclad composure crumbles when the casket disappears below the earth. Bodhi's hand slowly reaches for hers. When she takes his hand, he turns, pulling her into his embrace.

Mom squeezes my hand again. "No, sweetie."

As much as I want to be by Bodhi's side to comfort him, I know that's not my place right now, so I climb into the limo and head back to the Malone's house where family and a few close friends gather for a lunch that my mom arranged.

I disposed of the prescription bag and bottle two days ago, but when we arrive at the house, I make a quick sweep of his bedroom and bathroom to make sure nothing got missed.

"Hey."

I jump, turning away from the vanity in Barrett's bathroom, easing the drawer shut.

"Hey." I step right into Bodhi's body, wrapping my arms around him.

"What are you looking for?"

"Aspirin. I have a bit of a headache." Closing my eyes, I inwardly cringe at the lies that slide off my tongue so easily. I hate it.

"Sorry." He kisses my head and rests his cheek on it. "I know the past few days have been really difficult for you too. I hate that you had to be the one to find him. I should have been the one to try to wake him up that morning. I should have—"

"Shh …" I lift onto my toes and press my lips to his to silence him.

We stay idle like this for a few moments until he relaxes.

"No apologies." I kiss his neck, his jaw, and his lips. It's loving, not sexual.

It's truth. Beyond all the lies, I hope he will always know that my love for him is truth. I hope no lie will ever matter more than this truth.

"Bodhi?" Bella calls from the family room.

I step back, giving him a soft smile.

"Aspirin is in the other bathroom."

"Okay."

When he turns, I lean against the counter and exhale. Today I hurt, not just my heart, but my whole body. My back feels like it's ready to break, so I worm my way through the people in the living room to the table next to Barrett's chair. When no one seems to be looking, I retrieve the joint he saved for me and the lighter. I escape to the back deck. It's much smaller than the front porch, but it's also devoid of people. It's a beautiful afternoon. Maybe that's a sign. Even on a bad day, there is something good.

I light the joint and take a drag while sitting on the top step that gives me a clear view of Duke's and Etta's trailer.

"You owe me, Barrett." Holding the joint a few inches from my lips, I stare at the cloudless sky. "In another life, you will owe me."

A red-tailed hawk flies above, making a hoarse screech.

"Don't argue with me, old man." Giggling, I take another hit. "To you, Barrett. I hope you're reunited with the love of your life. I can't imagine ever being separated from mine again."

After a final hit, I lie back on the warped boards, extend my arms into a T, and close my eyes, letting the warmth of the sun blanket me like one last hug, one last goodbye from Barrett.

"I love you too," I whisper.

CHAPTER FORTY-SIX

"WE SHOULD GO through his stuff," Bella suggests after the last family member leaves.

Bodhi lifts the bag of trash from the plastic kitchen bin and ties it. "Not tonight."

An uncomfortable tension lingers between them, but the feeling of that tension has shifted. Before, there was an obvious pull from opposite directions. Now, there's this empty void that they fill with confrontational comments. It's as if they don't remember how to get along, how to just be siblings.

"Bodhi, I want to go through his stuff before I go home."

"No one said you have to go through his stuff at all. I'll do it when I'm ready."

My high has worn off. Too bad. I'd rather not be here for this conversation. From the kitchen table, I nibble on leftover veggie tray carrots as they go back and forth—Bella leaning against the counter by the kitchen sink, Bodhi by the back door, holding the garbage bag.

"I *want* to go through his stuff. Did you ever think that maybe there's something sentimental that I might want to keep?"

"Fine. Go pilfer through his stuff. I'll deal with the leftovers later."

"Pilfer? Jesus. I'm not stealing anything. Why do you have

to be such a dick about it?"

My gaze follows the volleying of their jabs.

"Yes. *I'm* the one being a dick about it. There was nothing dickish about you packing up and leaving after the accident."

Bella pushes off the counter, planting her hands on her hips. "Oh, did you *accidentally* get high and shitfaced? Did you *accidentally* need Dad to come get you? I think the days of calling it an accident are over. You fucked up because that's what you are—you're a fuckup. He would have beat the cancer had he not been in a wheelchair."

Bodhi drops the bag of trash. "Oh, really. What doctor told you that? None? Oh, that's right. You weren't here to go to the doctor with him. Leaving was your stupid explanation for punishing me. Well guess what? I didn't want you here anyway. The only person you punished by leaving was Dad. He busted his ass for years making *your* dreams come true. Have you looked at the sign at the end of the property? It doesn't say Bodhi's Stables."

Her jaw clenches. "You killed him, and you damn well know it. That's on you. You weren't even here the morning he died. You left your pothead girlfriend to find him."

"Shut the fuck up about her!"

I freeze. No longer feeling hungry, I let the carrot in my hand drop to the tray.

"It's on your conscience, Bodhi, not mine."

"You killed him by never fucking being here! Maybe if you would have been here more, he would have felt more loved by you and felt like he had a greater reason to fight!" Bodhi's voice booms as he clenches his fists, taking another step closer to Bella.

She doesn't back down. With two quick steps, she shoves his chest. "Murderer!"

"Don't you fucking touch me!" He grabs her arms.

"Let go of me!" She wriggles. "Are you going to kill me too?"

"I. Didn't. Kill. Him!" He shakes her.

"You did! You killed him, and mom, and your own god-damn life, and—"

"I KILLED HIM!" I bang the table with my hands as I shoot up, sending my chair backward, crashing to the floor.

Their heads whip toward me, slowly releasing their holds on each other.

My hand flies to my face, cupping my mouth, as my heart booms in my chest. Tears burn my eyes. Barrett would hate this. "It was me," I say softly behind my cupped hand.

Bodhi's forehead wrinkles as he shakes his head and stutters a barely audible reply, "What?"

Bella blinks rapidly, jaw slack.

I nod a half dozen times before inching my hand away from my mouth, tears streaming down my face. Maybe it's Barrett or the residual effects of the marijuana, but in spite of my racing heart and endless tears, I find a steady, almost eerily calm voice. "He wanted to die, but not because he was in a wheelchair and not because Bella moved away. He wanted to die because cancer is torturous and unforgiving to those who have it and the people who love them."

"You *killed* him?" Bella starts to step toward me, but Bodhi grabs her arm.

I shake my head. "The cancer killed him."

She wriggles out of Bodhi's hold and slams me against the

wall with her hands pressed to my shoulders. "Did you suffocate him with a fucking pillow?" Tears fill her eyes as she screams at me.

"Get off!" Bodhi pulls her away again with such force that Bella nearly stumbles to the ground.

"You're going to jail! Do you hear me?"

Bodhi pulls me by my arm out the back door. I nearly trip trying to keep up with him as he wordlessly drags me toward Alice. With less force than Bella used, he presses my back to the door and slams his hands on either side of my head against the window. "Jesus, Henna ... what the hell did you do?" His voice is tight, like a band ready to snap.

This is the unforgivable. It has to be. We will never be Henna and Bodhi again. I will be that girl who killed his father, the girl who betrayed him, the girl who lied to him.

"Physician-assisted death," I whisper.

Bodhi shakes his head, eyes narrowed. "I ... I don't understand. That would have required him to see more than one doctor. And the money for the medication, I would have seen that come out of his account. I ... how ..." He continues to shake his head as if doing so will erase everything that has happened.

I stare at him, unblinking. He's smart. He knows the answers, even if he doesn't want to admit it after a long day.

Bodhi averts his gaze to the side, jaw clenched, eyes red with emotion. "When I—" He swallows hard, nostrils flared. "When I asked you to come over Monday morning, did you know ... was he already dead?"

"Yes," I whisper.

His head drops to his chest, face contorted with pain as he

closes his eyes. "How could you?"

"It's what he wanted."

"He didn't know what he wanted!" He slams his palms against the window next to my head several times, accenting each word.

My heart stops as every muscle in my body stiffens.

"He was depressed, Henna!" he yells just inches from my face, squeezing more tears out of me.

My head inches side to side. "He was dying, not depressed. There's a difference."

"Shut. Up." Each word rips from his throat like he's on the verge of wrapping his hands around my neck. "Just ... shut the fuck up. Understood?"

Biting my lips together, I swallow past the boulder of pain in my throat and nod, willing the sobs to stay inside.

He closes his eyes, stepping back and letting his hands fall limp to his sides. "I can't look at you."

I don't breathe. One breath will leave me a mess of destruction on the ground. Through tear-filled eyes, I take one *last* look at Bodhi Malone. Silent sobs reach my soul as *goodbye* whispers in my heart. Peeling myself off Alice's door, my wobbling legs carry my lifeless body down the long drive.

CHAPTER FORTY-SEVEN

Bodhi

BELLA SPENDS SEVERAL days threatening to have Henna arrested. For what? I don't know. She did nothing illegal. When my sister's not ranting, she's crying while going through Dad's stuff. I have more emotions than I can handle. It could take more than one lifetime to untangle them, put them into manageable little compartments, and piece together what I'm really feeling.

I'm angry.

I'm frustrated.

I'm confused.

I'm hurt.

And I'm just exhausted.

"I'm leaving," Bella announces while dropping her suitcase just outside of the kitchen.

I pour a cup of coffee. "Do you need a ride to the airport?"

She shakes her head. "I called a taxi."

Leaning against the kitchen counter, I take a sip of coffee.

Bella's gaze falls from mine, her shoulders collapsed inward. I feel as defeated as she looks.

"Bodhi, I don't know how to fix us. I don't know how to

look at you and not see our parents' graves. I don't know how to forgive you or *her*."

I don't know how to forgive *her*—Henna—either, but I also don't know how to convince my heart that I don't love her anymore. It acts on its own free will.

"So I'm just going to go." Bella forces her gaze back to mine.

It hurts. I hurt for her. As angry as I am at her for holding on to the past and abandoning Dad, I still hurt for my sister, because when I messed up years ago, I changed her life forever too.

"If I can work through this, then maybe we can ... I don't know." She shrugs.

I nod slowly. She doesn't have to finish. I know she's saying goodbye. Maybe a final goodbye.

"I'm sorry for everything, even for having to say *I'm sorry* again. But I do love you. And I also understand that sometimes love isn't enough. So ..." I set my coffee down and walk to her, pulling her into my arms. Tears burn my eyes. "You were a victim too. And I'm just ... so ... sorry."

Bella slowly pushes away, quickly wiping her eyes and finding a brave face. "I took everything I wanted. If you sell the house or the ranch ... it's yours."

She cuts *all* ties.

I get it, even if it hurts.

Bella turns, grabs her suitcase, and walks out the door.

After my coffee, I head to the stables to take Snare out for a ride. Taped to his saddle is a large envelope.

"What the hell?" I pull out the cash—a lot of cash. Then I pull out a folded piece of paper.

Bodhi,

I wish I had some great wisdom to pass on to you with my final words. I don't.

Instead, I have a few secrets, some incredibly honest gratitude, and one last request.

Secrets I promised your mom I'd take to my grave …

Your first word was *Dada*.

Your first steps were to me.

You ran to me every time I walked through the door after a long day.

You tiptoed into our bedroom at night and nestled into my chest.

I don't know what I did to deserve your love.

Mom cared for you all day. Fed you. Changed your diapers. And kissed your boo-boos. She wiped your tears and made bringing you joy her full-time job.

Still … you were my boy.

Thank you for staying. I know you didn't do it out of guilt. You did it because you are and always will be my boy.

Thank you for taking my pain and making it your own.

Thank you for being my friend.

I'm sorry it took me so long to realize that it was unfair to ask you to help me die.

You are my boy, the whisper of my name, and the hand always holding mine.

You are an undeniable, physical, eternal part of me.

But ... the pain was real and the end was imminent.

It was just time to go, even if the goodbye felt impossibly unbearable.

Thank you for Henna. She gave me peace. She took the pain you couldn't take from me.

Thank you, my dear boy, for never letting go.

Now, I need you to do me a favor. Get on a plane and go live. Live for me and live for your mom.

Live because it's the only thing you have left to do in your life. Don't try to rewind. Don't try to fast forward. Honor my memory by living your best life. And whatever you do ... DON'T LOSE THE GIRL!

Forever your favorite pain in the ass,
Dad

CHAPTER FORTY-EIGHT

Henna

Two Months Later

"MY FAVORITE MEMORIES of us are on this beach."
I turn toward my dad's voice.

"Forgot your hat." He sets the white, wide-brimmed hat on my head.

My lips find something like a smile to give him in return. Joy still feels foreign to my heart, but I'm trying. I stare at the foaming waves settling around our feet. "Memories ..." I grunt a laugh. "Too bad we can't be more selective with them."

"Your mom and I were in love. The timing, our ages, the circumstances ... none of it mattered. It was real. It was forever."

I look up.

He gives me a sad smile. "Yes. I still love your mom. I will love her forever. What they say is not true—you don't have to let go to move on."

"Is Bethanne your *moving on*?"

Dad grins. "Yes, I like her ... a lot. But I moved on in other ways long before Bethanne. The day your mom married

Zach was a pretty official moment."

We stand together for a few minutes, just taking in the moment.

"Did you get to say goodbye?"

I shake my head slowly. It still hurts. It will always hurt. "I waited until school was out. Then I baked cookies—the kind that only give you a sugar high."

Dad smirks.

"Walked to his house. Knocked on the door. No answer. Did that for a week straight. His van was parked in the drive, so I just assumed he was refusing to open the door to me. But then Duke, the stable manager, told me Bodhi was gone."

"Gone?"

I nod, taking a deep breath to soothe the emotions that are still so raw. "Gone. He said Barrett had set aside a stash of money for Bodhi, but the money could only be used for traveling, which seemed odd since Barrett asked for money for his *final* medication."

"That is odd. So Bodhi is traveling?"

I shrug. "Guess so."

"That's different than moving. He'll be back."

"Maybe." I turn back toward the ocean, soaking up the salty breeze and late day sun.

Spending the summer in California with my dad was a good idea. For the first time in my life, I don't want to be in Colorado.

"Selling many paintings?"

"Yep. I feel like an actual grownup with a steady paycheck. Totally sucks."

He chuckles. "How's your back?"

"I see an acupuncturist and chiropractor on the regular. Massages weekly. Herbs. Kinesio taping. It's actually better than it's ever been."

"Pot?"

I glance over at him, giving him a smirk. He's always hated that I've spent so many years relying on edibles for pain relief. "No. I actually stopped when I needed it the most. But ..."

My gaze finds the endless blue horizon again.

"But?"

Forcing steady breaths, I find the words without allowing the tears to take over. I'm tired of crying. "But I wanted the pain. All of it. I thought I deserved it. I knew Bodhi and Bella were in pain. I knew they wouldn't get high to escape it, so I didn't either. Eventually, my heart went numb, and I realized my back still hurt like hell on certain days, so Mom got me a different kind of help."

"You're clean?"

I grin, shaking my head. "You make medicinal marijuana sound so terrible. But yes, I'm blisslessly sober."

"I'm not sure blisslessly is a word. You should have stayed in school."

I grin. The real kind. It feels good. It also feels wrong. What if Bodhi hasn't found his smile again?

He nudges my arm. My foot shifts a bit to keep my balance. "Have you called him? Texted?"

"He thinks I killed his dad. What would I even say?"

"It's been a couple months now. He's had time to rationalize what happened. There's no way he still thinks you *killed* his father."

"Then why hasn't *he* called me?"

"Maybe he's waiting on you to apologize." He nudges me again, making me sidestep a few paces.

I shoot him a narrow-eyed scowl. "I can't apologize."

"Why?"

"Because if given the chance, knowing the outcome, I would do it again. It was the right decision."

Dad's eyes widen, lips part.

"What?"

He shakes his head. "I'm proud to call you my daughter. You risked something really important to you for the greater good. I know men my age who still haven't mastered that concept."

"Thanks." I nudge him back. "And even if it makes me *blisslessly* miserable, I hope he finds a life. A real one with a wife and kids. Maybe a dog or goat to hang out with his horse."

"Stop." He nudges me harder.

"Dad!" I stumble into the breaking waves, my hands sinking into the sand and water crashing against me. My hat takes off on its own.

Scowling, I grab a handful of wet sand and throw it at him. It hits his knees.

"Be your age, Henna. Be pissed. Brokenhearted. Bitter. Jealous. Be Hell." He scoops me up and walks a few feet farther into the water. Then he tosses me.

I squeal as the water engulfs me. When I break the surface, he's wearing the biggest grin. Wasting no time, I attack him, dragging him down with me. We wrestle in the waves until we're both out of breath. I hop on his back since it's a bit too deep for me to keep my head above the water. Hugging his neck, I kiss his cheek. "Thank you."

"For what?"

"For respecting my feelings."

"And how do you *really* feel?"

"I feel like it's easy for Bodhi to walk away from me. He's done it before. When I left, I had to tear myself away from him, but I didn't do it without a goodbye. I didn't do it without handing him a part of my heart to keep him company. I did it with tears. A kiss. And a promise of coming back. He didn't even leave me. He just closed his eyes and ..."

And they're back.

Tears join the salty drops of ocean on my face. "He said he couldn't look at me."

"That's his loss."

"Says my dad."

"Yes. But that doesn't make it any less true."

"I want him to *want* me. Like the epic kind of love where he comes for me. The kind where he doesn't take no for an answer. The kind that involves begging and groveling. I want him to chase me. *Need* me. I want him to hold me in his arms the way I've held him in my heart."

CHAPTER FORTY-NINE

A month later.

"PACK A BAG. We're celebrating your birthday in style this year." Juni plops down on my bed.

I glance up from my canvas, dipping my brush in deep blue. "I'm good."

She frowns. "You're not good. You're drab and boring."

"Love you too, *Mom*."

"You're turning twenty-two, not fifty-two. Let's do this." She jumps up, tearing through the clothes in my closet.

I keep painting.

"Cute dresses and bikinis. That's all you'll need."

"Sounds like shaving will be required. Not sure I'm in the mood to shave."

Tossing clothes onto my bed, she rolls her eyes. "I already have appointments for us. Tomorrow we're getting waxed, mani-pedis, facials ... everything. Then we fly off to party on The Juniper."

"That's a weird name for a yacht. Don't you think?" I smirk.

"You think The Henna would be better?"

I nod, gathering my brushes because clearly I'm done for the day. "Now that's a solid name for a grand vessel."

Her lips twist. "Do you want a yacht?"

Chuckling, I carry my brushes to the kitchen. "No. I don't."

"I feel you submitting to this." She follows me. "I anticipated an argument. But you're not really arguing with me. Does that mean you're onboard with your birthday party?"

"Sure." I sigh. "Nothing keeping me here."

"Yes! That's my girl. Our appointments are at nine tomorrow morning. Be packed and out front by eight."

Italy

I LOVE ITALY. Of course, this is where we're celebrating my birthday.

"Wow, you invited all *your* best friends to my birthday party." I frown as we make our way to The Juniper where all of Juni's and Zach's friends are already sipping champagne and relaxing in the sun as ZIP's helicopter flies in and out with more guests.

"Don't be grumpy. You know them too."

"I'm not grumpy. I just thought it would be the three of us."

"What if I told you it's just going to be you and Mario."

"Who's Mario? And what are you talking about?"

"Mario is that fine man over there." She points to the smaller yacht next to The Juniper. It has high sails and a man in white with a captain's hat. "He's your captain."

I stop, making the guy carrying our bags behind us nearly ram into my back. "What do you mean *my* captain?"

"Happy birthday, Henna." Zach catches up to us and kisses me on the cheek before continuing toward the pier. "Your mom came up with the name," he calls over his shoulder.

I take a few more steps to see the name on the side of the yacht.

Hell and High Water

"Oh my god ... you bought me a yacht. That's so ... wrong."

She loops her arm around mine, pulling me down the pier. "You paint and draw. You love to sail. You love the Mediterranean. A yacht was the obvious choice."

"This is insane," I murmur.

"Go check it out. Get settled in. There are all your favorite foods waiting for you. Meet Mario, but he's married, so keep that in mind." Juni winks as she stops at the gangway of The Juniper while I take reluctant steps toward *my* yacht.

Fucking insane. I don't want a yacht. They don't keep well in the Rockies. I know plenty of rich people. I can always borrow one in a pinch.

"Welcome aboard, Miss Lane. I'm your captain, Mario Garza. If you need anything just let me know. And..." He takes off his hat and gives me a slight bow "...happy birthday."

"Thank you." I smile, but it's a little forced. I don't want a captain.

As I explore the yacht, my two bags are loaded onto the vessel for me. Just as Juni said, there are all my favorite foods and drinks.

California veggie rolls. Those are a little bittersweet to see.

After I overeat, I grab an hour nap then shower and dress for my party on The Juniper before we set sail for a week of port jumping around Italy.

"Happy birthday!" Everyone cheers when I step on board wearing a short blue cocktail dress, complements of Juni and Stella McCartney.

"Nice shoes." Juni shakes her head before sipping her champagne.

I glance down at my silver Birkies and shrug. "Hmm …are these not the ones you bought to go with the dress?"

"Funny girl." Holding her glass out to the side, she pulls me in for a hug and kisses both of my cheeks. "You look beautiful. Always."

I get a little teary-eyed when I see hers fill with tears.

"Darling …" Zach pulls me in for a hug. "Twenty-two years. I'm just so happy we're celebrating another year of you." His emotions bleed through his words. I don't think either one of us will ever forget the day he saved me, the day he gave me a second chance at life.

"I love you," I whisper just before he releases me. "Thank you," I say to both of them. "I love Hell and High Water."

Zach slides his arm around my mom. "You're welcome. Don't ever stop living."

I nod, taking a glass of champagne that's offered to me.

"Presents. There are more presents." Juni jabs her thumb toward the front of the yacht.

"I don't need any more presents."

"Not from us. They're from everyone else."

I follow them to the front of the mammoth yacht where a crowd of people mingle around small tables, music drifting from the large speakers. Their friends shower me with celebratory hugs as I make my way to a chair surrounded by more presents.

"Crazy …" I grin at Juni. She's still so teary-eyed. Must be hormones.

I open one elaborate gift after another, reading cards, extending heartfelt thank-you's, and feeling loved, overwhelmed, and still a little sad and empty.

"There's one more." Zach stops me just as I start to stand. He hands me a small box.

"No card?"

Zach shrugs, taking a step back. I glance around. Everyone is leaving.

"What's going on?"

"It's a very personal gift."

I lift an eyebrow. "Personal?" Oh my god … my mom has tears sliding down her cheeks. "Mom?"

She shakes her head, backing away from me. "It's fine." She smiles.

"Love you, darling." Zach winks just before taking my mom's hand and leading her away.

I'm alone with a *personal* gift as the sun sets over the beautiful blue water. I pull the gold ribbon and unwrap the blue paper that matches my dress. It's a wood box. My fingers ghost over the smooth surface with a tree carved into it. I open the lid. It's filled with postcards—from Bodhi.

The top one is from Helsinki, Finland.

Dear Henna,

I'm in Finland. My parents were going to travel here for their twentieth anniversary. I'm still mourning the loss of my father. The fact that I just said that means I'll never actually mail this postcard to you.

I'm a mess. How's that for honesty? I don't know what happens next in my life. So, I'm taking a page from your book and just trying to "live."

Bodhi

Gotland, Sweden

Dear Henna,

Today I hate you. The fact that I just said that means I'll never actually mail this postcard to you. The grieving process is painful. Today I feel like blaming the world. I guess this means that I still think of you as my world. What do I do with that?

I guess I'm still a mess. Trying to live, but it still feels like I'm not really alive at all.

Bodhi

That one hurt. *Today I hate you.* Tears fill my eyes. I'm certain my heart is squeezing them out.

Cologne, Germany

Dear Henna,

Today I met a woman at a coffee shop. She made me smile. It felt good. I bet you don't want to know this, so I'll never actually mail this postcard to you. She gave me her phone number. I'm not sure if I'll call her. If I don't plan on staying here long, it seems pointless. But I'm supposed to be "living," so maybe I'll get the courage to do it.

Bodhi

As I set this one aside, I choke out a sob.

Prague, Czech Republic

Dear Henna,

Did it take you long to choose my dad over me? Were you planning on telling me? Or did it just come out when Bella and I were arguing? Did you think blaming you was going to make things right between Bella and me? I'm certain Bella will take her hatred for me to her grave.

I wish you wouldn't have said anything. We were always a dream, but I liked that dream. You ruined that. Sorry, it's just my truth right now. Looks like I won't be mailing this postcard either.

Bodhi

I wipe my eyes and look around. It's still just me. This feels like a very cruel birthday gift.

Budapest, Hungary

Today I miss you. It might be because I spent the day in the hotel bed. I'm not feeling so well. I think I picked up something on the plane. Your name on my skin doesn't make it easy to forget you. Who am I kidding? You are the most unforgettable moment of my life. And that means a lot because I've had some very important moments in my life.

I should send this postcard to you, but at this point I don't know if we can really ever be an "us" again.

Love, Bodhi

A new round of tears come hard and fast as I cover my hand with my mouth. Love—he signed this one *Love, Bodhi.*

Lake Geneva, Switzerland

Dear Henna,

Today I didn't grieve my father. It was a truly good day. I also forgave someone for something they did that changed my life forever. It was a long time coming.

I forgave myself.

Not living my life to its fullest is not fair to my father, and it's not fair to me. If I get the chance to be a father someday, I hope I can love my children the way my dad loved Bella and me.

I hope you're happy.

Love, Bodhi

"Oh my god …" I whisper, looking all around as my heart pauses because the last postcard has a picture of Positano, Italy. *I'm* in Positano.

Positano, Italy

Dear Henna,

I forgive you for taking my heart. I forgive you for ruining me for any life that doesn't include you.

Thank you for doing what I couldn't do. I suppose it's true that if you really love something, you'll set it free. You set my dad free. You set me free.

I guess that means I don't love you as much because I can't set you free. And no matter how much I try to hate you—I will always love you more.

My tears blur the ink, so I swipe them away and move the box before I can't read his final words.

It's funny ... I write on these postcards for you, but I never say a word about the places I've visited. I'm not sure I've taken a single picture. Nothing I've seen has come close to taking my breath away like you do. The world is a big place. You could get lost, forgetting where you came from, not caring where you go.

Not me. My travels have taught me only one thing ... every place I've been has simply been a place without you.

SafetySuit, "Never Stop"

Love, Bodhi

"Where are you?" I yell, setting the box aside and jumping to my feet. I turn in circles, looking at the other yachts and the people on the pier.

When I don't see him, I take off running toward the back of the yacht, pushing and shoving my way past Juni's and Zach's friends.

"Henna?" My mom tries to stop me. Her tears are gone, replaced with a wrinkle of confusion because I'm clenching my fists and gritting my teeth.

Am I mad? No. I'm livid.

I run off their yacht and down the way to Hell and High Water. Stopping, I let more tears fall as Bodhi comes into view on the back of my yacht. He's dressed in a blue suit with a white and gray tie. I hate him for looking so incredible.

"No." I shake my head. "You can't be part of my life when

it's convenient for you. Christmas? My birthday? No. Not okay. You sent me a fraction of the postcards that I sent you." I run my hands through my hair, releasing a painful laugh. "Hell, you didn't even send them to me. You were too fucking chicken to say all the words that needed to be said, even if they hurt."

"Henna ..." He steps toward me. "I'm sorry."

I continue to shake my head. "Nope. Not good enough. Your favorite line has always been *I don't deserve you*. Well, guess what? You're right. You don't deserve me." Turning, I stomp off. I have no clue where I'm going, just away from Bodhi Malone.

"Jesus, Henna ..." He chases after me.

I speed up my walk, but my dress is tight, constricting my stride.

"Wait!" He grabs my arm.

I don't turn.

He steps around me, positioning himself in front of me. "What will it take?"

This pisses me off more. I brush past him.

Again, he grabs my arm. "No!"

I clench my teeth, fighting back the emotions that have plagued me since the day I met Bodhi Malone. I fell so fucking hard for him; I'm certain it will be impossible to recover in this lifetime.

His hands grab my face. "Anything. I will do *anything*. Do you want me to swim after your yacht? Beg? Plead? Promise my life to you in blood? Lasso the moon and capture the stars?"

We remain statuesque and unblinking.

"Yes," I whisper.

In spite of the emotions reddening his eyes, he narrows them a bit as if he can't believe I just said yes. "Yes to which one?"

Tipping my chin up to let him know I'm no longer his secret, his forbidden, his undeserving indulgence, I draw in a shaky breath. "All. I want it all. I deserve it all. You said SafetySuit, 'Never Stop.' Do you know the lyrics? Because I do and they're big. They're begging and pleading; they're lassoing the moon and capturing the stars. They're endless."

He nods slowly, blinking away his emotions as the corners of his mouth turn up a fraction.

"You'd better make this matter, *Mr. Malone.* You said you can do the right thing, or you can love me. I will *always* choose love. I will always choose you."

Bodhi's hint of a smile turns into the real deal, and he drops one knee and then the other. "Forever, Bodhi and Henna," he whispers, bowing his head to my stomach as he rests his hands on my hips.

"Dave Matthews, 'You and Me?'" I whisper, running my hands through his hair.

He eases his head side to side. "No … Train, 'Marry Me.'"

My breath hitches as I shake my head. "Don't say it unless you—"

"I mean it." He looks up, those blue eyes shining like the sunset on the sea. His hand reaches into his suit coat pocket, pulling out a ring. "Henna Eve Lane—"

"Yes."

He frowns. It's adorable, especially when he's on both knees. Looking over his shoulder toward the crowd gathered on The Juniper watching us, he sighs. "You're killing me, babe. I had a whole big speech planned out. They're over there waiting for the big proposal."

"They're waiting for you to slide that ring on my finger and kiss me. They're waiting for you to carry me to that smaller yacht. They're waiting to see us sail to the end of the world because that's our happily ever after."

Bodhi slides the ring on my finger, twists my hand, and presses his lips to the inside of my wrist. "I think they're finally one and the same."

"What is?"

He stands.

The crowd cheers. We grin.

"Loving you is the right thing to do. It's the only thing to do."

I slide my arms around his neck and pull him down to me so we're a breath away from kissing. "You smell like lemon."

Bodhi grins. "This girl told me I needed to come to Italy for the best lemon drops."

I ghost my lips over his. "Take me to the end of the world, Bodhi. Let's make little rock stars. Let's be limitless."

"Bodhi and Henna," he whispers. "Sounds like my favorite kind of Hell." Blue eyes come to life, and his white teeth peek through his grin two seconds before he kisses me, sweeps me up into his arms, and takes me to our forever.

The world *is* big, but our time here is small and precious. Life is meant to be lived, not solved. And love ... well, it's like a white T-shirt with french fries and ketchup. It's messy, but worth the risk.

EPILOGUE

Bodhi

"PUT ME ON your shoulders so I can see!" Henna tugs at my hand as everything goes dark for the band to take the stage.

"If you wanted a better view, then we should have stayed backstage." I smirk, knowing there's no way Henna wants to watch this performance from anywhere but immersed in the middle of the sold-out venue. "Baby, I'm getting too old to carry you around on my shoulders." I lift her up, and she ignores my comment.

A single spotlight shines on a beautiful, seventeen-year-old girl from India. The crowd goes insane screaming "Zoya" as she remains statuesque with perfect posture, left hand high on the cello neck, bow in her poised right hand. When the bow hits the strings, it silences the crowd, except for my wife.

"Oh my god, Bodhi … that's our baby." I don't have to see her face to know that it's marked with streams of happy tears.

After a classical solo, the rest of the stage lights up, and the other three band members join in, bringing the rest of the venue to their feet. It feels like the most incredible Bach and Mozart mashup with edgy rock undertones of Metallica and

The Rolling Stones.

The world of Bodhi and Henna has been filled with tragedy, obstacles, and a whole lot of *life*. After years of failing to conceive a child, we decided to adopt a three-year-old girl from India, who we met on our travels when she was two. Her name was Zoya which means shining or *life*. She instantly took a liking to Henna. She even cried when we had to leave—so did Henna.

It was a long year of jumping through all the adoption hoops, but a week before Zoya's third birthday, we brought her home to California. Yeah, we live in California now, just outside of L.A. so we're close to my VP job at ZIP Tunes, close to Zoya's grandparents, and close to her other band members.

Henna's bracelet-adorned arms shoot up in the air. "That's our rock star!"

Zoya has no interest in singing, but from an early age, she's had sick talent at playing any instrument we put in her little hands. And her music-loving family has given her the opportunity to play *all* the instruments. Cello is simply her favorite.

So, Zach and I set out to find some up-and-coming talent who would complement her gift, and that's how the band A World Away was born.

Four members from four different countries on their first U.S. tour, and their debut album has already gone platinum.

"Yeah," I say, knowing no one can hear me over the music, "that's our girl." It's not just my sappy wife—tears burn my eyes too as goose bumps shoot up along my arms.

How is this my life?

I steady Henna's legs with one arm while taking some video of our daughter then turn the camera to take video of her mother on my shoulders. I send the short clip to Henna with a single song message.

Me: *OneRepublic "I Lived"*

A few seconds later, her fingers lovingly run through my hair.

Henna

WE GET LESS than ten minutes to congratulate Zoya and her band members after the concert before they're swept onto the tour bus.

"You're my idol, baby girl. We'll see you in Seattle tomorrow." I give her a big hug.

"Thanks. Love you, Mom."

Bodhi pulls her into his arms, lifting her off the ground and swinging her around. It makes my heart do funny flips because they are so close. He's devoted his life to her. I remind him every day that he's a wonderful father just like his father.

"Dad, I was so nervous."

He kisses Zoya's cheek and sets her back on her feet. "That's how you know you're living. If your heart's not racing, if your teeth aren't chattering, then you're not doing it right."

She curls her long, black hair behind her ears and grins. "Then I was doing it *so* right." She raises both of her arms to him for high fives.

When he lifts his arms, his T-shirt rides up enough for me

to see the bottom part of his two tattoos—his world connected on his torso.

H

E

N

N

Z O Y A

When the buses pull out of the parking lot, Bodhi reaches for my hand, and we interlace our fingers like we've done for the last twenty-three years together. He lifts our joined hands and kisses the inside of my wrist over my *permanent* tattoos.

Z

B O D H I

Y

A

Yeah, some things in life *are* permanent, like the love I have for my husband and our daughter.

"I love you more, baby," he whispers over my skin.

I grin. The *hate*, the immaturity, the fear, the pain ... it's no longer part of *us*. Henna and Bodhi are simply more. More love. More days of living. More nights of passion. Just so much more …

"I love you always." I turn into his body and press my lips to his sternum.

It's been twenty years since Barrett died. Twenty years since we realized we were more than *us*. We are the people and the circumstances that surround us. We broke more than once, but love and time put us back together—and family.

Bodhi lived his own nomad life after his dad died, and he did it because Barrett swallowed his pride and asked for a huge favor from Juni.

"Bodhi will not understand why Henna helped me die. He will need time and distance. But … he will come back to her. I know it in my heart. So, I guess I'm asking you to make an investment in our children's future."

And she did. Juni made sure Bodhi got on a plane. She made sure he didn't know it was her paying for his travels. She took him away from me, trusting that it was the only way he'd truly come back to me. Then magic happened. Fate? Maybe. Bodhi contacted my mom with an idea to do something special for my birthday … and the rest is history.

It wasn't until after we were married that Juni told us about her conversation with Barrett, and how he had a hand in putting Henna and Bodhi back together. She did it because it bothered Bodhi that his dad watched them struggle with money, yet apparently had a greenback-stuffed coffee can hidden somewhere.

I tip my chin up. He looks down at me. We share a few moments of silence where so many things are said without saying anything at all.

He grins.

I grin.

"Hi. Remember me?"

Bodhi rubs his lips together and nods slowly. "I'm pretty sure you're still my greatest memory."

The End

ACKNOWLEDGMENTS

Thank you to my readers. If you're reading this, I assume you didn't DNF. My family gives my words meaning, you give them purpose. It's an honor to share my imagination with you.

Kambra, thank you for taking my forbidden romance idea and adding legalized marijuana. If I ever get high, I want it to be with you—and Mom, of course.

A special thank you to Dustin for making my office/home a beautiful and inspirational place to write—and for encouraging me to keep writing since I went so far over budget.

Thank you to the usual suspects and a few new ones. Leslie, Kambra, Monique, Shauna, Sherri, Sian, Bethany, and Amy, my words would not shine without your sharp eyes. And a special thank you to my editor, Max, I started this sentence with "and" just to piss you off. I love working with you.

Thank you to Cleida for keeping my stories alive on Facebook. You are a dearly treasured friend.

Jenn, Sarah, and Brooke with Social Butterfly PR, thank you putting my books in front of so many bloggers and readers.

Sarah with Okay Creations, you did it again. Beautiful cover.

My Jonesies, you are my people, and I have THE BEST people. Thank you for your encouraging words and sharing your love of my stories.

AND THEN ... there is Jenn Beach aka The World's Best Assistant—I'm out of words to accurately show proper gratitude for everything you do. So I'm going to keep it simple and just say *thank you* for giving me boobs, abs, and bad-ass biceps in 2018!

Tim, Logan, Carter, and Asher, you give every breath true meaning. I love you beyond words, which says a lot because words are my thing.

ALSO BY JEWEL E. ANN

Jack & Jill Series
End of Day
Middle of Knight
Dawn of Forever

Holding You Series
Holding You
Releasing Me

Transcend Series
Transcend
Epoch

Standalone Novels
Idle Bloom
Only Trick
Undeniably You
One
Scarlet Stone
When Life Happened
Look the Part

jeweleann.com

ABOUT THE AUTHOR

Jewel is a free-spirited romance junkie with a quirky sense of humor.

With 10 years of flossing lectures under her belt, she took early retirement from her dental hygiene career to stay home with her three awesome boys and manage the family business.

After her best friend of nearly 30 years suggested a few books from the Contemporary Romance genre, Jewel was hooked. Devouring two and three books a week but still craving more, she decided to practice sustainable reading, AKA writing.

When she's not donning her cape and saving the planet one tree at a time, she enjoys yoga with friends, good food with family, rock climbing with her kids, watching How I Met Your Mother reruns, and of course…heart-wrenching, tear-jerking, panty-scorching novels.

Made in the USA
Coppell, TX
01 June 2024

33004873R00223